JUST LIKE ME

Carica go out
from School and
work with others.

Aunt

JUST LIKE ME

❀

Beyond the Thousand-Yard Stare

The story of an infantryman in the battle of Okinawa

Archie Morrison

Writers Club Press

San Jose New York Lincoln Shanghai

Just Like Me
Beyond the Thousand-Yard Stare

Writers Club Press
an imprint of iUniverse, Inc.

For information address:
iUniverse, Inc.
5220 S. 16th St., Suite 200
Lincoln, NE 68512
www.iuniverse.com

ISBN: 0-595-22611-6

*This book is dedicated to all the men and women—
friend and foe—who served on Okinawa during
those bloody days between April 1 and
August 6, 1945.
It is especially dedicated to the memory of my comrades in arms—Lee, Jake, Cook, John, Nealy,
Martinez, Mitch, and Earl. All are very real; however, some appear in this book under other
names.
All of the events and emotions depicted in this
book—from muddy battlefield trenches to hospital
cots—are as vivid to me as life itself.
In the 55 years since I returned from the war, I have
become increasingly convinced that bloody battles
between nations are an outmoded way of dealing
with differences, and the more you get to know
about your enemy, the more you discover that he is:
Just Like Me.*

Acknowledgments

❀

I would like to thank my wife and family for putting up with a veteran whose mind has been all muddled up for these many years. I would like to thank my editors, Denzil Walters and Don Duncan. Their help with advice and encouragement meant more than I can say. Without their assistance I could never have finished this book, let alone submit it to a publisher. Thanks to Richard Prince for the sharp eyes he brought to my voyage. Thanks to my readers, Tearle Beal and Carol Laudmill.

I thank John Olsen, M.D., and his assistant, Donna Lawson, for their diagnosis of Post-Traumatic Stress Disorder and their follow-up. Their treatment called for me to write my feelings, no matter how difficult it was. I thank the Veterans Administration Hospital staff members for their on-going treatment for PTSD. Thanks to my cardiologist, Nathaniel Arcega, M.D., and Alcoholics Anonymous for helping in my recovery from alcoholism.

Introduction

❀

Denzil Walters

While Archie Morrison was working on the final pages of *Just Like Me*, teachers and parents were debating the appropriateness of selections in a book about a war. The war was Vietnam. The course was history. Disputants concentrated on two broad issues. One issue was truth: objectors said writers had distorted reality. Those given to impassioned opinions found it difficult to express unbiased stands on truth as they know it.

A second issue was the relevance of fiction in a high-school history course. One critic of the course readings argued that no work of fiction belongs in a history class.

Those who take that position are apparently unfamiliar with novels and short stories, some among the greatest works of fiction, that have wars at their center, in the background, or threatening. Consider *The Charter House of Parma*, by Stendhal, for a description of political events in France and Italy while this nation is taking form on the American continent. Go to *Uncle Tom's Cabin*, by Harriet Beacher Stowe, a story foreshadowing the Civil War. Take up *The Red Badge of Courage*, by Stephen Crane, for an account of one man in the Civil War.

Move to the William Dean Howells short story, "Editha," for a view of the loss extracted from a woman as wife in the Civil War and mother in the Spanish-American War.

To this short list add Tolstoy's *War and Peace*, Hemingway's *For Whom the Bell Tolls* and *A Farewell to Arms,* and Remarque's *All Quiet on the Western Front.* Has any careful reader reached the second chapter in one of these books without formulating images of the characters, and thus becoming concerned for their fate? Is that concern not likely to lead the reader to ask questions about the actions of men who heard the drums and went to war?

Events in Italy, the setting of *The Charter House of Parma,* build an understanding of Europe when princes, princesses, counts, and countesses see themselves as under siege because of the popular appeal of Napoleon's declarations, an appeal continuing after Waterloo. For the central figure in Stendhal's novel, war is a short excursion into misadventure. For Henry in Stephen Crane's work, war is grim, the anticipation of adventure only a dim memory of his frame of mind when he walked from his mother's farm to enlist in the northern army. Readers follow the boy with illusions of heroism into fire and out of the fire. Numbed in close-quarter attack, he stumbles from his place in a broken line. A serious reader who knows little about the Civil War will be drawn to read the non-fiction that will explain the background. A reader with sympathy for Henry will want to know why anyone would sign up for five of his dazed minutes.

In 1995, the 100th anniversary of *Red Badge of Courage* was marked at the United States Air Force Academy with a conference giving a platform for delivery of scholarly papers on Crane's novel. A statement explaining the mission of the literary journal published by the English department at the academy provides a rationale for study of that novel and others that take readers into battle, dubious and heroic. The academy journal centers on "a topic many find abhorrent," the founders state. But even "the least prescient reader must realize the creative result of individual war-time experience," the journal says in presenting the case for its special literary interests.

From his war-time experience Morrison has created a work that tests a reader's capacity to endure at a distance the abhorrent conditions that were his to live day after day. In *Just Like Me,* he has written a book that is as realistic as Crane's novel of the Civil War. In a key respect, it goes beyond the realism of Crane's novel. Authors in our time are less restrained than 19th century novelists in describing in plain language life in battle. *Plain* here means the words originating with people living close to the earth, without the sensitivities encased in words borrowed from polite languages spoken by those living higher off the ground. Staying alive in holes in the earth day and night, for weeks on end, while friends are dying, reduces the premium put on certain courtesies. Add quickly this: not all courtesies. Together in close quarters, soldiers work out understandings to raise the odds of survival. Unprinted rules govern.

Morrison's forthrightness in the language of soldiers is consistent with his openness in setting down his boyhood conflicts. He takes the reader into his world as he reveals the thoughts of a young man given to question what others accept as truth.

As a young boy, he doubts the doctrine he hears pronounced from the pulpit of the church of his parents. Later, in war, one certain unequivocal biblical commandment spins in his head. Duty calls upon him to kill enemy soldiers. As he performs the role instilled by training, he questions the thrill he feels as he kills.

Morrison, unlike Crane, did not rely on imagination alone to picture battle. As a young soldier on Okinawa in World War II, Morrison fought from the beach to the hilltops. His descriptions come from his memory. He is determined to tell the truth.

While reading his words describing hand-to-hand killing, I was carried back to the feelings I had as a boy in the 1930s studying pictures in the Sunday paper showing World War I trench warfare. Morrison's scenes are as jarring and unforgettable as the photographs of men dead face down in mud, men draped over barbed wire, their mouths gapping, their eyes vacant. The publisher of the Hearst papers expected the photographs to increase support for the movement to keep America out of a second world war, then looming on the horizon.

Morrison's way to reconciliation of civilian beliefs and military duties on the battlefield took form under stress. At wit's end, he imagined a second self. In his way he was following the technique of the novelist in a time when he was not a novelist but a soldier driven out of his mind. Reality under those circumstances was sometimes neither here nor there. Truth was out of the picture.

The writer William Kennedy has described the process leading from truth of one kind to truth of the kind that is translated into literature. One truth takes form through observations. The second comes after early observations have been transformed by later experience.

In a New York Times column, Kennedy said, "Fiction demands the necessary falsity, the essential lie that the imagination knows is truer than what your rational self thinks is true about your experience...."

Replace Kennedy's word *fiction* with the word *sanity* as a way to understand Morrison's travels of the imagination. By creating "the necessary falsity," Morrison the young soldier worked his way through mental disorder. Years later, as a novelist, he has constructed from the rubble of the irrational a world in which two men in armies at war can overcome the training that impels them to kill each other.

In his column on writing, Kennedy cites a comment of Henry James on perspective that applies to Morrison's *Just Like Me*. More than five decades have passed since Morrison lived the war he writes about. Could he have written this novel when he was 19 years old? He could have written a novel, but it would not have been this one. Morrison needed time to arrive at the perspective suggested in the statement of James on writing. He said that "...art blooms only where the soil is deep...." James went on to say that "it takes a great deal of history to produce a little literature."

Morrison's novel in a narrow sense comes from the individual histories of scores of men among thousands over part of a year. In a larger sense, Morrison's narrative takes its shape from issues that began with human consciousness. His profound questions draw from history's beginning.

When a thoughtful writer is brought to relive grim days of war, he may yield to a despair deeper than the first he experienced in combat. But despair vanishes from Morrison's work at the place where his imagination takes over.

Morrison leads the reader into the mind of a man who after months of combat, suffering conflicts of conscience, creates a new reality. He embarks on a dangerous journey. In his adopted role, he sees lands and people as he would not have seen them while in the uniform of a soldier.

The friendship of a man in the uniform of the enemy enables him to test his beliefs in principles he cannot reform to fit the demands of war. He sees the world with an understanding that is unpatriotic, even treasonous, in wartime. In peace, the principles are given another chance to gain adherents and prevail.

CHAPTER 1

❀

"Now hear this!
"Now hear this!"

The squawk box sounds. I glance at my watch. It is 0230 April 1, 1945.

"This is Major McMullen speaking. Men, this morning we hit the beach. Breakfast will be served in 30 minutes. All black-out regulations are to be maintained.

"The first waves will head for the beaches of Okinawa at o-three-hundred. We will have breakfast in our regular two sections. The first section will return to quarters after eating and be on deck with battle gear, ready to debark, by o-four-hundred."

Men in the fourth wave will eat in the second section.

Three young men who have gone through basic training together at Camp Roberts, California, listen quietly to the major's words. All are Pacific Northwesterners—Ralph from Tacoma, Jim from Seattle, and I (Archie) from Anacortes, Washington, and Vancouver, British Columbia.

There is no need to wake us. We have slept little, wrestling with fears we can neither understand nor talk about with our friends. Today I am to go into combat as an infantry rifleman. I am just 18 years old and this could be the last day of my life.

I look around at my comrades. Are we all going to be here tonight, or will some of us be dead? Ten months ago I graduated from Lord Byng High School in Vancouver. I felt so grown up I didn't bother to attend commencement exercises. I remember the close friends I walked to school with—Gordy, Ken, Mary, and Angus.

"Arch, quit worrying," I say to myself. "You're here. You have good friends. Just do your best, whatever lies ahead."

I picture the letter from the President that landed me here:

"Greetings, from the President of the United States of America:

"You have been selected by your local draft board of friends and neighbors..."

The letter, addressed to my home in Vancouver, British Columbia, orders me—a U.S. citizen—to report to my draft board in Bellingham, Washington, at 0830 June 5, 1944. From there I am to be transported to the Induction Center in Seattle to undergo a physical examination and be sworn into the U.S. Army.

I asked for early induction since no one eligible for military service is being hired in British Columbia for summer work. Besides, I'm in full rebellion against the almost suffocating religious fundamentalism and demand for conformity in my parents' home.

Canada's draft age is 18 years and 6 months, half a year later than ours, so I'm rather special among my Canadian friends.

I am met at the Bellingham train station by Uncle Clarence and Aunt Elizabeth, who take me to their large home on Chestnut Street. I spend the night there before reporting to the draft board.

At the draft board I find myself with 10 other men, each with a small bag of personal belongings. We have been told not to bring extra clothes because we will be issued uniforms later in the day.

Eight of the men are about my age—17 to 20. The two who are older stand apart. One looks to be about 30. We are all dressed differently—slacks and sports coats, bib overalls, suits and ties. I am wearing corduroy trousers and a sweater.

A local draft board member introduces us to the sergeant who is to accompany us to Seattle, then hands out train tickets and meal vouchers.

The sergeant lines us up in two rows and we march to the railroad station. People going to work wave as we pass. Some shout, "Good luck! Kill those Japs!" Others make Winston Churchill's "V"-for-victory sign with their fingers.

I spend two hours on the train, traveling ever farther from home. Seated next to me is a young man from Lynden, Washington, who never has been away from the farm and hardly can talk about his mother and father without becoming emotional. I, on the other hand, feel a tremendous sense of freedom, even though I'm apprehensive about what lies ahead.

My immediate fear is not of the war or that I might be killed, but that I might not be able to keep up with these men, all of whom appear bigger and stronger than I am. I make up my mind to do the best I can.

Army non-commissioned officers with stripes on their sleeves and ribbons on their uniform jackets meet our train at the busy train station in downtown Seattle. We are joined by more inductees from throughout the Pacific Northwest, each carrying a bag of personal belongings. Mine contains a razor, shaving cream, washcloth, and towel. My mother has carefully chosen the latter two items, saying, "You must have your own."

Mother and Dad have given me a *New Testament*, insisting that I carry it always in my left shirt pocket, for protection. Since I couldn't go on a train without something to read, I added two books to my bag—an A.J. Cronin and Sir Walter Scott's *Ivanhoe*.

We walk four-abreast from the station up Fourth Avenue to the Induction Center—out of step, talking all the way. At the Induction Center the recruits are herded into a large room with benches around the perimeter. A corporal tells us to remove all our clothes, place them in a paper bag, and print our name on the bag.

One inductee asks, "Sir, do you mean my underwear, too?"

"I want you naked as a jaybird," the corporal replies. "You're in the army now and we all look the same without clothes or in an army uniform."

I do as I'm told and join a single line for my medical checkup. Everyone in the room is a stranger to me. The boy immediately behind me is about my height, but skinnier. Behind him is a good-looking, taller kid. Never having been naked before with a group of men we don't know—except in high-school gymnasium showers, where everybody knows everybody—we are anxious and tense.

The three of us introduce ourselves: Ralph. Jim. Arch. After our eyes, mouth, heart, and rectum are checked, we are told to cough to see if we have a hernia. We also are given our first military short-arm inspection, to check for venereal diseases.

"I do what?" I ask, when the doctor describes how he wants me to squeeze my penis for him.

"You're in the army now, son. Your body's not your own any more. It belongs to Uncle Sam."

What seems degrading at the time soon will become a Monday morning routine following every weekend leave.

The medic at the end of the line pronounces, without looking up, "Soldier, I'm classifying you I-A."

I dress, report to a large room with the others and hear an officer say, "Repeat after me. I (we insert our own names) will defend the United States of America...wherever I am sent ...obey all orders.... (on and on he droned)...declare my duty to the United States of America.

"Now, say 'I will' and take a step forward.

"Congratulations, men. You are now soldiers in the Army of the United States of America."

The words mean little at this time.

Ralph, Jim, and I board a bus bound for Fort Lewis, about 40 miles south of Seattle, outside Tacoma. Upon arriving, we are issued uniforms and assigned to a barracks. I am informed that I am the lucky person designated to stand the first guard that evening.

It is beautiful outside when I go on duty. As the sun sets on 14,410-foot Mount Rainier to the east, the snow-covered mountain turns a striking pink. It is framed by colored clouds.

I carry a rifle they tell me is an M-1. I have no idea how to use it or whether it is loaded. My beat covers about four blocks. When a soldier approaches me, I try to look soldierly. As we pass, he orders me to halt.

I halt.

"How long have you been in the army, Private?"

"Since this morning, Sir." I could see he was some kind of officer, with eagles on his shoulders.

"Don't you know how to salute a senior officer?"

"No, Sir, I've never saluted any one. I don't know how to salute."

"God-damn-it, Private, I'll teach you."

The officer gives detailed instructions, then walks past me several times so I can practice.

"OK, Soldier," he says, "you've got it down. Don't let me catch you not saluting an officer again."

"No, Sir, and…thank you, Sir, I appreciate your time and instruction."

"That's OK, Soldier. What's your name?"

"Morrison, Sir." He writes it down in a small book. During what remains of my first guard duty I salute everyone, since I don't know how to recognize an officer.

After guard duty, I return to the barracks. Lights are out and mine is the only unoccupied bunk. The bed is small but not uncomfortable and I am tired. I hear someone not far away crying softly. I figure it must be home-sickness. Later, I'm awakened by someone calling out for "home." It's a strange night. Although I feel very much alone, I'm determined not to be like the homesick boys who cry in their bunks. If I miss home, I will never show it.

After a few days, I am sent to basic training at Camp Roberts—the hottest, dustiest place in the world. The routine calls for 12 weeks of hard infantry training in which we climb over logs, crawl in the dirt with live ammo flying over us, march endless miles and become proficient with a variety of weapons. The training climaxes with a bivouac 20 miles out of camp. There, we engage in war games, followed by a forced march back to camp with full gear. I do well, eat well and make up my mind that anything the others can do I also can do. Several in my platoon can't take it and are transferred out of combat duty or given a Section 8 classification (unfit for military service).

One young man from the hills of Oregon tells me that if his dad knew what they were forcing him to do, he'd come after them with a rifle. One night he tells me he's going home and if any soldiers come after him they'll be shot coming up the road to his house. The next morning he's gone. I never hear of him again.

I sort of enjoy basic training. I am with good fellows—Ralph, Jim, and John—and we sometimes discuss heavy stuff, like philosophy and politics. I even gain weight, beefing up from 127 pounds to 155.

After a short leave home, Ralph, Jim, and I ship out from Seattle to Hawaii for amphibian and jungle-intensive schooling. John is wounded in basic training and can't come with us.

🍁   🍁   🍁

So here we are, April 1, 1945, ready for our first combat.

Jim, in the next aisle of "bunks," which are actually canvas hammocks stacked six-high, calls out to me:

"You ready, Arch? Ralph and I are going topside. Get your ass in gear!"

"I'm on my way," I shout back.

We sleep in our OD skivies. That's olive-drab underwear to the uninitiated. It is not the sexiest stuff in the world. I pull on olive-green fatigues and heavy combat boots, with the laces untied.

The three of us silently climb the ladder to the deck.

On this, our personal D-Day, we know the target: the island of Okinawa.

We know we are to be in the fourth wave of the first day of an invasion. It must succeed, we've been told, if we are to have any chance of invading Japan.

We also know that we are going to be replacements for casualties in the first three waves, which means there will be lots of dead and wounded.

The first waves are on their way to the beach, accompanied by the thunder of heavy naval guns and the roar of planes from our aircraft carriers.

Although we have been told very little about the island itself, the army grapevine has provided a wealth of stories and rumors.

The island, we hear, has no less than 10 varieties of poisonous snakes. It is the home base of the Japanese Army's artillery school, which is why its gunners can hit any spot on the island with pinpoint accuracy.

Rumor also has it that the Japs have a secret weapon that they will unveil on Okinawa.

All of the stories are turning out to be partly true.

Ralph, Jim, and I line up in the ship's galley, holding stainless-steel trays.

"Wonder if we get the usual for breakfast," says Ralph, "the usual" being mush, toast, jam and coffee.

As we approach the chow table, we scarcely can believe our eyes. Before us are steak, baked potatoes, vegetables, milk, coffee, salad, and apple pie with ice cream.

I chuckle. The condemned man's last meal before execution.

We stand to eat at long, narrow, chest-high tables. Suddenly another announcement blares over the squawk box:

"Now hear this!

"Now hear this!

"This is your Captain. Major McMullen, your army commander, would like to say a few words."

The ship's captain and our Major stand at the far end of the mess hall.

"Men, I'm going ashore with you," the Major says. "I'm scared like you are. This is my first invasion. Let's do the best we can. Let's do our duty, for God and country! God-speed, men! I'll give you back to the ship's captain."

Ralph turns to me and says, "That sure as hell was different. I haven't heard an officer talk like that before."

Jim breaks in, "I do appreciate his attitude. He seems like one of us. It might not be bad to serve under an officer like him."

"I don't know," I say cynically, "He won't get up front like we will, and he knows that. He'll probably go back to Saipan to bring another batch of replacements and tell them the same story."

Not long after, the captain of our troop ship, the *A.P.A. Clarindon,* is back on the squawk box:

"Gentlemen, it has been an honor and a privilege to have you men aboard my ship. I wish you all the best, if that is possible. I'm not much with prayer, but I'm going to pray in my way for your strength, fortitude, and courage, because I know you will need all the help you can get no matter where it comes from. I hope that in the not-too-far-distant future, I will have the honor and privilege of having you aboard my ship again, not taking you into battle but taking you home to the United States.

"I salute you, men."

The captain, an athletic-looking man in his late 30s, comes to rigid attention and snaps off a salute.

We all cheer and go back to eating in silence.

Below deck, after breakfast, I quickly go through my battle gear: blanket, poncho, field jacket, socks, razor, soap, mess kit, toothbrush, toilet paper, rubber band around my helmet for extra toilet paper, matches, cigarettes, paper for writing stored between my helmet liner and my steel combat helmet, and a pen to write with.

These items go into my pack, with the blanket roll, and everything is covered by my poncho.

Then come the real essentials: M-1 rifle, cleaned and oiled, with a clip of ammo in the magazine and no round in the chamber yet; an ammo belt, filled with clips of ammo; an M-1 cleaning kit; a bandoleer of ammo to throw over my shoulder and, last, a first-aid pack, containing tape, iodine, tourniquet, triangular bandages, and pain pills.

Pack on my back, bandoleer around my neck, weapon on my shoulder and filled with the wisdom of 12 weeks of basic training, I join Ralph and Jim in climbing the ladder to the deck.

We are about to enter the battle of Okinawa.

The wind is blowing a bit topside, and our troop transport does slow rolls in the swells of the China Sea. I see flashes of the naval bombardment in the distance and hear the big guns just beyond our ship. Airplanes bomb and strafe the beach. The sea is filled with ships as far as I can see.

Amphibian Water Buffaloes, LCIs and LSTs circle our ship and other vessels, taking on troops and heading for shore.

A couple of Jap Zeros sneak through and make a run at the beach, strafing our incoming landing craft. Two-engined Jap bombers, called Betties, fly over the island, raining death on our incoming troops. Smoke rises from the shoreline.

I'm sure everyone in this chaotic scene, friend and foe, is doing exactly what he's been trained to do. All except me. I'm so frightened my senses are numbed and I'm acting purely by instinct.

It's as if I'm looking at a backdrop for a war movie and I'm the main actor. Some hero I am. I have already wet my pants.

We all move toward the railings—some to port, others to starboard. My turn comes. I lift my right leg over the railing where a cargo net is fastened.

Reaching down with my right foot, I feel a cross-rope. Finding a secure footing, I swing my left foot over the side of the ship. This simple maneuver, along with the roll of the ship, causes my pack to shift and I teeter precariously.

I stop and cling to the top of the net.

"Hold fast, don't lose your footing," I tell myself. No one talks. I must make sure my hands have a good grip and my feet are firmly placed on a cross-rope.

I quickly discover that every ocean swell and compensating pitch of the ship causes the cargo net, my personal spider web, to move away from the ship and then to come crashing back against the hull.

Fearful of being thrown into the sea, I take care not to move when the net swings back toward the ship. My body is taut. My heart pounds. Adrenaline flows. I tell myself I can either make the best of it or be over-come by fear and panic. I vow to hang on until I reach the Buffalo landing craft bobbing in the water below.

After a time, logic tells me that if I travel another 30 or 40 feet I'll reach the Buffalo. But when I look down, logic flies out the window. The distance to the landing craft appears to be more like 500 feet.

There must be a dozen landing craft on my side of the troop transport, with more waiting to come in as each pulls away with a full load of GIs.

Suddenly there is a scream to my right and my worst fear is realized. A soldier nearby loses his grip when the cargo net bangs against the ship. He plummets toward the sea and is pinned against the hull just as the landing craft slams into it.

I hear no more about him.

CHAPTER 2

❀

The ladder's footing slips as the boy reaches too high while hammering nails into the side of the building. He falls to the ground, striking his left elbow awkwardly. There is a loud, snapping sound.

The boy doesn't move. The arm is numb and tingly but he doesn't feel much pain yet. He looks up at the building he's been helping to construct. His father, owner of a sawmill in the lumber-and-fishing town of Anacortes, in Island County, has provided all the materials for the structure—a tabernacle to house the town's Pentecostal Christians.

The tabernacle is being built on several acres of land adjacent to the boy's family home, the same level field where a visiting circus set up tents the previous summer.

The circus had been great fun, and the circus workers very friendly, especially the young man who cared for the elephants and let the boy help with the watering.

I was that boy, and I had kept my father from knowing I was having fun. He expected me to devote my summers to chores and the Bible.

How strange for childhood memories to flash across one's mind when a comrade falls to his death. How strange to be in this place, undergoing my baptism in the kill-or-be-killed business of war, when just a few short years ago I was building a tabernacle for the Lord.

I wonder if the soldier who fell to his death knew the Lord. I wonder if he ever helped build a tabernacle as a boy, hammering nails along with the men and eating fried chicken, ham, baked potatoes, Jello salad, and apple pie provided by the ladies of the church.

I especially wonder if the young man, or any of the other young men going down the cargo net and being transported to the beaches of Okinawa ever knew anyone like Brother Jerry, the evangelist who conducted our tabernacle's first great revival meeting.

Brother Jerry was a master at preaching fire-and-brimstone, at getting the congregation to speak in tongues, at getting us to sing from the depths of our being such old favorites as "Just As I Am" and "Are You Washed in the Blood of the Lamb?"

When the time was right, Brother Jerry issued an altar call, a summons for all sinners—which meant most of us—to come down the "sawdust trail" spread on the dirt floor and give our hearts and lives to Jesus.

Of course, the collection plates were always passed. I remember one evangelist stopping the ushers while they were passing the plates and saying:

"I can't stand the sound of silver coins in the House of the Lord. Put only paper money in the collection plates. It's so much less disturbing and quiet in the House of God."

One of my friends told me of a traveling preacher who put a clothes line in front of the altar rail and told the worshipers to use a clothespin to attach their money for God. It's pretty hard for anyone to attach a coin to a clothesline.

I also think about baptism and speaking in tongues—things I don't really understand—as I lie on the ground and the numbness wears off and my arm begins to hurt.

Little Bill is working inside the building, wheeling sawdust down the aisle, when my ladder goes down. He comes around the corner shortly after the accident and sees his little brother on the ground. He's called Little Bill because his father—our father—is Big Bill.

"What's wrong with you, Kid?"

"I fell off the ladder and hurt my arm."

Bill picks me up carefully and takes me over to Dad's car. He drives me home, up Commercial Avenue, and we walk into the big house. I hold my broken arm with my good hand. It hurts too much to move it.

Mother listens to my story about how it happened and calls Dad at the mill.

"Archie's had an accident working on the tabernacle," she says. "I think he's broken his arm."

Dad tells Mother to call the preacher from our church and have him anoint me with oil and ask the Lord to heal my arm.

"Archie has been doing the Lord's work," he says. "The Lord will surely hear the prayer."

The preacher is called and he comes to the house. He anoints me with oil and prays to the Lord. Then he puts his hands on my head and pushes hard and says, in a loud voice:

"Lord, heal! Lord, heal! In the name of Jesus, heal!"

I wonder why he's talking so loud to the Lord and pushing down on my head so hard. I have never heard that the Lord is hard of hearing.

I am put to bed. My two sisters and my little brother visit and ask how I'm doing. Mary, who is 2-1/2 years older than I am, is told to read Bible stories to me.

"Has Jesus made your arm better?" my little brother asks.

Sister Mary tells me to think about something other than my arm. The next morning the arm is swollen and black and blue. Mother sees it and says nothing. But she immediately calls Dr. Cook.

We go to his office, where he tells Mother I have to go to the hospital. There, they give me chloroform and the doctor sets the arm under a fluoroscope.

Although I spend the rest of the summer in a cast, I am expected to do my chores: keeping the wood box filled next to the kitchen stove, feeding my 50 or so mallard ducks, helping big brother Bill with his chickens, and doing various tasks around the barn.

I scrape chicken manure off the roosts with a hoe and dump it on the manure pile. Brother Bill tells me there have to be a few roosters in with the hens if we are to have more chickens.

At night, after my little brother goes to sleep in our shared room, I lie awake and wonder why God doesn't heal my broken arm. Doesn't he love me? I don't tell lies. I follow directions when I paste pictures on our Bible-story posters. I especially enjoy the poster of Daniel in the lion's den. I can almost hear the lions growling and baring their terrible teeth. I saw our cat do the same thing in the barn when it tore a rat apart.

The Lord saved Daniel. Why hasn't he fixed my arm?

I listen quietly in our big living room on Sunday afternoons while Mother reads aloud from *Ben Hur* and from her favorite book *Pilgrim's Progress*. All five of us kids sit on chairs while mother reads, although sometimes she excuses Billy.

After *Pilgrim's Progress* Mother turns to a chapter in the Old Testament and then one in the New Testament. Each of us reads a verse until the two chapters are finished. Then we all kneel beside our chairs and pray aloud. Mother and Dad prompt us when we don't know what to say.

"Tell Jesus what a bad boy you were yesterday and ask Him to forgive you," Mother says on my behalf.

"Jesus, forgive me," I say. "I will not do it again."

"He will forgive if you ask," Dad says. "Now ask Him to protect you and He will."

"Dear Jesus, please protect me from all harm," I say. "I am not going to commit these sins again. Amen."

Dad then prays for about 10 minutes. Sometimes he prays longer. He seems to pray for everyone—each of us, our relatives, missionaries, the hungry, the poor, the sick. I often come close to falling asleep.

All that summer, while we were praying, I think to myself, "I have tried to do God's will, but He hasn't healed my arm."

When Mother lets me sleep with my brother Bill, I ask him about God not fixing my arm. Bill tells me to pray harder or to go ask the preacher.

When I'm in bed with Bill, he usually gets into his favorite subject: how humans enjoy the same mating habits as the animals down in our barn. He also explains the physical differences between boys and girls.

I ask whether Mom and Dad do the things that produce babies.

"They must, Arch," he replies. "They have lots of kids."

Bill makes me promise never to let on to Mother and Dad what we do and talk about under the covers.

Grandpa Andy and Grandma Minnie, my mother's parents, are very good to me. I often ride my pony to their farmhouse several miles from our place. They like to talk about the early days in Kansas before they came west.

When Grandpa Andy develops heart problems, they move to town to live with us. Grandpa becomes born-again at a revival meeting and immediately quits smoking and drinking. He spends a lot of time listening to news on the radio, where his favorite commentator is H.V. Kaltenborn.

Grandpa says there's going to be a war. The war will be caused by the Democrats, led by President Roosevelt, and the anti-Christ, Benito Mussolini, will take over the world.

"Mark my words," Grandpa says, "it's all in the Bible."

All my aunts, uncles and cousins on Dad's side are Republicans. Everything I hear at home and in the church's interpretation of the Bible convinces me that Democrats are the source of most of the country's evil.

Other people in our town put Blue Eagle stickers in their windows to show support for Roosevelt's National Recovery Act (the N.R.A.). I'm told at home that this particular eagle is the mark of the beast from the Book of Revelation.

Even at a young age, I wonder how so many people can be wrong while my family knows what's right.

Sometimes I wish I could be like the other boys at school. They make fun of our church and call me a "Holy Roller." They laugh at my clothes because I don't wear bib overalls. Their folks are all Democrats; their fathers work at the mill and belong to the union, the Wood Workers of America. Dad hates the union. He says the only reason unions have become powerful is because they are favored by "the Democrats and their president."

Discipline is strict in our home. "Children should be seen and not heard!" Obedience to Mother and Father must be unconditional—no questions asked. That's what the Bible says.

Punishment is Biblical, too. "Spare the rod and spoil the child!" Dad does little with the rod, preferring the thick leather strap on which he sharpens his straight-edge razor.

Dad sometimes employs simpler methods of punishment. If I fail to clean my dinner plate, he grabs my ear and twists it, causing considerable pain, then marches me down to the wood pile in the basement. I sit on a chopping block, while Dad force-feeds me. I often gag and throw up on the floor, the woodpile, and even Dad's pants. He pays no attention, talking on and on about the starving children in China.

Dad travels a lot on business, to get lumber and box orders for the mill. He goes by train to New York, Chicago, Philadelphia, and places in California. When he's gone for any length of time, the punishment is left to Mother.

Mother's methods differ from Dad's. She isolates me in a dark closet, behind one of the bathtubs. The closet is filled with pipes and valves and fingers of plaster that come through the lath like monsters.

The closet terrifies me. I lie on the floor with my eyes closed, kicking and screaming. Sometimes I'm left there for several hours with the door locked from the outside.

"You're going to be a good Christian boy now. Apologize for being disobedient. The devil makes you do these things. You don't want to go back in the closet do you?"

But I still love her. This is what Mother and Dad think is the proper Christian way to teach children right from wrong. Their beliefs cannot be shaken. They are right!

God is right, because He loves us and if we don't sin, He will protect us from all harm. He will answer all our prayers. He will provide for all our needs. And, finally, He will give us eternal life.

All I have to do is give my heart to Jesus, obey my parents, pray for forgiveness of my many sins, receive the baptism of the Holy Spirit and, like the missionaries, tell others about Jesus. I think I've done all these things.

Mother does a lot of Bible study with her children. She has books of commentary on the Bible, along with many translations of the Bible and printed sermons by preachers who agree with her beliefs.

She often disagrees with the preacher at our church.

Once the disagreement was so intense she left the church for a time, and others in the church who agreed with her came to our house for church services.

The usual Sunday morning service at church is preceded by Sunday school for the youngsters. On Sunday evenings there's an evangelical service to "bring sinners to God." On Wednesday evening there's a prayer meeting, at which time those moved by the Holy Spirit "speak in tongues," which sounds like a lot of babble to me. Friday night is "Young People's Meeting," a time for gospel songs, testimonials and baptisms, followed by a "tarrying time" during which worshipers stand around and talk further about their sinful ways.

Testimonials are the most fun, especially when young people stand in front of the congregation and tell what bad, evil, disobedient sinners they have been. This is where I fall short. I keep certain secrets to myself—like the things Billy and I do and talk about in bed—telling only those things that make me out to be just a little bit of a sinner.

Some kids tell everything—about smoking, drinking, swearing, dirty language, lust, and fornication. I have to look in the dictionary to learn the meaning of some of the words. Even then I'm confused, so I ask big brother Bill to explain.

Of course, the wilder the stories the more people like to hear them. One can gauge how a testimonial is going over by the number of interruptions by people shouting "Praise the Lord," "Wonderful Jesus," and "Amen."

When a testimonial is finished, the congregation—young and old—lets loose with "Hallelujah" and "Jesus forgive, Jesus forgive." Then we sing hymns. "God Will Take Care of You" and "Trust in the Lord" are favorites. Those who have testified are considered officially forgiven.

One hymn we call "The Salad," because it is a mixture of a whole bunch of hymns:

I'll be Walking on the King's Highway
Tell Me the Old, Old Story
I Love Him Better Every Day
Hallelujah.
If You Only Follow Me
I Will Make You Fishers of Men
So, Trust in the Lord
And Do Not Despair…

The rest is gone. Gone from memory.

One night, at the end of the young people's service when folks are tarrying, two older women order me to kneel by a chair and pray with my arms raised to heaven so the Spirit can fill me. The ladies say they will stay by my side to help me "get through and find God." I say, "I didn't know he was lost."

When I get up from kneeling, I notice my brother Bill in the back of the room with his arm around a girl. They are very close.

Night after night I pray and nothing special happens to me at these meetings. A year or so after the kneeling experience, I decide I've seen enough "spirit fillings" and heard enough "speaking-in-tongues" to do these things myself, in public.

For a week, I go out to the barn with the chickens and ponies to practice. My speaking-in-tongues soon sounds as good as anything I've heard from the old ladies at church. If this works I won't have to go to all those night meetings and I can play baseball. But what if they think I'm faking? Will I then have to stand up and tell everybody?

I decide to take a chance. It will be my secret with Jesus. On Friday night, I decide the time has come.

Kneeling by a chair in the tarrying room, with two elderly ladies by my side, I suddenly thrust my arms in the air, fall on my back, and do a great imitation of the gibberish I've heard so often and perfected in the barn.

I continue speaking in tongues for about 10 minutes, finally thinking to myself, "Arch, you'd better cut this off or they'll surely know it's phony."

It goes over big, really big. I am a convincing success. The room is in an uproar. The familiar words ring out from every corner: "Praise God," "Jesus," "Hal-le-lu-jah," and "Praise the Lord, finally he's one of us."

This marks the end of my attendance at church meetings three nights a week. I am formally filled with the Holy Spirit.

🍁   🍁   🍁

My father manages a lumber and box mill on Fidalgo Bay, just below our big house. Dad goes to work early and usually comes home for lunch with my two uncles. The three of us elementary-school kids walk home for lunch.

Dad prays a long time before we eat. When we take our lunch to school we are told to ask God to bless the food before we eat or it will give us a stomach ache.

Supper is never eaten until Dad comes home. At the table are Mother and Dad, five of us children, Grandpa Andy and Grandma Minnie, and the hired girl who is pregnant and came to Jesus and to us through the church.

There is often an out-of-work preacher at the table, too. If a man who has the calling can't find a church to support him, Mother and Dad will.

After dinner we all go to the living room, where Dad reads a chapter from the Bible. Then we all kneel by our chairs and each of us prays.

We usually complete our devotions in about 45 minutes on weekdays. On Sundays, it takes up to two hours.

Dad goes down to the Sound every Saturday to dump our garbage in the water. Then he goes to his office building, across the railroad tracks, to work on ledgers and check the progress of his orders.

One Saturday he asks me to go with him. While looking around his office, I spy a round hole in his desk and four more in the windowsill behind where he's seated. I ask what caused the holes and he replies, "Archie, those are bullet holes made before you were born."

Dad continues: "I was shot at by bank robbers and God protected me. The bank downtown, the only one in town, was robbed. The bandits were escaping. The only road off the island went by this mill office. The chief of police—there were three policemen on the force and only one car—called the mill and asked your Uncle Ben and me to block the road with our cars. And that's what we did, although as soon as your Uncle Ben got out of his car he took off fast down the railroad tracks.

"I returned to the office and was working at my desk when I heard the robbers drive up in their get-away car and come to a halt before the barricade formed by our cars.

"They got out of their car, saw me and fired their rifles at me. The bullets came close but didn't hit me. The bullets are what caused those round holes in the desk and windowsill."

"What's a rifle, Dad?"

"A rifle, Archie, is an accurate gun that's usually used for hunting animals, not to kill humans. Your Uncle Ben hunts deer with a rifle. Remember when he brought us a side of venison?"

"Were the robbers trying to kill you like an animal?" I ask.

"I think they were."

"I wonder what it would be like to be killed with a rifle."

"It would be a quick death, Archie, if the bullet hit your heart or your head. But if you were 'saved' you would be with the Lord and that would be wonderful. Absent from the body is present with the Lord."

❦　　　　　❦　　　　　❦

At home, I don't like sharing a room with my little brother and wish I had a room to myself, like Billy.

I wish I could play an instrument the way Billy plays the accordion. He is always being asked to play at young people's church meetings and high-school assemblies.

The high school he attends is the same one Mother attended when she married Dad. Mother and Dad think Billy is the greatest. If I can be like him maybe they'll love me as much as they love him.

I once heard Mother say to Aunt Elizabeth, whose two sons attend a Calvinist college in Wheaton, Ill.:

"All I want for my boys is for them to grow up as Christian gentlemen."

That's what Mother and Dad think little Bill is, a Christian gentleman. But what about the girls, and my little brother, and me?

Billy is good at manual arts, too. He made Mother a cedar chest in woodworking class at school. The chest is at the foot of her bed. It's where she stores clothes she doesn't want bugs to destroy.

In the third grade I had a teacher named Miss Jones. She had a wooden leg, which is probably why I remember her so well. That, and I thought she was also quite old. I think she liked me, because she was always helping me.

Ralph, my best friend in school, walks either to his house or comes home with me after school. When he comes to my house it's something of a problem, because Mother wants us to read Bible stories.

Sometimes I'm allowed to go to Ralph's house after school if all my chores are finished. Ralph lives down by the bay, near the mill. I've never seen his father. He's always working at the mill.

Their house is very small. The living room has older furniture, but it's "neat as a pin," as Grandma Minnie would say. When I go home with Ralph, we walk with other boys who live in small houses and have dads who work at the mill.

The Mitchell boys—Earl and Rex and an older brother—sometimes walk with us. Rex is in my class and Earl is a year older. Their father was killed in a mill accident a few years ago. But the boys never talk about him.

Rex and Earl wear bib overalls as most of the boys do. Mother and Dad insist that I wear yellow corduroys, with a nice shirt and jacket.

Boys my age are really close. Girls don't matter. With boys, you put your arms around each other and plan adventures. Rex and Earl and I build forts, climb trees, and talk boy-talk.

When I'm with my friends, having a wonderful time, the war Grandpa Andy says is coming seems very far away.

A girl named Sylvia sits across the aisle from me in school. She has just two dresses. She wears one for two days and then switches to the other, so they are always clean. Her shoes are not very good. The soles are almost gone.

I like her and think of her as a good friend. Smart too. I guess she's the first girl I've really liked. I enjoy talking to her. I would walk home with her, but the guys would laugh.

Why can't she have shoes like my sisters'? If only I could give her a pair.

I go home one day and ask Mother what she does with my sisters' outgrown shoes.

"Send them to the cousins in Coulee City (in Eastern Washington) and Mossyrock (in Southwest Washington)," she says.

"Could I have the next couple of pairs?"

"Why?"

I tell her about Sylvia's shoes and that I feel sorry for her. She laughs and says I'm a little young to have a girl friend and we must take care of the cousins.

I tell sister Mary about Sylvia and she finds two pairs of old shoes and says Mother will never know. I put them in a paper sack and place them under Sylvia's desk at school. She doesn't say a word, but the following day she puts her foot out and I see she's wearing my sister's shoes. She gives me a big smile and I feel good.

Billy's bedroom is a long way from Mother and Dad's room, which gives us a lot of privacy. The nights I sleep in his bed he continues my education on subjects I would never talk about with Mother and Dad. I figure that's the way most older brothers are with their kid brothers.

In June, Bill graduates from high school and goes to Seattle to Bible School, where he also takes classes on diesel engines. His dream is to be engineer on an Alaska fishing boat.

That summer I learn that even our family has secrets. When Dad starts bringing his brother Ben home in the evening, Mother sends all of us kids upstairs with a warning not to come down. We hide quietly on the stairwell, listening, and watching as my uncle grows louder and louder and laughs at nothing at all. When he starts to get up, Dad has to hold him upright.

Billy tells me later, when he's home from Bible School, that our uncle is a drunk and Dad has to look after him.

"What's a drunk?"

"Well, kid, you ask tough questions. Drunk is when you drink whiskey and it makes you feel good but you lose your head. It's also sinning, the same as smoking."

Bill tells me Uncle Ben has a place out at the beach where he has a girl friend. That's where he drinks his whiskey.

"We'll talk about it some night when you're in bed with me."

Dad, his brother Ben, and their brother-in-law Clarence sell the mill in 1938, blaming their decision on labor unrest caused by the Democrats, President Roosevelt's New Deal, and Roosevelt's wife, Eleanor.

During a strike at the mill, the workers dumped one of our cars into the Sound.

"We pay them a fair wage, what do they want?" Dad asks. "They get a turkey at Christmas. I give them extra for overtime."

The only thing to do, my father says, is move out of the country. He sells the big house and we move to Vancouver, British Columbia, away from Roosevelt, the "ungodly" Democrats, and the Woodworkers Union.

Dad builds a beautiful home in West Point Gray, an affluent part of town, and buys a hardware store. I lose all my friends—Ralph, Rex, Earl, and Sylvia—and go to a new school, Queen Mary Elementary. I have to make new friends, go to a new church, still Pentecostal, and live in a new country. It takes a while to start over.

Even in the new house, my little brother and I share a room and sleep in bunk beds. A third bed in the room is for Billy when he's home and his fishing boat is safely in the harbor. My two sisters also share a room.

Mother is devoted to her new church, The Seventh Avenue Tabernacle. Grandma and Andy come to stay with us after visiting my uncle in Los Angeles. They are given the downstairs bedroom, with their own bathroom.

One morning in the spring I'm awakened early by a lot of activity in the house. My sisters tell me Grandpa Andy had a heart attack and is going to die. The only time I had heard about death was when Dad told me about being shot at like an animal.

Andy going to die? I talk to him a lot that week. He tells me to be a good Christian boy, that he loves me and will see me in heaven. He dies a week after his heart attack. It is the first time I have seen a dead body. He looks very still and gray lying in bed with his eyes open.

The men come with the funeral car and put him on a cart and take him away. The funeral is back in the States and we kids don't get to go. Before the body is shipped south, we are taken down to the mortuary where Andy lies in a wooden casket looking as if he could get up and walk away. I ask Grandma Minnie why Grandpa looks so good. She tells me the mortuary men fix up the bodies before a funeral.

Mother says, "Dad is with the Lord, praise the Lord."

I wonder. I don't want him dead with the Lord. I want him back. How can they say, "The Lord took him?" Does the Lord give heart attacks? Does the Lord kill people? This God of love, comfort, and understanding, this God we sing about at church. He will take care of you! Trust in the Lord, he is a friend so true! What a friend we have in Jesus! A friend that gives Andy a heart attack and takes him away. Did I really want a friend like that?

School is not going well. I have no motivation. I know hardly anybody. My Mother is called and told I'm not doing well enough to stay in my grade. They put me back a year. In my new class, I quickly make friends—Evan, Peter, Mary, and Gordy. Mother hires two women, the Crake sisters, to tutor me on Saturdays. I like them a lot. They get me going and I don't stop.

In the Canadian schools we are ranked scholastically in class and sit in that order. My class has 29 students. At the first of the year I'm ranked

26th. By the end of the year I'm third. School is no problem from then on.

My physical-education teacher is a husky, aggressive young man. Although he likes to hear my American accent, I don't care for him.

Evan, Jack, and Peter are with me in the boys' choir, under the direction of Mr. Cummings. We come in second in a British Columbia choir competition. I have a feeling of acceptance. I dress like the other boys and nobody in the choir works for my dad.

I'll never forget September 3, 1939.

A newspaper boy races down our street early in the morning calling out:

"Extra! Extra! Canada, Britain at War With Germany. Extra! Extra! Canada at War!"

The whole family is awakened by the boy's shouts.

Billy is in Northern British Columbia on a fishing boat at the time. If he stays in Canada, he'll be in the Canadian armed forces. My sister is soon to be married to a young Canadian who also will be affected. He immediately volunteers for the Royal Canadian Air Force and becomes a pilot. His greatest desire is to fly a Spitfire.

That winter, before Bill decides whether to return to the States or be inducted into Canada's armed forces, his fishing vessel is caught in a violent storm south of Seymour Narrows, between Vancouver Island and the mainland, entering the Straits of Georgia.

The seas are so turbulent and the vessel so overloaded with fish that the aft deck soon is awash. The fishing vessel sinks from sight and three crew members are lost, among them brother Bill.

It is devastating to Mother and Dad, even though they say it is God's will. Dad goes up on a search boat and finds an oil slick where the ship presumably went down. All he says is that Billy was a wonderful Christian young man. I keep my secret about our relationship in bed.

For all my Mother's faith, trust, and religious belief, she never recovers from Billy's death. She puts his clothes and his Bible in the cedar chest at the foot of her bed and there they remain.

Visitors who come to our house to offer condolences ignore the younger children. I'm alone in the top bunk, looking across at an empty bed. My big brother is dead. He'll never come home again.

I cry myself to sleep many nights after his death. I return to school the following week. My physical-education teacher, who acts so tough, says, "Morrison, you've missed a week of school. Were you back in the States with your anti-war people?"

"No, Sir," I reply. "My brother died."

The class grows quiet. It is the last time the teacher speaks to me.

CHAPTER 3

❀

I can still hear the scream of death from the soldier who fell from the cargo net when I jump from the last horizontal cross rope into the landing craft bobbing in the China Sea.

There are about 50 others aboard. We all look pretty much the same in helmets and fatigues, carrying ammo belts, grenades, and rifles. Some are a little taller or heavier, but almost all are 18 or 19 and scared shitless at the prospect of going into combat for the first time.

The landing craft has no radio communication. When it leaves the troop ship, it circles until it receives a semaphore signal from shore saying it's time to begin the dash to Hagushi Beach.

Our Buffalo landing craft has considerable firepower, which helps when you're heading into enemy-held territory. Also, unlike earlier landing craft—which cannot get past the coral reef that guards the shore—the Buffalo is fully amphibian; with its tracked propulsion it easily maneuvers over the coral and goes right up on dry land to deposit its frightened cargo.

A faint glow in the eastern sky signals the imminent arrival of another sunrise when our Buffalo ends its circling, turns, picks up speed, and heads for shore.

From where I'm standing on the port side, it's hard to see through the salt spray that cascades over the blunt nose of the Buffalo. But there's no missing the billows of black smoke on the beach.

The first two waves of troops, which went over the coral reef at high tide, are already ashore and moving inland. Large parachute flares (star shells) hover over the beach.

"What are the flares for?" I ask one of the Buffalo's crew.

"They're fired by infantry mortars," the seaman replies. "They tell the pilots and navy gunners how far the troops have advanced up the beach. Weapons are adjusted to fire over our infantry troops. Your outfit probably will be firing flares this afternoon and hoping the navy and the fly-boys see them."

How right he is.

The seaman adds: "I've got to make sure the tracks of our landing craft hit the coral at the right angle to keep us upright. I'd better quit talking and pay attention."

As we near shore, I look over at Jim and Ralph and wonder how long we'll be together.

Large colored squares—orange, red, and yellow—mark our landing spots on the beach. Despite the noise of the naval bombardment, which covers a 10-mile front roughly 100 yards ahead of our advance infantry, there is no major enemy defense of the beach. Most of the Jap Zeros have been quickly shot out of the sky.

Our Buffalo comes to a stop near some trees. The acrid smell of gunpowder fills the air. The noise is deafening, a mix of naval guns, landing-craft engines, aircraft and machine guns.

But there are no human sounds—no voices, no shouts.

"Out, men, and keep moving up the beach to cover," someone shouts. As we spill from the landing craft, it quickly pivots, churning up sand and spewing gasoline exhaust as it heads out to sea to bring other groups of young men from a harbor black with ships. We run across the sand toward a depression we hope will afford some protection.

On a bluff to my left, enemy mortars and machine guns fire at, and hit, several incoming landing craft. Before long, their location is zeroed-in upon by the Navy's big guns, which thunder and send great clouds of dirt and mud high into the air.

The enemy guns immediately fall silent.

As we get our bearings, LSTs (landing ship tanks)—resembling giant whales with their mouths open—disgorge trucks, jeeps, artillery, ammunition, rations and assorted provisions that will be needed to support 100,000-plus fighting men.

To the acrid smell of gunpowder has been added the sickening-sweet smell of exhaust fumes and the pungent odor of ruptured gasoline barrels.

Noise continues to be our constant companion, dinning in our ears, confusing our minds. It comes from the land, sea, and air.

While we are in the protected area, we are told to report to a replacement officer, a master sergeant who has set up operations a bit farther inland, in a large dip in the ground, surrounded by trees. The Army calls such protected areas "defilades."

The master sergeant assigns us to various divisions in need of replacements. Ralph goes to the 27th Division, Jim to the 96th, and I to the 7th. We say our good-byes. It's a difficult, emotional farewell since we've been together since basic training. As soldiers we try to show as little outward emotion as possible, putting on brave fronts, but I am churning inside.

And now, heading into combat, I wonder if I will ever...?

The words remain unspoken. I say to myself, "Don't think that way, of course you will."

Our job is to replace those killed or wounded in the initial assault. I know none of those assigned to the 7th Division.

When the replacements arrive at division headquarters, they are sent to various battalions, companies and, finally, squads, the basic fighting unit. I'm assigned to the 184th Infantry Regiment, Second Battalion, Company C, Second Platoon.

The Second Squad is to become my family. We will live together and possibly die together during the next few months.

The 184th's mission is to spearhead the 7th Division's advance across Okinawa to the Pacific Ocean side. Our first target is Kadena Airfield. The Second Squad is already at the edge of the runway.

I report to the squad, informing those within hearing distance that I'm the new replacement. One of the soldiers replies, "Just stick with me, Kid, and you'll be OK."

He's a soft-spoken man, sturdy, about 5-7, clean-shaven except for a small black mustache, with dark piercing eyes and a wonderful smile. He's wearing fatigues with pockets stuffed with grenades, and he's carrying his M-1 rifle at the ready. His ammo-belt is filled, and more grenades and ammo are stuffed in the bandoleer around his shoulders. I can tell he's from the West Coast by his accent.

I do what he tells me. I stick close by.

"Kid," he says, "we're going to run across the airstrip one at a time. There will probably be rifle fire. We think there are Japs on that rise at the end of the runway. I'll tell you when to take off. Go fast, as fast as you can. Run with your head down. Zig-zag if you can."

"OK," I reply.

"Now, take off! Fast!"

As I run, enemy bullets kick up dirt on the runway to my left and in front of me. I hear the whine of ricocheting lead.

Many thoughts race through my mind:

-Somebody out there is firing at me! Somebody out there is trying to kill me! That somebody is the enemy, the Japs! They're people I can't see, that I don't know!

-I'm reminded of what Dad told me about the bank robbers shooting at him. "They tried to kill me like an animal."

Our squad makes it across the airstrip, each GI running low and fast. We gather in a wide ditch on the far side of the runway, realizing there is no real organized resistance, just small-arms fire.

"You did great," says my new friend. "You run low and fast. That's the way to stay alive. It looks like we're going to be together."

His name is Lee. He introduces the others hiding in the ditch.

"This is our first replacement," he says, "We really don't need him since it's been like duck soup so far today, but we can always use a good guy. Kid, this is Cook."

Cook is a 200-pound, 6-2 farm boy with a blond crewcut, blue eyes, rosy cheeks, and a big smile. Despite his size, he looks younger than 18.

"Sarge S here is our squad leader," Lee says, continuing to point out the various squad members. "Sarge has been with the outfit all the way. Attu, Kiska, Kwajalein, Leyte, and now here. We just call him Sarge S."

"Lieutenant Estes over there with the captain, getting our orders, is the platoon leader. He's a good guy and doesn't expect us to do anything he wouldn't do. He's always with us.

"And this is John, from San Francisco. John's the brains of the squad. He carries books with him and speaks good English. He was just 16 when he got out of high school and he had two years at San Francisco State College before being drafted..He was president of the college debate club."

Unlike Cook, John is on the small side—5-6 or 5-7—and slender. He has dark brown hair, dark eyes, and a heavy beard that gives him the look of someone always in need of a shave. He gives a quick hello and a nod of the head, but no big smile like the others.

"And this guy is Jake," Lee says, moving on. "He's from a coal field somewhere in the South."

"You know it's West Virginia, shit-head," Jake snaps.

"Jake got married at 16, has two kids and worked in the coal mines. His wife and two boys moved in with her parents and grandparents when he joined the army. As a coal miner, he's used to living in a hole."

Jake is about 6-4 and lean, with a mop of curly red hair, sky-blue eyes and practically no beard.

"Jake got by without shaving all through basic training," Lee says. "Look at his feet. I think the boots are size 15s and they look even bigger with his skinny legs. One thing you'll notice about Jake is his continuous outpouring of filthy language; profanity just pours out, despite John's attempts to teach him proper English. Jake's a rough boy, but he has a heart of gold. You'll find there's nothing he wouldn't do for the squad."

Without waiting for an introduction, a young man behind the others begins to speak, very rapidly:

"I am Jose Rodriguez from Modesto, California. I have a beautiful wife and four children. Glad to have you with us. My family works in the fields in the San Jose Valley. We live in a very small house. My parents, too. But it is wonderful. We all love and take care of each other.

"My wife and children are wonderful. I miss them very much. We have a wonderful church and a great priest. My mother is from Fresno and my father came from Mexico."

"That's it, Kid," Lee says, shaking my hand. "This is your home and we're your brothers."

I hadn't been called Kid since Billy drowned. He used to call me his "kid brother."

Estes, our platoon leader, returns with our orders.

"We're to defend this corner of the airstrip," he says. "We're not expecting a large counterattack, but there probably will be infiltrators we must prevent from getting through tonight and in the morning.

"Defensive positions will be set up on higher ground, at the south end of the runway. We'll form a protective perimeter with foxholes to guard the company position. Let's get with it."

The airstrip is visible and secured from east and west. Several enemy bombers smolder on the runway.

Lee says, "Kid, you're going to be with me. We have to get some protection for tonight."

He and I dig my first real foxhole. As we work, Lee says, "You'll have to forgive me for not asking your name. I should have asked earlier. I called you Kid because you remind me of my kid brother."

"I'm Archie Morrison, but just call me Arch. I'm 18, but I'll be 19 in June."

"Mine's Lucian Lee. My Dad got the Lucian from my grandfather. He's Portuguese. Everybody calls me Lee."

Our foxhole is not deep enough and the rocks prevent us from digging farther; so we collect some fairly large rocks and pile them in front of the foxhole and around each end. When I'm on my knees all that can be seen above ground is the top of my helmet.

We know the Japs could be watching and planning their infiltration. But there is no harassing rifle fire and no evidence of the enemy.

Lee tells me, "The Japs on Leyte let you dig in and they're watching you all the time, memorizing how to get to your hole. Then, after dark, they try to crawl to your hole and quietly eliminate you. If the Japs infiltrate behind us they can cause all kinds of hell.

"We don't want to have any light at night, since we don't know where they are dug in. We want to be all set up before dark."

We eat dinner in shifts, half the squad on guard protecting us from small-arms fire and the other half down the hill eating. We have two O.D. C ration cans. One can contains the main course—hash, or beans and franks, or meat and spaghetti, or scrambled eggs and sausage. I hope we get the eggs for breakfast. The second can contains condiments—crackers, cheese, powdered coffee, a tropical Hershey bar, powdered lemonade, and 10 cigarettes with matches.

That's 30 cigarettes a day for each man, and there are extra Chesterfields and Old Golds in the ration boxes. The squad has a small gasoline stove to be used when it can't be seen by the enemy and there is actually time for cooking.

At dinner I meet two more members of the squad, Goldsmith and Frances. They were on scouting detail when I arrived.

My C ration can contains cold hash. Cold hash is hard to swallow, but that's all there is here. Rations and more ammo are brought up from division supply by small trucks or weasels. The latter are jeep-like vehicles with tracks so they can go through mud.

Just before dark, Lee and I return to our hole and he gives me some survival tips.

"I learned them from a good friend on Leyte when I came in as a replacement," Lee says.

We'll take three-hour turns standing guard. I'm to be first. After three hours, I'm to wake up Lee.

I have a watch I got for high-school graduation the previous June. Lee doesn't have a watch. He'll use mine when he stands guard.

First, the most important tip:

"You have to keep a cigarette going all the time, so you can give it to me when you wake me, Arch," Lee says. "If you light a match at night or show the glow of your smoke you wind up dead. I've seen it happen. The Japs are out there and that's what they're looking for—anything to show where you are. They have accurate rifles and know how to use them. Let me show you how we smoke at night."

Lee gets down in the bottom of the hole, cups his hands, lights his cigarette, and holds it backward in his hand in the bottom of the hole. When he wants a drag he puts his head down to his hand and takes a deep pull on the weed. I practice while he watches and it's still light. Two or three tries and I hear, "Great, Kid, you've got it down."

I wonder what happened to the friend who taught Lee how to stand guard on Leyte. He doesn't mention him again. You don't ask certain questions.

The important thing is that Lee is willing to be my foxhole partner and share his battle experience, and he has confidence in my ability to protect his life tonight.

I tell Lee about the Japanese-American (Nisei—second generation, born in the United States) soldiers I met on a troop ship out of Seattle. One of them, named Nairi, told me to find someone in my squad who'd been in combat and learn all I could from him.

"I'll do my best, Arch," Lee says. "I think we'll be a good team. Let's start with tonight. Night guard is very important. It can mean our lives.

"You set out an area you're going to watch. Look at the area right in front of us, Arch. Study every little thing in view. Rocks, trees, bushes, everything. Be very observant and vigilant.

"Now, set out your boundaries. If you can make contact with the men in the holes on either side of you, communicate with them. Make common landmarks for the boundaries of your perimeter. Then you know the area you must guard.

"Count all the objects in your defended area. Memorize any outline you can see after dark or when our artillery drops parachute flares.

"Let's look out in front of our hole. On the left we have that big rock.

"Cook is in the next hole, so I'll let him know that rock is our boundary.

"On the right we have that tree, the one with the branches all gone on the left side where a shell has gouged a crater. You let Goldsmith, in the hole over there, know that the left half of the tree is our right boundary. He gets the other half.

"Now, count every object between your boundaries."

"I count eight," I say.

"And I count nine," he replies. "Let's go over them and see what you missed."

I quickly re-count and say, "I see it, Lee. That little stump. I missed it. There are nine."

Lee says, "Now you write that number down on paper and you put it in your helmet to keep it dry, so you won't forget it. When the action starts, I don't trust my memory.

"At night I count the field objects to see if there are more than nine. If there's one more, it's a Jap who wants to kill us.

"I watch each of the now 10 objects—the trees, bushes, and rocks I have designated to see which of them moves. I wait, watch, and prepare for action.

"Just remember, be silent and no movement above the hole on your part. When the moving object is close enough to line up with your eye, you pull the pin on a grenade, release the handle, and then just roll it out of your hole toward him, very quietly. You have five seconds. Any noise you make could give away your position and mean you're dead. Get down low in your hole and wait for the grenade to explode. The shrapnel goes over you.

"I hope we can practice this tomorrow. Grenades don't give away your position the way the flash of an M-1 does. The other Japs in the area won't know your position. But if you fire your rifle, the muzzle flash gives you away and you can expect a grenade, knee-mortar shell or even a Jap in your hole. And a bullet through your head the next time you look out.

"The explosion and shrapnel from your grenade, you hope will kill, wound, or in some way eliminate further attempts by this soldier to kill us.

"To be sure, you carefully count once more—when it's all quiet—the number of objects in your perimeter."

Lee goes on to explain that Jap soldiers carry a piece of wood, like a long rifle stock, with a sharpened bayonet strapped to the end. They crawl on their bellies, probing with this makeshift weapon to locate the edge of your hole. When they find it, they jump up and drive the knife into your hole and scream "banzai."

"One more thing to remember," Lee says, "is that the star shells released by our artillery light up the whole area for a few minutes. When that happens, freeze in position, using only your eyes—no head movement—to search the area for anything that moves. Make a mental note of where you see the movement, but do nothing until the flare has gone out. When the flare is dead, plan your defense.

"Look, Arch, if you're suspicious of anything happening tonight or if you think you see something moving on our perimeter, very quietly wake me up and I'll help you."

We light cigarettes without showing any light. The night is uneventful.

Our battalion is held in reserve until April 6, the day we begin our assault on the Pinnacle and Hill 178. During our wait, I gain confidence and combat skills while on patrol and pulling night-defense guard duty.

I'm also able to gain insight into the different ways soldiers prepare mentally for the life-or-death situations that await them.

While we're on reserve, a thousand yards or so behind the front lines, our food is upgraded from C rations to Ten-in-One rations. The latter come in large boxes with meals for 10 men and full packs of cigarettes instead of the half-packs we get in C rations. We use our squad stoves and have hot meals and hot coffee, along with fires at night.

One night around the fire, Jake talks about his wife and kids. He's been married two years and his kids are two years, six months, and one. Jake will be 20 in November.

"Shit, Kid," he says to me, "we have to start early in the mountains of West Virginia. What I've been wondering is, shit, what's my wife doing tonight. If I ever find her with another man getting into her I would kill him faster than I would a Jap, and you all know how I want to kill those yellow bastards."

Cook says, "Jake, don't talk like that. I got a girl I'm going to marry when I get home. She's the only thing I think about. The last night I was out with her was my 18th birthday, just before I left for basic. I wouldn't tell you what we did, but I will never forget that night.

"She's a wonderful girl and I don't have the thoughts you do, Jake, because we love each other. I can't believe you can even think like that. The only wish I have is to get back to her so we can marry, settle down, and help Dad on the farm. I'd like to start a family. I know my folks would like to have grandchildren. The whole family loves my girl and knows she'll be a wonderful wife and mother. She'll fit right into the family."

"You're a weak motherfucker," Jake says. "You just wait till you see me in action. I mean real action."

Lee joins in. "You guys know I've got a great little girl." He fishes a photograph out of his pack. The picture is of a girl seated on the grass with her mother in a park in Los Angeles. In the background are palm trees and flowers.

"I took this picture on my last leave," Lee says, choking up.

"She's beautiful," I tell Lee.

John is seated on the other side of the fire reading a book, paying no attention to us. It seems John is always reading or writing something. Some of the guys call him "professor."

Jose, seated next to me, says, "Arch, let me show you my family pictures."

He pulls out two dog-eared photos, one of his four children, all about a year apart, and the other of a very large family of children, young adults, and older folks.

"That's my wife," Jose says proudly, pointing her out in the picture. "She is beautiful. We say in Spanish that she is bonita esposa." He points to an older woman and says, "This is ...my mother." Tears trickle down his cheeks.

After a brief pause, Jose continues, "Arch, I hope I will see them again. I don't know. My father came from a fishing town in Mexico. My grandparents are still there. We hope to bring them to California after the war."

"Let's get some more coffee, Jose," I say.

It is quiet and getting dark. We get our hot coffee and listen to the artillery going overhead. The shells land and explode not far in front of us. We look up at the night sky full of stars.

"The sky is beautiful," says Jose. "I hope my esposa is looking at the same beautiful sky. She could be looking at the same moon but at a different time of the day. I told her before I left that when I look at the moon, I will send my love and kisses to her. She said she would do the same."

Mike Frances looks intently at me and then at another of our squad members, Fred Nealey, and says, "You know, Fred, I think the kid's older than you.

"When were you 18, Kid?" Nealey asks me.

"Last June."

"Shit. I won't be 18 until the first of May."

"How did you get in the army?" I ask.

"My dad volunteered me because I knocked up a 40-year-old woman back in my home town—Everett, Washington. They didn't want me around. I'll bet you haven't even had a piece of ass yet, Arch. And you've probably never been drunk either. Be honest, Kid. You look like you're just out of some holy-roller Sunday-School class."

How do they know? Does it show that much? I want to drop into the deepest hole I can find.

Lee comes to my rescue: "That's OK, Arch. When we get you back to California, Cook and I will take care of you. We'll find you a nice girl and teach you how to drink. But life's not all sex and drinking. There's a lot more to it than that.

"Jose and I make the sign of the cross. We're Catholics, and Jake laughs at us. But that's OK. Each of us has his own way of handling the war. Jake's a lot of bullshit. But that's his way and that's OK."

Jake snaps: "Wait and see how much protection you guys get with the sign of the fuckin' cross, your Bible in your pocket or a crucifix around your neck. My faith is in my God-damned M-1 and all the fuckin' grenades I can carry."

"That's the fuckin' way I feel, too," Nealey says.

Lee says, "By the way, Arch, you haven't formally met Nealey. I don't know where he was when you joined us. It looks like you've already gotten to know each other."

I take a closer look at Nealey. He's a little guy, maybe 5-5, but wiry and strong. His skin is swarthy and he has black hair. He doesn't shave yet.

I don't find out much about Nealey's home or the older woman he left pregnant, but he seems a nice enough kid. He hangs around a lot with Jake, who's always sharpening his bayonet.

After a few jokes, we head for our holes on the perimeter. The next day our squad is sent down to a little town on the coast. We're still quite far behind the lines in reserve.

John and I check out a village in search of buildings the army can use for a laundry or other support facilities. We find a building that seems OK and could be maintained by the gooks, our name for Okinawans.

John discovers a vegetable garden behind the building. He pulls up carrots, cabbages, and tomatoes.

"What are you doing?"

"I'm fixing us lunch," John answers.

He takes the squad stove from his pack and starts to cook the vegetables. The aroma is wonderful. While the food cooks, we smoke and relax in the sun. All of a sudden a bullet kicks up dirt by my left side. Then another and another.

"We've got to find cover and get out of here, John."

I turn and see a Jap on the hill behind us. I fire a few rounds and he takes off running. John turns off the stove, dumps out the food we can't take with us, opens the fly of his fatigues and pisses on it.

"Arch, damn it, I can't eat it and I can't fuck it so I'm just pissing on it."

The comment is so unlike John that the phrase sticks with him from then on.

On the way back to the company area to report our findings, John spies an elderly gook woman—small, bent over, trudging up the hill with a big load of wood. She's wearing the typical baggy tunic with gook pants, narrow at the bottom, and a round straw hat that comes to a point.

Heavy bundles of wood are attached to both ends of two poles slung over her shoulders.

I'm up the hill ahead of John. I look back down the valley, watching John trying to talk to the woman, waving his arms as a form of sign language. He finally takes one of her poles and puts it on his own shoulders. He begins to slog up the hill, trailed by the old woman.

The woman, who is about half John's size, laughs and points her finger at him because it's all he can do to carry those two bundles of wood up the hill.

When he finally puts the wood down, she easily picks up the second pole, with its two bundles of wood, and trots off toward her house.

"That was really dumb, John," I say. "How do you know she didn't have a weapon? She could have killed you. You can't take that kind of risk."

"Look at that little old gook lady going over the ridge, Arch. She's beautiful. She wouldn't harm anybody. I'm going to write about her tonight in my journal."

"You have a journal?"

"I try to keep some kind of record of what's going on in my life out here. It's not much, but if I don't get back, Arch, I want you to have it."

"Sure, John, but I don't like to hear you talk that way."

We learn that night that the rest of our division is having a rough time. We're to be briefed by our captain.

That evening Captain Brokaw pays us a visit. Japan's defensive strategy has become known to us, he says, thanks to captured Japs, civilians on the island, intercepted radio broadcasts, and propaganda leaflets dropped by the enemy.

Now that all the troops are on the island, the Japanese plan to go after our ships in the harbor with kamikaze-suicide aircraft. If they're successful, they'll have cut off further supplies and be in a position to mount a massive counter-attack on army and marine forces trapped on the island.

Their goal is simple: kill as many of us as possible and drive the rest into the sea. It would be their greatest victory of the war.

The kamikaze attacks have already begun, and our navy has taken significant losses.

Meanwhile, the captain says, the 7th Division's objective over the next 10 days is to take Hill 178. And we're to be in the assault group.

The captain unfolds maps of the Pinnacle and Hill 178, names he says will become very familiar in the days ahead.

Our job is to first secure the Pinnacle, providing cover for the battalions attacking Red Hill and Triangle Hill.

Then we move on to Hill 178.

There are lots of questions.

"Can we get hand-held flame throwers?" Jake asks. "I'd love to get my hands on one and see the Japs fry."

Goldsmith asks, "What about the navy, Sir, are the losses significant?"

Capt. Brokaw replies, "The navy is in good shape even with the losses it has suffered. The navy will provide all the support we need. We'll be pushing out at 0500. Get a good rest, men."

Jake, John and I sit around the last fire drinking instant coffee.

Jake says, "My father's been down in the coal mines since he was a boy. He used to work with picks and shovels, the only tools he had to break the coal from its seams. He was paid 20 cents a ton. A skilled miner could dig 10 tons a day.

"I left school after the eighth grade and went to work in the God-damned mine. The wages I got were some better than my dad got when he started. I got a dollar a ton, but at first I could mine only five tons a day.

"John L. Lewis and his mine-workers' union helped the God-damned miners a lot. Better wages and conditions. I think the world of old John L. with those big bushy eyebrows.

"It's fuckin' hard work even with explosives and more modern equipment. I was always standing in water and had to watch the fuckin' little birds in their cages. They are the sentinels for gas that reduces the oxygen down there. When the birds keel over and die, you get the hell out of there before you die, too. There's also methane gas that can explode and trap you.

"That's the way my father and grandfather worked and then I did the same. It's a rough life and all you've got to do when you're out of the mine is drink 'shine and fuck your girl. That's why I got married young, sort of shotgun, and I've worked hard to support the wife and kid.

"I hate Japs and want to kill every fuckin' one of them. My brother was three years older than me. He volunteered for the navy in '41, the day after Pearl Harbor. He was on a carrier at the Battle of Midway. The motherfuckin' Japs killed him. I never loved anyone like I loved my brother. I'll do anything to kill Japs.

"I'd like to knock out their gold teeth and take them home to show the other miners what old Jake can do. I've thought of collecting their ears, cutting them off with the bayonet I keep sharp all the time. I heard this was done by the knights of old. During the Crusades, I think, when knights had to prove they'd really killed the enemy. They brought home ears the way Indians brought home scalps.

"I want to kill as many Japs as I can and bring back teeth and ears to show the guys in the bars at home. The Japs are animals. I'm thinking of cutting off their cocks and shoving them in their mouths. I hate those motherfuckers."

I nod and say, "I lost a brother, too. He was drowned when a fishing boat went down. I miss him. I know what it's like to lose an older brother."

We sit silently for a long time, then John says, "You know, Jake, what you say about canaries in the mines is also the way it was during the last World War. Our side had canaries whose only purpose was to detect the gas, which the Germans dropped in canister shells so it would drift over our trenches. When the little yellow birds dropped over, they saved soldiers' lives.

"A British infantry platoon leader wrote a poem about it that I memorized. It's called 'Dulce et Decorum Est.'"

"What the hell does that mean, John?" asks Jake.

John ignores Jake and goes on: "Since it's quiet and we have a little coffee left, and you guys have nothing else to do, let me first tell you about Wilfred Owen.

"As I said, he was a platoon leader, a lieutenant, and after a year or so in France he was sent to a hospital in Scotland to be treated for shell shock. We call it psychological breakdown or combat fatigue in this war. They'll probably have another name for it in the next war.

"After treatment Owen was sent back to France to his old outfit and was killed going over the top a few days before the armistice in 1918. He wrote this poem about seeing his men gassed."

John read the lines quietly. He stopped after the first two words, then started again:

> Bent double, like old beggars under sacks,
> Knock-kneed, coughing like hags, we cursed through sludge,
> Till on the haunting flares we turned our backs
> And towards our distant rest began to trudge.
> Men marched asleep. Many had lost their boots
> But limped on, blood-shod. All went lame; all blind;
> Drunk with fatigue; deaf even to the hoots
> Of tired, outstripped Five-Nines that dropped behind.

Gas! Gas! Quick, boys!—An ecstasy of fumbling,
Fitting the clumsy helmets just in time;
But someone still was yelling out and stumbling
And flound'ring like a man in fire or lime...
Dim, through the misty panes and thick green light,
As under a green sea, I saw him drowning.

In all my dreams, before my helpless sight,
He plunges at me, guttering, choking, drowning.

If in some smothering dreams you too could pace
Behind the wagon that we flung him in,
And watch the white eyes writhing in his face,
His hanging face, like a devil's sick of sin;
If you could hear, at every jolt, the blood
Come gargling from the froth-corrupted lungs,
Obscene as cancer, bitter as the cud
Of vile, incurable sores on innocent tongues,—
My friend, you would not tell with such high zest
To children ardent for some desperate glory,
The old Lie: Dulce et decorum est
Pro patria mori.

"Again, what does that last line mean?" Jake asks.

"It's a quote, in Latin, from Horace," John says. "It means 'How glorious it is for a young man to give his life for his country.'"

Everyone was silent until Jake spoke again:

"You know, guys, I understand what this Wilfred guy was trying to say. Who will remember how glorious it was for my brother to give his life? The only ones that ever remember my brother are his own people, our mother, our dad, who's now 73, and me. Is that the way it's going to happen to us? Will anybody ever remember us?

"Sometime, John, tell me some more about Wilfred Owen."

"Sure, Jake."

We empty our canteen cups of cold coffee and leave in silence. It's raining. We go to sleep in wet bedrolls on wet ground, covered with wet ponchos.

CHAPTER 4

✿

By the night of April 3 we have advanced to the narrowest part of the island, about four miles from east to west. The 7th Division is responsible for a narrow strip of low land along the east coast and the adjacent hills to the west. The 96th Division is to take care of the central segment of the front. The 1st Marines are on the west coast.

The 184th, our battalion, is in the hills to the west behind elements of the 96th. We're to pass through the 96th and continue south and east.

With two regiments abreast on a 3,000-yard front, we are to press on to higher ground overlooking the coastal plain. We expect a coordinated attack down the coast and along the inland central valley.

On the following day, our gains are measured in hundreds of yards rather than the thousands of yards we covered each of the previous three days. We are slowed by intense rifle and machine gun fire and heavy and very accurate artillery fire from a ridge to the southwest, parallel to the coast.

My squad is on the right flank, poised to cross the open central valley and take the heavily defended ridge. The squad is divided into teams of three: Lee carries a carbine and ammo for the BAR. Cook has his M-1 rifle. I've been designated to carry the BAR (Browning automatic rifle).

To our right are Jake, a bazooka man, and John and Nealey, both riflemen. A second BAR team is in position with the third squad.

We watch our mortar and artillery shells explode in the open valley in front of us. Our orders are to wait for a smoke screen to be dropped, then the BARs are to provide cover fire over the heads of the advancing riflemen. When the riflemen find protected positions in the open valley, they'll provide cover fire for the two of us with automatic weapons and we'll advance and join them. The operation is then to be repeated.

Everything goes as planned. After several of these covering maneuvers, the squad crosses the valley and reaches the southwest ridge. We find good cover in a muddy irrigation ditch about shoulder deep. We run toward the ridge, crouched low in the ditch. The ditch ends in overgrown brush, which provides excellent camouflage.

We can observe, undetected, a dozen or more Jap soldiers on the ridge in two light-machine gun positions. We call for artillery and smoke to hit their positions, and I hear Estes on the phone say:

"I need an accurate five-minute action, and I mean accurate. We'll move out exactly five minutes after the first shell hits and the smoke is laid. If you're not accurate in both timing and range we're all dead."

After five minutes, the artillery with the smoke cover subsides. Our squad moves up under the protection of BARs and machine-gun fire.

The Japs, no more than 50 yards away, are caught by surprise. I see them and open fire with my BAR. The rest of the squad fires M-1s. As I look through my gun sight and fire in rapid bursts, I see enemy soldiers fall.

It takes such a short time. Then all is quiet. The Japs are dead, and they didn't even see us. I have no idea how many of the dead are attributable to me, but it must be a lot since I had the only automatic weapon in the squad.

I think to myself:

"Arch, you just killed young men you didn't even know, young men who probably were drafted just like we were. You're now a combat veteran, a killer."

I am tormented by the thought. I feel as if I am going to throw up. The crotch of my pants is warm and wet with urine.

Yet, I also have a feeling of euphoria such as I have never known. It's a bit like the time I hit a home run in a high-school baseball game and everyone cheered and my heart pounded and my palms were sweaty. I literally floated around the bases.

Now, in my excitement, I check out the bodies around the machine gun. Some apparently fled toward the higher ground of Castle Hill. Eight are dead, the bodies ripped apart by automatic fire. What a repulsive sight. One hangs over the machine gun. Another has been hit in the face and no longer looks human.

I go behind a tree and become sick again.

I have survived my combat baptism. I am learning the sights, sounds, and smells of battle—exploding artillery, small-arms fire, dying men, and mutilated bodies.

Our success is short-lived. Our frontal attack is halted by heavy machine-gun fire and repeated artillery barrages. Our squad is sent with part of Company E through a defilade area to probe for an alternative approach to the higher ground of Castle Hill.

While we reconnoiter, a Jap machine-gunner spots us and opens fire. Company E's commander and a platoon leader are killed. A few minutes later several of our men are wounded. The reserve company is sent in. Its soldiers give us fire protection. Jake, carrying a bazooka, has the sole of one shoe torn off by a rifle shot. Jake responds in typical Jake fashion:

"If these motherfuckers think they can stop me by shooting the shoes off my feet, they have another god-dammed think coming!"

Our immediate objective is a small piece of exposed open ground between us and the base of the next ridge. We cross the open space, one by one, zig-zagging while a Jap machine-gunner has some practice with moving targets.

I run fast and low, mud kicking up as bullets hit the muck around me. We all make it to a trench at the base of the ridge. We are safe enough in the trench, if we stay on our knees. But we can't move forward. The slightest movement brings heavy enemy fire and there is no way to bring in additional support.

By late afternoon we are told to fall back to a better defensive position. We wait until night to return to the rest of the company.

The day's action accomplished little. Company E has lost two officers. Five other soldiers are either dead or badly wounded.

They are the first deaths of American GIs that I have witnessed since joining the company. I have a strange, bewildered feeling when they bring a poncho-wrapped body past me. The head is exposed, the eyes open and the mouth open and filled with blood.

Our platoon has only one wounded man. Goldsmith, from our squad, is sent to a field hospital. During the night, Lee, Jose, and I are together in a deep trench occupied the previous night by Jap soldiers.

Lee takes first guard, and Jose and I talk a bit before turning in.

"Arch," Jose says, "I can't talk about what happened today. I now know what a dead man looks like. It could have been you or me. This is the first time I've seen someone I know lying dead. Do you believe in the Bible, Arch, in the Ten Commandments?"

"I suppose so. I was raised with the Bible and was told to believe it all. Why?"

"I don't think I can kill another man, Arch. The Bible says, 'Thou shalt not kill,' and I don't think I can. I'm afraid of what it will do to me. How can I go home and tell my boys that I killed another man who might have had a wife and children like me?"

"All we can do, Jose, is try to stay alive each day. The Japs are going to kill you if you don't kill them first. It's either you or the Jap."

"I'm going to pray tonight and ask God to help me with this problem."

Jose tells me again how much he loves his family and misses them, but he doesn't know if he can kill for them.

"What will I tell them?" he asks.

"You won't be able to tell them anything if you don't protect yourself," I answer.

"What do you think happened to Goldsmith?" he asks.

"He's in a field hospital back on the beach," I answer. "I have to grab some sleep, Jose. I'm next on guard and I don't want to talk about today. Lee told me to learn to accept what happens and go on. I try to do that. I'm going to put everything that happened today in the back of my mind, learn from it and stay alive tomorrow.

"Now for some sleep. If I don't sleep, I won't do my best on guard. And I'm responsible for you and Lee."

There is enemy activity throughout the night, but it is limited to artillery and small-arms fire. There is no sign of infiltrators.

The Pinnacle, our objective, is a natural rock-bound defense site, with caves, pillboxes and trenches connected by an intricate system of tunnels.

The caves and tunnels are so well guarded, with such heavy firepower, they appear to be impregnable. The plan is for Companies B and C to move up one side of the Pinnacle through a network of deserted trenches.

They are to fire phosphorous grenades into the mouths of the tunnels, then blow up the tunnel entrances with explosives.

The operation is to be assisted by air strikes. I watch through binoculars as Company B soldiers begin moving up the hill to place orange markers showing their forward position and where they want our aircraft to strafe and bomb.

The corsairs come in low and fast before the markers can be placed. The Company B soldiers wave frantically to the pilots to let them know they are Americans. The pilots begin to strafe, unable to distinguish friend from foe.

In the mix-up, 12 men from Company B are hit. One dies.

The tragedy drives home the importance of placing those large orange-canvas markers showing our forward positions.

I am shaken by another reality of war. Mistakes happen. The pilots might even have been from the hometowns of the boys they strafed.

We pull back again. A day later we call for more intense firepower. On the evening of April 13, while we are eating cold C rations, our sergeant calls us together to tell us "important news" he learned at a briefing.

We expect to hear about the next day's plans and what has happened to the rest of our troops. Perhaps kamikazes have destroyed our Navy as the Jap propaganda leaflets claim. Or maybe the Japs have broken through on the other side of the island and we are cutoff from our supplies on the beach.

It is none of those things.

The sergeant says, "On April 12, U.S. time, President Roosevelt died." There is silence.

Finally Jake says, "Our Commander in Chief, the only President I have ever known, is dead. Son of a bitch. What's going to happen?"

In combat the soldier's horizon narrows. He thinks only of the now. The rest—home, politics, the President—all stay the same. Roosevelt was special. He was part of the family, even though my dad hated him. He had been around almost forever. We can't imagine being without him.

John says, "I can almost hear his Harvard-accented voice coming over the radio on December 7th, 1941. 'A date which will live in infamy.' When F.D.R. heard Winston Churchill's famous words, 'We shall fight on the beaches, we shall fight in the fields, we shall fight on the streets, we shall never surrender,' he answered, 'They have asked for arms and we shall give them arms; they have asked for ships and we shall give them ships.'"

John pauses, then goes on:

"We all seemed to know that with F.D.R. in the White House, in the end everything would be all right. 'There is no armor against fate; death lays its icy hand on kings.' I think that's from Shakespeare."

John knows how to say things. I realize the importance of what my grandfather once told me. "You will find that there are moments in life where time stands still and every detail remains etched in your mind."

I could count these days on one hand. May 14, the day the circus came to town. September 3, when England and Canada went to war. December 7, when the Japs bombed Pearl Harbor. April 1, when we invaded Okinawa. And now April 12 (13th when we heard it on Okinawa), when we hear about the death of President Roosevelt.

It is as if a big black cloud has blotted out the sun and plunged us into darkness. We can't possibly win the war without Roosevelt. I think of the storms when I was out on my dad's boat—the wind, rain, darkness, and fear. I would go down to my bunk, cover my head, eat hardtack and sometimes fall asleep. I hoped that when I woke up things would be better.

I thought of home and how my folks would feel when they learned that the President they had no confidence in, the President that had caused so much trouble for them, the President they said wasn't a Christian was now dead.

I will never talk to them about how I feel about the President. The loss hurts. It takes away hope. Now I'm not sure I will ever get out of this hell alive. But still we have to keep going.

The Sergeant tells us Harry Truman is now our Commander in Chief. We've never heard of him. Meetings are taking place in Washington, D.C., to decide how to conduct the war without Roosevelt. It is a sad time. Jose comes to Lee and me that night.

"Can I be in your hole tonight?" he asks. "I am more scared than ever before."

Jose tells me he hasn't killed a man yet and wonders if have. I tell him I know I have killed and I don't want to talk about it tonight.

Jose says, "I can't do it, Arch. I can't do it. I don't think I can ever kill anybody."

"Even to save Lee or me?" I ask.

"I just don't know. I've seen what a dead man looks like. It's so final, and I would be responsible for causing it."

"Just stick with Arch and me, Jose, and we'll try not to let you get into a situation where you have to kill anyone," says Lee. "But it will be your decision. Pray about it and use your rosary. It helps me."

Sarge S briefs us on our next objective, now that the Pinnacle is in our hands. It seems practical, he says, to hold our present position and prepare to dislodge the Japs from Hill 178, which must be taken before the whole division launches an assault on Skyline Ridge.

On the morning of April 21, Companies E and F push off to initiate an assault on Ouki Hill, to secure supply lines to the base of Skyline Ridge. Company E is to start the attack. Company F (ours) is to pass through Company E and continue the assault.

Company E stops when one of its men sees a group of Japanese defending an embankment with a heavy machine gun positioned in the mouth of a cave at the summit of a rocky knoll, Ouki Hill.

Lee, Cook, Jose, and I watch from a defilade. We are up to our knees in mud. Our company is to move out as soon as this embankment is taken.

Cook has binoculars and excitedly shouts, "Look at that guy, Arch, to the right about 75 yards ahead."

"I see him," I answer.

"What the hell's he doing running up that embankment. Hey, I think I know him."

We see one of our riflemen get up from beside a companion who has been hit. He runs up the hill toward the machinegunner firing from the cave in the rocks. Our rifleman throws grenades, one after another. He's able to get the grenades inside the rock barrier, silencing three enemy riflemen.

The enemy machinegunner is unable to tip his weapon low enough to prevent the GI rifleman from continuing up the hill. The GI slides back down the hill for more grenades. He repeats the action a third time, grabbing his injured friend's BAR and firing all the way back up the embankment.

Lee calls out, "He's got only a few more rounds. The BAR's jammed."

The GI throws his BAR at the Jap-occupied pillbox and slides down the hill. He grabs a carbine and starts back. The machinegunner is still firing.

"This guy's amazing," I say. "He's firing point blank into that machine-gun nest."

"He's still alive; he's still firing!" Cook shouts.

Suddenly the firing stops.

"I think it's Rich, Arch," Cook says. "You know, that quiet guy in the Second Platoon of Company E."

Jake screams behind us, "Great, kill the motherfuckers or I'll come up and help with my fuckin' bayonet."

We watch Rich as he dismantles the machine-gun nest.

"That damned guy is throwing the machine gun down the hill," Cook shouts. "There go two mortars over the top, Arch. Now he's pushing the body of the dead Jap machinegunner down the hill."

We watch as Rich runs down the hill to meet his platoon coming up.

"Why wasn't he hit with all that fire?" Lee asks.

"I guess that's just another of the many questions about battle that will remain unanswered," says John.

It's the sort of response we'd come to expect from John.

We leapfrog through Company E and make good headway toward Hill 178. Beyond the embankment we meet a solid network of defensive trenches, tunnels and machine-gun emplacements on every rise. Pillboxes and trenches are strategically placed to provide crossfire for every approach to the hill.

We're able to utilize the trenches the enemy left behind. I haven't seen Jake for most of the afternoon and wonder what he's up to.

We set up for the night in the Jap trenches. Cook is with John. Lee and I are together. Jake crawls into a hole just before dark.

"Where the hell have you been?" I ask.

"Arch, I started my collection," he replies. "Look, I'll show you."

Jake opens a long coin purse with a snap closure at the top. Inside are gold-filled Jap teeth, some with bone still attached to them, from where Jake smashed them out with his rifle butt.

"You haven't seen it all yet, Arch," Jake says. "Look in the bag again."

I look again. I see five or six ears, covered with dried-blood from being cut off. Waves of nausea sweep over me. I shake my head in disbelief.

"You're soft, Kid, if this makes you sick," Jake says with a chuckle. "Remember those Japs on the embankment? Well, I got part of them. I tested how sharp my bayonet was. The ears came off with one swipe.

"Next time I'm going to cut off their dicks and put them in their mouths so they can be real God-damned cocksuckers forever. Every time I look at my collection I'll think of my dead brother."

Jake's a strange guy. But I don't know what I would be like if the Japs had killed my brother.

Night is anything but quiet. Artillery goes over us all night, from both sides. Spotters calculate the flash positions of the Jap artillery and then order rounds to hit those positions. I suppose the Jap spotters are doing the same thing.

Pushing off at 0700, we crawl in a deserted Jap trench toward two machine-gun positions on knolls separated by a draw. We can make out the movements of gunners, but the trench gives us some protection.

From the end of the trench there's an open space of about 50 yards and then a cave-opening just below a knoll. There are Jap soldiers in the cave and a Jap machinegunner is in a pillbox just above the cave.

John, Lee, Jose, and I reach the end of the muddy trench. We motion to the rest of the squad to lie low. We're too close to ask for artillery. We send word of our situation back to our Company, hoping for help.

We have been lying in the mud for 45 minutes, waiting for something to happen, when a Jap sneaks into the end of our trench and heads for Jose.

Jose raises his head to look for danger. He sees the Jap. The enemy soldier starts toward him. Jose stands and raises his rifle to fire. Then he freezes. The Jap keeps coming.

John realizes what's happening and fires at the Jap soldier. He's too late. Several of John's bullets hit the Jap, but the Jap bayonet goes into Jose first.

John and I crawl to the end of the trench, where both are dying. The bayonet is in Jose's chest. The Jap has fallen on top of him. We push the Jap's body off Jose and out of the trench. John, seated in the mud in the bottom of the trench, cradles Jose in his arms and says the Lord's Prayer. Jose looks at us for a moment and then he's gone.

John and I both make the sign of the cross on Jose's chest. Then we start dragging his body back down the trench. Lee calls: "Drop the body. They've spotted us."

Bullets fly.

Lee calls again: "Keep low and crawl back. The protection's better back here."

We're trapped and can't call for help. John's rifle fire gave away our position to the machinegunner on the knoll.

As we lie in the mud with Jose, I remember his photographs—his wife, children, and mother. How he loved them. What strong faith he had in the Catholic Church and in his priest.

Jose no longer has to worry about the dreaded decision of whether to kill another human being. But he has given his life for his indecision. Maybe that's the way God takes care of such things. Jose's war is over.

A scout crawling flat on his belly reaches us from the Company, some 50 yards to the rear. Our orders are to stay put. Calls have gone out for tanks with flamethrowers to help us out.

As the message is passed along the squad, the scout rises to run back to company headquarters. He's spotted by the Japs, who open fire. I see the scout drop, but don't know the extent of his injuries. We can't get to him, because enemy fire has us pinned down.

John says, "Let's see how accurate those Japs are."

He puts a stick in his helmet and holds the helmet just above our trench. It draws immediate fire and the helmet bounces down the trench. When John retrieves the helmet, it is air-conditioned by bullet holes.

"Now this is a real combat helmet," John jokes.

We're pinned down throughout the rainy night. Every time a flare is thrown up to show us the way back to our company, the gunners on the knoll start firing. All I can think of is how Jose died. His body is still with us.

About 0400 I awake to the sound of our first artillery barrage. I am hungry and wet and amazed that I had slept at all. The surprising thing is that the Japs don't try to wipe us out. I know they could.

At about 10 o'clock the next morning three of our tanks start coming up the draw behind us. They draw enemy fire from above and return it with their own 50-cal. machine gun and 75mm. cannon.

Suddenly three enemy soldiers come running from the cave at the base of the knoll. Tied around their bodies are satchel charges, bags of explosives with incendiaries that explode and burst into flame on contact.

We begin firing and hit one charge on a Jap. The satchels explode. When the smoke clears there is nothing. No satchel charge. No soldier.

The enemy machinegunner begins shooting at us. Two of our squad are hit. The rest take cover in the same trench that has been our home since the previous day.

The two remaining enemy soldiers carrying satchel charges throw themselves under one of our tanks. We hear the ground-shaking explosion, see a blinding flash of light, and feel the heat of the fire.

The tank stops and burns. The hatch opens as the four crewmen try to escape. We give cover fire with rifles and two BARs. The other tank fires as well.

The four crewmen run toward our trench. One man is on fire. Another is hit and falls. But three, including the man on fire, make it to our trench. The man on fire almost falls on me.

The tanks move in front of the fallen crewmember. Lee runs out behind the tanks and drags the man back to the trench. I grab my poncho and wrap it around the man who is on fire. He screams with pain. Still another member of our squad is hit in the firefight.

The other two tanks, one a flame-thrower, devastate the two knolls. We choke on the thick smoke and the fumes of burning fuel. Explosions shake the ground beneath our feet.

We use our first-aid kits to care for the wounded the best we can. The tank crewman who was on fire when he jumped into our trench is still wrapped in my poncho. I carefully unroll him. His arm is torn and bleeding. I bandage it, employing the minimal skills I learned in high-school first-aid.

The hair is gone from the left side of his head and skin on that side of his face is charred. His left eye appears to be badly burned. There are extensive burns on his legs and groin.

I cut away the clothing from his burned body. We use every bandage in our first-aid kits to cover his burns and keep off the flies. Lacking medications, I can do nothing more for the burns.

"Thanks, I made it," the burn-victim says softly. "God-damn it, I made it. Do you have any water and maybe one of those pain pills?"

I give him the last water in my canteen and my last two pain pills. I make him as comfortable as one can possibly be in a wet trench in which friend and foe have eaten, smoked, pissed, and crapped.

The burn victim continues to say, "I made it. I made it."

Lee is doing the best he can with the crewman he dragged in.

After 20 minutes we hear only the rumble of tank motors, no machine-gun fire. When the smoke clears we see the two blackened knolls. Sarge S calls out, "Let's move out. We can take those knolls."

John and I, with Steve, one of our new replacements, head for the cave at the base of the first hill, while Lee, Cook and another new guy go for the machine-gun positions. As we pass Jose, we bow our heads. John makes the sign of the cross and we push on.

The entrance to the cave has been burned out by the flame-throwing tank. We see five or six Jap bodies so charred they look like meat left too long on a barbecue. The faces resemble the mummies one sees in a museum. The smell of burned flesh fills our nostrils.

Taking no chances, we throw several grenades—regular shrapnel and phosphorous—into the cave. Ammo and satchel charges inside the cave explode, and rocks, dirt, and debris fly out the entrance.

White smoke fills the network of tunnels, spewing out of gun positions on top of the knoll. When the smoke clears we inspect the cave. The dead men inside are not burned like those at the cave entrance; except for phosphorous burns from our grenades they are unmarked. Death resulted from suffocation when the flamethrowers took all the oxygen out of the air in the cave.

Our squad, which has secured the two defensive knolls, is ordered back to the Company area while others take over the assault. On our return we watch medics remove our casualties on stretchers.

The tank crewman raises his good arm and says, "You guys put up a damned good fight and thanks for taking care of me. I'll never forget you." It sounds as if the pain pills have taken over.

We walk slowly back to the Company reserve area with the medics. The dead are on stretchers covered with ponchos. They will be removed by "body trucks." A couple of Weasels (tracked jeeps) evacuate the wounded.

It is a good afternoon. We have hot coffee. Even the cold C rations taste good. A meal without bullets hitting the dirt in front of your trench is like dining in a good restaurant.

Steve, the new replacement, says, "God-damn it, we made it, son of a bitch, son of a bitch we got through and I'm still alive." He starts to cry. Lee and I sit with him and tell him. "It's OK, Kid, just go ahead and cry and you'll feel better."

Emotions are extreme following one's first experience with battle, close combat, and death. I know. I worry that I'm becoming addicted to the adrenaline that pumps during combat.

The blood-thirst during close combat changes a man's personality. When I look into the frightened eyes of the enemy and he looks into my terrorized being, we are both transformed. The intermingling of fear, excitement, noise, and chaos makes the destruction of a human life an orgasmic experience. There is a rush, a high, a euphoria I had never experienced before.

I have done things I never thought I could do. It is strange. It is tremendous. It is a feeling of strength, of unlimited power.

A short time later, I hate myself for what I have done. I hate myself for having become a killer.

I feel great. I feel terrible. Which is it to be?

Sitting around at dusk, while setting up a perimeter in old foxholes, we drink hot coffee and say little. Our thoughts are on those who are missing from our squad. But we talk around what's on our minds.

Lee says, "Arch, there are still a few of the old guys around." Silence. "For how long?"

"Until we're called back to the front."

Jake and Nealey are nearby.

"That's the first time I've seen anybody die, and it was one of them and one of us," says Nealey. "I got sick. I couldn't help it."

Jake says, "God-damn it. I hate them all the more. I am fuckin' angry about Jose. I could kill them with my bare hands. He was such a loving guy. He had everything I don't have and not much of what I do have. I'm sure going to miss him.

"Have you seen the start of my collection, Nealey?"

"No."

"Let me show you the start."

That evening a Weasel comes up from somewhere north.

"Is this part of the 184th?" someone calls out. "I have a bunch of mail. Some is for Company F."

The soldier in the Weasel calls out the names. It is a sad mail call. Lee, Cook, and I answer. Goldsmith, Frances, and Rodriguez do not. Nobody ever writes to Jake.

I have four letters, three from my mother and one from a high school friend, Mary. Everyone knows my mother writes almost daily and someone invariably says, "Mother's boy got more letters." This time there's one that isn't from my mother.

"Hey, guys, Arch got a letter from a girl," says Sarge S.

Mary lived down the street about four houses. I won't say she is a tomboy, but she could kick a football farther than I could, she could throw a baseball as hard as I could, and on roller skates she could shoot a hockey puck more accurately than I could.

I put aside the letters from my mother and open the one from Mary. Lee and Cook watch.

Cook says, "Hey, Arch, who's the girl you haven't told us about? We all know you're a lover boy. Tell us about her. Goddamn. What do you think of that? Arch got a letter from a girl."

Lee breaks in, "Lay off, Cook, we have to hear about your girl all the time."

I go down the hill and sit on an ammo case and open the letter:

March 2, 1945
2536 Crown St. Vancouver, B.C.
Canada

Dear Archie:

It seems a long time since I walked to school with you last June. We all knew you had to graduate early because you were going to be drafted back in the States. You took all those correspondence courses so you would get your junior matriculation. I was so proud of you.

I used to look forward to our walks to school and would wish you would ask me to go walking on Sunday afternoons or take me to a ball game to see the Capilanos. But Archie I miss you and I don't know if this war will ever end.

I know you might not come back but I hope you do because I so want to see you again. The whole neighborhood is praying for you. The war has been going on for so long since we were back at Queen Mary grammar school. In 1939 when all this started who would have thought you would be in the battles. Is it ever going to end? I never thought that one of our gang that walked to school would be thousands of miles away fighting the Japanese.

Every morning when we all walk to school we stop and call on your house and ask your mom what she has heard from you. Gordy, Ken, Bill, and I ask what she has heard. Usually it is nothing. She is having a difficult time since you are gone and your brother was drowned.

I remember that day in 1939 when the newspaper boys came down the street calling "Extra Extra, Britain at War, Canada at War." Arch, did we ever think we, well you, would be fighting that war. We were only in grade school. I still think of you as one of us but you have prob-

ably grown up since I last saw you. When you come back, if you do, I shouldn't say that, maybe we can go walking out on the trails by the University and you can tell me all these things you have learned about the war and what life means. We are getting ready for graduation and the prom and all that. I do wish you were here.

Could you find time to send a letter? All of us would like to hear from you and tell us what we don't read in the newspaper or hear on the radio. It would be wonderful to just hear from you.

Our annual just came out. It isn't large, just the pictures of the seniors. We don't have the materials. The honor roll is a new page. It is the names of the boys in last year's class that have been killed in the war. There are fourteen names. I know you will know most of them.

I went to visit my cousin at Shaughnessy Hospital. You may remember him, Angus; he was at our house often before the war and kicked a football farther than you or I. He joined the RCAF about two years ago and trained with your brother-in-law at the air force base in Regina. He was shot down over the channel, rescued but badly burned and has been in the hospital since. They sent him home to this Vancouver hospital since it has one of the best burn treatment centers.

I walked into the room and didn't recognize him at all, his face is so bad and they don't have it bandaged. His upper legs and waist are burned also, and they have a frame to keep the bed clothes off him. I realized I was going to break down and cry, but I knew that wouldn't help him at all, so, I got hold of myself and was able to have a good conversation. I cried all the way home on the street car. I know he enjoyed my visit and he asked me to come back again. He said, "Everybody that comes to see me never comes back. I guess it is too rough to see me this way but I am the same guy." That hospital has a lot of boys just back in bad shape and I decided to visit others every week when I go to see Angus. I pray that something like this will not happen to you.

You probably want to hear a little of home. Something not so down. There isn't much to tell. We go to school all week and a movie on the weekend, everybody is just concerned about the war.

The other day Father Enright stopped me, you know the priest from the Catholic church across the street and asked about you. If you could send a letter to me I would share it, or parts of it, with all your old friends and even Father Enright though you are not a Catholic. He remembers you when you went to CYO without your folks knowing with the Applebee boys.

Bobbie Borrie quit school and signed up with the RCAF. He wants to be a pilot like your brother-in-law. Remember he is the one who went to bed with a rifle the day Pearl Harbor was bombed.

Mr. Hilltoo your social studies teacher asked me about you. I don't know how he thought I would know anything. When you write I can tell him about his favorite student.

I have to call your mom for your APO number. I heard on a Seattle radio station announcing not to forget we have to put that number on letters to U.S. servicemen overseas. Please write. I miss you and I would love to hear from you.

Mary

After reading Mary's letter, a wave of nostalgia sweeps over me. Or is it homesickness? I immediately put it out of my mind. I am starting to get better at putting those things in the back of my mind that could interfere with survival.

The next morning I go down the hill by myself and write a letter to Mary and shorter one home.

∾

April 24, 1945
Somewhere in the Pacific

Dear Mary,

I can't tell you where I am in the Pacific, but if you look in the Vancouver Province you should know. We should have been in the news if they even cover the Pacific war in Canada.

I am not going to try to tell you what war is like. If I did the censor would probably black it out or I would get court-martialed.

The sergeant made quite a deal when he saw a letter for me that wasn't from my mom. All the guys were kidding me about having a girl friend and they called me lover boy. It's all in good fun. They are great friends all about my age except for the old sergeant.

Thank you for dropping in on mother. I know that will help her a lot. It is very thoughtful of you. I want you to know it was just wonderful to hear from you way out here. You will never know how many times my thoughts return to those happy days with you and the others. You will never know how much your letter has meant. I will never forget all my friends at school and on the old home street. I have gotten to know some wonderful friends here. Wish you could meet Lee and Cook. They have taught me so much that has kept me alive so far. If it wasn't for great guys like them I wouldn't be around. I would never have gotten your letter. I am so thankful for the kind of men I am with, we all help each other. If I survive this hell we are having to go through, I will be able to tell you a lot more than I ever could have told before. If I ever get back, I do hope we could have some time to talk together, but if not I want to thank you for taking the time to write to me. It is wonderful to hear of the things that are going on in Crown Street when they seem so distant and remote from this killing and death.

I think it is great that you are visiting your cousin, he needs you. So see him as often as you can.

Greet Mr. Hilltoo in social studies and particularly Mr. Westmacott in English at school and tell the rest of the gang you got a letter from me and if they write they may possibly get one back if I am still around.

All My Love,

Arch

Three days later we move to the front to relieve Company G, which has advanced only 500 yards since we left. We make little, if any, progress the next day. We're in a defilade in front of Hill 178, and we can see the 32nd approaching Skyline Ridge to our left.

The draw between is known as "Gunshot Pass." It can't be crossed until we have taken 178.

That night, John says, "Arch, this is like calisthenics. We peep over our hole to look for infiltrators and then duck down when we hear one of the Japs' 'feupbang' guns firing down that God-damned pass."

What we call 'feupbang' guns are believed to be firing 77mm. shells. Unlike the big artillery shells the Japs lob at us, these shells come in on a flat trajectory and sound like loud crinkling paper. "Fe-uu-uu-p, then the big ba—ng." They come in so fast a soldier doesn't have a chance. They are terrifying.

The next morning I hear a foxhole of Company E was hit by a "feupbang." There was just enough left of the GIs to put into a ration box.

We hear rumors the 184th is to be placed in reserve, but nobody confirms it. Before midnight the Japs open up with the heaviest shelling of the operation so far. That makes for a no-sleep night, another night of John's calisthenics.

Our counter-barrage is even greater than the one unleashed by the Japs.

At 6 o'clock the next morning, fog settles in as we push off for the final assault on 178. As the fog lifts, I have an eerie feeling. There is no resistance. We walk up the devastated hill and find nothing. What a contrast to the noise and the dying of the recent past.

How ironic that the defenses we tried to break, that cost us so many wounded and dead, have simply vanished. The Japs have given up and retreated across the broad valley toward Conical Peak. There is no equipment left and their wounded and dead have been taken away.

Gunshot Pass and Hill 178 are now under our control. Lee, Cook, and I sit on the north side of the hill and look back to the beach where we landed.

Lee says, "Remember that first day we were together, Arch?"

"Do I ever. That's the day you told me, 'Stick with me, Kid, and you'll be OK.' We're still together, Lee."

CHAPTER 5

❀

The 184th has been out of action, in reserve, for six days. What a six days it has been: hot coffee, sleep at night, even sitting around fires and talking.

As I trudge along the road returning to the front, Lee in front of me, Cook behind, I think how great it is to have clean clothes from the skin out.

Just a few days ago, Lee, Cook, John, Jake, and I went down to a stream east of our bivouac area. We found a grassy slope where the water was deep enough for bathing and washing clothes.

We removed our clothes, and while they soaked in a pool the four of us fooled around in the stream, pulling each other down, spraying each other. We looked like anything but soldiers capable of fighting a war and killing the enemy. We looked, in fact, a lot more like happy school-boys skipping class on a warm day and skinny-dipping in a favorite swimming hole unknown to parents and teachers. The noise of the water and the vegetation around the pool made this a peaceful oasis totally removed from the chaos of war.

Someone had brought along soap. While we scrubbed each other and our filthy underwear, I spotted something moving upstream. I jumped from the water and grabbed my rifle. I quickly put it down when I saw that the moving figures were three gook women, who giggled and pointed at the four naked young white men.

They approached the pool, reaching for our clothes and soap and began scrubbing our GI skivies and fatigues while we sat, naked, on the grassy bank.

What a sight we must have been. Only John, who had a great deal of black body hair, bothered to hold his hands over his crotch. As usual, John carried one of his books. Unlike John, the blondish Cook had almost no body hair. Lee, the shortest of the four, was well-built from having worked with his dad. Jake, with curly red hair on his chest, had a muscular Charles Atlas build, except for his long skinny legs and big feet. As always, Jake talked a lot, and every other word was profane. As for me, I was pretty much average in every way.

The women never did stop laughing and pointing at us as they scrubbed our clothes. When they felt the clothes were properly washed and rinsed, they spread them out carefully in the sun. Then they picked up their huge bundles of wood, waved goodbye, and headed up the hill—still waving, still laughing and still pointing at us.

We were amazed at how these little women could carry such heavy loads, all the while holding their backs straight and heads erect.

Too soon it's back to war, as the 184th moves up with its new replacements to swap positions with the 32nd Infantry Battalion, which had been in continuous fighting for many days. The 32nd is to fall back and replace us as a reserve unit.

All we have left is memories of the good times while we were on reserve and free from guard duty.

I am fond of sitting around a campfire and drinking hot coffee while we express our feelings unashamedly far into the night.

Lee tells how he met his wife. "It was in San Pedro where my dad had his fishing boat. I always say I live in L.A, but it's really San Pedro. I helped Dad on the boat fishing for tuna after high school before the army. One Sunday two years ago, I went to early mass and sat by this young lady and her mother. They were new to the area. I hadn't seen them in church before and I couldn't keep my eyes off her—the young one, not her mother. This was something I had never felt before. I felt tingly and good all over, and I knew I had to get to know her. Before leaving the pew, I introduced myself. Her name was Ann.

"'That's on my way home,' I blurted after learning where Ann and her mother lived. 'May I walk with you?'

"It was a lie about being on my way home. I think I saw Ann every day for the next six months, and then we were married. Before I left for the army, my dad helped me get a nice apartment for Ann and our little daughter."

Lee brings out his pictures again, and we all act as if this is the first time we have seen them.

These thoughts go through my mind as I follow Lee's pack during our return to the front. In an almost hypnotic state, I watch his boots move rhythmically up and down in the mud. I try not to think of what's ahead.

Part of the 32nd passes us as we move forward. They are dirty and unshaven, their boots and clothes caked with mud, their fatigues torn.

Many of these 18-year-old boys have the now familiar combat stare, their eyes seemingly focused on something a thousand yards away. But some are so tired they simply stare at the ground. All are a worn-out, depressed-looking bunch of soldiers.

Nobody says a word. The fighting 32nd kept pushing to the end to gain every meaningless foot of ground they could before turning the battle line over to us. Late in the afternoon, long columns of gear-laden men of the 184th, including my squad, move up a shell-pocked valley that is almost unrecognizable as the valley we left only six days earlier.

Lee turns to me and says, "Arch, this is the same valley where we called for tanks and flamethrowers for the first time, remember?"

"Do I remember!"

"Over there, by those trenches and that little rise, is where we lost Jose."

"You're right, Lee." I pass the message back to Cook and Jake, who are a short distance behind me. It's easy to pick out Jake. He's taller than most and his razor-sharp bayonet gleams from its fixed position on his M-1. Jake worked on that bayonet with his sharpening stone almost every night during the six days we were in reserve. The rest of us carry our bayonets in holsters on our belts or on the side of our packs. Jake wants his to be seen.

Jake says that he thinks of his brother with every stroke of the stone as he sharpens the steel. A sharp bayonet, he says, not only goes in easy but is easy to pull out of a body.

We had two days of bayonet training from a sergeant and a corporal back at Camp Roberts. We sat under eucalyptus trees in 100-degree-plus temperatures. The title of the first session was "The Spirit of the Bayonet." The sergeant said he'd studied techniques in the "British Manual on Bayonet Training" and thought it the best he'd ever seen. He'd quote the manual while a corporal pointed to the words and the large colored diagrams:

"To attack with the bayonet effectively requires good direction. The bayonet is essentially an offensive weapon. In a bayonet assault all ranks go forward to kill or to be killed, and only those who have developed skill and strength by constant training will be able to kill. The spirit of the bayonet must be inculcated into all ranks so they go forward with aggressive determination and confidence of superiority without which the bayonet assault would not be effective."

Not only were the sergeant and corporal skilled in the art of homicide, but their eloquence lifted killing to new heights. The corporal hung burlap bags filled with straw from the eucalyptus tree to simulate an enemy body. Then he put on what he called his "killing face" to instill fear in his enemy.

The sergeant then told us: "We have to create the thrust, stare at the enemy's eyes with our 'killer face' and thrust forward with arms and body weight to jab the life out of the animals we call Japs. Every Jap you kill is a point for our side, and every Jap you kill brings victory closer. Kill them! Kill them! There's only one good Jap and that is a dead Jap. Remember, if the Jap kills you he is closer to victory. So work hard these two days and become a killer!"

We walk quietly back to the front, trying not to think of what is ahead. My mind doesn't let go of the past, however.

It goes back to the night Jake and the rest of our squad learned I was not only still a virgin but I also had never been drunk. Jake promised to rectify both shortcomings when we went on leave together.

As we march back to the front, I ponder the two questions: Will I ever make out with a girl? And will I ever get drunk?

The truth is, the most important questions are almost never spoken aloud. Will I be one of the wounded, in pain in a hospital? Will I lose these men I love? If I do come back, will I have my arms and legs? Will I have a sane mind?

I return to reality. I remind myself again that what's past is past and what the future holds I cannot know. All that's real is the present.

We are almost at full strength with our new replacements. More troops from the 32nd pass, returning to divisional reserve. They are a sad-looking group like the others: dirty, unshaven, with torn clothing. Some have cigarettes hanging from the corners of their mouths. But soon they will be in reserve, eating hot food and drinking hot coffee.

The switch of the 184th and the 32nd goes smoothly until our platoon's Company E is caught in a vicious crossfire in the open ground between a ridge and the small town of Kuhazu.

Only one squad has reached its objective. The rest of the company is pinned down by mortar and machine-gun fire. It is impossible to carry out the relief of the 32nd until the enemy position is eliminated.

Our company is called upon to take the pressure off Company E by moving into Kuhazu and drawing enough fire for Company E to take the offensive.

Cook, Lee, and I crouch low and run across open ground to the village. The rest of our squad and company are to follow. The plan works and we draw considerable mortar and machine-gun fire.

The three of us find holes as soon as possible and lose contact with the rest of our unit. I lie in the mud with Lee, trying to locate the enemy machine-gunner. Cook keeps a lookout for mortar shells. I finally spot my man. Lee hands me a magazine of ammo and I fire most of it.

Cook calls out, "Quick, move down to the hole to the left." Just as we hit the dirt, mortar shells hit the side of the hole we just vacated. My fire at the machine-gun nest has attracted the mortar shells, but I'm pretty sure I've eliminated the machinegunner.

The trapped Company E squad, free from fire, now can take over.

It is getting dark. We have no chance of getting into a more secure defensive position, so we set up a perimeter where we are, without knowing the exact location of the rest of our company. There is little sleep and much vigilant watching this night.

Cook and I are on guard about 2 o'clock when he sees three Japs coming to the right of our hole. Cook points to where they are. There could be more. We don't know. We make no sound. We know what we must do.

My heart is pounding so loudly I think the Japs can hear it 100 yards away. If they can, it will give away our position. My hands grow sweaty. My mouth is dry. I hope the grenade won't slip out of my wet palm with the pin pulled. If it does, I'm dead and so is Cook.

The moonlight is enough for us to make out the three Japs, crawling on their bellies in the mud. They are close together, and as they push their rifles ahead of them, I can see, in the white light of the moon, that they have shiny fixed bayonets. I can now see their shoes, too, soft like gloves, with the big toe separate from the rest so they can push themselves forward.

We can see them and they have no idea where we are. Our plan is for each of us to pull the pins on two grenades, one in each hand, and release all four together high over the Japs. If we time it right, the grenades should explode in the air above the Japs or just as they hit the ground.

It is a tricky maneuver. You release the handle of the grenade and count one-two-three and get rid of the thing since it explodes on five. We hope they were manufactured with accurate five-second fuses. The Japs won't have time to throw the grenades back at us if we count carefully.

We throw them together and dive to the bottom of the hole. The explosion wakes Lee. Cook puts his hand over Lee's mouth. If one of the Japs survives, we don't want him to know where we are.

I take long drags on my cigarette and conceal the smoke. I hand my cigarette to Lee and wait for what we think is five minutes. Cook, barely looking over the edge of the hole, says, "I can't see any movement."

We count the objects on our perimeter. There are no extras. We count again the next time a mortar flare lights the area. Again, no extras. All three of us watch silently for the rest of the night.

At daylight or just before, our artillery begins hitting the town ahead of us and enemy shells explode behind us on the flat. We check the damage we caused. To the right of our hole are three bodies. The Japs don't look dead. They are not blown apart. When grenades are thrown and timed, the victims usually die instantly from the shrapnel projected down from above them. One of the men is in a crawling position, his knee pushed up and the other leg straight, feet still dug into the dirt. His hands still clutch his rifle with its long bayonet. His head is up a little, as if he's still looking for our hole.

This time we see them first, just 10 feet away. We cautiously look over the foxhole, beyond the infiltrators' bodies, and see no enemy. Our movement hasn't drawn small-arms fire. All we can do is wait quietly, hoping the enemy doesn't know we are out here with no support. In about an hour, we hear voices to our right and rear.

"Arch." It's John. I see the top of his helmet in a drainage ditch nearby. It looks like good cover. Cook decides to make a run for the ditch. As he runs, low to the ground, rifle fire kicks up mud around him.

"Goddamn it, Arch, he made it," Lee says. Lee spots the location of the enemy rifle fire and shoots a few rounds from the BAR while I run for the ditch. Behind us a barrage of small-arms fire hits the enemy position as Lee makes his dash for the ditch.

There we find John, Jake, and Cook. They have a couple cans of rations and some water.

Jake asks, "How the hell did you dumb bastards get out into this motherfuckin' place? We thought you s.o.b's were blown to shit. It's God-damned great to see you. Don't you shit-heads know it's dangerous out here? It's fuckin' dangerous. You got to realize, you dumb shits, there's a war out here."

We hear from Jake and the others that our company suffered some casualties in the flats we just crossed, that they were in real trouble until they found cover in the drainage ditches.

During the rest of the day and early evening we secure the area with few problems, carrying out the dead and wounded through drainage ditches knee-deep with mud.

It is one of the roughest days of fighting I have experienced. Our battalion has 11 men killed and 32 wounded. The ditches we are using were used previously by the enemy for eating, sleeping, taking a crap and carrying out the dead and wounded.

It is almost midnight before we finish setting up our defenses. Lee and I feel somewhat protected in our ditch. We are able to get another box of C rations, using the empty box and our helmets as toilets and throwing the waste over the top of the ditch. Then we settle down in the darkness to watch…wait…and smoke.

April 27, 1945. Our platoon is depleted, discouraged and trying to recover from a week of heavy fighting and losses. We have taken our objective—Skyline Ridge.

From the ridge, I look back and think back.

To the north, just behind that muddy little knoll, is where we called for an armored bulldozer to create a makeshift road so our tanks could direct 75mm cannon fire against the Jap machine-gun nest. We blew the Japs to hell.

To my left, I can make out where Sergeant S and our squad manufactured our own explosive charges by filling mortar-shell casings with packages of TNT taken from Jap satchel charges. We stuffed in handfuls of cordite, then fastened white phosphorous grenades to the lid as detonators. A rope was tied to the contraption, and the grenade-armed bomb was lowered over the crest of a cliff to what we calculated was the location of a Jap stronghold. We don't know exactly what it did to the Japs, but the explosion shook the place like an earthquake and silenced their knee-mortars.

The next morning, April 28, we awake to discover the Japs have retreated during the night and we now occupy the entire ridge all the way back to Conical Peak. It is shaped like Mount Fuji, but too far south and not high enough for snow.

The Japs have taken advantage of the peak's 1,000-foot elevation to use it as an observation post for heavy and light artillery, both of which can fire a flat trajectory into and over our ridge. The mountaintop is riddled with caves and tunnels to provide protection.

Skyline Ridge overlooks a large valley and we look directly at Conical Peak. The valley runs all the way to the ocean at Nakagusuku Bay, where the city of Yonabaru is nestled in a quiet little cove. The battleship New Mexico is positioned off shore in this calm, peaceful cove just beyond the fishing boats. Most of the boats swing at anchor. It resembles a picture in the *National Geographic* and is a reminder of better times.

I am an observer today, with my own field glasses. My duty is to report anything unusual. I see the people of the town of Yonabaru who have not fled. They are doing their daily chores—getting water from wells, collecting firewood, and caring for their children.

These people, who have lived on this island for centuries, seem to take no notice of the invading foreigners—the Japanese troops on one hill, the Americans troops on the other, both aliens—preparing to further devastate their homes and landscape.

The valley between Skyline Ridge and Conical Peak is the largest I have seen so far on Okinawa. Once fertile farmland, it is now nothing but a barren no-man's land pocked with artillery craters.

We have established a line of defense just over the top of the ridge. I am a scout in a hole over the crest of the ridge, peering through my field glasses, connected to company headquarters by telephone. I report in every half-hour.

"All quiet" was my last report.

It has been dry for a few days, a break from the incessant rain. That means less mud to slip around in.

Everything is so quiet. I look off toward Conical Peak, which resulted from a volcanic eruption long ago. Although the volcano has long been inactive, it is in the Pacific Rim of Fire and one never knows.

Meanwhile, it is being eaten away, bit by bit, by our artillery. Its trees have been displaced by dead bodies, its wild flowers blown away. Nobody at home will ever understand this. Not unless their mountain is nibbled at by artillery, hour after hour, day after day.

The Japanese are sweeping south with fire and destruction and we are sweeping north with fire and chaos on a scale never seen before, not even during the eruptions of the now-quiet Pacific volcanoes.

Young men of two continents and two vastly different cultures fight over the prize that is Conical Peak. They are there because it joins Shuri Castle and Naha on the China Sea side of Okinawa to form a natural line of defense. We must have it if we are to control Okinawa. And control of Okinawa, we have been told, is vital to an invasion of Japan.

Our squad is in the middle of our company's defense perimeter. We have received replacements and our ranks are not as thin as we were after Hill 178, when we struggled up to Sky Line. But we are not yet a full squad. There are just 12 of us, even with the new replacements. And the new men are only 18 years old.

I almost said those words out loud around some of the replacements, until it hit me that I'm also 18 and a replacement myself. But I've been here since the beginning. And I'll be 19 in June. Maybe.

Artillery goes over us as usual. It sounds like crinkling paper, like somebody taking a newspaper and wadding it up, or tearing the paper off Christmas gifts and crushing it.

In a way, it's a good sound. If you can hear them, you know the shells are going over you. It's the Jap shells that make the "feupbang" sound, the kind we first encountered while trying to take Hill 178, that strike terror in you. One second you hear the noise, the next you're dead.

The "feupbangs" are 77mm. shells, like the German 88s. They fire straight at you—with no arc—destroying everything within 20 yards when they hit.

Three of those shells hit the squad next to us on Hill 178, almost wiping out the entire squad. I can see the feupbang guns up on Conical Hill, pulled out into the open, no longer inside the caves.

I report this and watch the fire from both sides. When one of our artillery shells comes near or hits one of the 77s, the Japs rush to pull the piece back into a cave. I give the artillery company the target position by telephone as accurately as I can. I enjoy being an artillery spotter for a while.

For the most part, it is a quiet time for me. Nobody is shooting directly at me and I am not moving forward or using my weapons. We can heat our C rations. It has been quite a while since we tasted hot food. Of course, hot or not, it is still just warmed-up hash, spaghetti and meatballs, or beans and franks. Still, hot beans and franks for breakfast are a hell of a lot better than cold hash. The hot Nescafe is fantastic. Cold coffee gets old fast.

One of the sergeants has been acting as our platoon leader. Headquarters has just filled the position with 2nd Lt. Ken Schram, a "90-day Wonder" fresh from officer training.

Soon after he arrives, Lieutenant Schram calls the squads together for a briefing. It is evening and we are in a safe area on the backside of the hill. Mortar shells can reach us, but we feel protected. The new platoon leader, who has his rank painted on his helmet and lieutenant's bars on his shirt, says:

"Men, the Japs are planning a large counter-attack. Army intelligence is expecting the attack tonight or tomorrow night, since April 29 is Emperor Hirohito's birthday. This information confirms there will be attacks by land, sea and air."

Jake calls out: "We know all that shit. They've been dropping leaflets telling us that crap for the last three weeks. Let me show you the propaganda leaflets, but I want them back."

Schram snaps at Jake: "How do you speak to an officer, Soldier?"

Jake replies: "Oh shit, Sir, come off it."

Schram stiffens: "You, Soldier, see me after the briefing. You need a lesson in military discipline."

We all know the enemy is preparing to counter-attack. We don't know exactly when, but it will be soon. We didn't know April 29 is the Emperor's birthday.

Our new platoon leader isn't finished: "Men, we have to be ready! Tomorrow I will have a rifle inspection at 0800. I want all you men to be prepared. The counter-attack may not be just a frontal attack but also an amphibian landing behind our lines. Landing craft have been seen around the point from Yonabaru, and a heavy concentration of troops in the protected hills behind Conical Peak is preparing for an assault. I want my men prepared. That's why I'm calling for a rifle inspection in the morning.

"Good night, men. And I want to see you." He points at Jake.

The two disappear around the hill. Jake returns in a short time.

"That cocksucker is going to report me to the captain for insubordination," says Jake. "We have to do something about this motherfucker. Who's going to do it?"

Jake repeats the words, this time in a shout that can be heard by everyone, ending with "Who's going to do it?"

Cook says, "That 90-day wonder is a real shit. Who's going to clue him in? He'd better shape up by morning or who knows how long we're going to have a platoon leader."

"You guys don't have to do anything," Jake tells us. "I'll take care of him when I get a chance."

The squads end up appointing me to inform the captain how we feel.

"Come on, you guys," I say. "How about Sarge S? He's been around the longest."

Sarge S fires back: "That's why, Kid. I let others do the shit duty, like telling our great new leader the facts of life, or should I say the facts of death. I'm leaving this up to you, Arch. You speak well. Maybe you can help the poor kid. He's about your age, maybe a little older, but a hell of a lot younger when it comes to combat experience."

I have no choice. It's up to me to save face for my guys and maybe save this 90-day wonder's life. I go back to the company command post, salute and ask for the lieutenant. Captain Brokaw calls me by name and tells me to go over by the ration dump. He says the lieutenant will be along shortly.

I sit there for about 10 minutes, looking at the hills and valleys to the north. It is a quiet and peaceful evening. As the sun sets, the island takes on rose and orange hues. The beauty, however, is marred by memories. I can see Hill 178, where we lost Goldsmith, Francis, Jose and the tank crew.

How am I going to talk to this kid lieutenant asking for a rifle inspection? Looking around again, in the twilight, I see the trench where Jose fell and where I wrapped the burned tank soldier in my poncho.

My thoughts are interrupted by the arrival of the lieutenant.

"Morrison, you want to speak to me?"

I jump to my feet.

"Sit down," he says.

"You're Morrison, the captain told me. You're in my platoon."

"Yes, Sir."

"What do you have to say? It's late, and we need our sleep."

"Your three squads, Sir, asked me to speak with you, Sir."

"What about, Morrison?"

"Well, Sir, you see the hills north of us? That one, the highest one, the naked one with all the vegetation blown off is…Sir, do you know anything about that hill, even its name?"

"No, let's get to the point."

"That's Hill 178, Sir. There was quite a battle, Sir."

I tell the lieutenant about the men in our squad, and the men in the rest of our platoon, what they have been through. I tell him of Jake's collection and I think he will get sick. Then about the loss of Jake's brother and how he sharpens his bayonet. I tell him of the reaction of my friends to his briefing tonight.

I try to impress on him how he could be a good officer with these men. He has the training that we need, and he is intelligent. He can help us all stay alive and maybe some of us will be lucky enough to go home after this is over.

I show him the hill, looking north, where we carried our friends' bodies, wrapped in ponchos, down the hill to be collected by the body detail. I tell him how we gave them, in our way, their last rites. I show him where Lee, Cook, and I took our wounded out of danger. I show him where members of the tank crew were burned. I show him where Jose was bayoneted.

"You can see all these areas looking north, Sir. This is where we have been. This is what has made us combat veterans. You ask us to be prepared. Sir, we are prepared. Are you? This treatment of Jake, this rifle inspection you call for is an insult to your men! Your orders must be rescinded, Sir."

The lieutenant was silent for a moment. Then he spoke:

"I think I understand you, Morrison. I'm scared, not only of the enemy but of my own men. What do I have to do? I didn't know what to do when I met you men."

I answer: "I want you to stay alive as long as you can, Sir. I take each day one at a time myself, and we help each other stay alive."

After about 45 minutes of discussion on becoming a combat officer with combat troops, the lieutenant asks what he has to do to become one of us.

"Sir, you have to earn the respect of your men. To become one of us, you must be one of us. You must be willing to sacrifice your life for your brother and your brother must be willing to die for you. If that happens, you become a member of the combat fraternity."

"How do I start?"

"You can begin by giving me a letter rescinding your order of a rifle inspection in the morning. When you come to have C rations at 0600, be ready to honestly apologize to your platoon, particularly to Jake. You should drink cold coffee with us. You should smoke and tell dirty stories with us. You should remove your lieutenant's bars from your uniform and the painted bar on your helmet. They are Jap targets. You must be one of us to stay alive."

The lieutenant writes the letter and hands it to me to read to the men. It cancels the rifle inspection and asks for a second chance to join our platoon.

Then he thanks me for our time together. Taking the orders, I stand, salute and say, "Goodnight, Sir." He says, "Let's cut the salutes and no more 'Sirs.' I'm Ken, and I thank you more than I can say, Arch." We shake hands and I start back to the platoon. It is getting dark. I hear my name called and see our captain.

He says, "Thanks, Morrison. It was better coming from you than from me. Maybe you saved his life."

"Thanks, Captain."

The next morning, Lieutenant Schram arrives in our area and asks if he can share C rations with us. His bars are gone from both his helmet and his shirt. He asks to be called Ken and tells us he has a lot to learn since he has only a year of college and just 90 days of officer-training school. We share our hash breakfast, instant coffee, cigarettes, and battle experiences in a constructive way. When he leaves to go for the day's briefing, we give him a hand.

The ridge is quiet. It seems strange after the struggle to get here. The sound of battle is gone. The smell of battle is missing. The Japs removed their dead during the night. We eat behind the ridge, where there's a fresh breeze off the ocean. Lee and I are lucky to have a good defensive hole prepared. It is larger than most and we find large rocks to put around the front, with spaces where we can see between the rocks without putting our helmets above the hole or showing any movement. We hope we can remain here the next few nights.

I am on watch in the afternoon, the only one on duty in our company's sector. I again have a pair of field glasses and a field telephone. Through the glasses, I see Japs on the hill to my right. Some are preparing food, one is shaving, another conversing, a few are taking it easy. One is standing, taking a piss.

One of their men has field glasses similar to mine. He is probably watching our men just as I am watching his.

We are just young men taking time out from the business of killing. Nobody seems overly concerned about anyone else. It is as if the war has taken a break.

I have a bizarre thought. What if all of us, on both sides, just went on strike like the men who worked in Dad's mill? Without anyone to fight it, the war would simply stop.

My eyes wander, taking in Conical Peak and Shuri Castle, the ancient capital of the Ryukyu Islands. The castle, we hear, has thick walls and beautiful gardens and temples. I understand it has been the home of kings since 600 A.D. I can also see Yonabaru, on the coastal plain. But just out of sight is Naha, the island's largest city.

We have been told that Naha, Shuri, Yonabaru and these heavily fortified hills may be the launching point for the massive counter-attack the Japs have promised.

CHAPTER 6

✿

We don't know whether our assault on Conical Peak or the Japanese counter-attack will come first.

The Japs like to tease us. A Zero, which we call "wash-machine Charlie," flies over every night and drops leaflets saying our navy has been destroyed by the heroes of the war—the Japanese kamikaze pilots.

Soon, they say, we will have no supplies, ammunition or food; and we will never see our mothers and girlfriends again. The Emperor's troops will be on the march soon, very soon.

The Zero seems to come out of nowhere. There isn't supposed to be a decent airfield left on Okinawa

Our Intelligence briefings confirm that enemy action is imminent.

It is the evening of May 1. May Day. One month since we came ashore.

Lee, Cook, and I are together in an excellent defensive position. Replacements make it possible for more concentrated defensive coverage. With three men in a foxhole, we get more sleep and are more alert on guard. There has been little action the past few days. We have time to regroup.

With the battleship *New Mexico* looming out in Nakagusuku Bay, we feel secure. Its two 12-inch guns, fore and aft, give us firepower. The guns fire flat into the hills, blowing up tunnels and concrete fortifications. The *New Mexico* has moved in close since the Jap Navy no longer is a problem. But the battle in the air continues.

Cook shouts, "Look!"

Out of a cloud to the northeast come two kamikaze planes, heading for the battleship. Cook says, with alarm, "They can't knock out that ship. It's our heavy guns. It's our security. It's more powerful than their artillery. Just yesterday we saw a Jap 77-artillery position get hit by one of those 12-inchers and the artillery piece was pulverized, the men annihilated. God, I hope we don't lose that power."

Every anti-aircraft weapon on the battleship and on two destroyers nearby opens fire. The two planes stay on course. The anti-aircraft fire leaves puffs of smoke in the sky. Through the smoke, we see the Zeros continue on their mission.

The encounter is far enough away that we hear little sound. But we can see it. It is like watching a struggle between men and machines unfold in a dream.

"Is this real?" I say to Lee. "I wonder what's going on in the sailors' minds. Are we going to see our battleship blown out of the water and over 1,000 men go down with it?"

Lee says, "I suppose the sailors react like we do in combat, Arch, doing what they have to in order to stay alive and save their ship."

A flash lights the town of Yonabaru. Smoke rises. Explosions follow as the kamikaze planes crash. Have they hit the ship? How could the pilots find their targets through all that flack?

There is a deathly silence. Nobody says a word. We can't see anything for a while. Then, as the smoke clears, we see the ship. It's still there, but the stern is gone from just aft of the gun turret. There are lots of men in the water. They are swimming. Oil fires burn on the water.

Aboard ship, we see water stream from fire hoses, billows of oily black smoke, and running corpsmen. It is a chaotic scene, not only as viewed through the field glasses but with the naked eye as well.

"It's like watching a newsreel, Arch," Lee says. "The big difference is this is real and we're the commentary."

"This is just like our action, Lee, quiet one minute and then all holy hell breaks loose."

Twenty minutes later, the ship is still afloat and the fires are being brought under control. Men are being pulled from the burning water. Even though the old battleship can no longer move, her guns look serviceable and may be able to fire for the rest of the operation. We don't know how many men have been lost in the attack, but we send up a prayer.

To whom? I don't know. Certainly not to the God I thought I knew, not to the God back in the tabernacle, where I fell from the ladder. Maybe a prayer to the big guns on the deck of the New Mexico, the big guns that may keep us alive for another day.

Can the 12-inch guns be my new God?

I am sure those big guns have a better chance of keeping me alive and safe than the God Jose worshiped and asked to keep him alive. His God afforded him no protection when a Jap decided to run a bayonet through him. John was just a fraction too late in shooting the Jap.

I wonder what kamikaze pilots, diving to their death, think about.

Is it something like "I have done the ultimate for my Emperor"? I remember my mother saying, when brother Billy died, "Praise the Lord. Billy is with Jesus."

Is belief that powerful?

Out there, on a ridge in Okinawa, watching the hell of war, I feel the Christian faith is blind to reality, just as those kamikaze pilots are blind in their faith in Shinto and Buddhism.

Neither faith faces up to life as it really is. I no longer know what I am or what I believe. But I do know I will not have a faith again that can't look squarely at life and death.

The kamikazes never return to the *New Mexico*, which is dead in the water but not dead in combat. The sight of that wounded ship continuing to fire its big guns will be burned into my memory as long as I live. What a memorial to the navy men we watched die in the explosion of fire and oil.

Before I can answer my questions about the faith in which I once felt such certainty, there is another evening visit from the Zero that seems to come out of nowhere. Once again, the leaflets tell us our navy is sunk and soon there will be no food or ammunition.

We spend another night watching and waiting. Lee, Cook, and I are in our foxhole. Nealey and John are about 75 feet farther down the hill as scouts. We are connected by a shallow trench and a telephone line.

It is Nealey and John's job to warn the company by field phone if there is any activity or hint of an assault. They have rifles and a couple of cases of grenades.

Tomorrow is Nealey's 18th birthday.

John takes his books, even on scout duty.

They phone and ask for another case of grenades and more cigarettes. I crawl down the trench with their supplies, pushing the case of grenades ahead of me.

When I arrive, John is reading a poem by Sassoon.

"Sassoon wrote it about going home after the First World War," John says. "Do you want to hear it, Arch? There's plenty of time."

"Why not?"

"It's titled 'They.' That's us," says John, who begins reading:

> The Bishop tells us: "When the boys come back
> "They will not be the same, for they'll have fought
> "In a just cause: they lead the last attack
> "On Anti-Christ; their comrades' blood has bought
> "New right to breed an honorable race,
> "They have challenged Death and dared him face to face."

> *"We're none of us the same!" the boys reply.*
> *"For George lost both his legs; and Bill's stone blind;*
> *"Poor Jim's shot through the lungs and like to die;*
> *"And Bert's gone syphilitic; you'll not find*
> *"A chap who's served that hasn't found SOME change."*
> *And the Bishop said, "The ways of God are strange!"*

"That's great, John," I say. "I want to know more about Sassoon."

"I think there's time for another," John answers. First, you need a little background. In modern wars, governments use all the conventional ways of influencing public opinion. The creative people who put together the ads to sell soaps and cars in peacetime have another job to do in war. They put together clever words, they paint pictures, they put them together to whip up hatred of the enemy. That's half of their job. The other half? Make war look romantic. Where people used to see posters for circuses, they see posters designed to boost recruiting.

"Sassoon wrote a poem as a response to a poster of English women watching troops march away. The women are waving the men off to war with a song. 'Go!' 'Go,' they sing, 'for King and your country.' They promise cheers and kisses for the men when they come back."

John says, "Now, Arch, I'll read Sassoon's response, titled *"Glory of Women"*:

> *You love us when we're heroes, home on leave,*
> *Or wounded in a mentionable place.*
> *You worship decorations; you believe*
> *That chivalry redeems the war's disgrace.*
> *You make us shells. You listen with delight,*
> *By tales of dirt and danger fondly thrilled.*
> *You crown our distant ardours while we fight,*
> *And mourn our laurelled memories when we're killed.*
> *You can't believe that British troops "retire"*

When hell's last horror breaks them, and they run,
Trampling the terrible corpses——blind with blood.
O, German mother dreaming by the fire,
While you are knitting socks to send your son
His face is trodden deeper in the mud.

After John has read the line addressed to a German mother, I push the toes of my boots in the dirt.

"All we have to do, Arch, is change the name to Japs and this is our war, right? If you like, take this little book back with you. I'll pick it up in the morning."

"Thanks, John, that's great. Have a good night and I'll see you in the morning."

I work my way back, crawling on my belly to the hole I share with Lee and Cook.

I pull my first guard duty at 0100. Cook gets me up, gives me my watch, which he's been wearing, and slips me his lighted cigarette and ammo clips. A light rain is falling, just as it always seems to do at home, in the Pacific Northwest. I ask Cook to clue me in on our perimeter.

"What are your marks on the right?"

"That rock you see, and on the left that blown-off stump."

"OK, how many points between?"

"Twelve."

"Thanks."

Cook rolls up in a blanket in the hole, covers with a poncho, and goes to sleep. The rain on my helmet sounds as if it is landing on a tin roof. Maybe it is the same as what our chickens used to hear on the metal barn roof back home. The rain on my face feels as it did when I used to go fishing early in the morning or when I watched a baseball game at Capilano Stadium and hoped it would be canceled.

There are no rainouts here. I take a puff on the cigarette, inhale deeply, and hide deeper in my hole. When the cigarette is down to where my fingers start to burn, that's the signal to light another.

Like a chain-smoker, I start one cigarette from another, never showing anything but two glowing united fags. We call it "cigarette sex." It is the only sex around.

By moonlight, as the rain clouds break, I see the holes on either side of us. Otherwise, I feel very much alone, with only my ever-present questions to keep me company.

Will I see tomorrow? Is there any other existence? Did I ever really have a home, a mother, a father, brothers, sisters, or is this all there is? Is the past only imagination, a dream?

Always, though, I return to the main question: Will I see tomorrow?

I wonder how many other 18-year-old men are having similar thoughts. Quite a few, I imagine. Some are halfway around the world, in Europe; others are 50 feet down the line from me.

But none of the other people in the world really matters now. My comrades are all that exist for me, the only ones I must protect. Ninety minutes after I start guard duty, the Japanese begin the heaviest artillery bombardment I have ever seen or heard.

A call comes on the field phone. It's John and Nealey. Something's going on out in front. They want parachute flares, not the small mortar flares our guys are using. They're so bright and short-lived that John's and Nealy's eyes don't have time to adjust to what's out there.

Pretty soon, everyone's awake as shells start landing around us. Our holes, just over the crest of the hill, seem relatively safe. But still we keep our heads down, to avoid being hit by "short rounds," which are shells that lack enough oomph to carry them to their target. They land short and kill troops unfortunate enough to be beneath them. Dirt rains down on our helmets.

Both sides throw up "short rounds," ours as well as theirs.

Artillery fights are hard on the nerves. There's nothing one can do about them. If you think too much, you go nuts. If you get killed, you get killed; if you survive, you survive.

After seeing what one artillery shell does to a foxhole and those in it, you know there's no pain. It's over in a flash.

Anxiety is what cracks men. We know that if we survive, don't get hit or crack, the artillery barrage eventually will let up.

When that happens, the enemy will be only a short distance below the crest of the hill, ready to attack with rifles and bayonets. We know this artillery attack is a prelude to the long-expected counter-attack. It is intended to soften us up, like ocean waves pounding on cliffs and scooping out a steep bank. I've seen it happen during violent storms on the Washington coast. There, powerful waves find every small crack in rocks. Then, wave after wave follows. The continual pounding eventually breaks off pieces of rocks. And in time, the waves pound those smaller pieces into sand.

As both sides fire artillery, the Japs are counting on us to soften. I'm counting on the Japs to soften as they did before our attack on Hill 178.

The noise is deafening and terrifying, and the smell of powder chokes us. When a hole is hit, the screams of the dying are chilling. The bombardment goes on, hour after hour. It seems to be even more intense than the bombardment we aimed at Hill 178 before the final assault.

Our fire is directed at the big guns the Japs have rolled out of the caves on Conical Peak. Spotters, like John and Nealey, tell our artillerymen where to aim. They call out, "five-degrees right," or "six-degrees left." It's called "bracketing." It helps us eventually zero-in on the target.

Lee, Cook, and I watch for any signs of enemy activity with every flare that lights our part of the valley.

At about 0400, Lee first sees, and then we all see, hundreds—maybe thousands—of enemy troops moving across the valley toward the base of Skyline Ridge. At sea, small boats move up the coast in an attempt to establish a beachhead behind us.

Our artillery changes to anti-personnel shells with fuses that trigger the explosive 10 to 15 feet above the ground. The explosions send shrapnel in all directions.

Even as the enemy fall, however, more troops keep coming. I over-hear a call from someone at company headquarters saying John and Nealey aren't to fire until they literally can see "the whites" of the enemy's eyes. Lieutenant Schram says on the phone, "As soon as we hear your fire, John, we'll all begin firing."

"OK, Ken," John replies.

The wait is short. The firing begins.

I find it almost impossible to fire over the head of Nealey, who is in a hole directly in front of us. So I fire on both sides of their hole, hoping they can protect the front.

I hold the trigger down, releasing bursts from the BAR. I see many of the on-coming enemy drop. But they always seem to be replaced by more, all coming toward us, as they move up the hill.

They hit the ground when we unleash rifles, BARs, and grenades. As soon as we stop for a moment, they rise and move forward again.

Ken is coordinating our operations. He crawls up to our hole and asks us to do all we can to protect Nealey and John. Their information has been great, he says, enabling the artillery to knock out an estimated 14 enemy pieces so far. He expresses amazement that so many Japanese have survived both our artillery attack and the anti-personnel shells.

Lee says, "Arch, you're doing great. Keep firing the BAR. I'll keep the ammo coming as long as it lasts."

"Thanks, Lee. Keep it coming."

Cook hollers, "I wish I had a BAR." He's keeping the enemy away from our hole with his M-1 rifle.

We see flashes of grenades from Nealey's hole. Minutes become hours.

Suddenly, a Jap soldier no more than 10 feet from our hole runs toward us with his rifle pointed down, bayonet fixed. Bullets hit the dirt in front of our hole.

Reflexes take over. Where the hell did he come from? How did he get this close? He's going to kill me? I've got to stop him. Do I have time? I can see his face. I can see the battle terror in his eyes as he probably can in mine.

It's either this Jap or me! I point the BAR at him and squeeze the trigger. I unload on him with a full clip of ammo, maybe 10 rounds. He drops not two feet from me. His face is contorted in agony. Blood foams from his mouth.   When he strikes the ground, the air is forced from his lungs. It sounds like a ruptured beach ball. His eyes and mouth are open. His arms go forward, releasing the rifle, which falls into our hole.

He makes a noise like that of a distressed animal. He doesn't move. I am sure he realizes that it's over.

He is dying and I have killed him! This is different from the others I have killed. They were far away. This one looks directly into my eyes. I cannot avoid his eyes. I lean over the side of our hole and puke my guts. The vomit runs down the hill toward him.

On the other side of the hole, Cook leans over and pukes, too.

Lee shouts at both of us, "You damn bastards get with it! You've seen this kind of thing before. There's more Japs coming."

I turn toward Lee, who gives me another magazine of ammo. I shove it into the BAR. While looking into the eyes of the dying man in front of me, I begin firing again. The crotch of my pants is wet. My underpants are dirty. There is vomit on my shirt. What a God-awful mess!

The Jap gurgles. It sounds like every gasping breath is a cry. My heart pounds in my chest like thunder. I want to stop his dying noise. Maybe I can reach out and stuff his mouth full of mud. Maybe I can fire more bullets to stop his misery. But I can't.

For more than two hours the soldier clings to life. The body, the man, the Jap I see on the ground not more than two-feet away finally stops making noises. He is finally dead, and I killed him.

Every flare that goes off lights the area so I can see his eyes. They seem to look right through me. The blood that foamed from his mouth and nose soaks into the ground.

He lies in the mud all night, arms outstretched, dark eyes staring at me.

The shooting stops. Lee and Cook pull blankets around themselves and fall asleep. I can't sleep, so I take the first guard. I know that some enemy troops have broken through our lines and I hope they will be taken care of by the reserve company. My job is to see that no more infiltrate our position. To do this, I must watch behind as well as forward.

As daylight breaks, I look for Nealey and John in the hole in front of us. The hillside is gruesome. Bodies are strewn as far as I can see. It is a massacre, worse than anything I could have imagined.

A helmet here, an arm or a leg there. Bodies in grotesque positions. Weapons from both sides intermingled and strewn everywhere over the hillside.

I see no movement in John and Nealey's hole. Lee and Cook join me in looking and praying. No one wants to say what we're beginning to suspect.

Lieutenant Ken crawls up to our hole to see if we're OK and ask if one of us can get down to John and Nealey's hole to check on them.

Lee volunteers. Cook and I cover him as he slides over the rim of our hole. There is no enemy fire. He returns in less than 10 minutes, alone.

His message is brief: "There are about 35 dead bodies in front of their hole. All their ammo is used, and the two cases of grenades are empty."

The three of us carry John and Nealey down the hill on ponchos later that day. Body trucks will pick them up. We kneel for a few minutes in silence. Lee makes the sign of the cross. Cook says the Lord's Prayer. I pray to the big guns of the *New Mexico*.

Nealey didn't live long enough to have his birthday.

I ask Lee and Cook, "Do you guys think it would be OK if...John gave me a book last night and I was to return it today. I would like John's other two books. He wanted me to have them."

"Sure, Arch, he'd want you to have them."

I cry as I search the clothing on John's lifeless body. I find his books and the journal he kept and stuff them into the pockets of my fatigues. Tears stream down my face as I walk slowly back up the hill. I stop once to look back.

I return to our depleted squad to continue the battle.

Cook goes with Jake to prepare their foxhole. Because of our fatalities and wounded, we're down to two in a hole again. Lee and I prepare for the coming night. But first we have to clear the area immediately in front of our hole. It is littered with enemy bodies.

The first to be moved is the closest, that of the Japanese lieutenant I killed. We know he isn't booby trapped, since we could see him from our hole the entire time. And we don't think he placed a primed grenade under his body.

But, taking no chances, we grab one of the Jap's favorite weapons, a four-to-five-feet-long pole, with a bayonet attached to the end. We crouch down in our hole and use the stick to roll the lieutenant's body over. When there is no explosion, we feel more confident.

We decide to create a row of bodies in front of the hole. Flies already cover the bloody areas on the bodies. They lay eggs that hatch into maggots that feed on rotting flesh. None of the bodies smells yet, but the skin that's visible is beginning to turn dark.

The lieutenant was wearing a belt with a holster and a .38 revolver. I remove the revolver. There is a bullet in the chamber.

I ask Lee, "Should we keep it or turn it in?"

"Let's keep it, Arch. We found it."

Lee pulls two flags and a wallet from the dead officer's pockets. He hands me the wallet and spreads the flags on the ground. Inside the wallet are some Japanese money and three photographs.

One is of a smiling woman about 50 years old. She is small, her black hair done on top of her head and she is dressed in traditional Japanese clothes.

Another photograph—this one in color—is of a beautiful, slender young woman, who looks to be in her early 20s. She is dressed in what appear to be wedding clothes. The final photo is of an adorable little girl of perhaps 18 months, dressed in embroidered clothes. She is seated on an embroidered pillow. It looks almost like a painting.

We study the pictures in silence. Lee says, "These family pictures are just like the ones in my wallet, Arch, the ones of my mother, wife and little girl. His family was just like mine."

"I wonder how long he's been married, Lee, and when he last saw his family. Maybe he was thinking about them when he died.

"I killed him, Lee. I could have stopped him by shooting him in the foot, and he might have become a prisoner and lived. I never thought of that. I just killed him."

"When you're in battle and the enemy is coming at you to kill you, Arch, you don't think of just wounding him. You shoot to kill, aiming at the chest. And if you're a good enough shot you nail him through the head."

"This time I was quicker than he was, Lee. I'm alive and he's dead. What will it be next time?"

"You can't think that way, Arch. You have to go on or you'll crack. Come on, we're still together. If you hadn't killed him, he would have gotten both of us. You've been face-to-face with the Japs before and you know his main thought was to kill us both. If we're going to stay alive, we have to destroy the enemy, not hurt him, or frighten him, or drive him away, or capture him. Just kill him. You never had second thoughts after you killed the others."

"But he has a wife, a daughter, and a mother, Lee."

"So did the others you killed, most likely. What about Jose? He had three children, a wife, and a mother. They killed him."

"Let's do something with the things he had, Lee, and we'll talk about it later. Why don't we just put his things in our packs and whichever of us survives can have them."

We make a commitment to each other: The one who survives, if there is one, will look up the other's folks when he gets back. This is the first time we've talked about living through combat. I take the bullets out of the Jap's six-shooter and put them in my pack, then shove the pistol in my pocket. Lee puts the flag and the wallet with the pictures in his pack.

"This isn't like Jake, with his big bag of ears and teeth," Lee says. "I can't see that."

"Jake's sort of like the kid in the first platoon who has all those gold teeth he knocks out of the dead Japs with his rifle butt," I reply.

"Let's just keep quiet about this, Arch, and not tell anybody else. I don't want to be thought of as a body-robber."

There's an evening briefing. Along with the 96th Division, we're going to make a night or early morning attack on Yonabaru and Conical Peak. We're to push off at 0300. The artillery will begin firing at 2300 and raise its fire at 0300.

CHAPTER 7

❀

The now too-familiar sound of someone vigorously crunching a news-paper or Christmas wrapping, but much louder, starts behind me, up north.

It grows increasingly louder, then gradually fades out in front of me, to the south, on the Jap side of the valley.

I see a flash and hear an explosion. The ground shudders as 155mm. shells explode into the enemy position.

I'm being shaken. It's Lee.

"Guard time, Arch," he whispers.

I glance at my watch, my high-school graduation present, inscribed on the back, "Archie, with love from Mother and Dad, 1944." It's a good watch, a Mido, marked with military 24-hour time. It is 2300.

"This is early," I say to myself. I cup both hands around the cigarette Lee gives me. Holding the half-burned smoke in my left hand, I crouch down in our hole and take a long drag. The butt burns my hand and fingers. It's time to light the next Chesterfield. I pull a soggy blanket over my head to hide the glow from the two cigarettes pressed together.

The artillery fire seems to be right above my head. It's different from the usual, more continuous. Hundreds of 155mm shells go over in a very short time. Lee is already asleep.

I say, out loud, "Goddamn-it, keep those things high enough so they don't catch the top of my hill." Sure, the orange markers are out to tell our guys where we are, but they're hard to see in the dim light of the moon without artillery flares. Our artillery use the last settings taken at dusk when it's still possible to see our markers.

I'm not supposed to get Lee up till about 0100. We're to move out at 0300. Right now, our heavy artillery shells are exploding a short distance in front of us and the Jap shells are landing a short distance behind us.

We're in the middle.

The night roars and flashes. I know the difference between the sound of ours and the sound of theirs.

After I wake Lee, we crouch in our hole for two hours, just listening to the shells going over. We smoke, eat a can of cold hash, and drink some water. I have to pee. I get on my knees, unbutton my pants, and put my helmet between my legs. After checking the wind direction, I pour the contents of the helmet down the hill. One of the new guys failed to check the wind and got the pee right back in his face.

Lee and I talk about surviving and dying, a subject we seldom mention. We both agree we have pretty much lost our fear of death. It might even be a welcome way out. Whatever happens, we'll carry out each other's wishes.

Lee, being Catholic, has his rosary, although he never says much about it.

I tell him a story I heard from old R.B. Westmacott, one of my high-school English teachers. Westmacott served in the Canadian Army during World War I and got acquainted with a fellow who took crucifixes off the bodies of dead soldiers after becoming convinced that crucifixes, Bibles, and St. Christopher Medals didn't do anything to ward off enemy bullets.

In fact, the fellow began using the crucifixes for rifle practice out in the woods.

"I'm Pentecostal, a holy roller, as you know, Lee. And I've been brain-washed to believe that since I give my life to Jesus, He'll take care of me. But did He take care of Nealey? Will He take care of you or me any better? Was it His will that Nealey and John were to die in that Goddamned hole out in front of us last night? Maybe God punished Nealey because he knocked up that 40-year-old woman somewhere back in Washington State.

"I wonder what kind of a father this God is. He lets his only son get killed on a cross while He watches. He will let us get killed out here in Okinawa while He watches. He has all the damn power to do every-thing. He's great. He's just. He's benevolent. He's loving. He's compas-sionate.

"He has the omnipotent power to protect and change all creation. He made the sun stand still. He parted the Red Sea. He has the power to control the world, the entire universe, everything. He supposedly cre-ated it all.

"Everything that happens is God's will. It's His will for us to be here killing other young men. It's His will that a bayonet was run through Jose.

"I think God's will is all a bunch of bullshit. We're here in a shit-hole of mud, the stench of bloating bodies and shit. He doesn't do a fucking thing but laugh at us. He doesn't care. He doesn't give a Goddamned shit.

"Nobody will ever understand or care about us, and I mean nobody. I heard before I left home that there are no atheists in foxholes. Well, I sure as hell know of one."

"I think you've got it right, Arch," Lee says. "What you say makes sense, even though I don't want to believe it. I don't know what to think. I just don't want to be killed like an animal. I will still keep my rosary around my neck with my dogtags and my prayer book over my heart.

"Arch, if I don't survive would you do something for me?"

"Sure, Lee, what? I'd do anything for you, you know that. After all, you've taught me what I need to know to stay alive. I've never known anybody with the patience you have."

"I'm only being selfish, Arch. I taught you so you could keep me from being killed. I sort of picked you out and thought, there's a sharp kid. I can show him what I know and maybe we can survive together for a while. As I told you when we first met, I had a buddy on Leyte who was my combat teacher.

"Anyway, I do have one request that's important to me."

"Go ahead."

"OK, if I die and you survive will you make the sign of the cross over my body and say the Lord's Prayer?"

"Sure, Lee. But it's not going to happen. Let's talk about something else."

I wonder what my mother would say if she knew what I'd promised to do. She was baptized a Catholic, but now she has no use for them. My dad's father was an Orange man. And here I am saying I'll make the sign of the cross and pray over my Catholic friend if he's killed. Well, I can't see how it's so terrible. He's the best friend I've ever had. Closer than a brother.

Ken whispers behind our hole, "It's 0300, let's get with it."

We start down the southeast side of Skyline Ridge. It's slow-going in the dark. I have to watch every step and whisper to the man behind me, "Rock…big drop left…deep hole keep right," just as Lee, in front, lets me know if there is anything in my way. We are extremely careful not to kick a rock, to step carefully over bodies, not to disturb anything that could be booby-trapped. Daylight is just breaking and we can make out the dirt and mud thrown into the air when artillery shells land in front of us.

Somebody shouts, "I got to take a shit, wait." He's to my left in another company. Somebody answers, "Shit your pants. Nobody's waiting out here in the open. We have to get behind that little hill before it's light. And keep your fuckin' mouth closed."

The poor guy has the "GIs," our name for diarrhea. He runs to the side, drops his pants and stumbles over a Jap body that's booby-trapped with an armed grenade.

The soldiers—one dead, the other taking his pants down—are both filled with shrapnel when the grenade explodes.

A call goes out for a medic. I don't know what will happen to the poor s.o.b., if he'll live or die. There are bodies everywhere, our own and those of the enemy. Some of our dead from Company H are still in their holes, where they were overrun by the enemy.

Yesterday was hot and wet. That speeds the decay process. The smell is putrid. Is this the last big push by the Japs? Lee seems to be reading my mind. He turns and says, "Arch, it really doesn't matter. It's never-ending. It goes on and on."

When morning comes it's easier to pick our way through the debris and bodies. There's a light rain and our combat boots sink into the mud and make a sucking sound as we pull them out. I can hear Lee's boots in front and Cook's boots behind. When my boot hits a pool of muddy water, the water splashes to my knees. It's difficult to tell whether the bodies I step over are ours or theirs.

A mud-covered body, I decide, looks like a large shell casing.

I see a U.S. combat boot sticking up from a mud-covered, rigor-mortised corpse. One of ours. I see another leg. I can't be sure whether it's a Jap with a two-toed shoe or a dismembered American leg in a combat boot.

I see an American helmet strapped to a head in the slime. One of ours. And nearby is a Jap helmet strapped to another dead body. One of theirs.

They are all somebody's sons, brothers, maybe even fathers. U.S. or Jap? Does it really matter? They're all dead, most of them boys from 16 to 19. Just like me.

The smell is so bad that some of us cover our noses, others throw up. It doesn't take long for bodies to disintegrate in this climate. First, the bacteria, then the maggots, flies, birds, and wild animals, all doing their part to eliminate the flesh of what a short time ago was a living human being.

I first smelled death when I was a kid in the islands of Washington State. My uncle, a neat guy with no children of his own, took me out in his big boat. We took a small boat into a beach. There, he shot a deer and gutted it, before putting the carcass in the small boat and taking it back to the big one.

Later, while we were pulling in crab pots—we keep the males, release the females, and re-bait the pots with chicken guts—I noticed a bunch of seagulls, crows, buzzards, and eagles hovering over something farther up the beach. There was this dreadful, putrid smell of decaying flesh, which made me so sick I felt like throwing up.

My uncle said a small whale, an orca, had died and washed up on the beach. The birds were eating its carcass. "Isn't it wonderful how nature takes care of things?"

"But the awful smell," I said.

"That will be gone in a day or so and all that remains will be clean white bones. What the birds don't get, the ants and maggots finish."

Vultures hovered overhead waiting for their chance to feast on the decaying meat.

❦   ❦   ❦

As we move toward Yonabaru, the smell is similar to that of the dead whale. And I feel just as sick as I did when I was a boy.

Lee's pack, in front of me, looks different. The pack and blanket roll are shaped the same, but instead of the usual olive drab, they are now black. Mine has turned black, too. Our packs are covered with what appear to be millions of black flies.

Mr. Brooks, my science teacher in high school in Vancouver, explained the process when he told us about an experiment conducted by Louis Pasteur, the famous scientist.

Pasteur took two pieces of meat to a Paris market place. He covered one piece of meat with a screen and left the other uncovered. Within two days, the uncovered meat teemed with maggots, whereas the covered meat was virtually unchanged, except for a little dehydration. This, Pasteur said, disproved the prevalent belief in spontaneous generation.

Mr. Brooks explained that what happened in Pasteur's experiment is how nature takes care of death and prevents diseases. The buzzards come, the flies come to lay their eggs, the maggots eat the protein, and, finally, the dead animal is gone except for its bones.

But Mr. Brooks didn't mention anything about what happens to your friends when they die in battle. When it's nothing but bones, then what?

Eternity? Heaven? Paradise? Nirvana? Hell? Eternal fire?

Or just death?

With Lieutenant Ken and Jake leading our squad, we round a hill, beyond which a flat plain stretches to the Pacific Ocean and the town of Yonabaru.

A Jap machine gun suddenly opens fire. Ken is hit and goes down. He rolls into a ditch deep enough for safety, Jake right behind him. The rest of us hit the ground.

Lee and I are protected on the right and able to go up the backside of the little hill. We can see where the machine-gun fire is coming from— four Japs on the edge of a shell crater just below us, no more than 35 feet away.

We hear them talking and watch their every move in silence. They have no idea they are in imminent danger of being killed.

I get on my belly and aim the BAR, trying to get all four in my range finder. As they continue to fire, we hear the familiar ra-ta-ta-ta-ta of a Jap light-machine gun.

Jake throws a rock from the ditch where he and Ken took cover. The Japs come into the open, firing at the sound of the rock. This is my chance. I catch all four with one burst from my BAR. I haven't shot even one clip, and all is quiet. Death is quick, final.

When medics take our lieutenant back to a field hospital, Cook says, "We'll miss him. He's a good officer, even if he is a 90-day wonder."

There is no more resistance the rest of the way to Yonabaru. The village is almost deserted. The only gooks left are those who refuse to leave their half-demolished homes and fishing boats. The Japs have retreated to higher ground southwest of town.

The town's docks, stores, and houses are leveled or barely standing. The guns and artillery of the disabled *New Mexico* have wiped out almost everything in sight. A breeze coming in from offshore blows away some of the odor of dead bodies.

Lee and I go through town, setting fire to partially destroyed houses. We have fun shooting off our weapons and burning things, another of those inexplicable emotional highs of the battlefield.

"Why do I enjoy burning down people's houses?" I ask Lee. "I must be out of my mind."

"What's that, Arch?"

"Nothing, Lee."

We come to the edge of town, toward the eastern hills where the houses are in better shape. We stop in front of one of the houses—a thatched-roof bungalow with no more than two rooms. We have seen similar homes in other villages. Each seems to have a small garden and some chickens and goats.

Lee says, "Arch, let's not burn this one. It's in better shape. Somebody could use this house."

As Lee speaks, an elderly man comes out of the house waving his hands and shouting. The old gook has a white beard trimmed to a point below his chin. His clothes are worn but clean. He is bare-footed and walks slowly. Although Lee and I can't understand a word of his rapid-fire Okinawan, we know from his arm waving that he's begging us not to destroy his house.

He motions us to the garden behind his home. We follow, covering him with our weapons. We walk slowly, watching for trouble, hoping the old man isn't leading us into an ambush.

We enter a sort of courtyard. Hedges enclose the yard and separate the garden from the animals. A goat shelter and a chicken coop are encircled by sturdy hibiscus with yellow flowers. A banyan tree stands in the corner of the garden, string-like aerial roots reaching the ground. A stream about three-feet wide runs behind the garden plot.

The sound of running water is pleasant. A large fan palm shades a well and stone bench in the center of the garden.

It is a lovely and peaceful yard, an oasis in the hell of war. Cook catches up with us in the courtyard.

"You guys are stupid to come in here," Cook says. "You could be killed. You can't trust these people."

The three of us watch as the old gook, ignoring Cook's outburst, uses a small hand winch to pull up a rope from the bottom of the well. Attached to the rope is a large metal teapot.

The old man goes into the back of his house and brings out some hand-painted blue cups with designs depicting events in Okinawan history. The cups are on a black-lacquered tray, along with rice crackers. He pours a colorless liquid from the teapot into the cups.

When all the cups are filled, he passes them around to us. Then he raises his own cup, says some words we can't understand, and drinks from the cup. We do the same. It's my first taste of sake.

We drink until the teapot is empty. By that time we all laugh a lot and feel no pain. When we leave the old man with his empty teapot in his still intact house, we give him some of our rations and assure him, in sign language, that he will be safe.

We rejoin our company in a happy mood. The mood is heightened when we hear that our lieutenant's wounds are not serious. He'll live to fight another day.

CHAPTER 8

✿

Knowing that Yonabaru is secure, we move west to the hills where we look down on the quiet harbor. Small fishing boats are at anchor in the bay or tied to the half-demolished pier. Farther out is the wounded battleship *New Mexico* with its two destroyer escorts.

Our battalion sets up defensive positions at several tombs in the hillside, some 300 feet above the town. The occupants of those tombs almost certainly had once lived in the war-torn village below.

The tombs, similar to ones we have used many times before, are ideal for machinegunners and night-time protection.

Okinawan tombs are unique: a vertical half-circle of stone or tile on the face of a hill, with a smaller half-circle opening in the center of the masonry; a small ceremonial area in front of the tomb juts from the face of the hill at 90 degrees.

Removing the large decorative-pottery jars of bones from inside the tomb gives us protection from attack and affords visual observation of up to 180 degrees.

There is just one problem with the tombs. They are full of fleas. The only remedies that seem to work are portable flamethrowers and phosphorous grenades, which burn out every living thing.

Before we can do this, however, we must follow company orders to investigate the tombs thoroughly.

Our squad is assigned to clear out one of the tombs. Lee and I go in first. With our flashlights, we see that the room is much larger than the ones we've seen previously. We call for battery-powered headlamps that can be held by hand or strapped to our helmets.

We strap ours to our helmets, freeing our hands to carry M-1s or throw grenades.

Lee says, "Arch, let's put a couple of grenades in the Goddamned tomb before we go in with the lights. The lights will make us perfect targets."

After the grenades explode, we crouch behind rocks on either side of the entrance. Hearing nothing, I turn on my light while Lee covers me and watches for movement.

It is immediately apparent that we have stumbled onto a tomb quite unlike the others we've seen. There are no big pottery jars of ancestral bones on stone shelves. And the room is very large, with connecting side rooms.

Seeing no movement, Lee calls the rest of the squad to join our explorations. We soon discover that the tunnels extend clear through the hill and exit on the other side.

In the largest room, which continues far into the hill, we can make out 100 or so cots and mats on the floor. On the shelves are what appear to be boxed medical supplies. An adjoining room is equipped like a surgery. Openings in the ceiling provide light and air. Jake calls me. "Arch, hold your light over here. I think this might be a generator. Steady, while I try to start it." Lee pulls twice on a cord. Nothing happens. He moves the choke and turns on the fuel, pulls the cord again, and the generator starts. There is light. We look on in amazement.

On the mats and cots are Jap soldiers, some with bandaged stumps of legs and arms, others with head wounds wrapped in cloth. All are dead, of course. But the manner in which they died is chilling. Some have single gunshots through the head. Others have committed hari-kari by plunging knives into their guts. We have seen a lot of carnage, but nothing like this.

Jake sickens and vomits. This isn't like combat. These men couldn't walk or get out of this tomb. They either killed themselves or were murdered by men who escaped.

Death apparently came within the last six or eight hours. The bodies haven't bloated or turned black. We know the enemy is not far ahead of us.

The tomb almost certainly was an underground field hospital.

Our company sets up observation posts on both sides of the hill. A company command post is set up inside the tomb, after the bodies and debris are removed.

Lee says, "Arch, it looks like we might get some hot food and a dry place to sleep tonight, even though we'll have a lot of silent company. I wonder if we'll ever know what really happened here."

"Maybe I don't want to know," I answer.

We heat cans of C rations that night, hiding deep in the tomb, not showing any light. I lost my spoon on the way from Skyline Ridge. Lee offers to share his, and we make short work of beans and franks. What a friend!

We have learned that it is much better for our health if we eat food, hot or cold, straight from the rations cans rather than putting it in our mess kits. The kits are hard to clean without hot water. A dirty mess kit is a breeding place for bacteria and a likely source of the dysentery and vomiting we call the "GIs." Attacks have been known to be fatal.

Lee, Cook, and I are as particular about our health as we can be under these conditions. We never keep a can after it has been opened, never use a mess kit unless it has been properly cleaned, and we scrub our spoons with GI soap and sand. We take Atabrine for malaria and use water-purification pills whenever we fill our canteens. Thanks to these precautions neither of us has been sick since we landed on the island.

We sleep on a hill above one of the cave's entrances. I am to pull my only guard duty of the night starting at 0400.

❧   ❧   ❧

I hear a strong wind, like a storm. I'm in my big brother's Model A Ford at the end of a road looking over the water. I see a storm coming toward me, across the Sound.

A blast of wind hits the car with such force that the Ford starts to shake. Rain is coming down in sheets, pounding against the windshield. It is cold, like winter at home; snow is mixed in the rain landing in front of me. I'm out of the car trying to see the islands across the Sound.

Big wet snowflakes, cold rain, and sleet hit my face, stinging my cheeks. Looking out over the water, I see a break in the dark cloud cover. The sun shines through the opening with bright, warm light. It is beautiful.

I am in the middle of a glorious rainbow. But there's something different about this rainbow. It rises out of the water and descends into the water, unlike anything I have ever seen before.

The rainbow is broken in the middle. It's a jagged break, not smooth. The rainbow can't be put together again. I try to pull it together, but it's impossible, no matter how much force I use. A part is missing.

Then, quite suddenly, the missing segment is filled with a bright white light. A young Japanese woman, about 22 years old, appears. She is dressed in a traditional silk wedding kimono, with a scarlet design and a violet hand-painted lining. Around her waist she wears an obi of regal tapestry, with gold and silver threads woven into it. Tabi [split-toe, thick-soled "socks"], geta [elevated wooden shoes], and an elaborate headdress complete her attire.

I call to her in a loud voice.

"I know who you are! I know who you are! I know who you are! You are the woman in the picture. You have a beautiful little baby girl. You are the woman in the picture!"

I struggle to get to my pack. I must show her the picture in my wallet, the one taken from the dead Japanese officer. I fumble with the pack and drop it. I can't find the picture. I call to her again.

"I want to talk to you. I didn't want to kill your husband. I didn't want to kill your little girl's father. What could I do? I murdered him! I'm a murderer!"

🍁   🍁   🍁

"What the hell are you talking about?" Lee says as he shakes me.

"I don't know, I don't know, Lee. It must have been a dream. Thank God it was a dream."

While standing guard and looking toward Yonabaru, I see the calm bay in the semi-darkness. Suddenly there is activity. Enemy troops are coming from the peninsula to the southeast in small civilian boats. They land and move quickly up the beach. There are about 25 of them.

I tell Lee. We can offer no resistance, he says, since we are the forward troops and don't want to expose ourselves. Besides, we are badly outnumbered.

I let our sergeant know. He says that even though our little squad has control of this hill, we're cut off from all support because we have no telephone communication and our only battery-operated radio is dead.

We continue to hold our fire, playing cat-and-mouse with the Japanese for three days, watching them take supplies left on the beach for our use. They take our food and ammo by boat back to the peninsula they came from, then return for more.

They could wipe us out in a minute if they knew we were here and how few of us there are. But they seem more interested in our supplies than in looking for enemy troops.

Meanwhile, our battalion has become aware of the little squad hiding out on the hill. We try communicating by semaphore. They send over a Piper Cub airplane, which parachutes K rations, cigarettes, water, radio batteries, and ammo on the back side of the hill, out of view of the Japanese.

On the third day, our artillery hits the nearby area with an all-night barrage. In the morning, Lee and I see that the enemy has left the beach.

"Arch," Lee says, "I hope our old gook in Yonabaru still has his home, his well, his teapot and his sake. It makes me feel good that we didn't burn his house. I have never burned for fun before. I'm really ashamed of what we were doing. It just wasn't right. We let our emotions take over."

"I feel the same, Lee. I don't know what got into us. I hope the old man's all right. He seemed very kind."

Several companies are on their way to relieve us. By noon we have re-established contact with the rest of the battalion. We hear that our whole company has been reported missing in action. This news, we learn, is being reported back home in the states; our families are being notified. What will my mother do?

That night Sarge S briefs us and says we're to move southwest, either behind or on the ridges south of Conical Peak. We will push off at daylight with Company A, which has just joined us.

The plan is to move straight south and cut off the peninsula. The company that joined us stands guard. Lee, Cook, and I get our first full night's sleep since coming off reserve. I have no dreams.

CHAPTER 9

❀

We push out the next morning to the south, where low hills and ridges with names like Jupiter, Kerodera and Chestnut are our objectives.

It is quiet. But rifle fire, the odd mortar shell, and sometimes machine-gun chatter occasionally break the silence and keep us on constant alert.

Big raindrops fall straight down, turning the ground into sticky goo. My clothes are wet, caked with mud and sticking to my skin. I haven't had any undershorts since I dirtied them during the counterattack. Unable to stand the smell, I threw them away. The rough fatigues chafe the skin in my crotch.

I've almost quit caring. I try to scrape the mud from my fatigues with my bayonet. My boots slip on the slick clay or stick in the mud. Every step is an effort. I fall several times, but continue to put one foot in front of the other without thinking.

We are the lead company, sticking to the mostly protected side of the ridge. When we arrive at the crest of the first hill at about 1000, Jake runs to a small outcropping to scout the way. He is greeted by a burst of machine-gun fire. Mud flies and water splashes as bullets hit just behind him.

Any little movement on our part draws more fire. Lee and I crawl on our bellies along the protected side of the ridge.

"Lee, I'm going to put my helmet on my bayonet and stick it up over the ridge. Let's see how accurate those damn Japs are."

The helmet is hit immediately. I grab it as it falls.

We move up to where Jake has found a protected area.

"Thanks, Arch, for the helmet," Jake says. "I spotted the Jap who shot it and we won't have that fuckin' gunner to deal with anymore."

Jap light and heavy machine guns have distinctive sounds. The heavies are much slower and have a deeper sound. The light-machine guns are faster and higher pitched than ours.

Orders come to hold our position until Company A moves through us. They arrive before noon and we are then able to take a position farther up the ridge. Our lunch is cold C rations on the run.

Our company starts up the hill, again with our squad in the lead. We leapfrog through Company A, which has suffered heavy casualties. While passing through our heavy-weapons squad, I spot a mortar man, Tim, who landed on Okinawa with me a lifetime ago. Tim turned 19 just ahead of me. Although he's much taller, heavier and strong as an ox, he looks exhausted. He sweats in the rain in mud-covered clothes as he throws shells into the tube of his mortar and then holds his hands over his ears to dampen the sound of the explosion.

Mortars are great weapons. A good mortar-man can drop a shell just over the ridge ahead of us. This keeps the enemy occupied while we move up the ridge.

The temperature is in the low 80s, with the rain still falling as I pass Tim on our way to secure the crest of the hill.

Tim is mired in mud to the top of his boots. He raises a dirty hand and calls out:

"Arch, I'll keep these Goddamn things coming for you guys as long as I don't have to go up that hill with you. Don't let those fuckin' Japs get through."

"I'll do my best, Tim," I answer.

I continue slogging through the muck to a higher, less-protected part of the hill. But it is not until 1600 that we secure the crest. Our mortar shells land no more than 50 feet beyond our position.

It is difficult to set up good, secure holes where we can see down the other side of the hill. Every movement on our part draws enemy fire. We work it with a system: one person digs while the other covers him with fire; then we switch jobs.

It takes patience and time, but we want to be as secure as possible for the night. When the digging is finished, we set up our perimeter defenses.

Tonight Lee is with Cook and Jake is my foxhole partner. Our hole is on the extreme left of the squad. To our left is an almost vertical cliff. I don't see how anybody can attack us by coming up that bluff. Still, I have never liked a position where one flank is totally exposed.

Jake and I take a pile of rocks as our left limit. Cook and Lee become our right-guard boundary. There are nine points between us.

I hear Cook call over before it is dark, "Arch, can I borrow your watch?" I don't answer, but crawl on my belly to their hole and give Cook my watch and wish them good luck for the night. It is quiet when we settle down for the evening.

Jake opens a can of rations and, while eating and drinking cold Nescafe, says:

"Arch, you know it's strangely quiet. That bothers me."

Night again. We anticipate the strain and the deadly tension that will continue till daylight. Jap shells explode in front of us and behind us while our 155s go over into the Jap positions. The shelling continues. Will it ever end? We look at each other in fear and say nothing.

It will end...perhaps.... But how will it end? Will we come through it? Are they going to attack? If their artillery suddenly quits, they'll almost certainly be coming up the hill.

I'm on guard at about 2300 when a bugle sounds and I hear Japanese words shouted down the hill in front of me. I get Jake up. He lights a cigarette from mine in the bottom of the hole. He takes a leak in his helmet and dumps it out. We whisper.

"Arch, one of the old guys told me the Japs sound trumpets after they're full of sake and ordered to make a banzai attack. Do you think that's what's happening?"

"I don't know, Jake. But if this is a banzai, it will be a new experience for me."

The only thing I know is what Lee has told me, and he lived through several banzai attacks on Leyte. Lee says the main thing is not to panic and be sure to hold your fire till the Japs are right on top of you. Don't give away your position until it's absolutely necessary.

The bugle sounds again.

We hear screams below us.

The noise is terrifying. That, of course, is their plan. They want to create so much fear we can't think straight.

The bugle sounds again. The screaming intensifies. This must be the start of a banzai attack.

We can see nothing in the darkness. All we can hear is the noise created by the enemy. Then, just as suddenly as it started, the noise stops.

Twenty minutes pass. The Japs play on our nerves. The silence is almost worse than the noise. We watch in the dark, trying to guess where they're coming from.

I'm sure I see soldiers moving toward us with shiny bayonets. I count my nine points. There are still nine. I'm seeing things.

Our mortars send up flares. Farther away, we see artillery flares. They light the area briefly. My heart pounds. It feels as if it's stuck in my throat. I'm in a cold sweat.

The bugle sounds again, followed by more screaming. Then it stops as suddenly as it started, and we are left in silence, an hour-long silence that seems like a couple of lifetimes.

The deathly stillness is broken when the Japs send up flares. This must be it.

I wet my pants and tell Jake. He laughs and says, "Arch, I did the same thing."

There is no more time for talk. The Japs start up the hill screaming, "banzai! banzai!" Bugles sound. Their machine guns fire from a nearby hill. They add rifle fire and mortar fire. And still the unearthly screams, "banzai! banzai!"

I'd been told the success of a banzai attack depends on how much confusion and chaos the Japs can create. They are certainly doing their best. If you let it get to you, you can go berserk, and a berserk soldier is not a reliable one. Someone calls for artillery flares. In the rain and confusion, I can't see a thing.

I whisper to Jake, "Keep down and wait till their machine-gun fire quits. They have to quit firing when their riflemen are just below us. That's our chance. We have to be ready with your rifle and my BAR. Let's line up ammo magazines and be ready, or we won't have a chance. We have to keep the Japs out of our hole. Keep your bayonet handy in case one gets in our hole."

"I'm ready," Jake says.

A parachute flare goes off and we can see for a short time. We freeze so they won't see us. I'm more excited than I have ever been in my life. My heart races and my chest heaves. Sweat stings my eyes.

"Jake, get the ammo ready for the BAR."

Another flare. We can see a bunch of Japs coming up the hill toward us.

"Hold on, Jake, I see one between the holes."

I see the dark eyes under the helmet as another flare lights the area. I pull the pin on a grenade and raise my arm to throw it.

The eyes of the Jap coming toward us are just like those of the Jap lieutenant I killed on Sky Line Ridge. For one insane second, I see the lieutenant's eyes as my grenade flies toward him and explodes in his face.

My mind is in a whirl. I have become a wild beast. I fight to defend myself against annihilation. I must kill. Death may hunt me. But I, too, have the power to destroy.

That power excites me. I can protect myself by killing. I want to scream and holler, "I killed him! I killed him!"

I can hold my fire no longer. I support the BAR on the edge of the hole. I call to Jake, "Keep the ammo clips coming." I begin firing, sweeping the area from right to left.

Jake shouts at me, "Fire at those motherfuckers. Fire, Arch. Kill for my brother. I can't stand this! I can't stand this! Shit, those Goddamned bastards are going to kill me. I'm not going to sit here and be killed. I want to go out there and kill with my hands. I'm not going to feed your BAR. Give me that BAR! No more of this shit for me. It's all over. It's all over. I can go out there and kill 20, maybe 30. I don't want to go on! I can't take any more of this Goddamned shit. My mother will have two gold stars in her window."

Jake swings at me and knocks me on my butt. Before I can get up and orient myself, he grabs my BAR with one hand and magazines of ammo in the other. He jumps out of the hole, firing right and left. I try to grab his leg just as a knee-mortar shell goes off to the right. I fall back in the hole and grab his rifle. My leg is numb. I fire on both sides of Jake, trying to protect him. Jake is in front of the hole, shouting, "I'll kill the motherfuckers for my brother!"

I shout at him, "Jake, remember, don't fire to the right. Lee and Cook are there."

Jake is a mad man, shoving ammo clips into the BAR, firing as he runs down the hill toward the on-coming Japs. Above the noise of the attack, I can hear him shouting, "motherfuckers—Goddamned—shiteating—bastards, that one's for my brother—here is another—"

A flare lights the area, and I can see him—farther down the hill now, out of ammo, his bayonet shining in the light as he falls.

Cook and Lee have been depending on my BAR, which is now gone. All I have is Jake's rifle. I tell myself not to fire unless I'm sure I can hit something. Cook and Lee throw grenades. We have to use every weapon we have.

Enemy troops are everywhere. I fire to my right, hoping I'm not too far right. Then I go back to my left. It's the first time I've been alone in a hole under attack.

Suddenly, I hear Lee's voice. "Arch, Cook is hit. I think it's bad!" I hear Cook's moans. I remember he's wearing my watch. I gave it to him just before dark when I crawled over to their hole.

Chaos and confusion reign, until suddenly the attack ends as quickly as it began, two-and-a-half hours earlier. A flare goes up. Bodies are everywhere—between our holes, in front of me, behind me.

Somewhere out there is Jake. We are all quiet, waiting for the next round. Cook is dying. I can hear him. It takes most of the night for him to die. Dying can be so slow. Fast, slow: I have seen it both ways.

The noise of dying is more animal than human. I experienced these sounds on Sky Line Ridge from the Japanese lieutenant. But the sounds tonight are being made by Cook, one of my closest friends, and the only person with him is Lee. The two of them survived the battle of Leyte together only to end up here.

I feel my leg. It's warm and wet. That means blood. It's also numb.

I cut my pants open with my bayonet and find a couple of small shrapnel wounds—three in one leg, one in the other. I wonder if the metal is still in my legs or if it went through. I pull out a first-aid kit, sprinkle the wounds with sulfa and wrap them with bandages, tight, right over my ripped pants.

The night seems to go on forever. I have lost the ability to figure time.

Is it the span of Jake's life? Or the conclusion of Cook's existence?

Over and over, I ask myself:

—Did I fire too far to the right in the heat of battle and kill my friend Cook?

—Did Jake, firing indiscriminately in his insane, final outburst, kill Cook?

—Does it make it easier if I can blame a Jap? Did I fail to protect their hole while watching Jake's final, mad moments?

—Will I carry the shame and stigma of my possible failure for the rest of my life?

—I do know this: If I did it, or if I caused Cook's death, it is murder. And if his death is murder, how about the deaths of all the Japanese I have intentionally killed?

I have run out of questions. My answers are always the same: I don't know.

There, in the darkness, I am back in a high-school English class where we are discussing a poem, "The Domesticated Cat."

The cat is a calm, quiet pet seated on a pillow in the lap of a beautifully dressed, attractive young woman. She quietly pets the cat, which purrs contentedly.

In a corner of the room, a mouse emerges from a hole in the wall. The cat goes wild, jumping to the floor, hissing, the hair standing up on its back. It runs toward the defenseless mouse and grabs it in its mouth, shaking it, tossing it into the air.

The cat doesn't immediately kill the mouse. It lets it go, then grabs it again, torturing it. The mouse is bleeding and in pain. Finally it dies and the cat brings the dead mouse to the feet of the beautiful woman. He returns to the pillow and the attractive woman resumes her petting.

The cat purrs.

Are we Homo sapiens really domesticated? Do we turn into animals when we are placed in a combat situation? What does the training our government has given us do to our minds? Do we, in the heat of battle, regress to the most primitive stages of evolution?

Have I lost my domestication? Have I become a killer, like the cat? I certainly act that way when I kill another human being, another 18-year-old just like me and afterward have no feeling of guilt or remorse.

The banzai attack was wonderfully exhilarating. At the time, I felt powerful and strong.

Now I am humiliated to think of what a fantastic time I had firing at those Goddamned Japs. What a blood-thirsty beast I have become—a man who enjoys killing, who gets a thrill out of it…. Who am I?

Will this night never end?

Did I kill Cook? Did Jake kill Cook? Did a Jap kill Cook? Does it matter now?

Cook and Jake are both dead. That's what matters.

When morning finally arrives, all is quiet. Lee and I lift Cook's lifeless body and lay it on a poncho. There is only one eyelid to close; the other side of his face is gone. I can see into his skull. We fold his hands over his bloody chest. Lee and I fold the poncho over him and silently carry down the hill one of the finest young men I have ever known or will ever know.

The man we carried was blond and tall, an Eastern Washington farm boy, with a mother and father and two sisters at home. He loved a girl from his high-school class. He would do anything for any member of our squad.

And now he is dead.

At the bottom of the hill, we kneel by the poncho. Lee puts his arm around me. He makes the sign of the cross. We both close our eyes to stop the tears.

I say, "I knew Cook when he was sad, reading a letter from his girl, and when he was happy from a joke, and when he was angry and violent in war. I knew Cook when he was quiet and when you couldn't shut him up. I know what he looked like clothed and naked. I know how he put on his boots. And now I know him dead, with half his face blown away."

After 10 minutes or so of silence, Lee and I walk back up the hill to war.

CHAPTER 10

❀

The next day is quiet. Lee and I don't say much, but we liberate a Luger from a Jap officer in front of our holes, along with a couple more flags. They don't mean much any more.

We put them in our packs and go on in a sort of daze.

In the afternoon we feel it is safe to go over the crest of the hill with a member of the grave-registration detail to retrieve Jake's body.

Both Cook's and Jake's families will be visited by army officers. One will drive up to the farmhouse where Cook grew up, carrying a flag and a gold star. Another will visit the coal-mining town in the mountains of West Virginia where Jake and his family lived. When he leaves, Jake's mother will have two gold stars for her window—one for Jake, the other for his brother.

Lee and I move into the same hole to spend the night. We smoke in silence, until I feel nature's call. When I return we open a can of hash, but neither of us feels hungry. A platoon member brings hot coffee up the hill and we fill our canteen cups.

That night, instead of sleeping, we peer into the blackness with the thousand-yard stare, men in combat who have seen more than we can bear, men looking for an enemy we cannot see, an end to a war we did-n't start but can't figure how to end. We pay almost no heed to the occasional flare or the sporadic sound of gunfire. I think the Japs have retreated to the next ridge to regroup.

After a cold breakfast, we roll up our wet blankets, check our ammo, and push off with the rest of the squad toward Hemlock Hill. It is a long, slow climb. Once again, we stay on the protected side of the ridge as much as possible.

The small-arms fire increases as the morning wears on. Our progress is slowed as we run from one rock outcropping to another. It seems there is no one left in our squad, just Lee and I.

Since May 22, our company has lost 83 men, either killed or wounded. We started from Skyline Ridge with 31 men. Now there are only 10 of us. Yesterday's banzai attack claimed three more, including Cook and Jake.

Nobody asks what happened to Jake's sack full of gold teeth and ears. We hear the company commander recommended Jake for a posthumous Silver Star for killing so many Japs. I know Jake really committed suicide.

We hear the familiar sound of Jap light-machine gun fire. When we move, we provide cover fire for each other. Lee and I are good at it. He taught me well. It's how we stay alive. I depend on him for my next breath. Could I ever fail him? With all my heart, I hope not.

So we cover each other throughout the day—one making a dash forward, the other firing steadily so the Japs will keep their heads down. Then the other making a dash forward and the other providing the same heavy fire.

Each time we land together, we nudge each other and speak to affirm that we're still alive.

"OK, Arch?"

"OK, Lee."

We run and stop, run and stop until about 1100. We're in the lead, ahead of the remnants of our platoon.

Lee takes off again. I give him all the fire I have. A Jap light-machine gun opens up and I can't tell where the fire is coming from.

I am desperate.

My heart pounds.

Won't that Jap ever quit firing so I can move up to where Lee is? I take off, running as low to the ground and as fast as I can.

The insistent ra-ta-ta-ta-ta of the Jap machine gun dins in my ears. Bullets kick up mud in front of me. I almost catch up with Lee. I have a full clip of ammo in the BAR. I can see where the enemy fire is coming from. I can see the Japs, two of them not more than 100 yards away on the rise of the next hill.

Through the rain and haze I turn my weapon, aim and fire at the machine-gun position. I run forward, close to the ground and drop beside Lee. The Jap firing stops. It is quiet. I must have hit the machine-gunner.

I slap Lee on the back and say, "OK, Lee, let's move."

No answer.

"Are you OK?"

No reply.

The last burst from that Goddamned machine gun got him. His pack has been blown off.

Lee is dead.

I didn't give him the cover he needed.

I got the Japs, both of them. But too late.

Lee's body is riddled with bullets from his neck to his belly. His insides are coming out.

I got them *after* they MURDERED Lee.

I MURDERED them too late.

I am angry. I have never been so belligerent and combative. Something inside me is telling me to go get the sons of bitches who killed Lee.

Go, run down the hill, find them and kill them with my bare hands. Kill them! Because if I don't, I will join John, Nealey, Cook, and Jake.

I scream every obscenity I have ever heard. I open fire with my BAR and fire five magazines of ammo at the next hill. Jake did the destroying during the last attack and was cut to pieces in two minutes. I'm still here, lying beside Lee's body, looking at him. He's a mess. If he hadn't been here, it would have been me. He gave his life for me.

I slowly move him, without showing myself to the enemy. I roll him over the top of the ridge to a safer place. I retrieve his bullet-riddled pack and put it over my shoulder.

I kneel again beside his body and cry. No, I don't cry. I sob. I mourn. I weep.

I make the sign of the cross on his lifeless body.

I put my arms around him.

I say the Lord's Prayer.

Lee is gone.

It is raining.

There is mud.

There is blood.

There are cries.

There is a jeep Weasel.

There is a field hospital.

There is more mud.

There are cots.

There are lots of men.

There are medics.

There is quiet.

There is death.

There are groans.

There is nothing.

There is silence.

Where the hell am I?

CHAPTER 11

❀

The temporary, hastily painted wooden sign above the entrance to a scattering of army tents bears the words "Camp Ernie Pyle."

The tents are round and large, with mosquito netting across the flap-opening. Each tent holds six cots, six small ammo boxes that serve as bed-side tables. Around a single, larger table are three wooden boxes fashioned into chairs. A light bulb hangs in the center of the tent over a larger ammo box. The floor is dirt.

I am lying on a cot in one of the tents. My rifle and two packs are stowed beneath the cot.

It is the same M-1 rifle I have had with me since the morning we hit Okinawa. The rifle barrel is shiny where the bluing has worn off. I feel it is safe on the wooden crossbars that support my army cot.

The two GI packs show the grimy signs of battle. One has 10 bullet holes through it and dark stains of dried blood. My dirty, mud-caked blanket is missing, but my slimy combat boots are beside my cot.

Five other men are in the tent with me. They are total strangers.

My mind is full of questions: "How the hell did I get here? Where am I? Who are these men? Where is my squad? Where are Lee and Cook?"

I have a clean blanket and a pillow, but no sheets or pillowcase. It is more comfort than I have known in a long time. Despite the rain outside, the dirt floor is dry.

Rising from the cot, I carefully smooth the blanket and make the bed, a carry-over from my spit-and-polish basic-training days. I don't have to dress. I am in the same fatigues, T-shirt, and socks I have worn since April. The only thing missing is olive-drab underwear. I threw my filthy shorts away long ago. My clothes were last washed by some laughing gook women while I took a bath in a stream with some of my buddies.

Is this a prison? I don't belong here, I'm sure of that. I must get out and rejoin my squad.

As I start to leave the tent, a smiling blond medic, about 20 years old and in very clean clothes, comes whistling through the door opening.

"You're up," he says in a cheerful voice. "I just came to get you. Have you gone to the latrine yet? Do you remember where it is?" I shake my head. I have no idea what he's talking about.

"Follow me. Then we'll go to breakfast."

The latrine has crude toilets and jerry cans of water for washing. The latter have "off" and "on" valves on the bottom. They hang above a wash basin fashioned from a trimmed-down bomb casing. The makeshift basin sits on a gasoline drum. GI soap and olive-drab towels are nearby.

On the front, where it is impossible to dispose of human waste—from friend or foe—it becomes impossible to maintain basic sanitary conditions. It isn't surprising that diarrhea is of epidemic proportions and is a major part of the horrible smell of the battlefield, along with the stench of decaying human flesh.

Since I seem to be in some kind of hospital, I expect they will be giving us a short-arm inspection. After all, we haven't had one since landing on the island.

The latrine has mirrors, and when I see myself I can hardly recognize the face looking back at me. I haven't shaved for weeks and I am filthy dirty. My face is skinny, my eyes sunken with dark circles under them, and gray is showing in my hair.

I look old and tired and I'm not 19 yet!

"Do you want to shave?" the medic asks. I shake my head from side to side. He takes a razor and shaving cream from the pack he's carrying and hands them to me.

"You can if you want to," he says. I shake my head again. He helps me clean up. It's the first time I have washed since April. He asks me to return the razor, which he puts back in his pack. I have the feeling he doesn't trust me with the razor.

Why would I try to kill myself with a razor when I have a rifle and two pistols under my cot?

"It's June the eighth," says the medic, who takes me to a large mess tent where they are serving breakfast. I take a tray, fill it with reconstituted powdered eggs, bacon from a can, good hot coffee, and toast with butter and jam. I follow him to a table, where several other men are already seated.

Fantastic food! The meager amount I am able to eat is tasty, but it nauseates me as I think to myself, "I don't deserve this food when my men are eating cold C rations in the mud up front."

I quickly get up from the table and run from the mess tent. I am no sooner outside than I throw up everything I've eaten. The medic takes me back to the latrine to clean up.

"This isn't the first time that's happened, so don't worry about it," the medic says.

Back in the tent, I go to bed.

"Stay here until I get back," the medic says. "I've got some other patients to get going."

While I lie on the cot, my mind races:

"So, I'm one of the patients he has to get going. I can get going myself, or…can I? Do I need somebody to help me go to the toilet? Do I need somebody to help me shave? Do I need somebody to feed me?

"Of course, I don't. I can take care of myself. I don't …belong here. This place is for sick people, for cowards, for those who forget their comrades. I'm not that kind of man. There has to be a way out of here. I don't belong in a place like this."

Slowly it begins to sink in. This must be a nut hospital, a place for those who can't take it, who crack under pressure, who have gone insane. They must think I'm one of them. What have I done to wind up in a lunatic hospital?

Thinking back, I remember that last day at the front. Lee is dead! Alone in the tent, I flop on my cot and begin to cry as I recall how much Lee and I meant to each other. The way he talked and laughed, the way he looked, how he taught me to survive. These things come rushing back to me.

Little things. Big things. Living in the same foxhole, dependent on each other for survival. Sharing a spoon to eat from a can. I got to know about his daughter and his wife.

We grieved together when our buddies died. We hated together. We killed together. And I had always thought we probably would die together.

My body shakes while tears fall.

I awaken some time later when the medic comes into the tent. Frightened, I jump off the cot.

"It's OK, take it easy. I just came around to see if you want to go for a walk."

I nod. Yes.

"You came in last week," the medic says. "I think it was May 26th. The medics sent you here from a field hospital down south. You're here for a rest and to get feeling better. You were found in the combat zone without any ID. No dogtags, just what's stamped on your clothes.

"Do you remember anything?" he continues. "Can you shed any light on this? Who are you? What outfit do you belong to?"

I shake my head.

"You've been sort of quiet, but I understand. You don't have to talk if you don't want to. This is Camp Ernie Pyle. Pyle was the war correspondent who was killed about five weeks ago on Ie Shima.

"The camp was named after him because the doctor in charge here was a close friend of Pyle's. Ernie Pyle did a lot to help infantrymen like you. He loved infantrymen. He got you guys the infantry combat medal. You know, the blue rifle with the cluster. He also got you guys a 10 percent pay increase when you're in combat."

I ask myself what good is 10 percent when you're dead? Ten percent of what?

The medic goes on:

"The doctor here knew Ernie wanted you guys to recover from what we call 'combat fatigue.' The doctor knows what it's all about.

"Do you know what combat fatigue is? It's what they called 'shell shock' in the First World War. The doctor here was a medic in that war; that's where he learned about 'shell shock.' Somebody will probably have another name for it in the next war.

"We want you to have good food, get rest, and get to feeling better. We cleaned the wounds in your legs and used a new drug called penicillin. Your legs have badly infected shrapnel wounds. I'll change the dressings every day. We think there's shrapnel still in there, but the doctor thought you could have it removed later. The medical people can't remove it while there's infection.

"I'll do all I can to help you. That's the only reason I'm here. My job is to help people get better. I don't believe in war. I'm a Quaker. The army let me be a medic."

We stop walking.

"We can go back to your tent anytime you want to go, and if you like I'll stay with you," the medic says. "Back to the tent?"

I nod.

When we're back at the tent, he says, "See you at lunch. Maybe we can take another walk this afternoon."

Later, while waiting for the medic to come back for lunch, I realize I don't want to eat. What is it with this guy? Why is he so congenial and considerate of me?

And yet, I sort of like him, and I'm looking forward to lunchtime whether I eat or not. I'm also anticipating the walk in the afternoon, even though I know I can't say anything, even if I try.

I can't tell him how I feel, what's going on in my head. I can't say anything. I know he can't comprehend what happens to a human being like me who has had everything shot out from under him. There is no past, no future, only this terrible, hollow feeling.

I am reminded of a T.S. Eliot poem. I am one of his "hollow men." Maybe that's why I feel comfortable around this medic. He seems to care and he is considerate without asking questions. If I answer, how can he understand? Maybe he's also one of "the hollow men."

I am alone in the tent again. I look under the cot and there is my M-1 rifle. I wouldn't have any other. It's been with me since we left Saipan. The two packs beneath the cot are undisturbed.

I reach for them. The first one I pull out is mine. I go through it. All the things I want, I put on my bed: the revolver with its ammo, the two Jap flags, the watch my folks gave me for graduation just a year ago. Cook was wearing it the night he was killed. How did it get in my pack? Lee must have put it there. He knew I couldn't take it off Cook's wrist.

Continuing through my pack, I see the Bible my mother gave me when I left home. I'm supposed to read it. I promised my Mother I would always carry it, and I have kept that promise.

The pack also contains four grenades, five clips of M-1 ammo, a picture of my mother, and some dog-eared letters.

All of these things are spread out on the cot.

The other pack is Lee's. How did I get it? I must have taken it off him after he was killed. No, I remember now, it was blown off him. I must have picked it up.

I try to open it and can't. I put Lee's pack back under the cot. Then I put everything back in my pack and replace it under the cot.

Sitting on the side of the cot, I plan how to return to my squad. They need me. I belong with them. The decision is made. I'm going back. Tomorrow night!

The medic's return to the tent interrupts my plans. He's a nice guy. I don't mind him coming around. I admire him for what he's trying to do. At least he isn't killing anybody or making others suffer.

He doesn't know what we do out there. Nobody could ever know unless he's lived through it. The medic brings clean GI underwear and asks if I want new fatigues. I shake my head. No! I have had these fatigues since April and they are a part of me. He doesn't press the issue.

"I'll leave the clean fatigues here, and if you put them on we can wash your old ones. Let's go for a walk and talk."

I feel I have to go along, or he won't trust me. We walk and very little is said. Time passes. Before I know it, it is time for dinner. This time I keep the food down.

That night they come around with the pills we're supposed to take. I put mine inside my mouth and turn and spit them out. I'm not going to be drugged. Later, after it's quiet and others are sleeping, I take Lee's pack out and combine his things with mine.

The Luger, revolver, ammo, two more flags, then his wallet, pictures of his wife and daughter and a few damaged letters with no addresses. Tears stream down my cheeks. There aren't many personal things, other than a rosary, socks, crucifix, and St. Christopher medal.

Not much. Not much to remember him by except the memory of someone who gave his life so I could live.

After putting Lee's things in with mine, I throw his pack in the garbage.

There are no addresses in the pack, not even the names of his wife and daughter. Just their pictures, which he had shown so many times.

Even if I manage to get back home, I won't even be able to look them up as I had promised.

Lee is gone. Everything. His past, present, and future.

I see an army officer, probably a captain, accompanied by a sergeant. I'm pretty sure that's the way they do it. The two of them will park a car on the street in front of the apartment house in Los Angeles where Lee's wife and daughter live. It would have to be in the evening, since she works in a war factory all day and his daughter is in a care center for kids whose mothers work in factories while their husbands are overseas. The army men will come up the steps of the apartment, find the right apartment number, then knock on the door. When it's opened they'll ask, "May we come in?"

"Yes, of course. Sit down."

After the officer and sergeant are seated and Lee's wife is also seated, with her daughter on the floor in front of her, the little girl might say, "You're in the army like my dad. See his picture on the table? Are you here to tell us my daddy's coming home?"

It will be time for the officer to speak.

"We have some bad news for you, Mrs. Lee. Your husband has been killed in action."

There will be a long silence....

"My daddy is never coming home? My daddy is dead?"

Lee is dead. A husband is dead. A father is dead. Why? Will they ask questions that can't be answered?

I'm the only one who can answer their questions, and I will never know this woman or this little girl who were so precious to Lee.

The captain will give Mrs. Lee a flag and a gold star to hang in her window.

The two soldiers will walk down the stairs and head back to the car. The captain will say to the sergeant, "What's the next address?"

Their car will pull away from the curb and head for the next house.

I decide to delay my escape from this place for another day. But sleep is difficult. I have difficulty distinguishing between being awake or asleep. Lee appears to me, a shadowy figure at the foot of my army cot.

"Why aren't you on line with our squad, Arch?" he asks. "Why have you deserted our men, Arch? You must return. You must return. Do it for me. But don't tell anybody about it. Just do it. You're not a coward. I went back after my friend was killed on Leyte, the one who taught me how to survive the way I taught you. You must go back. Teach a new man the way I taught you. It's the only way anyone will survive."

The next day is like the previous one. The mess tent. The latrine. Walks. I take some food back to the tent after lunch. It will come in handy when I escape tonight.

I check my pack again to be sure I have everything I'll need. It's all there. My new blanket, soap, cigarettes, ammo, grenades, and most important, my M-1.

That night I wait until the others in my tent are asleep. While lying on my cot, feigning sleep myself, I recall last night's "visit" by Lee.

I don't have to go back. Lee's command was just a dream. But if I don't go back, can I live with the thought of him standing at the foot of my bed? What would John, Jake, and Cook, who are all dead, think of me if I don't go back? And Sarge S. Where did he go? Did he just leave us? We thought he was a good soldier.

When I get home, which I know I won't, or when my family and friends find out I deserted my comrades, what will they think of me? A quitter. A deserter.

What will Nige and Evan and that girl, Margaret, who seemed always to be after me, think of me then? What will Arlene think? I used to enjoy being around her, just walking to school.

Then there's Mary. She could kick a football and throw a ball just like a boy, maybe even better, even though she didn't know the names of the big league baseball players—like Mickey Mantle and Whitey Ford. What will she think of me?

But why think of that. That world doesn't exist any more. There is only now, and I know what I have to do.

I don't want to let the medic down. He seems like a caring person. But I can't let that stop me. Maybe he can help some soldiers who really need him.

I don't need his help. I just need to get back to where I belong, where I'm needed and know what I'm doing. There must be a hell of a lot of screwed-up 18-and 19-year-olds for him to practice on. I'm sure another truck will roll into this camp tonight with more young GIs.

As for me, I'm going back to what I know, to where I belong, to where I'm sure I'm indispensable.

About 2330 I get out of the cot, dress, take my pack and rifle, and walk out under the "Ernie Pyle" sign. I head south down the road.

I'm going back—back to the only thing I know:

WAR!

CHAPTER 12

It's a lonely, solitary night—dark, raining, muddy, quiet. No stars. No artillery flares. I feel detached, as if I'm dream-walking.

I have only one purpose in mind: find my squad!

Having no idea which way to turn, I follow a hunch and go south. If I travel far enough to the south and stay on the Pacific side of the island, I tell myself, I should eventually find the 184th Infantry of the 7th Division.

If the hospital is somewhere in the middle of the 60-mile-long island, then the 184th could be as much as 30 miles down the island. The only way I know to get there is to walk.

Speaking out loud now, because there's no one around, I repeatedly tell myself, "I must return to the men I know." Then I add, "I am not a deserter; I am not a coward."

Once again, as in my dream, I clearly see Lee at the foot of my bed, and he's telling me, "You must teach a new man as I taught you. You have to go back."

There's only one way to do that at this time of night. Walk, and then walk some more. By tomorrow, there will be all kinds of traffic heading south to the front. I should be able to hitch a ride in a truck or a jeep, anything heading for Yonabaru.

About two miles into my walk, I see a jeep parked by a pile of supplies covered with tarps. The supplies almost certainly are being taken to the front.

"Maybe I can get a ride with them."

I peer under the tarps and see cardboard boxes of C rations and wooden boxes filled with ammo. I think of Dad and the wooden boxes they made at his mill, and how he used to say cardboard boxes would never last and pretty soon everybody would go back to wooden boxes.

Dad said of DuPont, which uses wooden boxes for its powder and ammunition, "Now that's a company that knows how to do things, and we know how to make their wooden boxes."

Out here on this dark night, on this lonely road, I think to myself that the DuPont company certainly does know its business, and its business is war, the same as the Krupp family of Germany. They seem to me to be two-of-a-kind.

My high-school history teacher spent some time telling us about the contributions the Krupps and the DuPonts made to what he called The Great War (World War I).

The jeep parked alongside the supplies has a top and a door, unlike the open jeeps used at the front.

I open the door and crawl inside to escape the rain. There's a carton of Lucky Strikes on the front seat. I break the carton, remove a red-and-white pack and recall that ridiculous Lucky Strike radio advertisement, "Lucky Strike green has gone to war!"

I pull out a cigarette. Just as I am about to light up, I duck my head below the dashboard and cup my hands around the match. I stop myself, laugh, and say aloud, "Arch, you dumb shit, you're not at the front; it doesn't matter how much light you show, you won't attract any sniper fire back here."

I wish I could quit talking to myself. I seem to be doing it all the time.

"I made it out of that nut hospital and I'm on my way back," I tell the dashboard. It says nothing back.

The rain falling on the car roof and the warmth of the jeep lull me to sleep and more dreams.

I'm back in my old room at home. It's just the way I left it—bed unmade, clothes on the floor, books on the nightstand.

Gordy, one of my high-school friends, is calling to me from our front lawn. I open the window and let down the string I have on my windowsill. Gordy ties a cigarette to the string. I pull it up into my room, light it and smoke at the open window while talking b.s. to Gordy, who is still on the lawn.

I tell Gordy my folks would be very upset if they caught me smoking. I would have to go to a young people's meeting at church and tell everybody. Then I would have to pray a lot to be forgiven.

Gordy, who is Catholic, says, "Gee, Arch, all I have to do is go to confession and say some Hail Marys and Our Fathers."

I toss the Lucky Strike butt out the window. But it's not the window of my room at home, it's the window of the army jeep. It's becoming hard to separate my dreams from reality. Nevertheless, I fall into a deep, contented sleep.

"Who the hell are you?" a voice asks, waking me about 6 o'clock in the morning.

I jump from the jeep and stand, shaking and frightened, before a sergeant.

The sergeant bellows again: "I said, 'What the hell are you doing sleeping in our Goddamned jeep?'"

Confused and startled by the interruption of my sleep, I have no idea where I am or who this sergeant might be, but I find my tongue and reply, "My name is Arch, and my serial number is 39480181."

Amazed that I can really speak to someone, I quickly add, "I'm speaking! I'm speaking! I can speak!"

"Of course you can speak, stupid. You're not a prisoner. What the hell's the matter with you?"

"OK, OK," is all I can say.

"Tell us how you got here and who the hell you are, Soldier."

"I had to get out of the rain. It's dry in here. You guys have a great jeep with a roof that doesn't leak."

I pause for a moment and then add, "I couldn't speak. Am I really talking? I know I couldn't say a word yesterday."

"What did you say?" the sergeant asks. "Are you all right? How the hell did you get here without us hearing you? What's your outfit?"

"The second squad."

"The second squad of what?"

"I don't know. I don't know."

"That's OK, Kid, we'll get you where you want to go."

Where has my memory gone? If I find the right place, I will know how to get back. If I can just find the place where Lee was…I'll find my squad. I seem to be talking to something way back in my mind. It isn't me. It seems like someone else is in there. In my head.

"I don't remember."

"That's OK, kid. We'll see what we can do, even though I don't quite understand you. Why don't you come on up to the base and have something to eat. Take my cup of coffee."

He hands me his canteen cup.

"Thanks. Something to eat sounds good."

The coffee is hot. It smells good and tastes even better.

This is a quartermaster group. There are big tents and huge amounts of supplies on the ground. All the supplies are covered with tarps.

There are tables in the mess tent and ammo boxes to sit on. The smell of food makes my mouth water. The sergeant says his name is Tom, that the men will be loading three trucks today. Tomorrow morning they will be heading south to Yonabaru, and if that is the way I am going, then I am welcome to ride along.

I tell him that Yonabaru is a familiar name, that my company was the first one to get into that town, that most of the civilians had fled and we burned the houses that were half-destroyed.

"You're infantry?" Tom asks.

"Yes, and I'm not a coward. I'm not a deserter. I haven't gone nuts. I should never have left my squad. There is nothing for me back here."

"How long have you been on the island?"

"Since the invasion."

"You've seen a lot of combat?"

"Yes, I'm in the infantry. The 7th Division."

"You must be a squad leader by what you say. But you're only a Pfc."

"There was nobody else and I had the most combat experience."

"You're a stupid dumb-ass to go back. You'll just get killed or wounded or your mind fucked-up even more than it is. Why don't you hang around here with us? We'll give you a job and nobody will know where you came from. You can attach yourself to anything you want. Who knows who you are? Let's see your dogtags."

"Of course. Of course, we all have dogtags," I answer. I check around my neck and there is nothing. What the hell happened to my dogtags? I have no identity. If I am killed, nobody will know who this body belonged to when it was living. I will have just disappeared.

I am wandering around with no identification. Nobody knows who I am. Maybe I don't know who I am. I could go anywhere and it wouldn't matter. I don't have a serial number. I remember my serial number, 39480181. That's what I am to give if I am captured—name, rank and serial number. Private First Class Morrison, 39480181. Why don't I just stay here and start all over?

No, I can't. I'm a squad leader and those men depend on me. I must go back.

On the other hand, if I could just forget my name and my serial number, I could be a new person with a new identity. Everything has an identification number, even those little Bakelite radios we have at home in the kitchen. There's a number on the back. There was also a serial number on the back of the stove, that old wood stove in the kitchen in

Anacortes. And there are numbers on the car. If the car needs new parts, you need the serial number in order to get a replacement.

Back in Hawaii, getting ready to go into combat, I had to stamp the last part of my serial number, 0181, on my clothing. My belt has that number stamped on the back. My field jacket has the same number. Everything I have.

I take off my belt and show Tom the number. I remember asking the corporal, back when we stamped the numbers on our clothes, why we were doing this. And the corporal, I think his name was Black, replied:

"You dumb shitheads, don't you know why we're doing this?"

And we all answered, "No, Corporal. Why?"

And he laughed and said, "If this is all we find of you, they will know you're dead."

That's why the numbers are on the car, on the stove, on everything. They can't communicate. When we can no longer communicate, when our feet, legs, arms, and head are gone, they'll still have our number to tell them who we were.

"Have you ever had to identify someone by the stamped number on their clothing?" Tom asks.

"There was one kid on Sky Line Ridge, a replacement who had just joined our squad few days earlier. A kid from California."

Tom interrupts, "I know Sky Line. We drove by there the other day on a supply run south. Lots of mud."

I continue, "There was a lot of mud, as I recall. It was hell. The artillery attack before the Jap counter-attack was massive. I was told the artillery that night fired more shells than in any other battle in the Pacific. That kind of shelling is horrendous. You just wait in your hole to see who gets hit. You never know where the next shell is going to land and there's no protection from a direct hit.

"The question is who the hell is going to be next? You hope it's not your squad. You hope the shells will land over there on the guys you don't know. You don't care about the 18-year-old kids over the hill, even though they're just like me. Or are they? It seems like after every attack somebody got it—killed, wounded or cracked up. You don't want anybody hurt, but your squad is the most important. You and your buddy are the most important of all.

"The question you can't answer is who is going to be next? This kid from L.A. was next, Tom. He came in as a replacement three days earlier, and we really didn't get to know him. He was just a dark-haired, 18-year-old kid, tall, good-looking. He seemed nice but didn't say much because he was still learning how to survive.

"I remember him saying, 'Arch, I'm scared shitless and really don't know what to do.' I told him to stick with us and learn from Lee and Cook, because they had taught me. I told him to get in one of our holes that night and he'd learn what to do. Here I was teaching a replacement after only a couple of months in combat myself.

"That night he got hit with an artillery shell. A direct hit, as he was crawling to our hole. We couldn't find much of him. Lee, Cook, and I got a ration box. You know, like the ones you load on your truck. We put what was left of him, at least what we could find, in that box. We couldn't find his dogtags, so we wrote his name on the box: Joe, from Los Angeles.

"We took the box down the hill for the body truck to pick up. We got down on our knees and didn't say anything. Lee made the sign of the cross. He was Catholic. In my mind, I said something. I don't remember what. Cook said a prayer about 'Dear Jesus.' Then we went back up the hill to our foxholes and back to war. We later found a piece of his belt with the last four digits of his serial number, just like the ones the corporal had us stamp on our belts. We went back down the hill and wrote '4265' on his box."

When I finished, Tom said, "Arch, we'll get you back."

The next day they load trucks, and they won't let me help. They say, "We know what we're doing. You just take it easy."

At 0600, June 10, 1945, the three trucks begin the trip south, toward Yonabaru, on a muddy road filled with vehicles taking supplies up to the front. It's slow going. Two of the trucks sink so deep in the mud we have to call for help.

Tom radios a construction battalion nearby to send some bulldozers. They pull our trucks out of the never-ending mud, and we're on our way. We learn that the construction battalion is making gravel from coral and dumping it on the roads to make them passable.

That night we find a level spot for the trucks and then bivouac beside the road on a plain about five miles northeast of Sky Line Ridge. A hot dinner is served off the tailgate of one of the trucks. Later we bed down in the back of the trucks.

Nobody stands guard. The men act as if they're in San Diego, sleeping in their own beds, not 10 or 12 miles from the enemy. It bothers me and I sleep very little.

At about 0300, I look out the back of the truck and see two Japs running between the trucks, one carrying a box of rations, the other with a small automatic weapon. I call for them to halt and fire a shot in front of them. Both fall to the ground. I jump down and cover them with my M-1. The rest of my group is awakened by the rifle fire. Tom and the rest of the men stand around looking helpless and frightened, staring in disbelief at the two Japs, who are now our prisoners.

The poor s.o.b.'s I've taken prisoner are hungry, dirty, and small. Their clothes are ragged. I suggest we give them something to eat and tie them up until morning. The rest of the group are so Goddamned scared they would have agreed to anything. These are the first enemy they've seen, and they're the first prisoners I've taken. Most of the enemy I've seen were dead.

The two desperately hungry enemy, trapped behind our lines and now taken prisoner, are also scared as hell.

Tom asks me, "What do I do with these Japs? I've never seen one before."

I reply, "They think we're going to kill them, and if we were at the front, they'd be right. We didn't take prisoners. However, this isn't the front. And, although I've never taken a prisoner, I think I know what we're supposed to do."

"OK, go ahead."

With my rifle covering one prisoner, I ask Tom to cover the other with his carbine. In sign language, I make them take off their clothes so we will know they're not hiding weapons. Then I let them put their pants back on after searching and finding nothing. We give them cans of C rations, which they eat like animals, digging the food out of the open cans with their fingers. We tie the prisoners to the wheel of the truck, and the sergeant posts three guards for the rest of the night.

The next morning we have no way of sending the prisoners back, so we tie their hands and feet and take them with us. They sit in the back of the truck, very frightened.

The convoy of trucks rumbles by the familiar hills. Riding in the cab with Tom, I tell him what happened on Pinnacle, Red Hill, 178 and Skyline Ridge. As our truck turns toward the flat land along the Pacific, Tom decides to call a halt and we bivouac behind Skyline Ridge for the night. The rain has stopped and the men make a great dinner from 10-in-1 rations. Our prisoners eat what we eat. We are far enough behind the combat area for a fire and hot coffee.

That is when I announce, "Today, the 12th of June, 1945, is my birthday. Today I'm 19."

Everyone cheers and claps. The guys want to know if I dream about girls, or if I would know what to do with one if I had one. I tell them, "Yes, and I even have a few good wet dreams."

Tom gets a bottle of Scotch from the glove box in the truck and pours a small amount in everyone's canteen cup. We all drink, and they sing "Happy Birthday."

Tom says, "I sort of confiscated this from the officers' mess supplies. Being in the quartermasters has its advantages."

We sit around a small fire singing war songs: "I'll Be Seeing You," "Blue Birds Over the White Cliffs of Dover," and "Don't Sit Under the Apple Tree."

This is my first hard liquor. After the first taste I know it won't be my last. It's not as good as the sake in the garden in Yonabaru. That will always be the greatest. But it's sure a lot better than high-school beer.

It is quite a celebration. We kill two bottles.

We bed down and, at my suggestion, post guards on three-hour watches. Feeling no pain, I don't wake up until 0600. The guards have had a quiet night.

When our convoy moves out, we pass the little airfield north of town and then go into Yonabaru. There is a lot of equipment and supplies and an M.P. tells us where to go. We pull up to an area to unload. Tarps are already on the ground.

We lunch with the M.P.s, who take custody of our prisoners. As the Japs leave, they bow to us. I think they're trying to say "thank you." The trucks are unloaded. The town is unrecognizable to me, even though I was there just a short time ago. By 1600 everything is unloaded and Tom and the rest of the crew say goodbye.

"You sure you won't join us and head back up the island?" they ask.

"No," I say. "I have to do what I have to do."

One says, "Arch, I've learned a lot and I hope to meet you again, in a different situation. Good luck, Arch."

Tom says, for the last time, "You're sure you won't go back with us, Arch? You would fit in well and maybe live a lot longer."

"Thanks, Tom. But the answer is still 'no.' I may regret the decision in a few days. I want to thank all of you for everything you've done. It's been great. I hope we'll meet again."

The last thing Tom says is that he doesn't want to spend the night here with me. The men working on supplies have tents behind Skyline Ridge in a protected valley. Before dark they head north to their camp.

I am alone.

The ration cases, I figure, will provide good protection for the night. I settle down behind a five-foot wall of C-ration boxes. I can see all around me while standing up, but I can quickly duck out of sight. Tom left a good dinner, extra candy bars, cigarettes, a box of 10-in-1 rations, and half a bottle of Scotch.

After dark, I take a couple of swallows of Scotch, roll up in my clean blanket covered with a poncho, and quickly fall asleep.

The sound of small-arms fire I know so well awakens me.

"What the hell's going on?"

My watch—the one Cook was wearing the night he was killed—shows 2315. I put my helmet on and look out over the ration cases. There are enemy landing craft on the beach and Japs running all over the place, carrying our supplies back to the landing craft.

I make no sound as I watch them fill their boats quickly with supplies intended for us. I hope they won't come as far as the cases surrounding me.

There are a few rifle shots from the hill to the south of Yonabaru. A mortar flare, then two more parachute flares light the area. Just as quickly as it all started, the landing craft pull out and head east toward the Chinen Peninsula.

There are more flares and the navy begins attacking the small boats with machine guns. I realize the Japs hit the town only for supplies. They are hungry. They take as much as they can and are gone.

I am puzzled and angry. It makes no sense to bring in piles of rations and ammo and then leave them unprotected. What a way to run an army.

But I understand, too. The quartermaster guys think their job is done when the supplies are delivered. They want to get back to safety as quickly as they can. They are sleeping soundly somewhere, oblivious to the fact that our supplies are being stolen by the enemy.

I cannot sleep the rest of the night. I think of home. If nobody knows what happened to me since I left the squad, or if somebody turned in my dogtags, I would again be reported as missing in action.

How long ago was that? I have no idea. Have I been reported missing all this time? Sometimes it takes weeks for someone to be reported either killed or missing and other times the report is made almost immediately. Notification could have been sent to my folks back home.

I get the paper out of the top of my helmet liner and write a short note home, taking care not to say anything that would be censored:

June 13, 1945

Dear Mother and Dad,

Had a great birthday celebration with a bunch of real guys.

Just think, I am now 19 and on the other side of the world. That's more than any of you can say. Weather is good out here in the garden land of the Pacific.

When I get home I will have to look up all the plants I have seen. There are snakes they say are poisonous, but that's the least of my worries and have seen only one.

Haven't got much time. I'm in the hospital not hurt badly. Out of action for a while. Have a good cot and good food. There is a doctor and some good-looking nurses.

I am walking and I have all my arms and legs. I am in fine shape. If you received any notice that I am missing in action, well I am found. It was just a big mixup that will take a lengthy explanation when I have time. I hope to get back to my unit soon.

Hello to everybody. Tell Mary Ree I got her letter. It is wonderful to hear from her and what is going on at school. Tell all the guys going to school in the morning I would love to be going with them.

Hello to Evan and George when you see them. Things out here in the Pacific are going about like you would expect. Greet the rest of the family. Tell my little brother Tom to hang in there and don't get drafted. They are picking up the mail so that's all.

Hope all is fine at home. Will write soon when I can.
All my love, Archie.

I give the letter to one of the truck drivers in the morning.

CHAPTER 13

❀

I sleep in. When I awaken it's a beautiful bright morning with mist rising off Nakagusuku Wan. Bright rays of sunlight shine through the vapor, showing spots of blue water. The *New Mexico* is at anchor in the harbor.

As I prepare breakfast and coffee, a jeep approaches on the ground-coral road. It stops near where I'm seated on ration boxes.

The two men in the jeep ask what I'm doing here alone.

"Where are the M.P.s and quartermasters that are supposed to be here?"

"Everybody took off last night."

The two join me for breakfast. They say they are war correspondents for *Time* and *Life* magazines. They are to rendezvous with a colleague who's with the 1st Marines south of Naha. After hearing my story, they offer a ride in the back of their jeep as far as they're going. Their plan is to take the old highway from Yonabaru through Shuri to Naha. This once was a good road, following a railroad. Now, thanks to the war, road and train tracks have virtually been destroyed.

From Yonabaru the remains of the road wind south of Conical Peak and up the hill to a plateau and then on to Shuri. Shell craters and the garbage of battle are everywhere. Most craters are filled with water.

Some are as large as small ponds, forcing the jeep driver to go around them. Several times we're stuck in the mud and have to be pulled out by construction trucks and weapons carriers.

We don't reach the ancient city of Shuri, the capital of Okinawa, until afternoon. The city's castle—which took hundreds of years to build and has served as the seat of Okinawa's government for over 1,500 years—lies in ruins.

The gardens, arches, and temples must have been magnificent, representing a great expenditure and sacrifice by the people. But war, as I am learning, is no respecter of art or culture. The once-grand castle must be imagined from the rubble that remains.

Just outside Shuri the road turns south. At the top of a hill is a wide turnout, bulldozed flat to serve as a staging area. A truck convoy has stopped here for lunch; we pull over and join them.

The view, taking in the China Sea and the city of Naha, is like an oriental painting gone wrong. This city, which had been home to 100,000 people as well as being the commercial and shipping center of the island, has been reduced to a shambles by the heavy guns of navy battleships, the dive bombers from aircraft carriers, and the army's heavy artillery.

The skeleton of a single building is all that remains standing along a once-busy waterfront. Ships are sunken in the harbor. There are twisted railroad tracks and parts of blown-up trains in the foreground.

A young marine stops in a jeep and asks if we need help.

"No," I reply, "we are just looking at the carnage."

He says the marines wore gas masks when they entered the city because the stench of rotting bodies and sewage was so bad. The city wasn't just destroyed, it was wasted. Most of the old men and women with children fled to caves in the south. Every living thing left behind in Naha—people, dogs, cats, and thousands of rats—perished.

The war correspondents who gave me a lift find their friend in the marine bivouac area. I'm on my own again.

I search the area, sharing rations and foxholes and asking questions about the various outfits. I locate my old unit and stumble into the 184th Regimental Headquarters. I ask about Company C of the 2nd Battalion. The sergeant at the command post asks my name and serial number. He checks names and serial numbers in the regimental records, then looks up at me with a dumbfounded expression. He picks up a file and re-checks the names.

"Here's your name," he says. "The battalion reported you missing in action back on May 26. 'Missing in Action' is all it says. You just disappeared in that battle south of Yonabaru where we had so many casualties. Your body was not found, so we sent in the report of 'missing in action.'

"We should be listing you as 'presumed dead' by now. Someone failed to check the records. We sent your parents a missing-in-action telegram, but didn't get around to listing you as 'killed in action.'"

"Well, thank God for that," I say, pleased my parents haven't been told I'm dead.

The sergeant asks where I've been and how I managed to get back to the 184th.

I told him about my hospital stay and of hitch-hiking down the island to rejoin my outfit. The sergeant directs me to my old company. But when I return to my squad, I'm greeted by seven men who appear to be total strangers.

"Where's the rest of the squad?" I ask.

"What do you mean?" a squad member replies. "This is all of us."

I'm stunned. There's nobody I served with back in May. I knew a lot of them were dead or wounded, but we had replacements that should remember me. I should recall some names and faces.

"Am I in the right place?"

One of the soldiers assures me that I am.

"I'm Mitch," he says. "My brother and I came in as replacements a few days before you and Lee were missing. You're one of the old guys in the outfit. Weren't you with the squad from the beginning? My first day, when we met, you told me to stick with Lee and Cook and I'd learn how to survive. Well, you guys didn't last long enough. I had to learn on my own, and I'm still here."

"We thought when we saw you coming down the hill from the company command post that you were our new replacement," another squad member says. "But when we saw your beat-up fatigues, your beard and that bullet-creased helmet, we knew you were a combat vet."

"I'm not a replacement," I say, "but I was once. This looks as if it's my old squad in name only."

"What happened to you? You were classified as missing since we couldn't find your body or ID. We knew Lee and Cook were killed. You just disappeared."

"How I got back would take a long explanation. It will have to wait."

I ask about the men I know. Nobody recognizes any of the names. But then, I don't remember a thing about the soldier who says I told him to stick to Lee and Cook to learn how to survive.

Earl, a rifleman who seems to be the spokesmen, asks my full name and where I'm from.

"Arch Morrison, and I'm from Anacortes, Washington."

"Did you by any chance go to the Nelson School?" he asks.

"Sure. White, two-story building at 28th and Commercial. Six classrooms, three downstairs and three up. The boys' toilets are outside in a little building back of the playground. I went to Nelson from the first to the sixth grades."

"Me, too. I'm Earl Mitchell. I was a year ahead of you in school. You were in the same grade as my brother, Rex, who's in the navy now. My older brother's been in the navy since '41.

"Your dad had the sawmill, the one on Padilla Bay, and you lived in that big white house about five blocks south of school. It was the biggest house in town. We always wondered how many bathrooms you had. We had an outhouse, a two-holer with a Sears-Roebuck catalog inside. Your folks were big in the Assembly of God Church—the Holy Rollers, if I remember right."

"That's me. I'm no longer with that church, so don't expect strange things from me."

I was mortified that the Pentecostal Church could follow me halfway around the world. I thought I'd left all that behind when I joined the army. I suppose it will always be my "cross to bear," as we Pentecostals would say.

The Mitchell family lived by Dad's mill. I stopped there often after school when walking to my friend Ralph's house. The Mitchell home was very small, with a wood stove in the kitchen and two bedrooms— one for the three boys, the other for their mother. Their dad had been killed in a mill accident before I knew them.

The house was always neat and clean, with a well-kept yard and garden enclosed by a white picket fence and gate. Flowers bordered a stepping-stone walk up to the front door.

Looking at Earl, I'm reminded of the "fancy clothes" my parents made me wear to school, while the other boys got to wear bib overalls. Well now we're equals, both in fatigues. The truth is, my fatigues—with their torn knees and pockets ripped from carrying grenades and ammo clips—are in much worse condition than his.

Earl gives me a slap on the back. "It must be six years since I last saw you before you moved to Vancouver."

We both have trouble believing that two young men who were in elementary school together would meet on a Pacific island thousands of miles from home.

Earl has blond hair and blue eyes. He's a bit shorter than I am and doesn't weigh more than 130 pounds. He's rather shy and never uses dirty language like Jake.

He introduces me to the rest of the squad. All are replacements, and all have questions about the men they replaced and the battles we fought. Hill 178. Skyline Ridge. The banzai attack.

"The only thing I can say is you're replacing some of the bravest, most dependable men I've ever known," I say. "My hope is that if I survive, my life will be worthy of their memory. It's wonderful to be back with the squad, to be back home."

I get to know a bit about the others in the squad.

There are twin brothers, Mitch and Mike, from Oregon. Both are about six-feet tall with sandy hair and ruddy complexions. They are skinny and friendly and shake hands firmly.

Bob from Sand Point, Idaho, is well over six-feet tall and also has blond hair and blue eyes. He looks a lot like Cook, with his football-player build. The resemblance frightens me. Instead of Bob, I see Cook's skull. I see where the bullets entered and blew off the side of his head.

"Arch, I'm not through yet," Earl says, noting that my mind is wandering. "This next guy is Jack, from Utah. He will let you know he's a Mormon, but he doesn't preach. Then we have Peter and Ken, from California."

Earl's 20. I'm now 19. The others are 18 or younger.   The platoon leader, Sergeant Long, interrupts us with mail call. "There's a pack of letters for Morrison," he says. "I hear the missing has returned."

I sit alone under a shelter-half and open the first letter from home.

ↄ

May 12, 1945
2512 Crown St.
Vancouver, B.C.
Canada

Dear Archie,

I have been in prayer most of the time since we received the telegram from the War Department in Washington, D.C., that you are missing in action.

The War Department gave no further details except that if they received any more information on your situation they would notify us immediately. I have called Washington, D.C. and have found out nothing more than is in the telegram. I know you are all right. God will protect you. The man in Washington said, "Look, Lady, we have hundreds of men missing and dead. We will get to you as soon as it is possible when we have something to tell you." My next move was to call the preacher at church. He has been a great reassurance to me. He came to the house and prayed with the family and particularly with your Dad and me.

The preacher has organized a prayer chain for the week. The hours are almost filled for the week. That means someone from the church will be on their knees praying for you every hour of the day and night for the next week.

That is wonderful…. I think to myself, as I look up from her letter, that a mother who has already lost one son must be in a frightful state upon hearing that her next son is missing-in-action halfway around the world. Her faith was tested when Billy died, but her blind faith, the unreasoning belief that everything that happens is God's will, brought her through that crisis. It must be wonderful to have "justification" (a word mother uses) for such faith. Faith that has no reason: all things, all events, all happenings, all eventualities, all circumstances, all life and deaths "justified" through blind faith.

Faith, as I remember from Sunday school, is hope for things unseen, for things we don't understand, for the unknown. I've lost that faith. I now view faith as a crutch for things we don't want to assume responsibility for. I see faith and belief as anchors that pull me down, keeping me from testing the limits of my ability.

War, for all its horrors, has freed me from the unrealistic bondage of faith and belief. I can only live in the present with no expectations. I can now act to the best of my ability without blind acceptance of God's will. But I can never tell my mother and dad what I feel.

The letter goes on:

∾

Dad and I got down on our knees and gave our problems to the Lord. We say together, "Not our will but Thy will be done. We are not of this world. We do not dwell on this day but on eternity with the Lord." We then sang together:

What a friend we have in Jesus. All our sins and griefs to bear! What a privilege to carry everything to God in prayer! O what peace we often forfeit, O what needless pain we bear, All because we do not carry everything to God in prayer....

I know every word of every verse. I think to myself that this is the belief I was indoctrinated with all my young life. I wonder how many people were praying for Lee. How many lit and paid for candles for Lee? How many "Our Fathers"? How many "Hail Marys"? Why didn't God save him?

Cook went to church, a Lutheran church, I believe. I wonder if they had a prayer chain for him with half his face blown off? Why should this all-powerful God, this loving God, this God that made the world, why should He protect me and not Lee, Cook, John, Jake, Jose? Well, maybe I can see why he didn't protect Jake.

On goes my mother's letter to its familiar conclusion:

∾

Archie, we leave you in God's hands, and we will accept His will. We know His will is the best for us all. All things work together for good to those who love the Lord. We know you love the Lord, so He will work things out for the good of all of us.

Love, Mother and Dad

A call comes, ordering our platoon to move up closer to the fighting. Our battalion is assigned to defend against infiltrators who get past our front-line troops.

The call is a surprise. Troops have a tendency to grow lax when they are in reserve. There is less attention to the dangers out there.

Headquarters has sent up a Weasel with hot food: 10-in-1 rations and steaming coffee. We drop our mail and enjoy a hearty early supper.

Our defense is set up to protect against enemy theft of our supplies, weapons, and ammo. The Japs have been sneaking in and making off with things every night.

I join Mike, one of the twins, for the night. The foxholes are large and deep. Army orders forbid the twins to be in the same hole at night, just in case.

There are quite a few letters from Mother, who writes often. After reading three or four of them, I realize how little I know or care about what's going on back home, and they sure as hell know nothing about what fighting a war is like.

There's no way the chasm between home and war can be bridged. Mother relates that my little brother, who is not a good student, has quit high school and run away from home. They hear from him after about two weeks. He is working in a pulp and paper mill up the coast. The way Mother relates it:

> *One of my boys is with the Lord, another is off fighting the war, and the third one runs away to break his mother's heart.*

My younger brother, two-and-a-half years my junior, hasn't had it easy. Bill, the oldest brother and the apple of his parents' eye, died at sea. I, the next oldest, was a good student and president of the senior class in high school, and now I'm fighting a war halfway around the world.

The only thing my brother could do to get attention from Mother and Dad was to run away from home. It worked! Mother is now on her knees giving another problem to the Lord.

My mother tells me in another letter that some of my high-school friends dropped by to see if there was any news from me. I think these friends give her badly needed support. George and Evan are mentioned in every letter; they are very loyal and I appreciate their concern for Mother.

The Canadian draft age is still eighteen years and six months. There has been controversy over conscription. Most of my school friends are a year younger than I. They are not in the military and will be going on to the university next year.

Mother writes that she's very proud of my sister's husband, Dudley, who volunteered for the RCAF and just received his wings, but she says he is very disappointed. He is being posted as a flight instructor in Regina when his greatest wish is to be a Spitfire pilot in Europe.

A letter from the Canadian government is enclosed with the letter from my folks. I open the envelope quickly and read the official notice:

> The Prime Minister of Canada and King George VI
> request that you report for active duty to the Royal
> Canadian Army on January 12, 1945.

The letter is a real-tension breaker in the squad. Everyone wants to see what a letter from the King looks like. They all think I'm special to have had two draft notices. I decide to leave the rest of my mail until morning. Everyone wants to know how I would like serving under a King.

"How are you going to get back to Canada, Arch?" they ask jokingly.

After putting the mail in my pack, I look up and see a young man walking toward us from Company Headquarters.

"Is this the Second Squad?" he asks.

"Yes," I reply, looking more closely at a young man a bit shorter than I am, with dark hair, dark eyes, and a black mustache. I am shocked to see a younger version of Lee—the same dark, bright eyes. The same light skin and winning smile. His talk, his gestures, his build, everything reminds me of Lee.

I quickly get back to reality, replying, "Yes, this is the Second Squad. I'm Arch. I'm the squad leader."

"I'm Merle, from Los Angeles, a new replacement."

I send Merle down with the rest of the men and sit on the ground, shaking as if I had just seen someone alive who is supposed to be dead.

Mike asks Merle to join us in our hole as we get ready for the night watch.

"Mike, how many points do we have on our perimeter?" I ask.

"What the hell are you talking about?" he answers.

"Don't you count the visible objects between our hole and the next?"

"Tell me what you mean, Arch," Mike says.

I give them both a lesson in protective defense, just the way Lee taught me. I tell Mike and Merle about Lee and what a great teacher he was and how I credit my survival to him—not only how to set up night defenses, but also how to cover each other under fire and react in combat.

I check the reference points, just as Lee taught me, and I make sure Mike, Merle, and I write them down and put them in our helmets.

I think to myself, Lee, wherever you are, thanks for teaching me. I hope I can be as good a teacher as you were. Is this the man you picked out for me to teach?

At 0600, I stand my last guard. It's light enough to read, so I peruse the last two letters. One has obviously been drenched with water, the other—dated May 16, 1945—is the last one from Mother.

The first is hard to read:

∞

Dear Archie,

....I follow the news in the paper and find very little from your area. I save all the articles....the news from the radio, particularly the broadcasts from the States...nothing gives me any idea of what you are going through...everything is focused on Europe....I was thinking

in bed the other night, when I couldn't sleep, that if my prayers are answered and you receive God's protection and safety, I would think God has answered my prayers. But what about other mothers who are praying for boys who are killed? God didn't give them his protection. Am I selfish in asking for your survival?

(This is the first time I have ever seen my mother question any of our Pentecostal beliefs.)

∽

All I can do is pray for all, but I do pray especially for you.... Evan dropped by again the other day and we had a chat...he is so faithful.... it's a relief and help to have visits from your high-school friends.... Your brother is back home ...don't have my approval.... friends.... sch

(I can't make out much more, so I open the last letter.)

∽

Dear Archie,

Last Saturday, the day before Mother's Day, the doorbell rang while I was washing vegetables in the kitchen sink getting them ready for dinner. I hurried down the hall as the bell sounded again. Opening the front door I found a large lovely bouquet of flowers for me. A young man was returning back to his truck in the street and called back, "Happy Mother's Day." The truck had printed on the side "Brown's Flowers."

I could hardly wait to open the card to find out who was sending me flowers. Nobody sends me flowers on Mother's Day. Your father always says it's extravagant. I opened the card and see your writing. They were from you. It's not possible, I thought. This can't be true, it is only the first of the week that we received the telegram from the war department that you were missing in action. I couldn't understand how this was possible.

This morning I called the florist and they informed me that you had ordered and paid for the flowers some time ago before you went overseas. I asked the date when the order was placed and found out it was when you were home on your last leave. I can't look at this beautiful arrangement of flowers. I don't know if you are even alive. I don't know if you will even receive this letter. I don't know if you will ever be home again. All I can do is pray and ask the Lord for strength. It seems so long since I have seen you. It seems so long since I have talked to you. You will never know what mothers go through with a son at war, which I am thankful for.

Fathers seem different. Your Dad just doesn't say anything and goes off to the hardware store where he says he can be alone. I wonder if he could stand the loss of his next son? The only way you will ever understand your Mother and Dad is if you have to send a son of your own off to a war across the ocean and wait to find out if he is alive or dead.

I pray to God this will never happen to you. To feel and experience our emotions, you would have to have a son in your situation and you waiting at home like we do to understand. I hope and pray that your son, my grandson, will never have to be a soldier in war and see the destruction and killing that you have seen and that will be embedded in your memory.

All I can do is trust in the Lord and be willing to accept His will.

We love you and miss you, Son,

Mother and Dad

I put the letters back in my pack in the bottom of my foxhole. As I lift my pack the Japanese lieutenant's wallet falls out on the dirt. Mike and Merle, my foxhole comrades, are awake.

"That's a strange wallet," one of them says. "Where did you get something like that?"

I tell them how I took the wallet from the body of a Japanese lieutenant I shot and watched die during the counter-attack on Skyline Ridge.

I told them it was a battle I would never forget, with soldiers from both sides dying all around me. I removed the pictures of the lieutenant's family from the wallet.

Upon seeing the photograph of the lieutenant's mother, Merle says, "I wonder what his mother's letters were like. I wonder if she prayed for him. I wonder if she knows he's dead. He's a lot like me, Arch. You probably don't think I'm old enough, but I'm married. We got married about a year-and-a-half ago when I was just 17 and we knew Jean was pregnant. Our little girl was born when I was in basic. I got to see her on my last leave. My mom is taking care of both Jean and the baby now. I'm just like this Jap with a little girl, a wife and a mom."

After our C rations, we discuss our night defenses: how to time hand grenades so they'll explode half-a-second before hitting the ground, how not to give away our position.

I try to show them all the tricks I learned from Lee and Cook, tricks that might mean the difference between living and dying.

I end my survival talk with one of Lee's quotes: "Terror can be endured so long as you can find a hole. But it kills if you think about it."

The squad digs in for the night.

CHAPTER 14

❀

The battle for Okinawa has been decided. It's only a matter of how long the Japs can hold out behind a well-defended natural escarpment of coral cliffs that crosses the southern end of the island.

The wall, 300-feet high in places, is honeycombed with caves and tunnels occupied by Japs, who believe it is the ultimate disgrace to surrender. They will fight to the end.

Our company is in a reserve role, assigned a responsibility quite different from anything I have experienced in the past. Instead of engaging in frontal attacks on the Jap fortifications, we have been ordered to destroy Jap stragglers and infiltrators.

Enemy troops, we are told, are hiding in every conceivable protected location. The Japs have no organization. At night, they sneak into foxholes, looking for food. They hide in artillery-riddled trees, bushes, and caves.

The Japs are desperate. They are hungry. Some are wounded, sick, and dying. They will kill to survive. They do not believe we take prisoners, which is almost true.

The civilians are similarly terrified. They hate Americans. They carry rifles and hand grenades, but use them only if they are in a desperate situation. Then they often turn the weapons on themselves. They have been told that if they are captured, the women will be raped, the men killed, and the children sent to slave-labor camps.

One hot, sunny afternoon Earl and Mitch bring a gook woman with two little kids back to our company area, where we are relaxing from our mopping-up operation.

Mike calls out, "Goddamn, look. Mitch found himself a family."

We gather around to ask questions, to find out where the enemy might be hiding and if they know anything about infiltrators in the area.

We learn nothing, despite trying every form of sign language we know. During the interrogation, some of our men bring tropical Hershey bars and other food to our prisoners. Even though we know they must be hungry, they refuse the food. Why should they trust people from a different culture who have put them through such hell, destroying their houses, gardens and towns?

Suddenly the woman, who is not over five-feet tall, lifts her tunic, exposing her bare body. In her hands is a small automatic weapon. She begins firing at us. I see three or four men go down as someone screams, "What the hell is she doing?"

There is much confusion. Shouts mingle with rifle and pistol fire. The sounds of dying, like the moaning of an animal or the noise of pigs being butchered, permeate the area. It is all over in a few minutes, although it seems like hours.

Seven bodies lie in the dirt, four of ours and the three gooks. Our medics rush in. One of our new replacements, a kid who just arrived yesterday—I don't even know his name—is among those killed. The other three soldiers are wounded; they are quickly evacuated.

The gook woman, a boy about 10, and a little girl are dead, shot to pieces.

One of the new replacements goes off to a few scrub pines still standing in the area and begins to puke. I follow and put my arm around him, holding him until there is nothing left to get rid of. I pass him my canteen so he can rinse his mouth and clean his face. He is shattered by what he has just witnessed.

"I got more than my mouth to clean up," he says.

"That's OK, Kid. I did the same thing the first time. I have some clean shorts in my pack. You can have them if you don't have any."

"I fired on them with my BAR," the young man says. "I killed them! I killed them! I could see those little kids' eyes when I fired. I could see the blood as I was firing. I could see their faces. I saw them convulsing on the ground. I'm a murderer! I killed them! I shot little kids and a woman! What do you do when you know you have murdered people?"

"I don't know," I answer. "I have the same feeling. It will probably haunt us forever."

"That Goddamn gook killed the only guy I knew in the squad. I felt like I could kill them all. I went through basic with Joe. We spent our last leave with his mom and dad. I came overseas with him. We're buddies. He didn't have a chance, did he? Killed by a woman with two little kids. I hate them. I hate them. I want to kill them all. I want to kill all those sons of bitches. Goddamn son of a bitch."

He starts to cry.

"What's your name?"

"Ken," he cries.

"Let's walk down the hill, Ken."

That night I eat my can of C rations with Ken and we stand guard together in a foxhole.

I wonder if this is the new young man I'm to train for Lee.

The next morning, the sergeant who is our company commander sends my squad—I'm now the squad leader—to flush the enemy from an area behind and north of our position.

There are rocks, caves, tombs, and groups of sago palms and scrub pines where we know the enemy can be hiding by day and wreaking havoc by night. Gladioluses and lily-like flowers that somehow survived the incessant artillery barrages bloom in the crevasses. Birds seem to be everywhere.

Our squad consists of Earl, Ken, Mitch, one of the twins, John, Peter, and myself. Earl and Ken are the BAR team. The rest of us are armed with rifles and grenades.

Whenever we find clusters of trees that have survived the war and might be enemy hiding places, we fire over the trees and call out:

"Come out with no clothes on and your hands behind your heads!"

I don't know how they are supposed to understand us. I never heard any of the enemy speak English.

I shout, "I will count to 10 before we start firing again. One…nine, ten."

If nobody comes out, we saturate the place with rifle fire. After firing, two or three of us go into the cover to see if we have eliminated any or all of the enemy that are hiding. We are told to be careful with the bodies, in case they are booby-trapped.

So far today, we haven't flushed out any Japs.

Caves and tombs we handle differently. We approach from either side, keeping away from the entrance. Then we throw in several phosphorous grenades designed to eliminate every living thing inside. To be safe, we don't go in until the next day.

Sometimes, if they are available, we use hand-held flamethrowers. Two guys with a flame-thrower burn out the cave or tomb, suffocating the hiding men. These portable flamethrowers are not as efficient as tank flamethrowers. In addition, they are heavy and lack sufficient fuel for multiple attacks.

In the first two clusters of trees we attack this morning, we find nothing. In the third, we find one dead Jap. And in the fourth, we find two more. All are enlisted men and there aren't any good souvenirs.

Jake isn't here to take their teeth and ears. In another brushy area, I fire over the top of the undergrowth of brush, call out the instructions and count to 10.

We hear noise in the beat-up pines and hold our fire.

Earl says, "There must be a bunch of Japs in there."

I call out instructions and receive no response. I count slowly to 10, and again there is no reply. We fire one more time over the top of the thick underbrush, before firing directly into it. Silence.

Earl and I go in and find a dead goat. We drag it out. Later we will take it back to the company area to cook.

Just before breaking for lunch we see an area in a small valley to our left with an almost undamaged stand of pines and sago palms. Earl and Mitch say it looks like a good place to hide. We come from three sides, weapons drawn, and fire several shots over the trees.

I call out as I always do, "Come out. No clothes on. Hands behind your head." I call out loudly a second time. "Come out, you bastards. No clothes on. Hands behind your head."

I start to count.

A loud answer comes back in good English,

"Don't shoot, don't shoot. We will come out. Give us time to take off our clothes."

I can't believe what I'm hearing. What do I do now? I have never been in this situation before.

Earl says, "Arch, ask how many are in there."

"How many of you are in the trees? Are you American or Japanese?"

"There are three of us. Two are wounded. We are Japanese and wish to surrender, to become prisoners of war."

"What do I do now?" I ask Earl.

"Tell him to send them out one at a time," Earl says. "This is great."

"Come out. No clothes on. Hands behind your head. Come out one at a time...."

"OK, but don't shoot," the Japanese answers.

I order the squad to hold its fire.

"Again, how many of you are there?"

"Three."

"You had better be telling me the truth. Now, come out one at a time. That's an order. And you, the one who's been speaking, you come out last."

"OK!"

"One at a time now. We have you covered on all sides with our weapons. We're not going to wait long."

The first one comes out, wearing no clothes. He is very thin, about 17 years old, maybe 5-3. His dark hair is long and matted and his bare feet appear to be ulcerated.

One leg is bandaged with dirty cloth from below the knee to his hip. He supports himself with a stick. The other hand is behind his head. He walks very slowly, his face showing terror, dark eyes wide open, his body shaking. He speaks rapidly in Japanese. I suspect he's begging for his life, fearful he'll be shot at any moment.

"Ken, take him over there in the open. Tie his hands and keep him covered. OK, you English-speaking Jap. Send out the next one."

The next man appears. He's older, maybe 20, a little taller and heavier. He walks well, but his head is bandaged, the hair stuck to his scalp with dried blood. He is in better shape than the first boy and shows less fear. I tell Mitch to take him over with the first prisoner, tie his hands, and then keep them both covered.

"OK, you s.o.b., come out," I say to the third prisoner, "then you can tell us how you learned to speak English so well. Keep in mind, you are covered every minute, so don't try anything."

I'm scared myself. It's the first time I have actually spoken with the enemy.

A young man of about 27 emerges from the trees. He has shed his clothes and has his hands behind his head. He is about my height and probably 135 pounds. Like the other two, he's dirty and unshaven, but he appears to be in the best physical shape of the three.

"OK," I tell him. "You are a prisoner of war. All you have to give is your name, rank, and serial number. Nothing more is required."

"My name is Tetsu Kazuki," he says. "I am a captain in the Japanese Imperial Army. I am a medical doctor. My number is 196650."

"Ken, will you write all that down," I say.

"OK, Arch, but ask him some questions. Let's find out something about him if we can."

"I'll try. Captain, you don't have to talk. If you want to tell us how you learned English and where you're from, we'll listen."

He answers, "First, can we get our clothes, and do you have anything to eat and drink?"

Peter and Mitch and one of the prisoners retrieve the clothes and everything else they find in the trees. They make the prisoner pick up the clothes and weapons, in case they are booby-trapped. They stay low to the ground as a precaution.

They emerge from the trees, after a few minutes, with clothes, two rifles, and two hand grenades. Meanwhile, the rest of us have put together a few rations and water. The prisoners are eating hungrily. They dress and the captain begins to talk:

"After school in Japan, at home in the city of Hiroshima, I went to live with my uncle in Los Angeles. That was in 1935. I was accepted at the University of Southern California the following year." He pauses, looks at me, and asks, "What part of the U.S. do you come from?"

We are all flabbergasted. We don't know what to say. Nobody in an enemy uniform has ever spoken to us so we could understand what he was saying. Now we have a captain who speaks English with virtually no accent.

I still think it may be a trick. Perhaps he's trying to con us. Maybe there are other Japs hiding nearby who are getting ready to ambush us. I send Earl and Peter out to check the area. They return shortly and report that there is no sign of anyone.

"Let him talk, Arch," the squad members say. "You talk to him, Arch."

"OK, I'll do my best, but you guys keep your eyes open. This could still be trouble. Remember that gook woman yesterday. Ken, write down as much as you can. OK, to answer your question, Captain, I'm from the Northwest."

"Where in the Northwest? Seattle?"

"No, but near there."

"I was in Seattle for a football game in Husky Stadium in the fall of 1940. We came up from L.A. to see if the Trojans could beat the Huskies."

"I attended that game," I tell him. "Give me the date."

"November, the second Saturday," he answers.

I can't remember the date, so I ask him to describe the stadium.

"It is on the campus of the University of Washington and the open end of the stadium looks out on Lake Washington. I remember, you can see a high mountain. I think they call it Mt. Rainier."

"That's exactly right," I say. "You had to have been there. OK, we'll take you back to the company area."

I take the officer with me. His hands are tied behind his back. He wears only his pants. His shirt, like that of the other two prisoners, is torn and dirty. He walks upright, but he is not arrogant. He shows no belligerence, seeming quite humble.

He reminds me of the Japanese-Americans on our troop transport when we left Seattle. They were coming back from army duty in Italy and were returning to their homes in Hawaii. They were the first combat veterans I had ever seen, and the ones I got to know on the ship were all highly decorated and battle-seasoned. They had been through hell, having fought at Anzio, and they were willing to teach me far more about combat survival than I'd learned in basic training. They also taught me how to shoot craps.

The enemy officer who was our prisoner would have looked just like the Japanese-Americans who fought in Italy if he had a GI uniform. Not only does he look like them, he also sounds like them.

If all three of the prisoners were cleaned up and put in our fatigues, you couldn't tell them from the decorated soldiers I met on our troop ship leaving Seattle.

Sure, these Japanese smell pretty rank right now. But I don't imagine dirty U.S. soldiers smell much different.

"How long have you been without boots?" I ask.

"That's OK," the captain answers. "I have walked a good many miles without shoes. It is not like I am back at USC."

"What's your name again?"

"Tetsu Kazuki."

"I'm Arch," I answer. "You're a doctor?"

"Yes, I got my medical degree from the University of Southern California in June of 1941. After graduation, and before my internship at Los Angeles County Hospital, I went home to Hiroshima to visit my family. I have a brother and sister. They were living with my mother and father. My father is a Zen-garden architect. He's a graduate of the University of Kyoto. I intended to stay for six months before returning to start my internship, which I hoped to follow with a residency in internal medicine. But I was drafted, just like you."

"Yes, I was drafted," I reply.

We talk little during the hour-long return trip to our company area. I am concerned about how the company will react to my prisoners. I am not going to kill them. I hear pretty much what I expect:

"Where did you get those bastards?" "What are you bringing them back for?" "Arch, we don't take prisoners." "You can share your rations." "You can stay up all night and guard those s.o.b.s; I'll kill them." "Have you forgotten yesterday?" "What would your dead buddies think of you now?"

"This captain is a doctor, a graduate of USC," I tell them.

Everybody laughs.

"We know, Arch, and you're a graduate of West Point. You bastard, you've gone fuckin' soft. Maybe you'd better go back to the hospital where you came from. You're no longer a soldier if you can't get rid of Japs and not bring them back to us. The hospital is where you belong if you can't kill those motherfuckin' sons-of-bitches when you find them."

I don't answer them. I'm beginning to question myself. Have I changed? Maybe I have. Am I different? Can I no longer kill? Just because this Jap is a doctor and can speak English doesn't make him different from the machinegunner that killed Lee.

The sergeant, acting as company commander, takes over and tells three guys from the heavy-weapons squad, three guys I don't know, to take the prisoners back to the POW compound a mile or so to the north.

The prisoners, their hands tied more securely, are pushed into line and taken away. I see them leave—the three prisoners in front, followed by the guards.

The little prisoner is hobbling on his wounded leg. He is followed by the one with the head injury. And behind him is Tetsu, walking upright, barefooted, wearing a pair of Jap army pants. He waves to me and doesn't say a word. I give him a sign of recognition I hope no one else sees.

They slowly wind their way up the muddy path to the top of the hill, where they disappear from view. I know it's a mile or so to the POW compound. I walk down the hill, away from the others. Sitting down, holding my head, I tell myself that I did the right thing, that I did the best I could to save the three prisoners.

My mind is confused. Why am I trying to save this Jap doctor? Is it because he was educated in the U.S. or because I always wanted to be a doctor myself? As a little boy going to bed at night, my prayer was that God would let me become a doctor to help suffering people.

But those were the prayers of a child, back when I had blind faith that God would do anything for me if I prayed enough. As far as I have strayed from my Pentecostal background, the old beliefs still have power. God can do anything, even make me a doctor if I pray long enough.

Then I think of how this all-powerful God told Abraham to kill his only son. And how He did nothing when His own son was murdered. How he watched Lee die and Cook die and still did nothing.

How can a God who rules the universe, parts the Red Sea, saves the Jews, and speaks from a burning bush be powerless when we need him?

How can such a God possibly help me to become a doctor when I will almost certainly die on this battlefield?

Tetsu is already a doctor. How, I wonder, would the Christian patients at Los Angeles County Hospital have reacted to having a Japanese doctor?

After all, the Japs bombed Pearl Harbor. They're sneaky. They can't be trusted. They have buckteeth. They have a strange language. And, they don't worship our God.

Never mind that Japanese-Americans fought the Germans in Italy in U.S. uniforms. Never mind that many died there. And that I liked the ones I met on our troopship.

Do I still want to become a doctor? I remember writing to Northwestern University and USC to ask for catalogs just before I was drafted. Would I ever go to college? Would I ever go to medical school like Tetsu?

The hospital we saw back in the cave near Yonabaru—the one with all the bodies—could Tetsu have been working there? Who was responsible for that slaughter? Could he have been the chief doctor in that cave hospital? And could he have been responsible for killing them?

Again, I think there's no morality in war! There's no just war!

Tetsu had said he was drafted, "just like you."

When my draft notice came, I really had no choice. I wonder how they found Tetsu on vacation. How did they know he was a doctor? Well, they found him and drafted him and he had no choice, just like me.

Is this dreadful war the price we must pay for living on the planet? Is it just a coincidence that we would meet here—a Jap doctor and an American GI who always wanted to be a doctor?

So many questions. So few answers.

As I sit, I lose all sense of time, place, and people around me. I find myself alone on a beach, watching a storm come across the water, a violent storm. Rain pounds on a window that protects me from the storm. I have no idea where the window came from.

The rain becomes mixed with large snowflakes. It continues to pound on the window.

Suddenly, to the south, a small bright spot appears in the dark sky. It grows larger and larger. A jeep drives up and parks in a non-conforming way, as if it's here to handle an emergency.

A young woman, wearing a beautiful long dress and no protection from the rain, jumps from the car and runs to the edge of the beach and points to the north. She shouts with both hands in the air as if she's receiving the Holy Spirit. "This is magnificent," she shouts.

The rain, mixed with snow and ice, is running off her head and shoulders. Her gorgeous black hair is wet and hangs in her face. Her beautiful clothes are soaking wet. I jump up and run toward her. She shouts and points north. I turn and look north and see, not 10 feet from me, a double rainbow. One end is at my feet, the other out in the water.

It's a different rainbow, broken in the middle. The woman tries to put it together again, but cannot make it whole.

"This is the greatest thing I have ever seen in all my life," she says. "It is the first time I have ever had a chance to be in the pot of gold at the end of a rainbow."

She runs toward the pot of gold. But she can never quite touch it. She holds her hand out to me. I recognize her. She's the Japanese woman in the picture—the wife of the man I killed. I want to go with her. I reach for her hand.

"I'll take you out of the storm," she says. "I'll take you to safety with my husband."

I cannot reach her hand.

I stand there and watch the entire scene begin to fade. The sun is enclosed behind the dark clouds and vanishes in a few minutes. It's dark again and the rain, ice, snow, and wind pound us. The marvelous experience evaporates.

The woman says, "Thank you for sharing this experience of life and death with me." She returns to her jeep and drives away, out of sight, into the storm.

I am brought back to reality instantly by the sharp crack of three rifle shots over the hill.

No.... No.... No.... No......Not......Tetsu!

CHAPTER 15

❀

The open can of C rations is still in front of me as I sit by myself. The rest of the men in the squad have already finished eating and are smoking and drinking coffee around a fire when they call me.

"What's wrong, Arch? Have we said something or done something? Are you pissed off? Come on over. We've got hot coffee."

"I'll be with you shortly," I say. "I'm just writing a letter."

When I join the group, there is no talk of the day's events. We break for the night without mentioning that three prisoners were shot.

Mitch says, "We better establish a perimeter even though we're not at the front. We ought to protect ourselves from infiltrators in search of food."

Earl and Mike—Mike is one of the twins—find an old net to hide their hole, which is very exposed. They anchor the back of the net with rocks and hold up the front with branches. They put leaves and branches on top of the net.

It is virtually impossible to detect the hole, unless you know it's there. They are proud of their ingenuity and hope it will allow them to enjoy a good night's sleep. They don't care if the Japs steal some food, but they don't want to lose any weapons or ammo.

185

The hole in which I spent the previous night is good enough for me. Tonight I'm alone, since we are back of the lines. We are short of men and not expecting any action.

Three foxholes that night are occupied by a single GI.

One will stand guard while the other two sleep. We draw straws to see who will be first. I draw the short one.

I follow the routine Lee taught me: counting significant landmarks, writing the numbers on a small piece of paper, and then slipping the paper inside my helmet liner. All is quiet. I'm alone in my hole.

I say to myself, "What the hell, I'm going to get some sleep. Nobody will know if I'm on guard or not. I'll wake up if I hear anything. I've always been a light sleeper."

Sleep? Who can sleep?

"Sleep that knits up the raveled sleeve of care." I think that's from *Macbeth*, something I learned in old R. B. Westmacott's class. My sister Mary is a great knitter. When she made a mistake on a sleeve, she would rip it all out and have a pile of yarn on the floor. Then she'd roll it up into a ball and knit a new sleeve without a mistake.

My mind is like that mess of yarn on the floor. All tangled. I can't get the Japanese doctor out of my mind. I think of Lee, Cook, the poetry of John. My mind is in turmoil.

Sleep? Every time I close my eyes I hear those three rifle shots. I see the dead bodies of three Japanese soldiers lying on the ground. My mind is unraveled, like the knitted sleeves Mary pulled apart. She could re-knit the sleeve. I feel I can never be knitted up or be made whole again.

I understand what Shakespeare was saying. Perhaps sleep can give me the help I need. I get John's book of Wilfred Owen's poetry from my pack. It's too dark to read, so I just thumb through the pages. It helps.

Nobody talked about the prisoners when I was with the squad tonight. They simply ignored the shootings, as if the killing of three prisoners meant nothing to anybody but me.

Tonight, in this hole—wet, but not too cold—alone with my rambling, irrational, and confused mind, I question the killings.

Was it necessary to kill the Japanese doctor, or the other two prisoners for that matter? The doctor had lived five years of his life with his American relatives in Los Angeles, working to get a medical degree. Why kill him? He wasn't responsible for the war. He wasn't guilty of the deaths of Lee or Cook. He didn't even have a weapon. Did they shoot him in the back? What a waste of a well-educated man.

No matter what happens, I'm going to get some sleep. I'm alone. Nobody's around. I finally fall into a fitful sleep.

Strange thoughts race through my mind. I am back at Fort Lawton, my port of embarkation when I left Seattle to come to the war in the Pacific. I found a hole in the fence at Fort Lawton, where a lot of guys were going AWOL to see their loved ones one more time before going off to battle.

I did the same. Night after night, I went AWOL to see my mother at the Edmund Meany Hotel, out near the University of Washington campus. I always made it back to the barracks in time for bed check. Mother knew that one evening I wouldn't show up, that I would be shipped overseas.

I called her when I arrived in Seattle. Since we were forbidden to tell where we were, I told my mother to visit some friends in Seattle. When I called the friends, they told me my mother was staying in the Edmund Meany.

One night I didn't show up to see her. That day we were taken to Pier 91 on the Seattle waterfront and boarded a troop transport, the USS Imperial, a merchant-marine freighter, a "liberty ship," converted into a troopship capable of carrying hundreds of 18-year-olds into combat.

After all the troops and supplies were aboard, the ship left the dock and moved out into Seattle's harbor, Elliott Bay, where it anchored for several days. Besides young replacement troops, the ship carried survivors of a battalion of Japanese-American soldiers who had fought in Italy and were now going home to Hawaii.

The battle-scarred group of Japanese-Americans, mostly in their early 20s, had received their overseas pay and were rolling dice between the six-high bunks deep in the ship and on the hatches on the top deck.

This little Pentecostal boy had never before seen that kind of sin! There were hundreds of dollars on the floor. I watched and learned the intricacies of craps, a game in which everything depends upon a roll of the dice.

They didn't seem to care who won or lost. They were going home alive and were overjoyed. They talked to us about combat. That afternoon, while the ship anchored in the Seattle harbor, one of the young solders, named Neri, described some survival techniques that he had used.

"Arch," he said, "Learn as much as you can as fast as you can from those who have been in combat. My advice is to find a good buddy, one with combat experience, and learn from him. Always stay alert, never get tired, protect your comrades, and don't worry about who you kill or about being killed. Follow this advice, Arch, and you will be OK. It's like the roll of the dice. You win or you lose."

That night, in my bunk, fifth up from the bottom, I heard the engine start and felt the ship move. We were heading out. Pulling on my pants and donning a field jacket, I climbed down the bunks and found my way up the ladder and through the blackout curtains to the bow of the ship. I couldn't see much of Seattle, which also was blacked out.

The ship passed all the landmarks I knew as a kid growing up in the area: the little town of Kingston, Point-No-Point Lighthouse, Double Bluff on Whidbey Island, Port Townsend's Point Wilson light. The lighthouses were still operating.

Our pilot went down the ladder on the side of the ship to the pilot boat waiting below. The pilot boat went to Port Angeles and waited for the next incoming vessel. Looking back, I saw Fidalgo Island and the lighthouse near Anacortes, my old hometown. After the ship passed Port Angeles, I went below. I didn't see Cape Flattery, the most north-westerly part of the 48 states. I climbed up into my bunk and slept. The next day I had to get up at 0400. My name was on the list for K.P.

At about 0120 I awaken from my dreams, sensing that something is different. I check my perimeter points, then check the number against the number written on the piece of paper inside my helmet liner. I count 12. The number on the paper is 12. Nothing has changed. And yet something's not right or I wouldn't have awakened.

I feel guilty about falling asleep. But what difference does it make now? I check my watch, the one Cook was wearing the night he was killed. My thoughts are again focused on the three rifle shots—one for each man I had taken prisoner, including Tetsu. And now Tetsu was dead, like Lee and Cook.

"Arch," I hear my name called from behind me.

I must still be dreaming.

I turn around and stare with disbelief.

If I'm not dreaming or sleeping, then I must be hallucinating, as I must have been doing when I saw Lee at the foot of my cot at Camp Ernie Pyle.

Surely I'm going mad.

Again I hear my name. "Arch!"

They say this sort of thing can happen when you are under stress for a long time.

But not me. I am fine. I am normal.

The stress isn't that devastating. I am back with my squad.

Is this combat insanity?

No. I look behind me as my name is called softly again.

Tetsu is standing at the back of my hole. In the moonlight, he isn't hard to recognize. Black hair. No shirt. No shoes. It must be Tetsu.

"Can I jump into your hole?" he asks.

Without waiting for an answer, he's next to me in my foxhole.

At first I can't speak. When I find my voice, I say, "You're dead. I heard the rifle shots yesterday afternoon. You're dead. It can't be you. If it is, I have definitely gone nuts. I've lost it."

"It's me, Arch. This is me, and I want to talk with you."

I must be out of my mind, cracked, insane.

I say, "God damn it, this is what I wanted to happen. But it can't be. I'm still dreaming. The combat fatigue the medic talked about at Camp Ernie Pyle has caught up with me. What will the squad think if I tell them about this in the morning? They'll just laugh and say I'm hallucinating and send me back to the nut house. I don't dare tell anybody what I am seeing."

"You can talk to me," Tetsu says, "even if you think I'm not real, or whatever you think I am."

"You're in my hole, on your knees, wearing the same pants, no shoes, no shirt. You must not have had anything to eat or drink since we fed you in the afternoon."

I give him my canteen and find a can of C rations in my pack. He eats and begins to talk.

"If you will be quiet, Arch, I'll tell you what happened after I left your company area."

"I'll shut up," I tell him.

"We had to walk slowly up the hill because of my man with the wounded leg," he begins. "Your soldiers were pushing us and cursing you, Arch, for putting them on this detail. They didn't know I understood English, since I hadn't spoken in English except to you and your squad. They decided to eliminate us as soon as we were over the hill and out of sight from your company.

"Realizing their intention, my plan was to drop on the first shot, hoping they would fire to kill us one at a time and not kill me first. They turned us around, our backs to them so we couldn't see them. My position was on the far left. The boy with the wounded leg was on the right. The one with the head wound was in the middle.

"Nothing was said. The boy on the right started to fall after the first shot. Then I fell just after the next shot was fired. Then the third rang out. I heard the bullet go over my head.

"The soldiers didn't bother to check to see if we were all dead.

"One said, 'Well, that's the end of this shitty detail. Let's get back for some chow and chew out Arch.'

"Another remarked, 'Why the hell didn't Arch do this in the first place so we wouldn't have to do his dirty work? He's gone chicken. Maybe he's had more than he can take. He's been on the island a long time. I've heard of guys that have been good soldiers and then, all of a sudden, they can't kill anymore. Maybe that's happened to him.'

"They sat down for a while and smoked and drank some water. I didn't make a move, hardly breathed. After they were out of sight, I moved slowly, no sound. I crawled up to the crest of the hill. There, looking down, I could see you and the platoon having rations and preparing for the night.

"I saw you, Arch, sitting away from the others. I memorized the position of the holes, watching where you went for the night. I saw you were in a hole alone, which seemed strange but fit into my plan.

"I figured out a route to your hole that I could manage in the darkness. At about an hour before midnight, calculating by the stars and moon, I crawled on my belly, using my hands and feet to push me along. I used the memorized checkpoints to make sure I was going the right way. I got here without anyone detecting my movements or falling into the wrong hole. Any mistake, and I'd be dead."

I look at him next to me in my foxhole and ask myself what do I do next. Tetsu has no boots. His pants are his only clothing. I give him my extra field jacket and old shoes. The boots are too big, but better than nothing. I received a new issue of boots and a jacket a few days ago, but hadn't gotten around to discarding the worn-out stuff.

What will be my next move? Whatever decision I make, I am faced with a dreadful dilemma. When morning comes and everybody in my squad finds me with a Jap wearing my field jacket and my boots, what will happen? Tetsu answers my questions. He tells me he wouldn't have put me in this position if he didn't have a plan.

"This is what we can do," he says, addressing both of our situations. "When morning comes and your men find me in your hole, wearing your field jacket and boots, you will be in deep trouble! You could be accused of harboring the enemy or even aiding the enemy. That's a very serious charge. You could be put in the stockade and court-martialed. Your trial would be conducted by officers who were in college while you were fighting their war. Imagine the headline:

"'Combat Veteran Goes Soft and Harbors Jap Soldier Who Has Been Killing Young American Boys.'

"What would they think of you back home? Your mother would think her son a traitor. Your friends, the ones you went to high school with, would ask, 'How could he do it?'

"The immediate problem is even worse," Tetsu continues. "Tomorrow morning, what is your squad going to think of you, bringing a Jap to the chow line? Their squad leader with a Jap! They already think you've gone soft, lost your ability to kill since returning from the hospital. I heard that myself. They might kill both of us like they tried to kill me yesterday."

Tetsu lays this on me. It is overwhelming.

"Let's first look at how we both feel," he goes on. "I am speaking for myself and I hope you feel the same way. We both have lived with the butchery of young men from two countries, two cultures, and two, maybe more, religions. We have been placed in a situation, not of our choosing, where we shed our facade of civilization and become animals in order to destroy each other.

"I have made up my mind that I can't go on like this. Can you? Can you keep on killing men like yourself? That leaves it all up to you, Arch. You have to make the gravest decision of your life. You are at a crossroads, and you have two choices. The first is to kill me now and push my body out in front of your hole to make it look like I was attacking you."

"That's impossible. I can't," I say.

"I won't resist you," Tetsu says. "I won't put up a fight. I'll make it easy. You just have to shoot me as you did all the others."

"Like my men shot two prisoners in the back and tried to shoot you."

Tetsu replies, "Those two wounded young men were the best I had in the war. They wouldn't hurt anybody. They didn't believe in violence. They had refused to carry weapons. That's why they were in the medical corps. They were wonderful men."

"I didn't know any of the Japanese soldiers I killed, Tetsu. They were just the enemy I hated. The enemy that had to be killed."

"I am 'just the enemy' and you are 'just the enemy,' Arch. I am just like you and you are just like me."

"Sure, you went to USC and you speak American. You're just like me."

"Why does that make anything different?"

"It means it would be murder to kill you. I can't do that. I can't. You're not attacking me. It would be murder."

"If I am a doctor, speak English, and talk to you, then I am not a Jap. Where the hell are you coming from, Arch? What kind of morality is that? Come on, Arch, let's get it over with. Do you want me to go out in front of your hole and then you won't have to move my body? I'll take off the boots and jacket. I won't need them after you shoot me."

"There has to be another way."

"I'll make it easier for you. Let me borrow a weapon and I'll kill myself. You will have nothing to do with my death."

"You can't have a weapon. You could turn it on me. I can't kill you. It's inconceivable. I can't do it."

"How is it, Arch, that we have been killing or helping to kill the enemy—in my case, Americans, and in yours, Japanese—and we haven't asked this question before? I think it is because for both of us to tolerate, condone, and participate in killing other men, we have to convince ourselves that the enemy is different. He's inferior. We're superior. He has a false religion. We have the true religion. He's against our God, and therefore he's the devil. He's a dirty Jap with buckteeth—stupid and deserving to die. He bombed Pearl Harbor. He kills women and children.

"We dehumanize the enemy—in your case, the dirty Jap; in mine, the white devils. Yanks that rape women and kill children. We can justify our own horrible acts because we are killing something evil. This works well until something breaks this dehumanizing myth and we recognize each other as human brothers. The blood of those we are killing is then on our hands, and we have to deal with the realities of death, murder, and destruction, which is difficult, if not impossible. We have come to realize that I am just like you and you are just like me. This has happened to us, Arch, through our chance encounter.

"I know you as a good person, and you know me as a physician whom you respect. Continuing to kill, or to contribute to killing, will, for both of us, create a terrible guilt in our minds that will drive us insane for the rest of our lives."

I tell Tetsu: "There has to be a way out of this. There has to be. If there isn't, I'll go insane, if I'm not already insane. I could never live with myself if I killed you. We must change the way we think about each other and about this war. We do the killing and all we really need to do is stop. If I kill you, then I will have to kill myself."

"That's no answer, Arch," Tetsu replies. "There is a way, if we accept the fact that we are changed men, that something has happened to us, that we no longer want to participate in the killing. To protect ourselves against this insanity of killing and suicide, we must remove ourselves from this diabolical war, in which both sides inflict carnage on the other."

"Impossible," I tell him. "We're in a hole in the ground, on an island surrounded by water, in the middle of the night. To think we can change history is bullshit."

"Well, that's your second choice, Arch. That is my plan."

"What is this Goddamned plan, Tetsu?"

"My solution to the dilemma we are in is for you to go with me to my home in Japan."

"That's impossible, Tetsu. You're a damned fool. I would be deserting and I would be in worse trouble than I am in already. When we're caught, which we will be, I will be put in prison for the rest of my life as a deserter or, worse, shot as a traitor. And you would really be shot this time, just as you almost were yesterday."

"We won't be caught," Tetsu says confidently. "I have connections on the island. Arch, you have two alternatives and not much time to make your choice. Kill me now—I won't resist—or desert with me tonight."

CHAPTER 16

❁

Darkness wanes and the landscape begins to change. I can see a little farther ahead, not just what is immediately in front of me. This time of morning is mystical. The brief span between night and day is like coming out of the water after skinny-dipping in a stream. I emerge from the stream, scramble up on dry land, water streaming from my body and feel a new beginning.

The night turning to day is what I think baptism by immersion is supposed to be—going under the water, closing one's eyes and being enveloped in darkness, then emerging from the water, pure and free of sin and into the light of God.

I expected that feeling when I was baptized in a tank in front of the whole church when I was 10 years old. The baptism was all wrong. I was forced backward, and, while I struggled to regain my balance, the preacher kicked my feet out from under me and said, "Get with it, kid. I have 15 more to dunk before lunch."

It was terrifying. Still, the minister, like Jesus, eventually did bring me back from fear and darkness into the light, while all the congregation praised the Lord and said, "Hallelujah!"

In my present situation, light is danger, darkness offers more protection. In the daylight, we must find places to hide where we won't be seen by the enemy. We continue to hide until, once again, we are given some protection by the darkness.

War turns everything upside down. We've always been taught that darkness is sin, light is right. "I am the light of the world," says Jesus. "Let there be light," says God.

Now light is a problem. But so is darkness. Even though the latter affords some protection, night in a foxhole can be pure hell and terror. Besides the threat of an attack, on the ground or from the air, a night in a foxhole also is a time for asking questions.

I used to pray, "Now I lay me down to sleep. I pray the Lord my soul to keep." Now I ask, what soul? Who is this Lord to keep my soul when I don't even know what a soul is?

"If I should die before I wake…." Let's face it. While that's quite possible tonight, it certainly wasn't likely when I was taught the prayer as a boy of four.

"I pray the Lord my soul to take." Again, who the hell is this Lord I'm asking to take my soul? What would he do with my soul? Where would he take it? And would I ever see my mother and father again?

It's when I am all alone in a foxhole at night that I come face to face with my inner-self. It is then that the questions come.

Everyone but me is asleep. I'm on guard. I must keep a cigarette going and be super vigilant, eyes sharp, hearing acute. I must protect not only myself but also my sleeping comrades.

I can't see anyone in my foxhole or in any of the other foxholes. All I can do is count the objects on my perimeter. If the number is unchanged, nobody is out there.

My thoughts are interrupted by a star-shell lighting the area. I freeze. Darkness returns. I return to my "self."

One side of me that I never knew before is the violent one, which causes me to function so much differently than I would if either the intellectual or emotional sides were in control.

My violent side is able to kill, and I have discovered that the killing gives me an emotional high such as I have never felt before. This blood lust, deep within me, is especially strong after I've seen my closest friends die at the hands of the enemy. At such times, I could kill any Jap in sight and enjoy doing it.

My emotions while in combat are a blend of fear, hate, excitement, and the confusion created by close visual and physical contact with the enemy. The latter makes taking a life an orgiastic experience. This is the side of me that hates, that wants revenge, that wants to kill. This is the side of me that is blood-thirsty, that uses wild profanity, that delights in slaughter and destruction.

At such times, I talk and act much the way Jake did before the banzai attack in which he was killed. Jake showed the side of me that could cut off a man's penis and shove it into his mouth. I have seen men do this and seen that they enjoy it.

This is the side of me that could emulate Jake by collecting teeth— but only the ones that have gold in them. Jake taught me how to break a dead man's skull with a rifle butt, split the bone around the teeth, crack the teeth out of their sockets in the fractured bone, and keep the teeth and the gold. The keepsakes are placed in a special bag that the soldier always carries with him.

This is the part of me that could cut the ears from dead bodies with a razor-sharp bayonet and put them in a leather sack, just as warriors of old did to prove how many of the enemy they had killed.

Jake took satisfaction in cutting off ears. I remember John telling us one time about the origin of the practice of sending home souvenirs of bones and skulls taken in war.

This is moral? This is war?

After I see Lee, Cook, Jake, John, and Jose murdered, I want to kill any Jap I encounter. How the killing is accomplished is not important. It can be with a grenade, a bullet, or a sharp bayonet.

They kill us. We kill them. They are dirty, rotten creatures—foul, immoral sub-humans. They are lousy, contemptible beings, unworthy of life. They are sordid, vile, inferior animals. They deserve to be tortured and killed.

I'm not proud that I have such savage, uncivilized feelings. After a battle is over, the rush is gone and exhaustion takes over. Then I feel remorse, shame, and a terrible guilt. How can I reconcile these sharply different sides of my inner-self?

My intellectual side is in command when I am able to reason that war is a return to our animal mentality.

The culture that over the years has been embedded in my mind has given way to a divided morality:

The only answer to war is love your enemies.

The only answer to war is to pray for those who spitefully use you.

The only answer to war is "thou shalt not kill."

The only answer to war is to treat one's neighbors as we ourselves would want to be treated.

"To be or not to be...whether it is nobler..."

How thankful I am to my high school English teacher, R. B. Westmacott, for his introduction to the world's great writers.

And, of course, words Wilfred Owen wrote after World War I, along with the words of Sassoon, are always with me, as well as the words in Shakespeare's *Macbeth* and *Julius Caesar*. All are contained in the books in John's pack.

When John saw a dead enemy he would call out to me, "Fey."

The first time we saw a face all shot up, he said it looked like a "gargoyle."

"What in hell does that mean, John?" I asked.

"Arch, you don't know what a gargoyle is? A gargoyle is a grotesquely carved head projecting from a roof gutter in the Middle Ages in France. Stick around me, Arch, and we can learn lots of great stuff even if I don't have many books."

I can still hear John's reciting Wilfred Owen's poem, "Dulce Et Decorum Est." I repeat to myself Owen's words. They tell how I feel:

> *Bent double, like old beggars under sacks,*
> *Knock-kneed, coughing like hags, we cursed through sludge,*
> *Till on the haunting flares we turned our backs*
> *And towards our distant rest began to trudge.*
> *Men marched asleep. Many had lost their boots*
> *But limped on, blood-shod. All went lame; all blind;*
> *Drunk with fatigue; deaf even to the hoots*
> *Of tired, outstripped Five-Nines that dropped behind.*
>
> *Gas! Gas! Quick, boys!——An ecstasy of fumbling,*
> *Fitting the clumsy helmets just in time;*
> *But someone still was yelling out and stumbling,*
> *And flound'ring like a man in fire or lime...*
> *Dim, through the misty panes and thick green light,*
> *As under a green sea, I saw him drowning.*
>
> *In all my dreams, before my helpless sight,*
> *He plunges at me, guttering, choking, drowning.*

I see again the Japanese lieutenant I killed and watched die in front of my hole, and I remember going through his uniform pockets, where I found pictures of what almost certainly were his mother, wife, and little daughter. Lee was with me then.

When my emotions are strong, I re-live kneeling by Cook's body and mopping the tears as they ran down my face. I see Lee make the sign of the cross and I pray. I can't recall much of what I said. I do know it wasn't any prayer I learned at home.

If in some smothering dreams you too could pace
Behind the wagon that we flung him in,
And watch the white eyes writhing in his face,
His hanging face, like a devil's sick of sin;
If you could hear, at every jolt, the blood
Come gargling from the froth-corrupted lungs,
Obscene as cancer, bitter as the cud
Of vile, incurable sores on innocent tongues,——
My friend, you would not tell with such high zest
To children ardent for some desperate glory,
The old Lie: Dulce et decorum est
Pro patria mori.

This is where my whole body revolts, where I puke up my guts, shit my pants, and piss down my leg after mortally wounding my first enemy and then watch him die—a human, a man, a father, a son, a boy. Just like me.

When my emotions are in control, I see once more the new replacement—just a kid—whose remains we put in a ration box and carry down for the body truck to pick up.

I remember when Jose received letters from home and went down the hill, far away from us, so he could cry as he read. Jose died because he couldn't kill the Jap who killed him.

I confront these memories in the foxhole at night when I am alone. I sure miss John in this foxhole tonight.

I look ahead at the body crawling in front of me. A Jap. No, Tetsu isn't a Jap. He's a young man caught in the dilemmas of war, just like me. He's my friend. We want to live, to be brothers.

We have been moving since about 0230—silently crawling, making steady progress. We're traveling northeast toward Yonabaru, where Tetsu says he has connections. Now we must find a hiding place to give us protection when it is daylight again, one that can't be seen from the muddy jeep road to our left. We have been following that road, but keeping our distance from it since shortly after leaving my foxhole.

It is the same road I walked down when I rejoined my outfit a short time ago. We are far enough back from the fighting front so that there should be no patrols in the area.

When it is night again, we can emerge from the dark like bats and continue our journey.

We come across a shell crater, partly covered with debris from a demolished house. The crater is open on the downhill side, so it is not full of water. We can sit up and not be seen. And, by pulling some thatch from the destroyed roof over our heads, we are protected from the weather.

The four cans of rations in my pack and a canteen of water are all the food and drink we have. We divide half our food and save the rest. We eat and take turns sleeping in three-hour shifts. There's no reason to count the objects on our perimeter because we can see everything in the daylight.

This is my first guard duty in a hole with an enemy soldier. It seems strange to protect a Japanese soldier and then to rely on him to protect me.

About four in the afternoon, Tetsu awakens me and points toward the road. About 400 beat-up infantrymen are heading down the road. Their fatigues are torn, their faces and beards caked with mud and dirt. They walk like robots. In their eyes is that far-away look I know so well. They pay no heed to the devastation around them. The dead—both U.S. and Japanese—lie where they fell.

The ground is pocked by hundreds of shell holes. The remains of humans and of dead farm animals give off a stench. Destroyed farmhouses yield no sounds.

From our shell hole, I see these men coming back off the lines—just as Lee and Cook and John and Jake and I did—plodding through the stinking mud, stagnant water and skeletons of burned trees. They are going back to the reserve area, just as we once did. But they will not recover as readily as the land, now poisoned by the rotting bodies and human waste left behind by two armies.

Two of the soldiers run to the side of the road and drop their pants to relieve themselves. What comes out is pure liquid. I know the feeling.

The whole company halts for a break.

"I hope they get better," Tetsu says of the two soldiers.

"A lot of our men just shit themselves to death," I reply.

"It's a diarrhea called dengue fever, which can be very serious," Tetsu says.

Watching these men pass, I am reminded of T.S. Eliot's poem about "the hollow men."

"What is this poem, Arch?" asks Tetsu.

"It's in John's book," I answer.

Reaching into my pack, I pull out John's book and read the poem.

"These men are going into battalion reserve where they'll get better food, medical treatment and some real rest before returning to the front," I say. "Maybe the battle will be over before they are sent back to the front."

The soldiers start up the side of the road toward us to find a place to lie on the muddy, wet ground and rest. Four of them come up the side of our shell crater and stop less than 10 feet away. We are quiet, hardly breathing, hoping they won't spot our shelter. We can hear them talking.

"I'd sure as hell like a cold beer," one says.

"All I want is some peaceful sleep," says another.

"I never thought I'd come out alive," says still another, adding, "It isn't the same bunch of guys we went up with. We left a bunch up there this time. I wish they were still with us. I miss Joe."

I'm sure they will see us and we will be taken prisoner. But after about 20 minutes they start down the road again. We once more are safe and alone.

I remember when I went on reserve—tired, dirty, unshaven, and foul smelling. We passed a group of replacements on their way to the front. How young and clean they looked. When they went by, not a word was spoken between us.

Tetsu and I drink some water from the canteen and wait for darkness to fall.

"What's our goal for tonight, or is that in your plan?" I ask.

"We should make Yonabaru. I hope to arrive in the early morning at my uncle's home. He lives toward the hills on the west side of the town, if he's still alive and the house still exists."

We start moving again when it grows dark. Without incident, we reach the home of Tetsu's uncle early the next morning.

Exhausted, we sack out in the yard behind the house. I awaken to the sound of birds. The sun is up and it is warm, not raining. In the backyard, a stream several-feet deep runs through a garden. Hills rise behind the house, and on a nearby hillside there is a Greek omega-shaped tomb.

The garden and outbuildings are bordered by hedges of sea hibiscus. It is obvious that similar bushes once had surrounded the entire house. But many have been mangled and crushed by the artillery, grenades, and rifle fire that leveled most of the town.

Behind the garden of carrots, cabbage, and sweet potatoes (called kamodes) are two enclosures—a pen for pigs and a stable for goats. Chickens peck at the boards of the two shelters. All that remain of the livestock are a single nanny goat and two half-grown pigs. It is obvious that while our men were here, they had fresh meat.

Near the house—sheltering a well—is a half-destroyed banyan tree, its many long aerial roots growing into the ground. The well is surrounded by a stone wall. Here, in better times, farmers could sit beneath the fronds of a fan palm while a cooling breeze blew off the stream on a hot day.

There is something familiar about the place—the well, the masonry bench atop the lip of the well, the small hand-made winch used to wind the rope and pull up the water. Have I been here before? Or is it another of my dreams?

Tetsu awakens and says we must go inside the house because it is not safe outside. We enter by the back door with our meager belongings. It is a typical small Okinawan farmhouse, with a thatched pyramidal roof and walls (called wattle) of interlaced rods and sticks.

There are two windows, both broken. The main hall is spacious with an earthen floor and patches of baked, colored-clay tiles. Mats and a jar of water, for foot-washing, are nearby. Beyond the hall is a large room with a wooden floor and screen dividers. Rushes and thin mats are spread on the floor. A charcoal-cooking hearth is set in one corner. Above it is a cupboard containing a few dishes and cooking utensils.

Bedding and sleeping mats, with matching head rests, are neatly arranged behind the screens. A simple family shrine (Buddhist or Shinto) stands in the corner across the room from the hearth. This neat, rural Okinawan home is to be my refuge.

An elderly gook sits beside a small stove, burning wood since no charcoal is available.

Tetsu introduces me. "Arch," he says, "this is my Uncle Aoki, my mother's brother."

Aoki looks at me and I at him. Suddenly he jumps up and runs toward me and throws his arms around me saying words I cannot understand. Then he starts to cry.

Tetsu stands there, saying nothing. The old man is shaking with emotion. Tears stream down his sun-hardened and wrinkled cheeks.

Tetsu breaks the silence. "Arch, my Uncle Aoki is saying thank-you and letting you know he will do anything he can for you. You didn't burn his house, and you saved his life once."

I can hardly believe what I'm hearing. I knew there was something familiar about the house. No wonder it stirred thoughts of Lee and

Cook. This is the old man we met outside his house, the one who entertained us in his garden, giving us sake to drink in a toast to peace.

I tell Tetsu how Aoki pleaded with us not to set fire to his house.

And then I say, "Tetsu, this is unreal. I remember your uncle seemed more concerned about his house and things than about his own life. Do you know what he did that day?"

And then I tell him about how Lee, Cook, and I, sitting around the well in back, joined in drinking his uncle's sake and toasting peace and how we returned to our squad that evening very happy.

Uncle Aoki, with tears in his eyes, motions us to follow him. We go out the back door and walk down the little path toward the well, where he says (Tetsu's translation):

"Fan palm trees purify the water. Water passing through their roots is made sweet and good. That is why you must always have a fan palm next to the well. It is said if we wash with water filtered through the roots of the fan palm, we will come out of the water a new person, compassionate and good.

"The war has destroyed most of my fan palms and most of my banyan trees, but the roots are still purifying the water and we must wash in this water to return to peace."

We sit on the wall of the well in the garden where I once sat with Lee and Cook.

Uncle Aoki says, "In ancient times when soldiers came home from war and killing, the priest of the village would take them out to water purified by the fan palm. He would wash the soldiers in the pure water to cleanse them of the blood on their hands."

Then he adds, "I would like to wash your hands, faces and feet with the water, if you would allow me."

Uncle Aoki then lowers the bucket into the well and brings up purified water. After washing our feet and faces, he says, "I am sorry I do not have new clothes for you."

Then, speaking directly to me, he asks, "Why did you not bring your two friends, Arch? I want to thank them for not taking my life."

"Lee and Cook were killed," I answer.

The three of us sit in silence....

I notice that the garden, even though everything shows the ravages of war, has been carefully tended and there's not a weed in sight. I like that. I love a well-kept garden. Uncle Aoki goes into the house and returns with rice cakes and cups. He uses the winch to bring up the large teapot from the well. He pours each of us sake. As we eat and drink, he says, "This we do to create peace and end war for us. I honor you two friends."

I feel that for the second time in my life I have been baptized in peace and have partaken of a real communion.

The first time it was the old man and three U.S. infantrymen. Now it is the same old man, whom I now know as Uncle Aoki, with a Japanese soldier and a U.S. deserter.

Uncle asks the names of my two friends.

"Lee and Cook."

Uncle Aoki repeats their names.

We go inside his house and Uncle kneels before his religious shrine and repeats the names: Lee and Cook.

CHAPTER 17

❀

In the night, my mind is in such a whirl over the day's events that it is impossible to sleep. While Tetsu and his uncle sleep, I get up quietly and walk out the back door.

I make my way in bare feet to the stone bench that circles the well. Moon and stars are bright in a cloudless sky. My heart pounds, a mixture of guilt and fear. I am a deserter. If captured, I could be shot.

I could have murdered my friend and been a hero. Now I could die because I spared his life.

I re-live the banzai attack. I am firing to protect Jake. It is terrifying man-to-man combat. Lee and Cook are in the next hole fighting for their lives. I hear Cook scream. The side of his face—the side next to me—is destroyed. The same old question arises again. Did I fire too far his way? Did I shoot off the side of his face? Did I kill him?

I'll never be able to go home again. I'll never see the U.S. again. Today my life changed. My beliefs have been turned upside down, or right side up. I'll never again be the Arch my friends and family knew. What would Lee and Cook think of me now?

Both sides in the war are victims of a wrong policy. Trying to solve violence with violence is hopeless. I don't want Americans to die. I don't want Japanese to die.

How can the conflict in my mind be resolved? I must have peace with myself before I can have peace with others. I cannot kill again.

I slowly and quietly return to bed. I fall asleep quickly, pushing aside my guilt and hoping I eventually can bury my shame.

CHAPTER 18

❁

Along with several of Uncle Aoki's friends, we sit on the floor of the Aoki home one evening discussing a plan of escape.

We sit on mats in the center of the room, because sitting and sleeping on the floor are as natural to Okinawans as breathing.

Water is warming in a small fire in the earthenware stove. Wood keeps the fire going, although it is very scarce.

I expect tea. Instead, Uncle Aoki brings out a package of Nescafe, stolen from army rations. Tetsu translates, "Uncle says, Arch, that he apologizes to you that he has no tea."

Later, Uncle makes a great vegetable dinner for us, consisting of boiled sweet potatoes and cabbage. These vegetables are straight from Uncle Aoki's garden, not stolen from the U.S. Army. Even better, the food is hot. There are no artillery shells crashing around us and no snipers' bullets kicking up dirt while we eat.

Uncle Aoki, a venerated community leader, can arrange almost anything with the people of Yonabaru. And he is trying to arrange for his nephew and me to be given one of the few fishing boats in Yonabaru to survive the massive U.S. naval bombardment, followed by our army's scorched-earth policy.

Tetsu gives me a little background. When the bombardments began, many residents of Okinawa fled to the south and collaborated with the Japanese. Others stayed behind, and, because most Okinawans never cared much for the Japanese, went to work for the Americans or set about rebuilding their homes.

Both sides hope to wind up with the winner. Is there going to be a victor?

The Americans gave the boats back to Okinawans even before the island was declared secured. That enabled the fishermen to return to their trade. Of course, with the young men taken away to serve in the Japanese Army or in work regiments organized by the Japanese, it is the old men who are doing the fishing.

The fishing vessels leave early in the morning, before daylight, heading out to the fishing banks north of the island. At dawn, the fishermen go around the battleship *New Mexico*, anchored in Nakagusuku Bay, the same ship I saw hit and disabled by two kamikaze planes.

Okinawans are among the world's great fishermen. Besides bringing in fish every day, they also have become adept at appropriating food intended for U.S. troops. They cleverly pilfer a few cases here, a few cases there, never enough to warrant any full-scale reprisals or too much concern about security.

Those who work for the Americans are careful not to antagonize their benefactors. They work hard and follow directions. They are paid in occupation money, food, and fuel for their stoves and boats. The situation differs little from my boyhood in Anacortes, Washington, during the Great Depression. Those who were out of work rode the rails looking for jobs, sometimes begging for food. My grandfather Andy kept a pile of railroad ties back where he tethered the horses. When "bums" came to the door in search of food, he would put them to work cutting railroad ties with two-man crosscut saws. Then they had to split the wood and stack it before there was any food. When they worked well, Andy let them sleep overnight in the barn.

Uncle Aoki's closest friends, men and women, worked for several days to arrange for one of the locals to give up his fishing boat for the escape of a Japanese soldier and an American deserter.

The people are fascinated by an American wearing Okinawan clothing who must have the Japanese soldier speak for him.

We burn most of our army clothes. We assemble our equipment at Uncle Aoki's home, sitting up late to work out our plans with the help of uncle's friends. Sometimes, when there is not time for translating, I see them just look at me and laugh.

The evening before we are to leave, Uncle Aoki tells Tetsu he's going to have a few people in for a send-off party. He and Tetsu use the cardboard from army supply boxes to cover the spaces where the window glass has been broken. This prevents light and noise from attracting the attention of U.S. military police who sporadically patrol the town.

Tetsu cleans the house and takes the mats outside, beating them with a flexible bundle of branches until they are dirt-free. He dusts the walls and scours the cooking area. He brings in scented wild flowers from the hill.

That night, he prepares a feast from "liberated" army C rations, along with raw fish steeped in Okinawan sauces. Uncle apologizes because he has no fruit.

Three couples arrive quietly. One of the women carries a large bag. Her husband has brought what looks like a banjo case. We sit in a circle, on woven straw mats, with a single lamp for light. The couple who brought the case and bag go behind a screen while Uncle Aoki begins serving:

The feast begins with a very special tea served in beautifully decorated china cups.

After a short time, the young lady appears from behind the screen in a traditional Okinawan costume. She is beautiful. Tetsu tells me her clothing is not a costume, but is very old and was used in bygone days for special rituals.

Tonight's ritual honors the two of us and asks for our protection as we begin our long voyage to Japan in the Okinawan fishing boat.

In the past, there would have been many girls in classic dress dancing to the music of the Shamisen. The people of Yonabaru, as elsewhere, have hidden their prized possessions in tombs for safekeeping during the war. We are honored that they chose to bring them out tonight.

I look more closely at the clothing worn by the beautiful young woman. The kimono is of heavy silk, with scarlet and violet hand-painted lining depicting early Okinawan mythology. Around her waist is an obi, a thick tapestry sash, with gold and silver threads woven into the cloth. Her tabi-style socks are painted with historical figures. Her elaborate headdress sparkles with depictions of gods embroidered in bright gold and silver threads.

"Tetsu, I have seen pictures in school books that are similar to this costume," I say, marveling at how much this beautiful young lady, in her fine clothes, resembles the photograph of the wife of the Japanese lieutenant I killed on Sky Line Ridge.

I think again of what happened on the ridge. Of Lee, Nealey, and John. It seems so long ago. I am brought back to reality by the sound of music. The husband of the beautiful woman has opened the case and taken out a three-stringed instrument resembling a guitar. His wife dances and sings delightful old ballads, based on stories of Okinawan mythology, on birth, life, marriage, and death. While she sings and dances, we all sit quietly and sip our tea.

There is a rap on the door. I look at Tetsu. He points to the bedding piled behind the screen. I quickly move there, hiding under the bedding. Tetsu, wearing fisherman's clothing, goes to the door and opens it. There stands a towering Army M.P., who asks in an unmistakably Southern accent, "What's going on here?" Tetsu replies in sign language and one word of English, "Birthday." The M.P. responds, "A birthday! Wonderful! Happy birthday!" He shakes Tetsu's hand, waves, and leaves.

Uncle serves a ceremonial meal of fish, rice, rice-flour cakes, and stolen army rations. Everyone bows to us and wishes us well. We pray for peace before the family shrine. The guests quietly leave the celebration, returning to their partially repaired homes—homes I had helped burn.

The three of us—Uncle Aoki, Tetsu, and I—sit in a circle after the guests depart to listen to family history. Tetsu interprets for me.

Aoki begins, "I am the oldest of the family. We lived on a little farm on the edge of Shuri, about a mile-and-a-half from the castle. Our house had a red-tile roof and more rooms than this one. We had nice wooden floors in most of the rooms and a baked-tile floor in the living room. Outside, we had a beautiful garden.

"The fields my father and we boys worked were some distance from the house. One large field was in a valley where we had enough water to grow rice. We grew sweet potatoes and other vegetables on the hillsides, which were terraced down to the valley. Higher up, on the sides of the valley, were pastures where the animals grazed."

"Would that be goats?" I ask.

"Yes, and horses," he replies.

"When we were trying to hide in what we call foxholes in this area, the goats would come over to nudge us," I say, explaining my question. "The animals were friendly, but it bothered me since they could give away our position. We often shot them for food."

Aoki continues his story:

"Father and we two older boys went to the fields each day while our younger brother and our mother took care of the home, garden, and animals. My mother and father were so happy to tell us that we now were going to have a little sister or brother. The sister came to our family in due course and was a joy to us all. The sister is Tetsu's mother. She went to school in Japan and met a young man who, after their marriage, became Tetsu's father. They now live in Hiroshima.

"I can remember when Tetsu used to come and stay for the summer and work on the farm with my father, mother, my wife, and me. My two brothers also went to school in Japan and did not come home to work. I remained here to help my father and mother. But after I married, I lived in the house of my wife's mother here in Yonabaru.

"What happened to the farm, your mother, father, and wife?" I ask.

Aoki answers: "Before the war, there was a sickness that went through the island. My mother died. My father, Tetsu's grandfather, remained in their home near Shuri until it was destroyed in a bombardment. My father and my wife then fled south with most of the people of this area. I do not know if they are dead or alive. I hope they are safe in some cave in the south of the island and will surrender soon.

"I am going to remain here and work for the Americans and try to stay alive a little longer. I am pleased to be able to help you. All we want and pray is that this killing will stop and peace will return to our island. I hope the family tomb near Shuri is still intact, because if anything happens to my father, I want him to have a proper resting place with his people."

"I hope so, too," I say.

I ask Tetsu's uncle to tell me about the family tomb. "Is it like the one up the hill behind your house?"

I listen until well into the night as the old man explains, through his nephew's translation, the ancient burial rites of his people.

"The rich people bestow far more time and wealth upon their family tombs than on their earthly abodes. These graves are really great vaults, built above ground or into the sides of hills. The tombs of the higher class, the wealthy people, are in the shape of the Greek omega, while those of the common farming people have straight pitched roofs.

"When a person dies, the body is placed in a squatting position in a small tub or metal pan, with the hands tied around the knees and the head tilted forward. The burial ceremony is performed in an area paved with stone in front of the tomb.

"After the ritual, the burial tub is placed in the tomb and the door is walled up with stone and mortar. Over the next three years, prayers are said and offerings are made at the entrance to the vault. At the end of that time, the tomb is opened and the remains are taken out.

"The women of the family have the honor of preparing the bones for permanent burial. Using special chopsticks, the women remove any remaining flesh from the skeleton. After the bones are cleaned and carefully washed with alcohol, they are packed in ornate earthen jars and placed in chronological order on shelves within the tomb.

"We honor our dead and believe their spirits have an influence over our lives. They give us advice and counsel, and we can ask for their help in time of need."

As Aoki speaks, I can see that our use of the tombs as pillboxes and places of refuge is a desecration of the Okinawan people's ancient myths and beliefs. On the other hand, in clearing the tombs and thus destroying bones of the Okinawans' ancestors, we may have saved some of our soldiers' lives.

Meanwhile, the fishing boat and supplies have been secured. The vessel, about 22 feet long, is like a Chinese junk, with a small sail forward and a larger one midship. A vaulted, semi-circular roof covers the area between the two masts. It not only protects the supplies, but also provides enough room for the two of us to have shelter from rain and sun.

The boat has the smallest outboard motor I have ever seen—a Yanmar one-cylinder engine with a drive shaft that extends both fore and aft. The aft shaft drives the propeller while the forward shaft has a pulley with a lever to engage the bilge pump.

The supplies are carefully stowed: U.S. Army blankets, ponchos, cases of C rations and 10-in-1 rations, a pair of army binoculars, dried fish, sweet potatoes, rice, fishing gear, and bait. Jerry cans of fresh water are placed on each side, midship, and jerry cans of gasoline for the engine are stashed in the stern.

A compass, clock, and map are our only navigation instruments.

Our plan is to get underway early in the morning with 14 other fishing boats. We will be part of the usual flotilla leaving before daybreak, heading for fishing grounds north of the island. We intend to stay with the fleet until well out of range of air patrols, which fly mostly over the southern end of the island. When we feel safe with no one to observe us, we will put up our sails, hoping for favorable winds to help us conserve our precious fuel as we head north to the next island.

Early in the morning, I put my pack into an Okinawan basket. I burn the rest of my U.S. Army clothes, even my olive-drab underwear. I don't have anything left that is army issue or stamped with my serial number. My dogtags have never been replaced, so there is no way anybody can find out who I am unless I tell them. I can tell anyone anything I wish. I am a deserter with no identity; I am going to try to pass as a civilian, a gook. I hide my pistol, ammo, and flags in the basket. I load six rounds of ammo into my revolver, leaving the chamber empty, and put it where I can get my hands on it at any time. Tetsu has already stored my M-1 rifle with ammo aboard the boat.

Tetsu calls, "Arch, are you ready? Let's go."

I shout back, "I'm on my way."

Telling Uncle Aoki goodbye with tears and hugs and bows, Tetsu and I go with the fishermen down the makeshift docks to our boat. The wives of the men go to the beach, as they have for centuries, seeing their husbands off to the sea.

It is amazing how well our Okinawan friends have prepared our boat, our home at sea for the next ten days. I know the risk they have taken. First, in "liberating" supplies from the U.S. Army, then in sacrificing from their few possessions to see that we're provided for.

I notice, upon going aboard, a gasoline stove just like the ones we had in our squad. At that moment, one of the fishermen bows to me and speaks to Tetsu. All is ready. We are prepared to depart.

Daylight is just beginning as the engines of all the boats start. The Okinawans wave to each other as the flotilla leaves and heads toward the

U.S. battleship *New Mexico*. As we pass the bow of the great ship, the sailors on watch wave to us. They see the fishing boats every morning and have no idea that a U.S. Army deserter is leaving for Japan this morning. The fishing boats keep close together as usual.

Rounding the old battleship, I see the damaged stern with gaping holes where the kamikazes hit the deck. The night it happened is still vivid in my memory. I remember Cook and me standing on Skyline Ridge, seeing all the smoke, the men in the sea, and the destruction.

I wonder how many were lost. I mean killed, drowned, burned, blown to pieces. Memories of my own lost comrades fill me with sorrow.

As we travel north along the coast, we can see the hills I know so well. At this distance, reality undergoes a transformation. How different they look from the water. How pastoral and peaceful the countryside looks from here—I could be passing any island in the world. What a seemingly small impact we have on the earth.

Surveying the terrain with binoculars, I can see many tombs in the hillsides. I mention this to Tetsu, telling him about the way we had used the tombs.

"Arch," he says, "let me tell you more about the tombs, the ones Uncle told you about last night. Interestingly, they are constructed like a womb. If burial rituals are done properly, we believe the spirits of ancestors will return to their surviving relatives to give direction to their lives. This may differ from the Christian religion in that the people who are now alive have a sense of belonging to an ongoing past, present, and future. However, change is occurring, and today some Okinawans are leaving the old traditions and accepting more contemporary burial, like cremation.

"In addition to these religious notions of immortality, I was taught in medical school, later, that we will someday find a protein in our reproductive cells that is passed on from one generation to the next through egg and sperm. I believe that is the reason our ancestors' spirits are still with us. Who knows? This could be the substance of eternal life. One of my professors believed we are close to discovering this protein in the nucleus of our cells. Its discovery will unlock a lot of the mysteries of life."

"I don't really understand," I say.

In the next hour, Tetsu teaches me about human reproduction. He describes the stages, the descent of the egg from the ovary, through the fallopian tube into the uterus. The ascending sperm unites with the egg. Cell division occurs, and an embryo is created. He talks as I imagine a doctor would talk in front of a class. I hear in his voice a seriousness that shows respect for the complexities underlying the words.

We continue on our journey for several hours until we reach the fishing banks where the boats gather in a circle. As we leave, everybody waves, just as they would back home in Yonabaru.

Tetsu and his deserter American friend head north along the Ryukyu Islands, toward, we hope, Tetsu's home in Hiroshima. We keep the engine going for the next half-hour before putting up the sails to conserve fuel.

CHAPTER 19

We are out of sight of the town of Hedo, on the northern tip of Okinawa, after just a few hours. I don't know what name to give the sea we're sailing on. The East China Sea is to the west, the Pacific Ocean to the east; nevertheless, out in open water with no land in sight, there are no dividing lines.

There's not a ship, boat, aircraft or anything in sight: all that exists is a circle of blue water about eight miles in diameter, the sun hovering overhead, and a little Okinawan fishing boat making its way north.

There is no war, except in our memories. And those memories are far to the south, fast fading over the horizon. There is no danger of being shot, taken prisoner, or being identified while escaping. There are no guard duties, no foxholes in which to seek protection, no perimeters with landmarks, no artillery sounding overhead, no fire from small arms or machine guns, no dead bodies, no terrifying battle cries, no terrifying battles.

The two of us are alone—a U.S. infantryman, private first class, and a Japanese Army physician, captain, enemies at war yet becoming friends and escaping their war on the open sea.

"How can you tell where we're going?" I ask. "All we have is a compass and that beat-up little map your uncle gave us. We haven't plotted a course the way my dad did when we took our boat to Alaska.

"I remember how we would travel for so many hours and minutes on a particular compass course at a given speed. Dad factored in the wind speed and the direction of the currents with the equipment he had. He was never quite right, but fortunately we had visual contact with the land."

Tetsu replies, "I sailed these waters with my family when I was young and we visited relatives who lived on the islands north of Okinawa. Don't worry, Arch, I'll get us to Yoron Jima. That's our next stop. If the wind keeps up like it is, I predict we'll be landing on Yoron tonight. Maybe, while it's quiet and we're sailing out here on this beautiful sea, I can tell you something of my life and we can get to know each other better."

I reply, "We met in a clump of trees, where you were hiding. You survived when you were supposed to be shot. You gave me two choices—commit another murder, yours, or come with you. I chose to make this journey. Getting to know each other just might change our lives forever, Tetsu.... This situation reminds me of a scene in the book *All Quiet on the Western Front*."

"I've read that book, Arch, in a translation from German to Japanese. What part of the story reminds you of our situation?"

"It's where Paul was out in no-man's land alone trying to get back to his own trenches and jumps into a shell crater to take shelter from a machinegunner. I can imagine a shell crater similar to the ones we know.

"A French soldier taking shelter in the same crater falls over Paul. Paul draws his knife and stabs the man, a reaction to kill the enemy. He describes his anger, how he goes to the far side of the hole and watches the man bleed to death slowly and with a lot of noise. Paul thinks he can run away, but the machine gun sweeps very low to the ground. I recognize what that's like. Paul thinks the French soldier is dead and it is just his body making the terrible noise until Paul sees the soldier trying to lift his head.

"It's like the Japanese lieutenant on Skyline Ridge. Paul goes to the soldier he's stabbed and tries to help him. He bandages the stab wounds of the dying man, then moistens a cloth with water and wipes the soldier's mouth."

"I remember that part," Tetsu interrupts. "Then, after the enemy soldier is dead, Paul talks to the body. I remember, perhaps even memorized, that part. In English, I think it would go something like this:

"I speak to him: 'Comrade, I did not want to kill you. If you jumped into the shell hole again, I would not hurt you if you would be reasonable. But before this, you were only an idea to me, an abstraction that called forth a terrible response. It was the abstraction I stabbed. But now I see you are a man like me. I thought of your weapons—your hand-grenades, your bayonet, your rifle; now I see your wife and your face and our fellowship. Forgive me, comrade. We always understand too late.'"

We are both silent for a long time. Then I tell Tetsu about the Japanese lieutenant on Skyline Ridge. I take the pictures from the lieutenant's wallet. Tetsu studies them, and tears run down his cheeks.

"You know, Arch," he says, "If we survive I think we should both re-read that book. Lew Ayres was the principal actor in the film. After playing the role of Paul, he became a pacifist.... I'm glad your squad wasn't successful in terminating my life or I would never have known you.

"I remember that in medical school we had several lectures on survivor's guilt. The research quoted by the professor was from the treatment of British soldiers in the first World War. The object was to prepare the men to go back to the trenches and do battle to rid themselves of shell shock and guilt. It didn't work. The officers who had 'shell shock' were sent to a hospital in Scotland. There were several rather famous writers who met in a hospital near Edinburgh. One was a poet named Owen. And there was his friend, Sassoon."

"Tetsu, have you read any of their works?"

"Yes, a few of Owen's poems and a little of Sassoon. Why?"

I reach for my pack, find John's books, and show Tetsu the poetry of Owen. He is amazed. Then I tell him what happened to the enlisted men who were afflicted with "shell shock." Those who could not go over the top again were called cowards and weak and were sent to prison. They were left in prison until they begged to go back to the trenches in France.

"We, Arch, are doing the only thing that research shows has any success in the treatment of 'combat fatigue,' the new name for 'shell shock.' That is to get away from battle. The Japanese Army calls the condition 'combat insanity.' They do not tolerate it.

"I would like to look at those books. May I?"

"Any time you want to. If we're going to live together on this little boat and get to know each other better, we had better get acquainted."

"Sounds great, Arch. I'll try my side first, starting with my family, O.K.?

"My father graduated in horticultural design from the University of Kyoto. He and my family live on the estate of the president of a large shipping company in Hiroshima. The home in which I grew up was given to my father as a reward for the beautiful gardens he created there. Father's job is designing and maintaining large estates with Zen gardens for some of Japan's wealthy people.

"He's a kind and considerate man. I think a great deal of him and wish I could be more like him. He has done much for our family and we, his children, respect and appreciate him.

"He speaks some English, as do the others in my family. Mother came from Okinawa, as you know, and attended the university in Kyoto, where she met my father. They were married after graduation. Later she returned to Shuri with her three children for summer vacations. During these visits I developed a close relationship with my grandfather.

"Grandfather taught me much of the history and mythology of the island. I spent every summer after I was six years old with my mother's parents. Looking back, I think those visits with my grandfather were some of the best times of my life. Father would take me on the train to the city of Kagoshima on Kyushu, the southernmost island of Japan. From there, the boat trip down the Ryukyus to Okinawa was a highlight of my youth. The ship stopped at all the coastal towns on the way to Naha, the final destination. There, Grandfather would be at the dock to meet me. We always rode to the farm outside Shuri in a buggy drawn by an old white horse.

"When I was 10, I was able to make the trip by myself. That's how I learned these waters and how to navigate. The ship's navigator, a friend of my mother's family, had lost a son about my age in an accident. The navigator was like a father to me when I was aboard his ship. He taught me how to navigate through treacherous waters, how to read a compass, to understand nautical charts, to plot courses, and, most of all, how to be a good sailor. I've never forgotten those lessons.

"The Ryukyu archipelago stretches in an arc for about 700 miles between Japan and Formosa. Commander Matthew Perry, who came from the United States in the 1850s, forcefully brought western culture and ideas to my people, and he wanted the United States to occupy the major islands as naval bases."

"So that's why you are so confident about where we're going?" I interject.

"Yes, but the real learning for me," Tetsu continues, "was from my mother's father. We spent hours on a hill above the farm, among the broad pines and clumps of sago palms, where the ground was carpeted with wild lilies and gladioluses. Sometimes one of his goats would wander by and nudge us as we sat together.

"Would you be interested in some of the mythology of ancient Okinawa, as I learned it from my grandfather?"

"What could be better while we're out here on this peaceful water?" I reply.

"Okinawa's mythology is a tangle of stories influenced by Chinese, Japanese, and Polynesian cultures.

"Sometime in the distant past, it is said, the Sun Goddess, Amaterasu, descended to a great cave on the island of Iheya Shena just north of Okinawa. She brought light into the darkness of the world.

"It is said, too, that the first Japanese Emperor, Jimmu, was born there without a male antecedent, a direct descendant of Amaterasu. The Emperor would, when he grew up, move north and east to conquer all the Japanese islands."

"That's just like Jesus being born of an Immaculate Conception, except Mary was only a virgin, not a Sun Goddess," I say.

"Wait, Arch, I'm just getting started. On Okinawa and in the central part of the Ryukyus, the Chinese Confucian philosophy, with some Polynesian influences, molded the legends of the Okinawan people. These legends are quite different from the mythology of Japan.

"The way my grandfather told it, the first people came to the island in rowboats. Probably they had been lost in a typhoon. They survived in caves on the Chinen Peninsula, south of Yonabaru, where commemorative worship services still are held every year.

"From a high promontory overlooking one of the caves, you can see a valley bursting with lush vegetation all the way from the rocky cliffs to the ocean. Two springs cascade over the rocks to the valley below and flood the valley in the spring and early summer, Okinawa's monsoon season. This makes it an ideal environment for the island's rice paddies and for cultivating fruits and grains, the kind probably brought by the earliest settlers."

I interrupt again. "The Garden of Eden. But where are Adam and Eve?"

"Patience, Arch, you're getting ahead of me. There's a great coral reef where the marines made a fake landing just before the big invasion. The reef protects the shoreline from storms and forms a lagoon that has an abundance of seafood.

"So, with protection, seafood, and fertile land for growing staples, it is no surprise that the ancient Okinawans commemorated their good fortune in finding the valley by holding a celebration similar to your Thanksgiving.

"But I've gotten a bit ahead of myself. I have the garden before the creation of my ancestors. To bring them on the scene…"

I begin to nod off in the warmth of the afternoon sun and the rhythmic slap of the waves against the hull—a feeling of peace, comfort, and security enveloping me with a gentleness I hadn't known for months….

After a reverie of undetermined length, I slowly open my eyes to see Tetsu, at the tiller, looking straight ahead, almost in his own reverie as he continues to speak:

"…From high on the hill, Grandfather and I would look down on his farm as he recalled his father…how he had loved the crops that moved in the breeze, like gentle green waves on the sea. To the west we could see Shuri Castle, the ancient center of a traditionally peaceful people who followed Shinto. In 1462, some Okinawan representatives returned from China to Shuri Castle with a copy of the Buddhist Canon, an enormous work said to consist of 11,000 volumes. These religious treasures were housed in four temples within the castle.

"The king, who lived in the castle, had been the keeper of sacred religious myths, and now the wisdom of Buddha and Confucius was superimposed over ancient Shinto rituals and assimilated into daily life.

"Still, many legends were passed down by song and by word of mouth. One poignant song I remember hearing at celebrations tells of a beautiful girl in a beautiful valley in northern Okinawa.

"It seems the king paid a visit once a year to her hamlet, just as he did other towns and villages. While there, he lived with the young girl. A song the girl supposedly composed about her relationship with the king is still sung. She tells the wind to be still and the wind to be quiet because the Shuri king has arrived. She falls in love with the king, but her love is unrequited. He leaves her. She throws herself from a cliff.

"The story goes on. At her death, there is a violent storm of thunder and lightning, and rain, even sleet and snow. The Gods accept her spirit. The storm subsides and there is a beautiful rainbow. The rainbow is different. It is broken in the center. The break in the middle of the rainbow is not smooth but jagged. The myth says a rainbow with a jagged break signifies impending tragedy, suffering, and death. The people of Okinawa still look at rainbows today to see if there is a jagged break.

"Shuri Castle was one of the wonders of the Eastern world. Okinawans put their imagination, skill, and wealth into its construction for centuries. It perfectly expressed a mild and generous people, proud of their island homeland.

"The castle grounds were covered with massive trees and beautiful gardens. It was surrounded by walls of cut stone, which were incorporated into the natural rock of the mountaintop upon which the castle sat. There was a moat, wide and deep, in front of the wall.

"The castle's main room was the 'Audience Hall of State,' the seat of government. The hall's concentric walls were beautifully lacquered and gated. Looking out from the hall, one could see the island's largest city, Nara [now Naha], with its active harbor, and Yonabaru, a smaller fishing village.

"Grandfather would take me to the castle for an entire day each summer, explaining its wonders as we walked through beautiful arches and gates, and flowering trees surrounded tranquil pools of water.

"That magnificent ancient masterpiece, which took countless years of technology and sacrifice to complete, was reduced to rubble in a few hours by the 16-inch guns of your battleships, firing from both the China Sea and Pacific Ocean sides of the island."

Tetsu falls silent for a moment before continuing:

"I didn't have the same close relationship with my father's family that I had with my mother's parents. They lived in Kobe and we visited them once or twice a year. Their religion was Zen Buddhism. So I developed a religious philosophy that is a combination of the various ideas I was given by my parents and grandparents.

"My belief system is probably quite different from yours. Maybe on another day at sea we can discuss our religious backgrounds and talk about how the war has changed our beliefs."

CHAPTER 20

✿

In the late afternoon, just a dot on the rim of our encompassing circle of the blue Pacific, land appears to the northeast.

"There it is," Tetsu exclaims. "I'm a little to the west of where I thought I'd be, but we didn't do badly with our little compass and my uncle's old map."

Tetsu points to an island he identifies as Yoron, which he says is about 75 miles north of where we began our voyage early this morning with the fishing boats of Yonabaru.

"There's a little village on the southeast part of the island with good sheltered anchorage," Tetsu says. "It will take us a couple of hours to get there in this light wind. But it should be before dark."

I move to the rail for a better view as Tetsu speaks.

"You know, Arch, I've been very lucky to have experienced two cultures. I learned a bit about yours while living for almost seven years with my father's brother, Uncle Shag, in Los Angeles. That was while I attended USC.

"Uncle Shag runs a large Japanese-food market on Pico Boulevard. He lives in comfortable quarters above the store, which attracts customers—Asian and Caucasian—not only from the west side of Los Angles but also from nearby cities.

231

"My uncle's three children attended UCLA. Los Angeles is a very large city, as you know. It was hard for me the first year, when I was not very fluent in English and was required to speak only Engl: while working in the store. I quickly signed up for English-language classes in night school. Before long I lost most of my accent and began sounding quite American."

"I know a little about L.A. myself, Tetsu. Camp Roberts, north of Paso Robles, is where I took basic training. Going down to Los Angeles on my first weekend pass to visit my uncle and nine cousins in Highland Park was a real adventure.

"While hitch-hiking outside Bakersfield I got stuck. No rides. And it was really hot. I stood on the highway for several hours in temperatures over 100 degrees before hailing a bus ride.

"At the downtown bus terminal I had what my father would call a 'worldly' or 'carnal' experience. I found a telephone and called my uncle to get directions to his home. He told me to walk to Figueroa Street and catch the red car to Highland Park.

"While walking the four or five blocks from the bus depot to the red car stop I met the carnal, sinful side of life—a real education for this little Sunday-school boy."

Tetsu laughs and says, "I know what's coming. I've been in that part of town."

I go on.

"I was approached by pimps, prostitutes, homosexuals, and probably a lot more I didn't even know about. They offered me a multitude of sexual activities. Scared, I almost ran to catch the streetcar. You know, Tetsu, I was just a pretty naive young man. I'd lived a very sheltered life. The only sex I knew about was what the chickens and horses did and what my brother had taught me. That was only last summer. How things have changed.

"When I arrived at my uncle's home, I interrupted their evening devotions. Uncle Bud is a self-educated Pentecostal preacher who received a call from God to go out and spread the gospel. The entire family was on its knees—nine kids, a pregnant girl, a visiting preacher, my aunt and uncle.

"I walked in wearing my uniform and was invited to join in the prayers. They were even more religious than my folks. I was finally given a very emotional greeting by my nine cousins following the devotions.

"The weekend was wonderful. I enjoyed the family, and my aunt was a wonderful cook. Los Angeles is quite a city. I remember that before I left for the Pacific my uncle took me aside and told me to develop a bad leg.

"He said, 'Arch, go on sick call every day with your bad leg. Limp wherever you walk. Fall out when in training. If you complain enough they will have to classify you as unfit for the infantry. Or you could be transferred and maybe given an office job. You could even be designated as 4-F or Section 8 and discharged as unfit for military service. God gave you a head. Use it, Arch.'"

"What's a 4-F, Arch?"

"4-F is a military classification that means you're physically unfit for the army."

"Arch, that would be an untruth. I couldn't do that."

"Neither could I, Tetsu."

"But this Section 8?"

"Oh, that's not good at all. A Section 8 means you are mentally unfit for military service, and that's before you even see combat."

"That's worse yet," Tetsu says, frowning.

I continue:

"I have trouble reconciling war with religion when a preacher tells you to be dishonest so you won't have to serve your country, even to pretending you're insane. At the same time, the church says it's a just war and God is on our side.

"'If God be for us, who can be against us?' is the way I remember it."

Tetsu says, "In both of our cultures we manipulate religion to justify our own ends. I learned in the States that almost all of your religions or denominations—except for the Quakers—talk about a 'just war.' This I can understand only as it relates to our belief.

"Since Shinto—influenced by Buddhism and Confucianism—became the state religion of Japan, our government leaders have used religion to shape the beliefs of our nation's students.

"You have to remember, Arch, that our Emperor is a direct descendant of the Sun Goddess, the giver of life. He is not only a king, but also our pope, our Christ. Like your Jesus, he is the Son of God.

"As for war, Japan believes it is a lover of peace. Peace is the natural ideal, the highest goal of man. But, even though war is not seen as honorable, our religion does not absolutely oppose it when it is undertaken in order to bring about peace.

"We are at war because both Shinto-Buddhism and the Emperor accept war as a necessity to bring about peace. In the schools I attended in Hiroshima, I was taught that Japan advocates peace and racial equality but we, its citizens, must never forget our allegiance to our state, our country, and the Japanese Empire.

"The Emperor is given to us by the Sun Goddess, and through him we exist. He is our state. Real peace cannot be expected if we forget our state, the Japanese Empire, in our love of mankind. If we forget our duty to our country, no matter how we advocate the love of mankind, nature, and the universe, there will be no peace.

"Is that much different than the Western belief and its justification of war for 2,000 years because God is on their side? The countries of the West don't want war, but must wage battle because the enemy is so un-Godly and un-Christian. Christians try to change everybody to their belief, and, failing, they destroy the heathen.

"Among the early English writers that I studied at USC, Jonathan Swift in his 'Gulliver's Travels' makes some wise commentaries on mankind in describing life in Lilliput, Brobdingnag, and Houyhnhnmland. When the Queen asked Gulliver about war on earth, this is what passed between them, as I recall it:

"Queen: 'I can understand war to take someone's land or cattle or money, but you say that is not your worst war. What then is the worst war?'

"Gulliver: 'Oh, the worst wars are religious wars.'

"Queen: 'What are religious wars fought over?'

"Gulliver: 'Over very important issues such as whether a stick of wood be a stick of wood or whether a stick of wood be a cross.'

"The Queen did not understand."

"It's hard for me to understand either the Emperor-based approach or the Christian-centered approach," I say. "Your nation's theology is a philosophy I want to know more about, but it doesn't seem to answer any of my questions about war.

"All I know now is that I am in an ever-continuing present. If it ends, I believe I will be dead like the rest of my friends. That's as far as I can go. I just exist and try to survive in this limbo. I hope to learn more about your culture and Buddhism, but I can't go along with either side's reasons for killing our young men and bombing our cities. To my mind, that can't be justified.

"If I were to be a true Christian and believe the way Christ taught in the Sermon on the Mount, and if you were to be a true Buddhist and work toward enlightenment, we would both be pacifists or be forced to deny our belief in Christianity or Buddhism. If we fought we would be hypocrites."

Tetsu takes his hands from the tiller, shakes his fingers, then repositions them, right over left. He says, "The world's people are suffering; we know that and have witnessed their anguish. But many people are not aware of the suffering of the innocents. They don't know that children are dying from hunger and the ravages of war, that unarmed civilians are being killed from the air. Nor do they realize that if they were born into the other person's culture and religion, they probably would act exactly as he does."

I sigh and say, "You sound as if you've given this a lot of thought. I hope we can get back to this subject again."

I look far out to the Eastern sky and see and hear beyond the approaching island, a large group of B-29 bombers heading northwest from their bases in Saipan and Tinian in the Marianas. The bombers have P-51 fighter escorts from the airfields of Okinawa. We know the planes are on their way to fire-bomb Japanese cities.

To the west the sun is sinking low on the horizon. A sunset glow colors and enhances the scattered puffy clouds. As the sun slips into the ocean, we enter a little harbor, a most welcome sight after a long day in our little boat. We anticipate a warm meal.

As we near the shoreline, a young girl rows toward us. As she draws alongside, she engages Tetsu in a conversation I do not understand. Tetsu turns to me and says, "She asks us ashore to her home for the evening meal and to meet her family. She says they have plenty of food and would like to know where we come from."

"Sounds great, Tetsu! I look forward to the experience."

After anchoring our craft near the beach, we accept her invitation to board her small rowboat for the short row to shore.

We introduce ourselves formally as Arch and Tetsu. She is Tomiko, and she lives with her mother, father, and sister. A brother was taken away by the Japanese to serve in the army. Her father is a fisherman. Her mother has a garden.

"Tomiko is also the name of my sister who lives in Hiroshima," Tetsu says.

As Tomiko makes for the shore, I remark that she rows well for a small girl.

As she pulls the boat out of the water and ties it to a tree, I notice that two P-41s, returning from an escort flight, are flying toward us. They must have spotted us earlier. This time they fly very low and begin firing with .50-caliber machine guns. Without a word, we run for cover, winding up in a ditch.

The planes are close enough for me to glance up and see the faces of the pilots in the cockpits, their fingers on the button that fires the machine guns. The pilot I see most clearly looks to be a year or so older than I am. Like me, his mother and father probably live in some small town back in the States. Why, I wonder, did they go out of their way on a return flight to try to kill us by strafing this little beach?

As usual, Tetsu seems to read my mind.

"I know what you're thinking, Arch," he says, "and you know the answer, don't you? We are the dehumanized enemy. We are no better than the animals hunted on an African safari. In the future, I imagine, hunters will use aircraft in the same way your air force hunts us.

"You, Arch, have become the enemy by taking on a new identity. They can't see that your eyes are not slanted or that your teeth don't stick out."

The planes make a tight circle and return for a second run. This time we have good cover. The planes depart to the south, probably to land at Okinawa's Kadena airstrip, where I saw my first combat with Lee and Cook. A hot meal is waiting. They can brag to their comrades about how they strafed some gooks.

This beautiful Pacific island, with its peaceful fishing village, has been turned into hell. Tomiko is hit but does not cry. She points to her leg and says only that something isn't right.

Tetsu tears his shirt apart to make a tight bandage and says, "I don't think the femur's broken, Arch, but there's a lot of muscle damage. I hope her folks have some medical supplies."

We find a stick and immobilize the leg with Tetsu's shirt. He bandages a bleeding cut on her face. While we carry her up the beach, a man and woman come running toward us. Tomiko identifies them as her parents. Tetsu calms them in an even voice that indicates "the doctor is in charge."

Back at the house, there are good first-aid supplies. Tetsu re-bandages the wounds and says that while Tomiko probably will have a scar on her face and never again will walk as well as she once did, she will certainly survive.

Later that evening we share a fish dinner with the family.

We stay with the hospitable family for the next two days, during which Tetsu shows the parents how to care for Tomiko's wounds.

It is a sad and emotional farewell as we sail away. We see our friends on the beach waving, becoming small and smaller until they finally disappear as we continue our journey north.

CHAPTER 21

❀

Two days should be enough for us to cover the 120 miles to our next island destination, which Tetsu calls Amami O Shima. That's what it sounds like to me. We hope to spend several days there, replenishing our water and adding some fresh vegetables.

We expect to land at Naze, a good-sized town with a fine harbor on the island's northwest coast. A strong wind from the south speeds our journey, but the waves throw spray over the stern and we cover our supplies with a tarp to keep them dry. The tarp has large letters across it, "U.S. Army." Tetsu settles down at the tiller and checks our position on the map and with his compass.

"Right on course," he says. "By my calculations, sometime this afternoon we should pass Tokumo shima, about halfway to Amami O Shima. And if the weather continues to be this good, we will arrive at Naze by noon tomorrow."

We have begun to take on a little water from the spray going over our stern. Fortunately, we have a good bilge-pump attachment for our engine. The trick is to be conservative in using the pump, since our fuel supply is limited. Besides manning the pump, I am also cooking our meals for the day.

I usually sit about midship, looking toward the stern where Tetsu has his hand on the tiller. It is quiet, even when the pump is running.

"Tetsu, since you were on vacation when you returned to Japan from Southern California, how did you end up in the army? If war had not been declared, you would have gone back to Los Angeles for your internship. Did the authorities know you were a doctor?"

Tetsu weighs whether to give a simple reply or to stretch it out a bit. He decides on the latter, since it is a quiet day and we have nothing else to do.

"I told you before that while attending USC I lived over the store run by my aunt and uncle. One of my aunt's brothers lives near Vancouver, British Columbia, and he owns several fishing boats in a small town near the mouth of the Fraser River, south of Vancouver.

"He has done very well financially and the family wanted me to visit him on my way back home to Hiroshima. Traveling north by train up the West Coast, I arrived in Seattle at the King Street Railway Station on the south side of downtown. I was to transfer from there to a Vancouver-bound train."

Surprised once more by the similarities in our backgrounds, I interrupt to say, "Tetsu, that's the same station where I arrived to be inducted into the army."

Tetsu goes on: "When I arrived in Canada, my relatives met me at the train station and we drove to their home. I discovered that the family works at fishing or gardening when time permits, and all my cousins are good students in school or college. It was a wonderful vacation for me. My relatives must have used a month's worth of rationed gasoline to show me the local sights."

Tetsu lists a number of places that I know well, including Vancouver's famous waterfront showplace, Stanley Park, with its giant firs and cedars and magnificent rose gardens. I tell him I went to high school on Burrard Inlet, at the west end of the park.

"You know all the places I was shown, Arch," he says. "It's amazing.

"I had to leave Canada after a week. My vessel was the *Empress of Japan*, a Canadian ship that travels from Vancouver to Yokohama. The whole family came to see me off, helping me carry luggage to my stateroom and taking a tour of the ship. I threw colored streamers to them as the giant ship began to pull away. As the streamers broke and fell into the water, nobody knew what that goodbye signified."

"Tetsu," I ask, "do you know what happened to your relatives after the war broke out?"

"No, Arch, neither I nor my folks have heard from any of our relatives in Canada or the United States since the war began in 1941, at least as far as I know."

"You know we've talked about the hatred in war," I say.

"Yes."

"Well, on the West Coast of the U.S. and Canada, everyone of Japanese ancestry—including those who were citizens—were rounded up and taken by trucks and trains to remotely located internment camps. They had done nothing to earn our distrust, but all had to leave behind their land, homes, and businesses.

"Many of the young men taken to these unofficial 'concentration camps' volunteered for the military. Most are still serving in Europe, but some are out here, too, as translators or in Army Intelligence. I came overseas with a group of Japanese-American wounded veterans, going home to Hawaii. Their units had fought against the Germans in Italy and they were among the most decorated soldiers in the U.S. Army.

"One of the men, I recall, was missing a leg and was resigned to walking with an artificial limb so he could get rid of his crutches and an empty pants leg. Your cousins could be from that unit.

"When the Japanese left the Vancouver area for camps in the interior of British Columbia, I was still in high school. There was nobody left to work in the salmon canneries. My friends and I from high school were recruited to take their place. We'd take the trams out to the cannery at the mouth of the Fraser River.

"I remember one Sunday morning when my good friend Evan and I sat together on a tram. Two well-dressed older ladies were seated in front of us. They opened their window and, by their conversation, we knew they couldn't figure out the cause of the terrible smell nearby. It was us, smelling like fish.

"By the way, Tetsu, how do I smell? I haven't cleaned up since my bath back on the island. I'm wearing clean Okinawan clothes."

"Arch, since you mentioned it, let's clean up."

We get a bucket of sea water to wash ourselves and then tie our clothes to a rope and let the clothes bounce in the water behind the boat. Using an old rag and salt water, we clean up. No soap. No razor. Our beards grow daily. Tetsu's is very black. I can't see what I look like. It's warm so we wait, comfortably naked, as our clothes dry in the sun and wind. When we finally put them on, they are a little stiff from salt water and lighter in color from being bleached in the sun, but we do smell better.

"I can't get my American and Canadian relatives out of my mind," Tetsu says. "I do hope they are OK. It's hard to think they would be badly treated since most are U.S. and Canadian citizens. Is that possible?"

I answer with silence.

As we continue on our way north, I fix us a simple lunch of U.S. Army rations. A heavy cloud cover makes it impossible to see land. But we know that we should be passing Tokuno Shima.

Tetsu continues his story in the afternoon.

"Arriving home in Japan," he says, "I found it a different place than when I left six years earlier. Most of my friends were in military training and those who were not were in some kind of war industry. No one of military age or with a skill that would be needed in the war effort was allowed to leave the country.

"It was only a matter of time until they would induct me into the military. I was able to stay home until September 1941, when I was conscripted into the Army Medical Corps.

"I was stationed in Miyakonojo, on the island of Kyushu in southern Japan. There I worked with other physicians to pre-package a complete field hospital, which was loaded aboard a large supply ship for deployment at any time.

"I had a week's leave at home with my family in November, and it was a sad departure. My sister Tomiko was just out of school and working in a munitions factory and my brother had been accepted into the Air Force Academy. I wondered if I would ever see any of them again.

"After returning to Miyakonojo, we immediately sailed south. Although we were not told our destination, we figured we were heading toward Singapore. You know how it is in the military, Arch. Even though where you are going is supposed to be secret, before long everyone knows where you are going."

"That's for sure, Tetsu. Before Okinawa, when I was on Saipan, there was a big black spot on the map on the company bulletin board from all the fingers touching Okinawa. We all knew where we were going. It was a just a matter of when."

Tetsu continues:

"One of my friends on the ship was Kido, the radio operator. I used to hang out in Kido's radio shack and listen in when he picked up short wave from all over the world. The closer we got to Malaya, the more British radio reports we received from Singapore. Because I knew English, I'd often translate the reports into Japanese for Kido.

"When we entered the Gulf of Siam, southwest of Saigon, we knew our destination was to be Kuantan, about halfway down the Malay Peninsula.

"It was in the shack with Kido shortly after lunch on December 9, 1941 when he picked up a very excited voice, static-free, on the shortwave radio.

"'This is Lieutenant Iki. We are coming out of the clouds at 400 meters. I can see two huge vessels. They must be the battleship *Prince of Wales* and the battle cruiser *Repulse*, both British.'

"Kido and I had intercepted an earlier submarine report that they were in the vicinity."

"Tetsu, the *Prince of Wales* was the pride of the British Navy. A few months before it sank, Churchill and Roosevelt met aboard her, off the coast of Greenland. You know, don't you, that Roosevelt is crippled?"

"Crippled? What happened to him?"

"He contracted polio as a young man. He can hardly walk, even with braces. Most of the time he's in a wheelchair. I wonder how they got him from one ship to another off the coast of Greenland."

"I don't know, Arch, but this is what we heard on the short-wave radio that day:

"'The *Prince of Wales* is hit and I think she is sinking, listing badly and dead in the water. She must have taken torpedoes from the first planes. The *Repulse* is OK and I am dropping down to get her. Over and out.'

"Then we heard:

"'This is base command. Lead your squadron in, Lieutenant. Report as much as you can. Over and out.'

"'I am down to 150 meters, I am now skimming the water at about 40 meters, getting closer and closer to the ship. The *Repulse* is the largest vessel I have ever seen up this close. The sailors are on the deck firing at us. I am releasing my torpedoes. I am pulling up. I can see the wakes of the torpedoes in the water.

"'Direct hit! Direct hit! I can see sailors flat on the deck. Kazu's plane behind me has exploded in a ball of fire.

"'We have scored two more hits on the side of the *Repulse*. I am looking down now. The ship is sinking fast!'

"Then, a little later, 'The bow of the *Repulse* is straight up in the air and the rest of the ship is underwater. It is horrible. It is the worst thing I have ever seen. There isn't a ship in sight. Both ships and over 4,000 men are gone.

"'I am on my way home. This is Lieutenant Iki. Over and out.'

"The whole battle, Arch, lasted less than 10 minutes and the British Navy's two largest ships were gone."

Tetsu falls silent. He adjusts the sail and then resumes.

"We later picked up a report from naval headquarters in Tokyo that went something like this:

"'It is difficult to imagine that two battleships could be eliminated in the open sea at a cost of only four planes. After our success at Pearl Harbor, and now the defeat of the British Navy, we have changed the concept of naval warfare forever.'

"We landed in Kuantan and unloaded the hospital unit. Truckload after truckload of tents, generators, surgical supplies, and operating tables were taken ashore. There was little resistance to our landing. Our troops and equipment moved forward rapidly.

"The field hospital followed in a convoy of trucks with trailers. It was days before we finally set up the hospital, far down the Malay Peninsula.

"We moved so swiftly that we commandeered trucks and bicycles, and any other means of transportation left behind by the retreating English and Indian infantry. There was little or no defense as we proceeded down main roads. We were in such a hurry that when our bicycle tires blew out on the hot pavement, our troops went as far as they could on the rims before leaving the bicycles behind.

"The Indian troops were deathly afraid of tanks, and the noise of the truck and bicycle rims on the roads sounded to them like approaching tanks. They ran as we approached.

"General Yamashita, called the Tiger of Malaysia, led the successful assault on the so-called 'impregnable fortress' of Singapore.

"I, along with three other doctors, came down this main highway with our field hospital in trucks, thinking we would take part in the siege of Singapore. We established our field hospital about the first week of January, 1942, just five miles behind the bridge to the island of Singapore.

"The city of Singapore, if you don't know it, is surrounded by water. It was said to have the strongest fortifications of any city in Southeast Asia. Coastal artillery was positioned in heavy concrete-fortified bunkers, believed to be impregnable. The biggest mistake was that the defenses were aimed out to sea, to defend against a naval attack. Our attack came from the rear, down the peninsula. Singapore didn't have a chance.

"The back-door tactics we used were similar to those employed by the British on the Plains of Abraham at Quebec and by Lawrence of Arabia against the Turks.

"And we took it in a week.

"Our army had had little trouble up to this point and we were able to establish a field hospital with almost no harassment from the British. The other medical doctors had heard the British would make a strong stand at the bridge to the island. We expected them to destroy the bridge by the time our troops arrived.

"Our air force had established an operational airstrip near the hospital and planes constantly took off to bomb the city.

"Our army took a lot of prisoners and established POW camps as we moved down the peninsula. A group of Swiss International Red Cross personnel were captured and placed in the custody of the doctors. The Swiss had been working in the area for some time prior to the war. Our casualties were so light that our hospital was only about half full. We had plenty of room to bring in the more seriously wounded POWs, so we could demonstrate to the Red Cross how well we cared for them. We also gave the Red Cross permission to use radios. But, of course, their broadcasts had to be filed and censored before transmission.

"One afternoon I was sent out with a Red Cross worker to observe a combat area. I was told to impress him with how well we cared for British and Indian POWs. The Red Cross worker was originally from Switzerland, but had lived in Southeast Asia for many years before the war. He spoke excellent English and French. As we approached the combat zone, our infantry was advancing on a squad of British soldiers who had been surrounded. I followed one of the sergeants to a group of tropical trees and undergrowth where they had the enemy confined. We could see several of our aircraft strafing the shoreline of the island to the south. The infantry were firing their weapons and throwing grenades into the trees while calling out for the British infantrymen to surrender."

"That sounds familiar, Tetsu."

"I thought it would, Arch. Well, lying flat on the ground next to the sergeant, I watched the action and didn't see how anybody in those trees could be alive. We finally called a cease-fire. In combing the area, our men found two British boys alive and dragged them out. One had a head wound, the other a puncture wound of his left lung and a broken leg. I quickly controlled the bleeding and the two men were carried on bamboo stretchers back to my ambulance. We had started back to the hospital when six British Buffalo aircraft came lumbering over to bomb our airstrip. Several of our Zeroes were in the air, and one of them was hit. We couldn't see it go down and didn't know if the pilot had parachuted to safety.

"Arriving at the hospital, I saw that the operating room was busy. The other surgical team was busy with the pilot who had, I learned, parachuted to safety but had serious wounds. The POWs would have to wait.

"When the pilot was finally taken to the recovery tent, my team went to work on the British soldier with the lung wound and broken leg. When we finished, we put him in the recovery tent next to the Japanese pilot. The Japanese pilot later asked, 'Is the boy next to me British?'

"I told him that he was, indeed, British, and was now a POW."

"'Can I talk with him?' he asked.

"He doesn't understand Japanese," I said.

"'Isn't there someone who could translate?'

"'Why?' I asked. "'I am Lieutenant Iki,' he said. 'I am the pilot who dropped the torpedoes on the *Repulse*. I want to apologize to the British for what we did. I know this is war, but I will never feel right myself until I let them know how difficult it is to be the one who causes such destruction and death. The morning after I led the planes that torpedoed and sunk those ships, causing the deaths of all those British sailors, I took off in my plane all alone and flew to the place in the ocean where I had last seen the British ships. I dropped down close to the water and dropped flowers. I want this British soldier to know how I feel and the respect I have for their navy.'

"The Red Cross worker took notes of the day's incidents, including the words of Lieutenant Iki, which were broadcast that evening.

"The hospital was across a road from the POW camp and it was my duty to provide medical treatment for the prisoners. The British boy with the damaged lung and broken leg was healing rapidly. The lung would be fine. He would never walk again as he had before, but at least we had saved his leg. I showed him how to do his own physical therapy and he was amazed at my English. I asked him to keep my fluency in the language from the rest of the staff.

"The Red Cross personnel from Switzerland were not allowed to leave. The British soldier—whose name was Gordon—was tall, slender, blue-eyed and just 20 years old. We often discussed philosophy and history in French, which he handled well. In fact, Gordon frequently acted as an interpreter for the Swiss, who spoke French but very little English.

"Gordon told us he lived on Highgate Avenue in north London and had completed his first year at the University of London before entering the army. The Red Cross team was able to let Gordon's family know he was alive and recovering from wounds in a POW camp.

"The day I told him that the Red Cross had notified the British government that he was safe, and that his government would, in turn, notify his parents, he reacted much as you and I would.

"'I can just see the telegraph boy pedaling his bicycle to our second-floor flat,' he said. 'My father will probably answer the door when the telegram is delivered. He will be very worried that I might be dead. Then he will open it and excitedly call my mum. I am alive. For a long time, I presume, all they've heard about me is that I am missing in action.'

"I told him about Lieutenant Iki and how he wanted to talk to him and apologize. He could hardly believe it. We were interrupted by one of the Red Cross team who had a plan for Gordon's escape.

"'Since you speak French so well, we can give you Red Cross clothes and disguise you as a member of our team,' they told him. 'You must speak French and play the role well or we will all be in danger. We have at last been given permission to leave Singapore for Spain. We're scheduled to depart in two or three days. We will let you know.'

"None of my fellow Japanese understood any French, so the Swiss had a good chance of succeeding. Two days after I first learned of the plan, I brought Gordon to the hospital for treatment of his leg. He changed clothes in the X-ray tent, walked out with the Swiss team and headed to the dock in Singapore to board a ship bound for Spain.

"Our Japanese guard didn't miss Gordon for three days. When he discovered what had happened, he was so afraid of being punished for letting a prisoner escape that he told no one. Six months later, I got a letter from the Red Cross worker in Switzerland telling me that Gordon was home safe in London.

"I found a poem written by an anonymous British soldier in the POW camp:

> *A mighty island fortress*
> *The guardian of the east*
> *Impregnable as Gibraltar a*
> *Thousand planes at least*
> *It simply can't be taken*

It'll stand a siege for years
We'll hold the place forever
It will bring the Japs to tears
Our men are there in thousands
Defenses are unique
The Japs did not believe it
And they took it in a week.

"I have kept it. Why, I am not sure."

That evening at sea was without the usual colorful sunset. It also had grown much cooler and there was a stiff breeze from the south.

There has been no sign of Tokuno Shima, and we know the island is behind us now. Tetsu sets our sail, checks our course with a compass and map and we settle down for our first night at sea.

My watch, from 2000 to 2400, is uneventful. The important thing is to be on the lookout for larger ships that could ram our little boat without ever seeing us. I have some difficulty keeping our little fishing boat on course in the rising wind.

Tetsu takes over at midnight. I awaken shortly before 0300 with rain splashing in my face. Covering myself with a poncho and moving a little under cover, I go back to sleep as if I were at home and am dreaming when Tetsu awakens me at 0400 for my next watch.

I hear Tetsu say, "Night guard is important. It can mean our lives."

"Tetsu, I have heard those words before," I reply. "They are the same words Lee spoke when he taught me how to guard a perimeter."

"Who is Lee?" Tetsu asks.

"Sometime, sometime maybe," I answer.

Tetsu rolls up under cover and is soon asleep. The wind becomes increasingly stronger. By 0600, I know we are in a real storm. The bilge-pump runs all the time and seems to be handling the spray coming over the stern and sides. I know we have to trim the sail and I'm not a sailor, so I awaken Tetsu around 0700.

The south wind is giving us great speed as we move with the rough sea. Tetsu cuts back the sail and tells me to keep the pump going and stay on course, even though it's difficult to see. When we're in the trough of a wave and spray is going over us, all I can see is a wall of water on both sides of the boat. Then, when we rise to the crest of a wave, I can see a short distance. The sky is as gray as gun metal and clouds reach down to the ocean. ,

We don't mention fear, but I doubt we'll survive. We have no life jackets, no radio, no survival equipment. Certainly no rescue team will come to our aid. We are all alone, out of sight of land in a terrible storm. I think to myself that this is a better way to go than to have a bayonet run through me. At least I will have a clean grave under the water rather than in the mud of Okinawa.

Our battle against the storm continues throughout the morning. Our little engine sputters occasionally but does not quit. Tetsu stays at the tiller while I act as the lookout. We say little to each other, except what is absolutely necessary. Our sole purpose in life is to keep going, to keep our little craft afloat. We are wet to the skin, but it is warm. The howling wind hasn't broken any of our supplies loose, and if we can just stay afloat and not break up, there's always a chance we can survive.

The noises are frightfully loud at times, but not as terrifying as the sounds of battle. And the smell of the fresh salt water dashing into my face is wonderfully stimulating. Yes, we are frightened, but not as if we were enduring the horror of battle. I am, in fact, exhilarated and excited while at the same time I am anxious about coming out of this alive.

About mid-morning, while our little ship rides the crest of a breaker, Tetsu calls out:

"Look to the east, Arch."

I can't believe what I see. Surely it must be a fantasy. I've read stories of seamen seeing phantom rescue ships in storms, but this is real life and there really is a large fishing vessel nearby. This ship is not a fantasy. I am sure it isn't. I hope it isn't.

The fishing boat, three or four times the size of ours, disappears momentarily in the spray even though it is not that far away. Meanwhile, Tetsu fusses around among our supplies. When we rise to the crest of the next wave, he sends up a small flare.

"Where the hell did you get that?" I shout above the wind.

"You have to come prepared," Tetsu answers with a smile. "Compliments of your U.S. Army."

We see the boat approaching ever closer. The men on board have seen our flare and are trying to call to us. But with the noise of the crashing waves and the howling wind it is impossible to hear them.

Finally they come as near to us as possible without hitting us. They ask our condition and tell us to follow them. The storm is getting worse, they say. If necessary, they will throw us a rope and tow us to shelter.

Violent winds begin to shred our sails, so we quickly lower them. I engage the motor to give us power. The fishermen slow a bit and toss us a line. After several attempts we are able to catch it and tie it to the metal ring on the bow of our boat. What a difference between yesterday's calm seas and today's treacherous weather. Tetsu puts his arm around me and says, "Arch, I don't think we're going to make it."

We sit quietly in the howling winds, under a slow tow by the larger vessel. Suddenly land is visible through the torrential rain. It is the island of Amami O Shima. We make our way toward a narrow inlet. I know from living with boats and weather in Washington State's San Juan Islands as a boy that we will have protection when we get land between us and the wind. We're going to make it.

Finding protection is a fantastic feeling, like hearing bullets going overhead while I'm safe on the muddy floor of a foxhole. For a brief moment, I'm back home in Dad's boat, with my big brother Bill at the wheel. Yes, everything is going to be OK.

The men on the big boat call back to us. "You're safe now. We'll keep you in tow up the channel to Naze."

We wave back and they pick up speed.

Naze is situated in a punch-bowl-like harbor with wooded hills rising from the water. It is a beautiful sight, even in stormy weather. The setting reminds me of paintings of Japanese cities I have seen in schoolbooks.

The dock consists of large floating logs covered with heavy planking. We secure a line to a cleat on the dock and soon find ourselves on the aft deck of the fishermen's boat. Hot tea is served while we tell our story and explain our situation. The owner of the big fishing boat, a man named Nakamura, says his own boat has sustained very little damage. He invites us to stay in his home while we repair our boat for the rest of our journey.

The fishermen unload their boat, pack the fish into carts, and pull them to the public market. Nakamura brings several fish with him to take home, then beckons us to follow him through a town untouched by war to his home up the hill from the dock. While passing through town, we see shops selling fresh vegetables, grains and fish, expensive cloth of pongee, and real silk from the silkworm caterpillars that feed on mulberry leaves.

It is so peaceful. Maybe we can stay here, far from war, and be happy for as long as we want. We find the house to be larger than the ones on Okinawa. The floors are tiled and clean. There are bedrooms, a living room, and a kitchen separated by screens from the other rooms. The entry is like a small courtyard, partially covered by a curved-tile roof. There is a large bowl filled with water; the water runs through a bamboo pipe for washing our feet. We leave our outdoor shoes in a cabinet when we have finished washing.

Nakamura introduces us to his wife, his three children and a friend, a young man about my age. I imitate Tetsu's bow when I am introduced and let Tetsu do all the talking. The conversation among Tetsu, Nakamura, and the young man becomes heated and Nakamura's wife takes me and the children outside the house and up the street to a neighbor's house. A few minutes later I hear loud voices and violent conversation in the street.

"I'll kill that white American devil," someone shouts. "I'll kill him." I look outside and see the young man from Nakamura's house running up the street with a sword. He is calling for me. Tetsu and Nakamura are right behind him. Tetsu's friend's wife is translating.

"I'll kill that white devil," he calls, over and over. "I will kill that white American devil with my sword. His people want to kill us with their firebombs. Our kamikaze men in their planes will conquer. Their navy will be gone. They will have nothing. We will kill all the devils with our swords. They killed my brother on Okinawa. I have to kill them for my brother."

Tetsu and Nakamura tackle him just as he gets to the front of the house where I'm hiding. He falls to the ground. They hold him. Tetsu takes the young man's sword. A crowd gathers. The young man has the support of the gathering people. They shout threats I cannot understand. Scared as hell, I stay in the back room, peering out the window. I wonder if I am to be taken into the street and beheaded, because I've heard that's what the Japs do with their prisoners. I can see the hatred in the young man's eyes. I am terrified. I am hated. I think of the night of the banzai attack, when Jake went berserk and ran down the hill killing to avenge the death of his brother. This young Japanese man is doing the same thing. But, then, why shouldn't he? For all I know, his brother could have been one of those that Jake killed. I wonder if Japanese mothers put gold stars in their windows. There's nothing I can do but wait.

The Japanese wife, in her poor English, tells me that if Nakamura brought me home they will protect me. Tetsu and Nakamura quiet the people and tell our story. One member of the neighbor's family is a teenage girl who knows some English. She tells me that the young man who wants to kill me is a kamikaze pilot whose plane crashed just off their island. A fisherman rescued him. All he can talk about is how he wants to kill Americans for the Emperor and avenge his brother's death.

"Can you understand?" she asks. "He was trained in Japan to fight and kill for the Emperor. I live here on Amami O Shima and haven't been trained by the army. I don't like this at all."

All I could think of was Jake and how he was so filled with hatred that he carried a sack of ears and a bag of teeth wherever he went. He, too, was trained by an army. And he, too, had lost a brother.

"We people of the islands are not filled with hatred," the young woman continues. "I know you saved the life of a Japanese soldier. I know there is a war, but I could never kill kind people, and you have been kind. Just hide and wait. Nakamura will calm things down."

I survived combat and the storm. Now I could be killed like an animal in this little fishing village. I hide in the far corner of the room, beneath comforters brought by my protector. In time, Tetsu and Nakamura restore order. Tetsu tells me later that Nakamura thinks we had better take our boat down the bay to his brother's home. He isn't sure it will be safe for me here after the kamikaze pilot has stirred up the people.

"I don't trust the young pilot or what he might do," Nakamura adds. "He's trained to die killing, and if he fails it would be a great dishonor."

Nakamura's wife prepares food for us, and her husband travels with us in the boat about five miles down the bay. We tie the boat near his brother's home and remain with the family for several days. The family, it turns out, has relatives on the island of Yaku-Shima, our next destination. The brother is certain his relatives will want to buy our boat and will readily agree to take us to Kyushu, the southern most island of Japan.

The food that night is wonderful, consisting of seafood and fresh vegetables.

The next morning the sea is calm and blue and the enormous waves and white breakers that had menaced us the previous day are nowhere to be seen. Nakamura's brother and his family enlist the help of neighbors to help us repair our damaged boat and mend the torn sail.

There is a farewell feast the last evening of our stay at the home of Nakamura's brother. The food is plentiful—various fish, crab, octopus, sea cucumbers, roe, vegetables, rice, chicken, and pork. With chopsticks, we drop the food into a hot broth. When it is cooked, we dip it into tasty sauces. There also are copious quantities of sake and tea.

The feast continues well into the night. The people seem remote from the war, even though we can hear B-29s high above us on fire-bombing runs on Japan.

I turn to Tetsu, "What wonderful people. How fortunate I am to be alive and to be with you celebrating this marvelous friendship."

On the morning of our departure, a crowd of islanders gathers to bid us farewell as we sail out of the long inlet into the open ocean.

As we sail out of sight, Tetsu says, "Arch, I have to show you a gift I was given the other night by a Shinto priest following my confrontation with the kamikaze pilot." I watch as he reaches into our supplies and extracts a heavy pillow filled with dirt rather than feathers or down. Tetsu says the Shinto priest told him that whenever he is at sea he carries this pillow and sleeps on it. As a result, he has never been seasick, lost or harmed during a voyage. The priest wants us to have the pillow, to provide health and protection.

I laugh. "What a bunch of b.s., Tetsu. If we were going to be seasick, we'd have done it by now. And if we were going to be lost or drowned, we would have done so in that terrible storm. Besides, who the hell is going to harm us while we're at sea?"

Tetsu says, "Arch, I'll take help any way I can get it, and you had better be prepared to do the same. We'll keep the pillow and share it. OK?"

"OK," I reply. We are soon out in the open sea, heading north.

CHAPTER 22

❀

Nakamura and his brother are amazed at Tetsu's navigational skills with such meager equipment, especially the way he enabled us to survive the typhoon, with, of course, some miraculous assistance from the fishing boat.

To help us avoid future problems, the brothers provide us with accurate new charts for the rest of our voyage. Our course has been plotted with compass readings. Buoys, lighthouses, and geographical highlights on shore have been marked. In addition, we have a letter of introduction to Nakamura's cousins at our next island stop, Yaku-shima.

When we are well on our way, I return to a nagging question.

"Tetsu," I ask, "do you know anything about an underground field hospital a short distance south and west of Yonabaru, toward Shuri? On those hills beyond your uncle's home?"

"Why ask about such things, Arch, when we're safe and relaxed on this calm sea?"

"It's just that I have a lot of unanswered questions, Tetsu. If you don't know anything about it, or you do know something and don't want to talk about it, that's OK."

"Tell me, what's bothering you?"

"Well, it was my unit that discovered the underground hospital. Inside, we found everyone dead, apparently murdered. An unbelievable slaughter. Someone killed those men. You being a doctor, I thought you might have some insight into what happened."

"I'd rather not talk about it now, Arch. Later, I might tell you what I know. What I will tell you about is how I happened to come to Okinawa.

"In 1943 the army transferred me to Okinawa as a medical officer for forces permanently stationed on the island. When I arrived in Manila from Singapore—on the way to my new assignment—I encountered repeated delays in my attempts to find transportation to Okinawa.

"First, I was assigned to be the only medical officer at a prisoner-of-war camp near Manila. It was the roughest duty I have had, Arch, watching men suffer when there was nothing I could do to ease their pain. I simply didn't have even basic medical supplies, and there were no toilets or any form of sanitation in the camp. The food consisted of rice soup, mostly water, twice a day. I protested repeatedly and was told to keep my thoughts to myself. These men were the enemy; they were 'white devils.' It was a concept I could not accept, because it was opposed to everything I had learned in medical school, where you are taught to treat all people who need your help.

"As bad as it was, Arch, I can tell you that I was never ordered to kill the 'white devils.'

"Lacking medicines, and with a poor excuse for food, I thought I might be able to help with my knowledge of Zen, which teaches that there is within each of us a desire to be non-violent, to show love and compassion for our fellow human beings.

"Since I could not practice what I believed, I requested a transfer. They put me on a ship taking prisoners to Japan. This was even worse. The ship was not marked as a POW ship and we were strafed and bombed, but not sunk, by U.S. aircraft. It was a terrible voyage. The men were crowded together and there was very little food, except for the now familiar watery rice soup of the POW camp. It was a small ship with just three decks, one topside and two below. The men sat on these decks, crowded so closely together that they had to spread their legs for the person in front to sit. They urinated, defecated, and died in that position.

"I was the only medical officer and I had only two assistants. The men were all sick and many died. We buried them at sea. After one attack, the ship was so disabled that we had to abandon it off Formosa. My time on that ship was, I believe, the most depressing experience I have ever endured. I became, as you are always saying, Arch, a walking zombie with that 'thousand-yard stare.'

"I deteriorated both physically and mentally, frequently overcome by a horrible feeling of emptiness and depression. I thought I was going insane. After I arrived in Japan, on a somewhat better ship, I was flown immediately to my new duty post, the army hospital on Okinawa."

"Tetsu," I ask, "did you learn anything about soldiers going mad in combat? Did Japanese soldiers break down psychologically like some of ours did?"

"While I was at USC, I did some work with a doctor who had served in the First World War. He had some interesting ideas on the subject. Let's see if I remember enough to summarize his ideas for you.

"First we have to agree that we are fundamentally alike—Germans, Americans and Japanese—in our ability to endure psychological stress, unless we are mentally ill to start with.

"It took approximately 30 days for a soldier in the First World War, under continual combat, to suffer what was called 'shell shock.' The professor used the term 'psychiatric casualty' or 'combat insanity.' It's a complicated condition with little research available. I was sent to observe a ward of World War I mental patients in the veterans' hospital in Santa Monica. I thought everybody was insane."

"In 1940, you saw shell-shocked veterans who had been hospitalized since 1918?"

"Yes, and they were still in sad shape."

Tetsu's account brought me up short. That's the way I could end up.

"I was in a hospital on Okinawa that I know was a nut hospital, Tetsu. I left in the middle of the night and found my way back to my outfit."

"Why were you sent there?"

"I can't talk about it."

"OK, that's all right. If you ever want to talk about the hospital, I will listen and I won't judge.

"You know, Arch, that among people who go through extreme trauma, some will go mad and never recover. During the time I spent in the Veterans Hospital in West Los Angeles, I talked with some of the men from World War I. Those who had deep psychological wounds were more disabled than the ones in wheelchairs with both legs gone. At least the amputees had a mind. It is unbelievable what happens to the strong, innocent young men who fight the wars for their nation's often greedy, power-seeking leaders—men who seem to have no desire for compromise because they are convinced their cause and their beliefs are the right ones.

"The first thing the leaders have to do is teach their young men, really boys, to hate each other. Just like that man the other night who wanted to kill you when he didn't even know you. He had been taught that Americans are white devils who must be killed, and since you were an American you, too, must be killed.

"On both sides of a war, we are taught to dehumanize the enemy. Our enemy thus becomes an animal or a species below us. We draw degrading pictures and coin degrading words to reinforce our hatred. All this is necessary for us to be able to kill.

"In 1940, during the Battle of Britain, when I was living in Los Angeles, I would listen on the radio to your President's 'fireside chats.' President Roosevelt said he was strongly opposed to the bombing of citizens in British cities. Then, after Pearl Harbor, he changed and was as ruthless as the other leaders. He dehumanized the enemy, just as they did, and seemingly had no problem ordering the killing of civilians."

"The same thing that happens to nations happens to soldiers, as you know, Tetsu. I have killed your soldiers. It is possible that I could have killed the kamikaze pilot's brother. So, naturally, he has to kill me."

I finally tell Tetsu about Lee and Cook and what they meant to me. I show him my watch, the one Cook was wearing when he was killed. And I tell him about Jake and the teeth and ears he collected and about John and his books. I show him pictures of Lee's wife and daughter and of the family left behind by the Japanese officer I killed.

I cry, my shoulders shaking as I dry my eyes on my sleeve. Tetsu puts his arm around me and also cries. We spend some time in silence.

At length, Tetsu says, "Let me make some tea." We sit quietly for a long time, looking out at the sea and slowly sipping our tea.

Tetsu finally breaks the silence, saying, "Let me tell you about my happiest time in the army, Arch. At least it started out that way. The army base on Okinawa, to my surprise, was a short distance from Shuri, a place that you know. It was a thrill to arrive in Naha, a city I knew so well from my youth, and it was unbelievable that I should be stationed so near to the home of my grandfather, a home where I spent so many wonderful vacations as a youth.

"Whenever I was off-duty, I hurried to the hills around Yonabaru—where I had spent those vacations—visiting the home of Uncle Aoki and seeing my cousins. Although it was just last summer, Arch, it seems like years ago, almost like a dream."

"I can certainly understand that, Tetsu. This whole year has been 'like a fantasma or hideous dream' for me."

"That's a quotation, isn't it, Arch? From what?"

"Shakespeare's *Macbeth*, I think. Something John told me."

Tetsu continues:

"A cousin was farming the old land and supplying the army medical people with fresh vegetables. While visiting the farm, I had a great time with my cousin's little girl. She was only six. I would give her piggyback rides in the hills. And I would tell her the stories my grandfather told me when I was her age. We would sit in the flowers on the hills where the goats nestled up to us just as they did when I was a schoolboy on vacation. I almost forgot there was a war going on. That all changed in April, as you know."

"After the invasion we moved to a field hospital toward Yonabaru, where we treated the casualties and sent them back to the big hospital south of Shuri. We couldn't send them back to Japan, since no ships could get through the blockade. The sick and wounded became a problem. There were more and more of them as the fighting continued and nowhere to put them. For us, the island was becoming smaller and smaller.

"Nobody thought the battle would go on for so long. Our leaders told us the kamikazes had destroyed your navy and we were going to counter-attack and drive your army into the ocean. We were getting reinforcements from Japan and our wounded would be sent back on the ships that brought fresh troops.

"The wounded died while we waited. As you know, our plan did not succeed. In desperation, we put the wounded officers and men in the cave you discovered. Even though the cave was expanded, it lacked the supplies and staff to treat anyone adequately. I was running out of morphine and had nothing more for pain. There was very little to eat. Men died from lack of plasma, food, and basic medical treatment.

"When our commander learned that your troops had taken Yonabaru, it was all over. You must understand, Arch, that these men had taken an oath not to surrender. To surrender is to be disgraced, the same as it would be for an American soldier to desert in combat. To surrender is to be a coward, a traitor. It is an honor to die for our Emperor, who, as I have said, is descended from God.

"Back in our hospital in the cave, my superior officer ordered my staff to destroy all the patients before your army arrived. I argued that I could not be a party to this.

"When I asked the major to allow me to surrender with the patients, he pulled his pistol and told me I would be shot if I did not carry out his order. I kicked him in the groin with all the force I had. He dropped to the ground, losing his handgun, which I immediately grabbed. Two other officers came running and began firing their weapons. Three of my ward boys tried to stop them. One was killed immediately. The other two were wounded but still capable of fleeing.

"We realized that our only chance of survival was to get out of the cave as quickly as possible. Throwing obstacles in the path of the officers, the three of us retreated toward the underground exit on the other side of the hill.

"Once clear of the cave, we ran until we came upon a dense clump of trees and a small cave. While we huddled there, I used undershirts to bandage the wounds suffered by the ward boys. One had been hit in the leg, the other in the head.

"It became clear that our best chance of survival was to stay where we were for the night and await capture by the Americans when they came our way. I told the ward boys that I could speak English and would talk to the Americans. I said I knew they wouldn't kill us, but would take us prisoner. I thought I knew that much about Americans, having lived with them for over six years.

"We were without food and our only water came from the rain. That night we heard voices nearby. A company of Japanese soldiers had set up camp. They were retreating to the south. We overheard them say the Americans were close behind.

"When they were asleep, one of the ward boys sneaked over to their camp to look for food. He found dried fish and cooked rice they had not eaten. Also some water, which was most welcome.

"The soldiers left early the next morning and we felt safe again. The next afternoon I heard English being spoken as a company of American infantry came through the valley and headed up a hill to the south of us. American artillery fire flew over our heads from several directions and aircraft strafed the next valley.

"I knew we were behind the U.S. lines and felt we soon would be safe in a POW camp. That night we went out and stole some food intended for the American troops. I lost track of time after that. It may have been three days, perhaps four, when I heard voices and looked out through the trees and saw your squad coming over a hill toward us. It was time for me to talk my way into a POW camp.

"I watched the five of you approach and waited to see if you would fire into the trees. I was going to call out in English if you started firing. I was greatly relieved when I heard you telling us what to do. I told the boys with me that we would follow your orders. I sent them out as you directed. Well, Arch, you know the rest of the story, because from then on you were the star."

"It turned out that the faith you had in Americans to make you a prisoner and do you no harm was misplaced, Tetsu."

"Arch, having lived in the U.S. and knowing how my fellow medical students valued life, I was certain we'd be taken prisoner. After all, we were medical people and hadn't harmed anybody. The only difference between us and your medics was that we didn't wear a red cross on our uniforms.

"I heard you tell our story after we were captured. Your soldiers either didn't believe you or they hated us so much they couldn't bring themselves to take us prisoners. I can't blame them entirely. Under great stress, the first thing that suffers is the ability to make rational decisions. That's when inhumane actions take over, actions one otherwise might never consider.

"There are, I believe, three basic reactions a soldier must defend against or he'll go mad. First, he must believe that what he does now will in some way affect what happens to him in the future. Second, he must believe that if he does his best and things don't get better, someone will step in to help him. This is b.s., and we know it, but we have a way of pretending it isn't b.s. Finally, men—especially young men—think they are invulnerable and will live forever. When they taste the reality of death, few can retain their sanity for long. A few crack immediately. Others take longer. But I have seen some of the bravest collapse and go mad. Often, our officers give orders to shoot such men, even though they were anything but cowards. Their minds had simply snapped."

"Tetsu, I think I was in a psychological hospital after Lee and Cook were killed. I couldn't stand the place and left. I hitchhiked back down the island and rejoined my outfit. If I hadn't, I never would have met you. I'm glad I did, because I wouldn't have missed your friendship for anything."

We remain quiet for a long time after our conversation.

It takes almost three uneventful days to reach our destination, the town of Kurio on the island of Yaku-shima. The directions by Nakamura are excellent.

During that time Tetsu and I develop a very trusting relationship. We share our feelings about life and death, religion, women, sex, and the hope that we both will survive.

Do we want eventually to have wives and families?

Tetsu says, "I never want to send a son of mine to war."

"It's going to be difficult to ask a girl to marry me," I reply. "I know that what I have done out here I will have to live with. I know these memories will not just go away. I will carry this with me, in my fucked-up mind, for as long as I live. What kind of father could I be after combat? I just don't know, Tetsu."

I don't tell Tetsu about Cook, about my fear that possibly I, in the heat of combat, might accidentally have killed one of my dearest friends.

Tetsu says, "Many in the war say they are working for peace, or they are fighting for peace, but they are not at peace. To make peace, our hearts must be at peace with the world. Trying to overcome evil with evil is not working for peace. To love your enemies, as Christ taught, is impossible unless you can find a way to understand him and to feel compassion for him. Only when that happens is he no longer your enemy."

I am amazed at the bond that has been established between the two of us. I have felt this togetherness, this mental cohesion with another person only once before in my young life. And that person was Lee. And the only thing that broke our bond was his death in combat.

Sharing close combat—with its terror and death—creates the deepest of all masculine friendships. I have shared these feelings with both Lee and Tetsu, with an American soldier and a Japanese soldier.

CHAPTER 23

❀

The Nakamuras' brother in-law, Mr. Kubota, is staying with his elderly parents on the island of Yaku-shima. The small farm where we spend the night with Mr. Kubota is very rundown.

He tells us: "My folks have not been able to hire any labor since the start of the war. When I grew up here, this was a productive farm with delicious fruits and vegetables. My father kept the farm immaculate, not a weed in any row. I love to come back to the farm. I hope I can leave my work and return before the invasion. This would be a safe place. That is why I would like to buy your fishing boat."

Tetsu says, "We need money to get to my home in Hiroshima. We don't know how we are going to make the journey, but we will find a way."

Mr. Kubota says, "I have a friend in Kagoshima. I can leave the boat with him. This will be my escape route from Japan when the big battle begins. There will be no need for devastation on Yaku, since it has no military value. I would just be a farmer-fisherman, not an executive of the Mitsubishi Corp. that manufactures the Zero aircraft and much of Japan's military equipment."

Tetsu asks Mr. Kubota, "What kind of transportation will be available to us on Kyushu?"

"I thought I had that all arranged," he replies. "I was hoping a company car would be available in Kagoshima, on the island of Kyushi to transport us to my office in Hofu, on the island of Honshu. That is impossible the way the war is going. Not only are company cars not available, but also the roads are in deplorable condition. The company is trying to arrange a compartment on the train. That is, if the railroad is still running and the tracks haven't been destroyed by bombs. Let's keep this all quiet until we are safe in our hotel in Kagoshima. We will say you two are men in my division of the Mitsubishi Corp."

After our arrival in Kagoshima, we leave our fishing boat with Mr. Kubota's friend. Mr. Kubota, after several phone calls, informs us that we have a compartment on the morning train.

"I want you, Arch, to stay in the compartment and speak to no one," he says. "It will be safe. It will take us two days and one night, if there are no complications, for us to reach Hofu and my home."

The train trip is uneventful, and we stay in Mr. Kubota's home in Hofu. His wife tells us she gets her vegetables from a farmer, a Mr. Kenzo, in Yamaguchi, about ten kilometers from Hofu.

The next day, Mrs. Kubota, drives us to the farm of Mr. Kenzo. Tetsu, Mrs. Kubota, and Mr. Kenzo talk for some time. They inform me later that Mr. Kenzo wanted to know more about me. He thinks maybe he should call the police, even though he knows I will surely be killed if he does. But after Tetsu tells his story, plus the fact that Mrs. Kubota is such a good customer and pays any price he asks, Mr. Kenzo says I can stay and do chores on the farm with Tetsu. I must, however, remain out of sight and do my work satisfactorily. I am to hide in the vegetation whenever there is a chance of being discovered.

Mr. Kenzo and his wife have two sons who helped to cultivate and harvest the crops before they went into the army. Now Mr. Kenzo and his wife must do all the work themselves with no power equipment. Although they have a truck, there is no gasoline to make it run. So they take their crops to market in a large horse-drawn wagon.

Tetsu and I put in a long day seeding, weeding, and harvesting the vegetables. I admire the weedless rows, the green foliage contrasting with the rich black soil. Rice, dried fish, and tea are brought into the field by the farmer's wife at lunch time.

After sunset we return to the farmhouse, bathe, and change into light cotton garments called yukatas. For the evening meal, we sit on cushions around a low table, Tetsu and I on one side, the farmer and his wife on the other. The wife does not look at me. Her husband talks to her for some time, after which she gives me a forced smile and turns away. I hope she can be trusted. I wonder what my mother would do if she had to live with a Japanese soldier.

The farmer's wife serves fresh steamed vegetables and chicken, all from their farm. The vegetables are delicious, crisp, and green. The chicken has a great aroma and a delicious flavor.

Mr. Kenzo and his wife never acknowledge my presence. It is as if I do not exist. I am the enemy in their home—to be scorned and yet to be tolerated. I am constantly anxious and fearful that Mr. Kenzo will change his mind. I can imagine a public execution with two star performers, Tetsu and me. I can visualize a large block of wood and an executioner with a sword. It would be one of those fancy swords with beautiful handles and razor-sharp blades. Who would be first, Tetsu or me? It wouldn't matter.

At the end of the week, we load the wagon the evening before leaving for the market in Hiroshima, covering with wet burlap the boc choy, egg plant, lettuce, and a few vegetables I don't recognize. About 2 a.m., after a breakfast of maso soup and vegetables, we begin our trip to Hiroshima.

I am relieved to be on our way. Tetsu and Mr. Kenzo are seated up front, on the driver's seat. I am behind, sitting on a wooden box that is filled with eggplant and covered by the wet burlap bags.

The old white horse, in worn harness, pulls us slowly. Though the wagon has inflated tires, it lacks springs and gives us a bumpy ride on the rough, dirt road. We frequently are forced to pull off the road as far as possible to allow convoys of troops and supplies to pass on their way to the army base in Hiroshima.

The sight of troops brings a terrifying fear of capture. This fear is shared by Tetsu and Mr. Kenzo, who know they would be executed along with me. They give friendly waves to the troops while I peer out occasionally from my hiding place.

As dawn approaches, we find ourselves on a hill overlooking the blacked-out city of Hiroshima. All we can make out are outlines. Mr. Kenzo tells us there has been no bombing in Hiroshima. At least not yet. He has heard that cities to the north are on fire.

As the old horse pulls on, Tetsu crawls over his seat and takes a place beside me, briefing me on his hometown.

"Hiroshima is a city of 320,000 people, built on the islands and shore of the estuary of the Ota River," he says. "The river flows from the hills, through the city, into the Inland Sea of Japan. Eighty-one bridges connect the delta islands.

"The city sits in a bowl, bounded on three sides by low mountains. The road we are on winds through the hills on the west side of the city."

"It's a large city, Tetsu," I say. "Where is your home?"

"We live about four kilometers from the city center on a hill overlooking the islands where the river enters the Inland Sea. Our home is on the estate of a very wealthy businessman who is a part owner of the Mitsubishi Shipyard. As I believe I told you before, my father designed the estate's magnificent Zen gardens and, in gratitude, was given our home."

The weather is overcast, the humidity oppressive, much as I understand it is in the eastern U.S. in the summer. Lush green vegetation covers the hills as we approach the outlying areas of the city in the early morning. Our horse-drawn wagon reaches the crest of a hill and starts down into Hiroshima. Tetsu grows increasingly excited. He is going to see his family again. This was beyond his wildest dreams a short time ago.

The cumulus clouds turn pink from the first rays of the sun. Through the early morning light, as the road tops the hill, we see spread out before us an almost mystical scene of river, islands, harbor, and city. It is nothing like my own hometown.

As we start down the hill, I notice that the homes are spaced farther apart and the gardens are larger than I had seen in other Asian cities. About two miles from the city center, Tetsu calls for the farmer to stop the wagon. We climb down to the road, pick up our meager belongings, and accept a few vegetables from the farmer as a gift to Tetsu's family. Then we say our farewells and watch the wagon slowly disappear down the hill to the city.

Tetsu says excitedly, "Arch, we made it. I wondered sometimes if we would. I don't think we could have done it alone. But we did it together. We did it." Tetsu turns and points down a long tree-lined lane and exclaims, "That's the way home."

I reply, "Tetsu, I'm worried about meeting your family. What if they don't accept me and call the police?"

"Over my dead body," Tetsu answers. "Not after I tell them how you saved my life. I don't remember whether I told you that my father speaks English. He learned the language from an English professor at the university in Tokyo. When the class ended, the professor invited my father to come with him to England for a year. My father went for a year and then returned home to be married."

We slowly walk together under cherry trees heavy with summer leaves.

"Arch, you should see these trees in the spring. Their fragrance and color are something to behold."

Rounding a bend in the road we come upon the walkway to the home where Tetsu spent his early years. How different it is from the big house where I was born.

Tetsu's home is surrounded by a bamboo fence. We enter the yard through a bamboo gate, and as we pass through the gate, I stop—overwhelmed by what I see. The walkway is of flat stones. Soft green plants cover the soil between the stones. A pool to the right is shaded by a large pine tree. The stream that feeds the pool is crossed by an arched wooden bridge. Summer flowers around the pool fill the air with fragrance.

"Tetsu, this is marvelous. I'm amazed at how the simplicity of the house merges with nature, giving one a sense of peace and serenity."

As I speak, a large fish swimming close to the pool's surface flashes in the sunlight.

"Arch, we can't stand here all day. Let's go in the house. My father will show you all this in detail, I can assure you."

Tetsu asks me to stop first in the entry room, which he calls the genkan. We sit on a wooden bench, remove our shoes, and select slippers from a rack.

Upon leaving the genkan we enter a hall with rooms on each side separated by shoji doors. We then enter a large room of 10 tatami mats with a low table toward one end. There is a broad recess in the wall at that end. It contains a simple scroll painting and a vase of flowers. On the far side of the room is a Shinto Buddhist shrine. On a small low table is a picture of the family tomb near Shuri on Okinawa.

An oscillating floor fan cools the air.

It is a strange scene, because three people—who turn out to be Tetsu's father, mother, and sister—are seated at a table, on pillow-like mats, apparently finishing a morning meal of rice, pickled vegetables, miso soup, and tea as we enter the room. Yet, not a word is spoken. Those at the table seem to be oblivious to Tetsu's return from the war.

The silence continues. Suddenly, they realize who is there. Two women at the table jump to their feet and run to Tetsu, embracing him and bursting into tears. The man at the table, Tetsu's father, finally rises from the table and comes to embrace his son. Tetsu bows. There are tears in his eyes.

At the conclusion of embracing and excited talk, all in Japanese, Tetsu turns and introduces me briefly to his family. I am his friend. That is sufficient.

The welcome, although a bit chilly, is not hostile. When the family returns to the table, we join them. Tetsu's mother goes into the kitchen and returns with fresh tea and cups.

While family members talk, I study each of them. Tetsu looks a lot like his father, Okumura Kazuki, who is slim, clean-shaven and has some gray in his black hair. The father is immaculately dressed in a dark suit, white shirt, and tie. I guess him to be about 5 feet, 6 inches tall—a bit shorter than Tetsu—and roughly 55 years old.

With Tetsu giving me family information, in English, as he talks with his family, I learn that his father has a degree in the art of Japanese gardens and horticulture from the University of Tokyo and is widely regarded as one of Japan's foremost garden designers. Tetsu reminds me again that his father studied for a year in England.

The father is soft-spoken and has a calm, peaceful demeanor. Because of the war, he now works as a bus driver, taking people to the factories early in the morning and driving them home again at night. He has the middle of the day free for his design work, and he still supervises the maintenance of gardens on large estates.

Tetsu's mother, Yoshiko, is not dressed in the typical formal Japanese dress of the woman I saw in the pictures carried by the lieutenant I killed. Instead, she wears practical dress pants and a tunic, similar to the clothing worn by native Okinawans. She is slender, about 5 feet, 1 inch and roughly 50 years old. Her well-groomed black hair is piled high on her head. Her joy at the return of her son is what one would expect from any American mother.

Because of the war, she cares for the children of mothers who are working in war factories, leaving home early in the morning, and riding a bus to the city. She arrives at the center long before the mothers drop off their children.

The third person seated at the table is Tetsu's sister, Tomiko, who is 22 years old, almost as tall as Tetsu, slender and very beautiful. She lives at home with her parents and works in a small factory, with about 35 employees, in central Hiroshima. She makes parts for Betty bombers.

Tomiko has little time off from work for recreation. She dresses simply, but with style.

Tetsu's brother, Seigo, a graduate of Japan's Air Academy, serves his country as a bomber pilot. He left home early in the war and has not been heard from in over a year. The last time the family received word from him, his squadron was on the island of Rabaul, north of New Guinea, surrounded by the "enemy" (our U.S. Navy).

With no hope of getting reinforcements or food to the air and ground troops on the island, the Japanese high command left them to starve or surrender.

After the celebration of the arrival of Tetsu, all eyes suddenly are on me. I can see the consternation in their faces as Tetsu explains at length how he came to be traveling with "this strange person in Okinawan clothing, who is definitely not one of us, but is my good friend, Arch."

It is all in Japanese and I don't understand a word. But when he finishes, after about eight minutes of talking, his parents and sister come to me and bow and say words that sound kind. I know that I am welcome.

Soon after our arrival, the family members leave for their jobs and Tetsu and I have the day to ourselves.

Tetsu says his first priority is to take a bath. "How about you, Arch?"

It sounds good to me, since I haven't had a bath, except in a stream or in salt water while on our boat, since April.

"I'll take you through the rest of the house first and then light the fire under the tub in back," he says.

As we work our way down the hall, Tetsu points out a study with a low, black-lacquered desk and a beautifully carved urn on the floor. This room is his father's, he says. He shows me the kitchen, the rooms for bathing, and the large rooms for eating, study, and sleeping.

"We sleep on futons, Arch, which you will find a hell of a lot better than the ground," Tetsu says. "You must air your futon and put it away in the closet each morning."

"That sounds great and very practical."

I see a small desk and book shelves in one corner.

"Is that your corner for studying, Tetsu?"

"Right, I spent many hours there before going to USC," Tetsu replies. "Now let's go light the bath."

We go outside where a large cedar tub rests on a metal floor. A small gas stove under the floor heats the bathtub and water.

While the water heats, Tetsu gets us some clean clothes. Then he explains the difference between American and Japanese baths.

To begin, we will sit on low stools and, with hot water from a bucket, wash ourselves with washcloths and soap. When we have washed, we will pour the water remaining in the bucket over our heads.

Thus, we will be clean and rinsed before getting into the tub for a relaxing soak. The family usually does not do this together. The father is first, then the boys, then the girls, and last, the mother.

Tetsu says, "I feel like a new person after the long soak in the cedar-scented hot water."

I put on a yukata and relax on Tetsu's futon. It is a wonderful feeling. I wonder if I'm dreaming.

The day passes quickly. Tetsu tells me much more about his city.

The houses of Hiroshima, he says, are of traditional Japanese wooden construction, as are many of the industrial buildings. There are, however, some Western-style, reinforced-concrete buildings in the center of town, housing government agencies, and retail businesses.

"I would like to show you Hiroshima Castle," Tetsu says, going to a window to point out a 400-year-old castle built on an artificial mound and surrounded by a moat. It is now headquarters for 40,000 soldiers in the Hiroshima area, serving as a training depot, a hospital, and an ammunition dump.

"Beneath the castle is the area's civil-defense headquarters where troops stand ready to direct anti-aircraft fire in case of an air raid."

As we look out the window, Tetsu directs my eyes towards the mountain that looms over Hiroshima. At the foot of the mountain, Tetsu says, is the headquarters of the Japanese 2nd Army, which has responsibility for the ground defense of Southern Japan, if and when the Americans invade "this fall."

"If an invasion occurs, Tetsu, it will be the greatest massacre of men in history. If only something could happen to stop the war."

"As long as we have our military government, Arch, Japan will fight to the death."

"This is quite a city, Tetsu," I say, "It not only has war factories and shipbuilding but also army headquarters. With so many military targets, it's strange we haven't bombed this area."

The family returns home at about 7 o'clock and bathes. Then we gather around the table, wearing our yukatas. Tetsu's mother brings dishes of vegetables, fish, and steaming rice. We eat quietly and slowly. Afterward, Tomiko clears the table and brings tea.

Tetsu relates some of his experiences the past year. His parents, in turn, tell some of theirs. Tetsu occasionally breaks into English to let me know what they've been saying.

The family's conversation about Tetsu's brother, Seigo, is filled with tenderness and concern. Their faces sadden when his name is spoken.

I am brought into the discussion and asked if I would like to see some photographs of trips the family has taken to Tokyo and Kobe to visit relatives, along with photographs of Tetsu in cap and gown graduating from medical school and of Seigo graduating from the Imperial Air Force Academy.

But the photograph that makes my heart jump is one of Tetsu's mother and father on their wedding day. She is in the same traditional dress worn by the wife of the lieutenant I killed.

"What a beautiful bride," I say.

After the photographs have been shown, I am told that there is some fear that Tetsu and I might have been seen when we left the vegetable wagon and walked to the Kazuki home. They tell me their nearest neighbors, a doctor and his family, are very good friends. But the family recently received word that their son, Imoto, a former classmate of Tetsu's, had been killed on Okinawa.

The neighbors say their son was murdered by "American devils," Tetsu says. "I know they would report you and my family if they knew you were here."

It is agreed that I will sleep that night in the bomb shelter beneath the house.

I wonder to myself how many American boys Imoto killed before he died. I suppose this question has no meaning to a Japanese family that has just lost its only son.

But it is a question for everyone. Do Japanese families and American families ever grieve for all the sons, brothers, and fathers on both sides who are dying in the war?

The madness of war destroys more than the lives of the soldiers who are fighting. It ravages everything in its path, so no one can escape its impact, not even someone as decent and compassionate as the family next door.

"So, Arch," says Tetsu, "when anyone comes or if we have guests we are not sure of, it would be better for you to stay in the shelter."

A trapdoor in the corner of the kitchen has a retractable stairway leading to an underground room about eight-by-eight feet. It contains a small desk, a wash basin, and a portable toilet, along with several futons.

Water and food are stored in wooden boxes. There is a large first-aid kit in a strong metal box near a stack of towels.

In the dark of night, and at times when visitors are unlikely to appear, I take walks through the estate. In the morning and in the evening, when the people are off at work or are returning to their homes, Tetsu and I watch them scurrying to catch buses or to step down from them.

One evening, when there is a full moon, we raise the blackout curtains with the lights out and see the moonlight reflected on the water beyond the city.

On such a beautiful and peaceful night, I feel like a member of the family.

CHAPTER 24

❊

Tetsu's father asks if I would like to walk with him through his garden. A light breeze drifts in from the east. The sun is midway in the western sky.

Tetsu has told me I would have to wait until I was accepted before his father would ask me to experience his garden. And even then, Tetsu says, his father probably will show me only a part of it, to gauge whether I properly appreciate the Japanese philosophy of eternal things.

The garden, owned by the Mitsubishi Corp, is seen by invitation only. It has taken years for Mr. Kazuki and his assistants to perfect it. I feel honored to be allowed to share this part of his life.

We wend our way on a slightly inclined path, covered with scented ground-cover plants, to a small bench cut from a large stone. The bench, under a large trained wisteria, overlooks a small pool with strategically placed stones and blooming water lilies. He asks me to sit with him.

Carp swim near the water's surface. The pool's edge consists of large rocks interspersed with pebbles, along with carefully placed low-growing plants. The scent of jasmine fills the air. It is noiseless except for the running water and the occasional sound of a bird singing in a tree or a fish breaking the surface of the water.

Tetsu's father says slowly, in good English:

"Someone once said, 'When we observe things calmly we notice that all things have their fulfillment.'

"My garden is a union between our culture and the environment with the past, present, and future of the cosmos, or maybe to you, the world.

"To me," he continues, "we must have communication, a unity—even what you might call a friendship—with the sun, earth, and rain. This gives us a relationship with plants, birds, flowers, rocks, trees, and all of what I think you call nature.

"To me, it is a union with the unknown, something beyond us, perhaps a fascinating unexplored part of our own thinking that we can reach in no other way than by experiencing the serenity of a place like this.

"This garden, quietly speaking, enables me to experience that serenity and, with it, the relationship between me and the source of existence, the total power of the energy of creation or whatever you choose to call it.

"The Zen garden can be of any size, very large or extremely small. But it must be of natural elements and design."

We walk slowly along a path covered with low moss-like plants that muffle the sound of our sandals. Edging the walkway are dwarf mint and thyme that give off a familiar, pleasant fragrance.

The garden is full of secrets. The stone lanterns, the positioning of the large rocks, the shade patterns created by the trees let me see only so much. As I walk on, I begin to experience a new breathtaking glimpse at every turn.

The simple beauty of the garden whispers, never shouts. I feel no need to talk. Communion with a setting such as this requires no words.

"See that small black pine on the stone pedestal?" Mr. Kazuki says, pointing to the tree. "My father began pruning and shaping that tree 25 years before I was born. I have been working with it since his death. I had hoped that Tetsu would learn the art of bonsai culture so he, too, would be able to care for the family tree after I am gone. Some black pines have lived over 400 years in the same family. Could this be our two-hundred-year family tree?"

He recites:

> *The pine tree lives for a thousand years,*
> *The morning glory for but a single day.*
> *Yet both have fulfilled their destiny.*

Mr. Kazuki says the author's name quite rapidly. It sounds like "chow," something familiar to GIs. He continues:

"Our culture of nature, in the Japanese manner, is part of the process of 'the way.' In a garden, a single flowering tree is 'the way.' In some gardens almost invisible blooms may be 'the way,' rather than a sweeping view of a broad landscape."

I tell him that when my brother died a long row of onion seeds was just beginning to sprout in our vegetable garden. Grass was growing between the sprouting onion seed, and it took time and patience to weed the grass from the onions because they look alike. It was good to be alone with my thoughts in a time of grief. When I finished, I felt I had left some of my sorrow out there with the onions, grass, and the soil.

"Arch," he says, "you know a garden and the spiritual benefits one can gain from communicating with the soil and plants. That's what a Zen garden is all about. Everything comes from the soil, sun, and rain, and everything returns to the soil to rise again. I can come out here any time of the year and find 'the way.'

"The word *shibui* is often applied to Japanese gardens, though the word relates to other things as well.

"Tell me about shibui."

"*Shibui* begins with the power of quietness, an understatement, especially in the use of commonplace things to create peaceful beauty. The quality of *shibui* invites prolonged examination with meditation, never revealing itself all at once, manifesting its serenity over time. It is slowly discovered rather than being immediately apparent."

He continues, "We must gain the understanding and realization that we are the ones that have overturned our original source of oneness and accord with nature and all the universe. But through enlightenment we can transcend to a peaceful and harmonious summer with nature and all creation."

We stop at a small bench cut into a boulder next to a stone bowl used for washing and purification. The bowl is overflowing with clear water, its contents constantly renewed by water entering through a piece of hollow bamboo.

"Before meditation one must prepare," my mentor says. "The critical purification agent is water. If it isn't naturally present, you must acquire it for washing and mouth rinsing from bowls such as this. The meditation area is completed with that old black pine over there that symbolizes the ancient creators of our life and culture."

He quotes the lines of a poet:

> When you hear the splash
> of water drops that
> fall into a stone bowl
> you will feel that all of the dust
> of your mind is washed away.

We overlook a small pool fed by a waterfall. The only sounds are the water, a koi breaking the pool's surface, birds singing, a light breeze moving through the trees.

After meditating in silence for some time, Tetsu's father says:

To every natural form,
rock, fruit, or flower
even the loose stones
that cover the highway
I give a moral life; I saw them feel,
...and all that I beheld
respired with inward meaning.

"That is what one of your poets says."
"Who is that?" I ask.
"The Englishman, William Wordsworth."
Walking along nature's serene garden path, we return home in silence.

CHAPTER 25

✿

The path leading back to the house divides as it leads from the garden back to the house. One way returns to the pool in front of the house, the other passes between two large Japanese red maples that shade a bamboo gate.

Beyond the gate I see a small, plain building. The path is bordered by crepe myrtle. Again, the scent of jasmine is in the air. I ask Tetsu's father about the second path and the small building.

"That path," he explains, "leads to the teahouse where I administer and take part in a tea ceremony with particular friends and family."

"My knowledge of the 'tea ceremony' is negligible, but I would like to learn more," I tell him.

"That pleases me very much," he replies. "The historical name for the ceremony is cha-no-yu. I would be more than happy to explain the ritual. It will be my honor to sometime serve you and my son tea in our teahouse. The poet says:

> *Tea has the blessing of all the deities.*
> *It promotes filial piety.*
> *It drives away the devil.*
> *It banishes drowsiness.*
> *It keeps the five viscera in harmony.*

It wards off disease.
It strengthens friendships.
It disciplines body and mind.
It destroys the passions.
It gives a peaceful death.

"Let me describe the ritual of attending the tea ceremony. You will first see a gate and path as you did in my garden. Our gate is of weathered bamboo and must stand ajar at all times. This indicates that you are welcome. A path leads through a small garden, simple, with nothing spectacular, not even flowering plants.

"You step on the simple stones as you approach to prepare the tea; you relax and free the mind of all activity. Our teahouse is plain, with a tatami floor and roof, just large enough for the host and his guests.

"There is an art alcove, with an appropriately inscribed scroll honoring the occasion. Near the scroll is a single flower in a bamboo container. The beautifully crafted kettle, with artwork reflecting the seasons, steams over a charcoal fire and is inspected as the visitors enter.

"The guests take their places on clean, crisp mats. Conversation stops in the subdued light. The host enters and bows to his guests.

"The utensils for the tea ceremony are kept in a cupboard. The cabinet's exterior is carved with scenes similar to those on the teapot.

"The host carries the utensils on a simple black lacquered tray and places them, in the order of their use, on a decorative shelf near the steaming kettle. The utensils consist of a water jar, tea bowl, whisk, tea scoop, caddy, ladle, waste-water jar, and a lid rest.

"The ceremony is initiated by cleaning the utensils with a clean silk napkin from the host's obi. He rinses the tea bowl and wipes it with a linen cloth. The cleaning process demonstrates the host's concern for his guests, his respect for the utensils and his willingness to serve.

"A small amount of tea and hot water is placed in the bowl. The bowl is wiped with the whisk. This tea is served to the first guest. The procedure is repeated with each guest.

"Guests drink their tea slowly in silence. After all have partaken of the tea, the guests examine the scoop and caddy. The host removes the utensils to the preparation room. He returns to his guests, turns and bows to his friends. The men examine the scroll and flower again and leave through the garden. Nothing seems to have happened, but much has. Each person, for a few minutes, has allowed his senses full reign. This is a unifying experience, employing sight, sound, smell, taste and touch."

"It's a beautiful ceremony," I say as I accompany him back to the pool in front of the house. We walk in silence, looking only at the path before us.

The next afternoon, Mr. Kazuki asks Tetsu and me if he can have the honor of serving us tea in his teahouse at three o'clock in the afternoon. Following the ceremony, he says, we will go to the shrine in another part of the garden.

Promptly at three, Tetsu and I join his father in walking down the path, through the open bamboo gate to the teahouse. Tetsu's father administers the tea in silence, as described to me the previous day. I feel the tea ceremony is similar to the sacrament of Christian communion, where we become one with our creator. After the moving experience of the ceremony, the three of us make our way to the family's Toma Shrine.

It is situated on a small open knoll not far from the tea hut. As we approach the shrine, I see three identical red-painted gateways, consisting of two sturdy upright poles on the sides, with two crosspieces, one curved upward toward the extended tips, the other straight across from one post to the other.

We walk through each gate in succession to reach the shrine's enclosure.

Tetsu's father says, "Arch, these gates are known as 'torii,' and it is said that when we pass under the timbers we are purified in heart and mind."

Flat stones form a path through the torii up to the simple square wooden building. On one side of the shrine's entrance is a stone bowl filled with water. A wooden ladle hangs from a peg on the wall. I follow the example of Tetsu and his father, taking the ladle from the peg, filling it with water, and rinsing my mouth. I spit the water on the dirt behind me.

After removing my sandals and washing my feet, I enter the shrine. There is an aroma of burning incense and sweet rice wine.

I follow my friends to a wooden platform where there is nothing but a plain wooden box and a blue rice bowl. The right wall of the shrine is covered with small pieces of paper, each containing prayers. I copy the actions of Tetsu and his father, walking up to the altar and clapping my hands three times, then reaching up to pull a thick braided rope attached to a wooden clapper in the ceiling. The wooden clapper moves horizontally and strikes the outside of a large bell. The sound echoes through the small building, a signal for me to close my eyes and bow.

Tetsu has brought sticky rice for each of us to put in the blue rice bowl. We leave the shrine in silence. Out on the green slope we sit quietly. Tetsu pours tea from a thermos. We share the last of my American cigarettes.

I break the silence, saying, "I hope that one day our countries will be friends."

"I share that hope," Tetsu says.

"I want what you hope. We want our friendships to be not unusual but the way for all," Mr. Kazuki says.

CHAPTER 26

❀

Tetsu's family invite their next-door neighbors, a doctor and his wife, for dinner. The neighbors are having a difficult time after the loss of their only son on Okinawa.

The families share their rations of fish, rice, and vegetables. Because I must remain out of sight, Tetsu's mother brings dinner to me in the bomb shelter, where I spend the evening reading.

I find it difficult to orient myself when I awaken in the bomb shelter. There are no windows to provide clues to whether it is night or day. But when I hear footsteps on the floor above me, I am certain it must be morning. It is dark, but it has been quiet. I turn on the one light and see it is 0600.

Family members move swiftly to ready themselves for their day's work. They always eat together.

When they have finished eating breakfast together, Tomiko leaves for the aircraft-parts factory, her mother for the day-care center, and her father for the bus barn. Later in the day, Mr. Kazuki will work as a volunteer in a nearby military hospital.

I decide to stay in bed until everyone has left for the day. I quickly fall asleep and do not get up until almost 0800.

While dressing, I examine one of Tetsu's medical books, opening it to a section on the treatment and prevention of trauma, particularly trauma resulting from burns.

Mrs. Kazuki has placed clean clothes on a chair next to my sleeping mat. I plan to take a bath this morning, since I'm alone and Tetsu spent the night at his girl friend's home several miles away from the city.

Wrapped in a yukata, and with the clean clothes under my arm, I pull down the retractable ladder and start up the steps toward the kitchen. I glance down at my graduation watch. It's 0815. I hope there is some breakfast left for me.

When the trapdoor is about halfway open, I'm struck by a blinding flash of orange-white light. A powerful white light follows. Then a tremendous explosion shakes the floor and the ladder, the shock wave knocking me back down the stairs and onto the bomb-shelter floor.

I am on my back, dazed; I am unable to move. The shock wave is infinitely more powerful than the one that knocked me unconscious when an artillery shell landed a few feet from my foxhole on Skyline Ridge.

I have no idea how long I lay on that bomb-shelter floor—groggy, trying to regain my senses and some movement in my extremities. But I do know I've been involved in something truly catastrophic.

When I finally stagger to my feet, my first impulse is to escape the claustrophobic little room. I pull down the stairs again and start to climb. I push on the trapdoor and it doesn't move. I push harder. It still does not move. I push with all my strength and nothing happens. Something must have fallen across the door as a result of the explosion.

Panic washes over me as I realize my escape route is blocked. What little water and food I have won't last long down here, nor will the air hold out indefinitely.

In desperation, I search for something to help me open the trapdoor. I suspect that it is blocked by a fallen roof beam. Surely the entire house couldn't have tumbled on it. Or could it?

What I need is a crowbar, the kind I used as a kid. Under the futons, next to the wall, I find some garden tools. A hoe-like tool, with a sturdy wooden handle and a 12-to 14-inch blade, catches my eye. While working on the Okinawan farm of Tetsu's uncle, I had watched workers swing just such a tool to break up clods of dirt.

Then I open the rugged metal box that contains the first-aid kit. I feel better. I have food, water, first-aid supplies, and a tool that might get me out of here. If not, then the family members can open the trapdoor when they return from work.

I wonder more about what sort of explosion could have created the blinding light and the powerful after-shocks. It was as if the bombs from hundreds of airplanes had exploded all at once. Perhaps it meant only that a bomb had scored a direct hit on the Kazuki home.

The worst thing that can happen to me, I reason, is that the family might have been caught in the bomb attack and be unable to return home to help open the door. What if they have been killed? No one knows I'm here. And if they do know I'm here, they'll either kill me outright or let me die in my concrete coffin.

The outlook is not good. I must find a way to escape. Then I must keep my disguise and try to survive by my wits, as a beggar or a thief.

It's hot. Hot enough to make me sweat. And it's getting hotter. The house must be on fire. I put my back against the trapdoor, bend my knees, and push with all my strength. The door lifts slightly, but I cannot hold it. I let it go and it slams shut with a loud bang.

I sit on the chair, my legs aching and shaking from the exertion. I decide to employ the hoe-like tool and the first-aid box in a final, desperate attempt to gain freedom. I place the box on the sill where the door will open, if I can shove hard enough. I bend my legs and push with all my strength. As the door opens ever so slightly, I insert the hoe blade in the crack. It's a start.

I come down the stairs again and put all my weight on the tool's handle, hoping it will not break. The crack widens, but I cannot hold it. I take a deep breath and try again, with all my strength. This time I raise the trapdoor a foot high, jamming the handle between the stairs to hold it in place. Then I shove the metal first-aid box under the door.

It will be a narrow squeeze, but I should be able to crawl through the small opening. Before I reach the opening, however, I'm hit by air so hot it might have come from a blast furnace. I retreat down the stairs, sit on my futon, and ask myself if I'm able to go back up the ladder and find out what really happened.

Meanwhile, I check the calendar on the floor next to my journal: 6, 8, 1945.

August 6, 1945.

Where is Tetsu's family? What has happened? Why is it so hot? Is the house on fire?

After a time, I decide that leaving the bomb shelter is much better than staying here. I brave the heat and wriggle through the narrow opening.

I cannot believe my eyes. There is no house. The beautiful home is gone. Shattered timbers are scattered over the floor. One large timber has fallen on top of the trapdoor. The roof tiles have been blown off and are scattered up the hill. There is no fire. Yet the air is so hot I feel as if I'm burning. I cover my face with my shirt, except for my eyes, and wonder what can possibly have happened.

It is as if a tremendous hot wind has swept everything away in its path. The typhoon we went through in the fishing boat off the coast of Okinawa seems almost ridiculously mild by comparison.

I free the hoe-like tool from the trapdoor and sit down on the timber that held me prisoner. I need time to clear my mind. What I see is astonishing, beyond my wildest imagination.

It is dark, but the dark is quite unlike any night I have ever known. A strange orange glow hovers, like a canopy, over land swept clean of standing buildings. Donut-shaped fires burn everywhere. Black water, in drops big as marbles, falls on a landscape that appears to have been stripped of any sign of life.

The garden in which Tetsu's father took such pride is gone. The estate's trees, stripped clean of foliage, are now just leafless poles stuck in the ground. The teahouse and shrine have vanished.

There is not a trace of anything that was there yesterday. It is a different world.

How could this have happened without hundreds of bomb-laden B-29s flying overhead? But if they flew over, why didn't I hear them? And why didn't I hear hundreds of explosions?

All I know is that where the city of Hiroshima stood just a short time ago, there is now only fire and smoke.

It is much too bizarre for me to comprehend. I've no idea how long I've been sitting here, numbed by what I've seen.

Suddenly, I think of Tetsu, and then of his parents and his sister. They will need help. I open the metal box, fill my pockets with first-aid supplies, and start out toward the city. I must find them and treat them.

I run down the lane Tetsu and I traveled when we arrived at his parents' home. This time there are no trees. I approach the main road into the city. I recognize the place where the farmer let us out of the wagon. I see that I am the only one heading into town. The road is packed with people running away from the city. No cars. No bicycles. Just people running, crying, and screaming. Many seem to have horrible burns. Flesh hangs from arms and faces. Ears dangle from heads. Noses are gone or hang just below the eyes, looking like overcooked meat. Women clutch babies that appear to be nothing more than dead flesh. Some women run naked, arms flung into the air. Others bear the imprint of flowered kimonos on their flesh.

I see a wall with the shadow of a human being burned into the masonry. I pass a boy, about 13, naked, his hair burned off, eyelids gone, groin pocked and pitted, one ear burned, skin hanging to his shoulders. He carries a girl of about three. Her body is terribly burned.

He stops in front of me, puts his precious burden on the ground and stands there, arms outstretched. His face is hideous, but he has beautiful dark eyes. In a calm voice, he speaks. I recognize a few of the Japanese words. Help. Sister. Water.

Oh how I wish I could do something. But I can't. I turn from the carnage and run. I run and run. Soon I am wet from the big black drops of rain. I have no idea where I am. The image of the little boy and his sister haunts me. Then there is another image—of a little boy and his sister lying dead, alongside their mother, on a field in Okinawa. Their bodies were riddled with bullets after the mother fired on us.

It is night. It is dark but not dark. Fire lights the sky. The smells and sounds of death and destruction permeate everything.

I come to the river. It is crowded with people trying to get relief from their burns. I am still running. Tetsu and his family are in my thoughts constantly. Where are they? How can I find them?

I don't know how long I've been running when suddenly I find myself back at the home of Tetsu's parents. Nothing has changed, except that I removed the timber from the trapdoor before leaving. I open the trapdoor in the kitchen floor and return to the tiny room that saved me from the fate of the poor people up above.

As the door slams above my head, I remember that Tetsu is out of the city. Perhaps he has survived. Falling on my futon, exhausted, I wonder if any members of his family possibly could have survived. I put my face in my hands and begin to cry. How can I lose any more friends?

Why not me?

Why Tetsu?

All I can think about is the line John taught me back in April.

Dulce et decorum est pro patria mori.

How wonderful it is to die for your country.

The old lie.

CHAPTER 27

✵

Something is shaking me. Is it an earthquake? Was the destruction, the catastrophe that destroyed Hiroshima, an earthquake? Are we having another?

"Wake up, Arch. Wake up. We need you."

I awaken with strange thoughts racing through my mind.

Where the hell am I? What happened to the bomb shelter? What happened to Tetsu and his family? I think I am completely insane. I am back in the war. I have no desire to be back in the war. I thought I was away from the battle. Do I have to go on with the killing and see more death and destruction?

Who is this man who is waking me? How does he know my name? I'm totally confused.

"Arch, get up. It's Jack. Are you OK?"

Jack is one of the new replacements in my squad.

"Arch, we need you! Now! Right now! Goddamn it, get your ass in gear. Earl and Mitch got in trouble last night. Real trouble.

"Tell me that again."

Jack looks at me as if he doesn't know me, as if he has never seen me before. As if there's something wrong with me.

"Arch, get with it, Goddamn it. What the hell's going on with you? Earl's calling for you. Mitch is dead. Will you get the lead out, or do I have to drag you out. What the hell's wrong with you? You remember last night, don't you?"

"I remember last night," I answer, trying to focus on where I am.

Jack spells it out for me: "Remember how we've been losing somebody or having somebody wounded almost every night, even though we're behind the front? The Japs are still getting through and giving us a lot of shit.

"Well, Mitch and Earl were going to be prepared. They took that old piece of netting they'd found and put up poles to hold it over the hole. It was great, Arch. You couldn't see them at all after they put foliage on the net.

"What it looks like, Arch, is that they were throwing grenades. We found two Jap bodies in front of their hole, killed by grenades. But it looks like one of Earl's and Mitch's grenades, fully armed with the pin pulled, got caught in the net and they didn't hear it fall back into their hole. They were riddled with shrapnel when it exploded.

"Mitch is gone. Earl's still able to talk, but not for long. He's asking for you, Arch. There's something he wants to tell you."

How did I get back here? What's happening to me? I don't know what's real and what isn't.

"Where's Mike?" I ask Jack.

"We haven't seen him since he found his brother dead, Arch."

The army had issued an order that the twins were never to be in the same hole at night or even in the same squad. But our company commander, at the twins' request, allowed them to be in our squad. Now I see why they shouldn't have been together.

I run over to Mitch's and Earl's hole with Jack. Mitch's mutilated body is lying in the bottom of the hole. I kneel beside Earl, wiping the blood from his face with my shirt and water from my canteen. His blue eyes move toward me. I reach out, take his hand, and mop beads of sweat from his clammy forehead. I hold the canteen to his lips. His body trembles as he tries to speak. At first I can't understand what he's trying to say. In time, I pick out a few weak words in the same voice I remember from our days in the first grade.

"Arch...please go visit her...if you get home see my mother...you know her...take my things home...don't tell her how...I died...."

Earl is quiet for some time. I continue to hold his hand and wipe his forehead.

"Don't tell her how...I died.... Just tell her...the Japs killed me.... There's a Jap flag in my pack.... Give it...go see..."

He squeezes my hand and then his hand goes limp, his blue eyes looking straight ahead without the eyelids twitching. He's gone. Dead. We used to walk home from school together. Why did I let them put the Goddamned net over their hole? It's another of the "if only's" of this awful war.

I lay my head on Earl's chest and cry. I look up after a time and see the whole squad in tears.

"You guys," I say, "get the ponchos out and take Earl and Mitch over to the company area and telephone graves registration. OK?"

"Don't we say anything for them?" Jack asks. "These are my first friends over here, and they're dead."

"Sure, go ahead, Jack."

"What do I say?"

"Anything you feel like saying."

Jack's voice is strong, but it sounds as if he's far away.

"Our Father who art..." Earl was small for his age and quiet in school.

"Hallowed be Thy name..." He was kind and caring.

"Thy kingdom come." His mother is a widow. His father was killed in my father's mill.

"Thy will be done on earth..." Is it God's will that Earl should die in a hole far from home?

"As it is in heaven…" I hear someone crying. Earl has two brothers. All the brothers wore blue bib-overalls to school. When I stopped at their house after school, his mother always had something for us to eat.

"Give us this day…" That's all we ask. Jack repeats, "Give us this day." He stops, unable to say more. All of us are on our knees, in tears. Some of us make the sign of the cross.

The bodies go down the hill on ponchos. All I can think of is the last words, "Give us this day."

That's all we can ask.

"Where's Mike?" I shout. "Where's Mike."

Nobody answers.

"Did anyone see him?"

A voice says, "I think he went down the hill, that way, Arch. I really don't know."

I run down the hill, calling "Mike! Mike!" It's daylight now, but cloudy. The hill is slippery from rain during the night.

When I reach the bottom of the slick slope, I skid into a fall, automatically putting my rifle over my head to keep it dry and clean. When I regain my feet, I look around and see Mike sitting by a stream, eating dirt.

Approaching him, I notice that he smells of excrement. He makes incoherent animal-like sounds. And his glassy eyes stare vacantly into the distance, the familiar thousand-yard stare of the GI who has seen too much.

I probably have it myself.

I sit down beside Mike and put my arm around him. We both give way to tears. There's nothing for either of us to say. I have the feeling we're in a deep, dark hole and there's no light, no way out. It's wet, but not cold. It's hot, but not uncomfortable. It's humid, but not sticky.

There are just the two of us, and nobody to pull us out of the hole. Drumming in my mind are Jack's last words—"give us this day."

Do I even want this day? Is this to be a lost day, or my last day?

I struggle against losing my fragile grip on reality. But I no longer have the ability to resist. I'm worn out, exhausted in heart, mind, and body. I long for death. I am not worthy to live. I am racked by guilt.

I see the Japanese wife. She's calling: "Take my hand and join my husband in peace."

I have survived so far. But for what? No matter what happens, death will never come to me. Everyone else can die. I can't die. I am floundering in the never-ending present. I wonder what I have done to deserve living in a perpetual hell on earth.

Is this my punishment? Did I fire too far to the right during the banzai attack? Did I kill Cook?

To know what this anguish is like, one must face an enemy in kill-or-be-killed close combat. The survivor is burdened by sorrow for friends who did not survive and by guilt for what he did in order to survive.

If we live through this war, we will never be able to explain adequately to anyone what it was like. So we'll seal these memories in the deepest recesses of our hearts and minds. There they will remain—out of reach of those who cannot understand—visited by us only when something reminds us of those we once loved and lost.

CHAPTER 28

❁

The sounds in a field hospital are strange to me. Gone are the artillery or small-arms fire, replaced by rain pounding on an olive-drab canvas roof, wind whipping through tent ropes, and medics scurrying around.

I'm frightened. I'm on a canvas cot, my rifle resting atop the cot's wooden crossbars. It's hot and so humid it almost feels as if it is raining inside the tent, which smells of dirty soldiers in dirty fatigues.

The tent holds 20 cots, 10 on each side of the center poles. The center aisle is muddy. I have no idea how I arrived at this hospital or how long I've been here. The last thing I remember is sitting in the mud with Mike at the foot of a hill.

My mind races, flitting from the valley to Mike to the lieutenant's wife in the rainbow. I talk with her.

"I can't go with you. I have to take care of Mike. He needs me. He's lost his twin brother."

"I will give you both peace," she says.

I hear someone coming down the aisle. I hear the sucking sound of his boots as he pulls them from the mud. I am moving off Skyline Ridge at 0400 with Lee and Cook.

"Lee, I want you to meet Mike. His brother was killed last night."

"Who's the new guy with you, Arch?" Cook asks.

"How is Lieutenant Ken?" I ask Cook.

"The medic says they don't think he'll lose his leg," Cook answers.

I hear a new voice.

"Just a little stick and you'll feel better," the new voice says. I feel a sting in my arm.

"Don't leave me. Don't leave me, Arch," Mike says.

How did I get here? Where's Mike? If this is a hospital it's not like Camp Ernie Pyle. That one was round, with six GIs to a tent and a lot of psychos.

The last time I looked, my rifle was on the crossbars beneath my cot. I look again, for reassurance, and it's no longer there. I panic. I'm afraid of an attack with nothing to defend myself. The Japs are coming over the hill where the artillery shells are landing.

"Who took my rifle?" I scream. "The rifle's mine. I need it now. It's been with me since the landing on April first. It has never left me. Where is it?"

A new voice calls loudly from the next cot.

"What's the Goddamned fuss about?"

"My rifle's not here," I yell loudly. "The Japs are coming over the hill, and I don't stand a chance without my rifle."

The soldier in the next cot says, "You don't need your rifle any more, soldier."

"But I do. I haven't been without it since we landed."

"Don't worry. You don't need it any more."

"I'll always need it. Somebody took it away from me. How did I get here? Where's Mike? Where am I?"

A medic hears the commotion and comes to my cot, injecting me with a sedative. Before the drug takes effect, I make sure my pack is still with me. It contains my pistols, flags, and everything I own in the world. Most important are the pictures of Lee's family and the Japanese family. All of my possessions and Lee's are in my pack. I ask the soldier next to me to be sure nothing of mine is taken while I'm drugged.

"I don't have my rifle, I don't have my rifle."

"Take it easy, Kid. I'll keep an eye on your pack. I won't let anyone touch it."

I make him promise.

"It's OK, Soldier. I'm a marine and as long as I'm able, I'll make sure everything of yours is safe."

The next thing I know, it's morning. Because the marine and I are able to walk, a medic takes us to the mess tent for breakfast. The marine asks how I feel.

"I have lots of questions."

"Can I ask you a favor?" he says. "You see my hands? Would you be kind enough to feed me."

"Sure," I say. "That way we'll each get every other bite."

"I've lost my spoon, Lee."

"That's OK, Arch, we'll use mine."

He gives me a knowing look, as we sit together on the side of our fox-hole.

"Who's Lee?"

"It's a long story," I say. "Maybe some other time."

"You were sort of out of it when you came in last week," he says. "But after I told you I'd take care of your things you settled down. By the way, my name's Bob. Sorry I can't reach your hand. My hands are out of commission in these Goddamned bandages. I'm with the 1st Marines."

The words spill from me like machine-gun fire. "I'm Arch," I say. "7th Infantry. I was with a member of my squad. His twin brother was killed. He's in bad shape. I have to take care of him. He needs my help."

"Slow down, Arch, so I can understand what you're telling me. When did you start to stutter?"

"I stuttered as a kid in the first three grades of school. Never again until I went to the hospital the last time. It doesn't bother me because I really don't stutter. People think I do."

I tell Bob about Mike. How I found him.

"Mike could be here," I say. "I have to find him. I don't know how long ago it was. We were together."

"Slow down again, Arch, I can't understand you."

"I slid down the hill. Mitch was dead. Earl died. The Japanese lady in the rainbow was there. Bob, the rainbow is broken. I tried to put it together again."

Bob looks at me as if I am nuts and says, "It's OK, Kid. I don't get all that, but that's OK. We'll talk more later. I had a guy in my platoon like you."

After breakfast Bob says, "We'll find out if Mike's in the hospital. Give me his name and I'll get someone to check the roster. If he's here the medic will find him."

That evening the medic comes by. "Arch, there are 25 Mikes in the hospital."

"It's Mike of Company C of the 184th. It's driving me crazy not knowing where he is."

"You came here from another hospital last week for evacuation," the medic says. "You're due for evacuation. Your friend most likely already has been evacuated to a hospital in Hawaii. You can be sure he's receiving good care."

When the medic left, Bob said, "When you were in the head, Arch, we were told that we're scheduled for evacuation as early as tomorrow if we're OK to travel."

"Where will we be going?"

"Probably the big fleet hospital on Guam. I hear that's where the wounded are being taken."

"I can't go! I can't go! I'm a squad leader. My squad is here. I can't leave them."

"I feel the same way, Arch. I'm a platoon leader. But until I get better I'm no good to my men and neither are you. Look at those bandaged legs of yours. What good are you with puss running out of your legs? How did they get that way?"

"The same way your hands got the way they are, Bob."

I try to remember just how.

"Jake, come back! Come back! Come back! Don't fire too far to the right. Get the Jap blowing the trumpet."

I'm trying to protect my hole and one side of Lee's and Cook's hole with just an M-1.

"Jake, you took my BAR. I feel my legs getting wet."

I reach down and touch them. There's blood. A piece of spent shrapnel protrudes from my left leg.

Bob slaps my face.

"Arch! Arch! Get hold of yourself. It's OK. You're all right."

"I'm OK, Bob. I'm OK."

"I don't want to hit you again," Bob says. "By the way, I watched your stuff last night and today. It's still all there. But I don't know what happened to your rifle. It doesn't matter now, since we may be out of here tomorrow. You can't take weapons on the airplane."

"Airplane? I've never been on an airplane. You can't take weapons? Listen, Bob, I've got two Jap pistols in my pack and I'm not going to let anybody take them from me."

"Let's just be quiet and hope some asshole doesn't go through our packs and find what we have," Bob says. "I also have some things they wouldn't want me to have, and I have no intention of giving them up. I have a pistol, too. And a prayer book one of my friends was carrying in the breast pocket of his fatigues. The book has a bullet hole right through the center of it."

"OK," I say, "let's just keep our mouths shut about the whole thing. If they don't suspect anything, maybe we'll be all right."

We remain silent, until Bob says he's afraid I might do or say something that will keep me from being evacuated.

"You have to get control of yourself, Arch," he says. "You can't act like you did last night and again this afternoon. I don't know what's wrong, but you made a hell of a fuss in your sleep. You keep that up and they'll lock you up and throw the key away. I'll wake you up if it happens again in your sleep. All you have to do is take five minutes at a time when you don't think.

"I know it's hard to let go of the past. I have terrible pictures in my mind, too. I don't know if I can ever be free of them. But let's hold on until we're out of here and in a place where we can get help."

"I don't know if I can do that, Bob."

"I'll help you, Arch. I want to be ready for the big push in November."

"What big push?"

"When we hit Japan, Arch. I want to be in on that. Isn't that the reason we're out here?"

"Maybe if I get better I can go in with my old squad, Bob."

I try not to sleep, because as soon as I doze off it's all there again—the paralyzing terror and lurid, violent dreams that are real enough to touch.

Hoping Bob is still awake, I ask him what sort of fuss I make when I'm asleep.

Bob repeats a few things he's heard me say, then adds, "The front's behind us now, Arch. But the battles have made a lasting impression."

I tell him, "Bob, the battle of Skyline Ridge pursues me wherever I go. If we survive the invasion of Japan who knows what new nightmares we'll carry around with us."

Bob answers, "I've been told there's a large hospital on Guam where we'll be rehabilitated and made ready for the big invasion. They say that battle will make Okinawa seem like a picnic."

"Let's not think that far ahead. Today is all I can handle right now, and I'm not doing a very good job of that. Let's clear our minds of all thought for the next five minutes, just as you suggested."

My legs are bandaged and packed with a new drug, an antibiotic called penicillin ointment. Bob's burned arms and hands are re-bandaged with the same medication. We both hope we're on the evacuation list for tomorrow. We understand two hospital planes will be flying to Guam.

The next morning I'm shocked to find my hands and feet badly swollen. I don't know what's wrong, but I'm sure if the medic sees them there'll be no evacuation for me.

I wonder if I've contracted some tropical disease. Or is it mental? Do I really want to leave Okinawa?

All I have to do is show the medic my hands and feet and I won't be going anywhere. The rest of my squad is still up there, even though the island is supposed to be secured. There's a lot of the enemy left to dig out, and I'm thinking about leaving them. The new guys are all replacements, and they don't know their ass from a hole in the ground.

They don't know how to watch for booby traps on dead bodies or in discarded clothing or in what they collect as souvenirs. I have to be there to tell them. I can't let them down. They depend on me.

No, I'm not going to do what I did last time when I hitchhiked all the way south. But am I ready to begin the journey back to the States?

If I leave, I'll always think I let them down. Do I want to live with that feeling of guilt the rest of my life? On the other hand, I could go on the plane to Guam, get better in a rest camp and rejoin my squad for the big invasion of Japan's mainland. If I did that I wouldn't consider myself a coward, a quitter, or a deserter. If I did that I might even find Tetsu, if I live through the invasion.

I think constantly about Tetsu. He was with his girl friend the night Hiroshima was destroyed. Maybe he lived. Maybe he's all right. He was, after all, on the other side of the hill. But the rest of his family was in the city. Anyway, I must find out what happened to them—some day.

I can't tell Bob or anybody else what happened at Hiroshima. He'd never believe me.

"OK," I tell Bob. "I've been thinking it over and I'll be able to travel today. I'll stay under control if you keep reminding me."

After lunch, the medic comes by and says, "You two get your clothes on and be ready for transport in 20 minutes."

"You," he says, looking at me, "We don't have a name for you or any identification. We couldn't find any dogtags on you when you came in."

"I don't have any dogtags. They were lost in battle."

"That's OK. Just give me your name and serial number."

I give him the information. He writes it down on my chart and on the evacuation list.

"Arch," says Bob, "you could have been anybody you wanted to be when he asked for your name and serial number. In fact, you could start a new life."

"I couldn't do that. It wouldn't be right. Let's get dressed."

We're wearing the same OD boxer shorts and T-shirts we wore when we hit the island back in April. Mine have been washed just twice—once in a stream, the other time out on the boat with Tetsu. My fatigues are on the bed as a pillow.

I help Bob dress. I slit the sleeves of his fatigue jacket so he gets his bandaged arms and hands inside. I button his fly and tie his boots. Then I use my bayonet, which is on the side of my pack, to slit my pants legs so I can get my pants over my bandaged legs. I leave my combat boots untied because my feet are swollen.

Bob gives me his field jacket. There's no way he can get his hands and arms through the sleeves. While putting it on, I notice the lieutenant's bars. All of a sudden, I'm an officer.

The ambulance takes us to Kadena airstrip, and more memories.

"Kid," Lee says. "Run as fast as you can. Keep your head down and zig-zag if you can. When you get across, jump into that trench where you can see the rest of the squad. Cook and I will give you cover fire. I'll cover you the best I can. Take off, Kid."

I see the dirt kicking up in front of me, alongside me, behind me. It's bullets. Somebody's trying to kill me. I could die crossing this airstrip.

I turn and give Lee cover fire.

Lee jumps in the trench after me.

"How did I do? I was scared shitless."

"Great, Kid. You didn't get hit, you're still alive and you gave me great cover fire."

"That is the first time for me."

"Arch, Arch," Bob says. "Stop your babbling and get aboard this aircraft. I don't want to slap you again."

Those who are ambulatory board the C-54 evacuation aircraft from the front, up a long flight of stairs; those who can't walk, because of internal injuries or missing limbs, are lifted on a platform by a forklift through a large cargo door halfway down the fuselage.

I am in a state of disbelief. I've never been close to any airplane, let alone one as big as a C-54. The space inside is outfitted like a hospital ward. There are seats for the "ambulatories" and stretchers with mattresses stacked three-high on both sides of the fuselage for those who can't walk. There's a nurses' station in the center of the aircraft and two nurses to manage it. There is one doctor aboard.

The airplane is better equipped than some field hospitals.

Although there is no hot food, we are served cold meals and coffee is kept hot in thermos jugs similar to the ones my family took on picnics.

My heart races with excitement when they start the engines. I strap myself into the seat for takeoff and show Bob my hands and feet, swollen out of shape by what look like giant mosquito bites. The welts force my fingers and toes apart.

"What the hell's wrong with you?" Bob asks. "How long have you been like that?"

"For some time now," I reply. "My hands and feet were this bad when I woke up this morning."

"Why the hell didn't you tell the medic so he could give you some medication?"

"I thought they'd cancel my evacuation."

"As soon as we're airborne, Arch, call the nurse over and see what she can do."

The airplane's four engines roar as we taxi to the end of the runway.

"Bob," I shout over the roar, "have you ever flown before? Does the airplane shake like this all the time? Is everything all right?"

"It's fine, Arch. I've flown several times. It isn't this noisy and the vibrations quit once we're airborne. It's OK."

We stop at the end of the runway for an engine check. Then the engines roar and the C-54 starts down the runway—the same runway I raced across on April 1. The forward thrust of the airplane pins me against the back of my seat. I'm scared but excited. When we become airborne things become smoother and quieter, just as Bob promised.

Looking out the window I see one of our two P-41 fighter-plane escorts. Through the mist I see Hill 178, then Skyline Ridge. Unable to hold back the tears, I start to tell Bob that's where all my good friends were...

"Don't do that, Arch."

"I thought I told you."

"Told me what, Arch?"

"That's where he died. That black hill over there, just north of Naha. That's where he died."

As Conical Peak and Yonabaru come into view, Bob sees the tears running down my cheeks. He puts his arm around me.

"It's OK, Arch. Hang on."

I see the hill where Lee and Cook died. We both cry when I show him the hill. As we move away from the familiar hills, they become smaller and smaller to the human eye, increasingly insignificant.

As we fly over the north end of Okinawa and the islands beyond, I see places that remind me of my journey with Tetsu. I have not told Bob about Tetsu, but it all comes back to me.

"Arch, get in the middle of the boat and you won't get wet," Tetsu says.

"See that island straight ahead? That's Yoron. There's a good harbor on the south end, if I remember right. Those two planes are going to strafe us. The little girl is rowing toward us."

"Get down," I holler. "Tetsu, get down. They're strafing us."

"Arch," Bob says, shaking me. "Cut it out. Hang on."

As clearly as if I were there again, I see the first island where we were strafed, where the little girl was wounded. But how can I tell Bob? He'd never believe me.

"Arch, who's this Tetsu?" he asks. "You say a lot of stuff I can't understand. Lee. Cook. Jake. Those names I can figure out. But Tetsu's a Jap name."

"I can't…"

I change the subject, remarking on how small Okinawa looks—a tiny speck in a huge ocean—as we leave it behind.

"Bob, it's getting so tiny."

"That island will never be insignificant in our lives, Arch. We've seen and learned things there that will be etched in our memories forever. Nobody can take them from us.

"Friends are dead who were closer than brothers. We took their bodies down the hill on ponchos and spoke our earthly farewells. They'll be with us as long as we live."

I wish I could tell Bob about Tetsu. Instead I say, "I know what you mean, Bob."

We sit in silence as the island disappears.

A nurse approaches. "Are you two all right?"

"I think so," I answer.

Bob asks her to look at my hands, adding, "He wouldn't tell anyone for fear he wouldn't be evacuated."

The nurse examines my hands and says, "Are you like this all over?"

"Almost."

She goes to the nurses' station, confers with the doctor, and returns with a shot of adrenalin and two pills to counter the effects of the penicillin.

"You'll be OK until we get to Guam," she says. "You have a severe attack of hives, caused by anxiety or an allergic reaction. The medications should cause the swelling to go down and the itching to stop."

She checks Bob's burns and my legs and tells us she thinks we need some sleep. She gives us medications so we will rest.

As we move farther from Okinawa, we fall into a light sleep.

CHAPTER 29

❀

A nurse taps my shoulder and softly says, "Wake up, soldier."

The plane has begun its descent to the naval airstrip on Guam, in the Marianas. Tires squeal as the C-54 touches down. Ambulances are waiting for us to come to a halt so they can transport us to the 111th Fleet Hospital.

At the hospital, I and other ambulatory patients are deloused in showers containing DDT. Combat packs and clothing are fumigated and returned. Before dressing in hospital pajamas and robes, we're lined up to be checked for venereal disease. I've always felt sorry for the medical officers sitting on stools and looking at a row of penises in what is called a short-arm inspection. We laugh self-consciously.

"They think we were fucking the gooks," a patient behind me says. "I could never do that. She might be hiding a grenade up there and I'd detonate it."

With our bodies deloused, clothes fumigated and genitals inspected, we slip into navy pajamas and bathrobes with USN on our backs and go to the mess hall for a hot meal. I'm at a table eating good food, not out of a can or sharing a spoon with someone, but using a knife and fork. The chow line has a wonderful array of foods: roast beef with gravy, fried chicken, mashed potatoes, assorted vegetables, bread, milk, coffee, salad, and ice cream and cake for dessert. Unbelievable!

Bob and I are still together. I feed him. Together we enjoy our first meal away from combat. After dinner we're taken to the doctors' offices. Bob goes one way, I go another. We wish each other luck and express a desire to see each other again.

As a corpsman takes me down a long hall, then outside to a Quonset hut, I'm suddenly back to April 1, when Ralph and Jim and I went ashore on Okinawa.

"We made it up the beach; Ralph, I'm going to the 7th Division, and Jim says he in the 97th."

"I'm in the 27th," Ralph says.

"What are you talking about," the corpsman asks.

"I didn't say anything."

The corpsman takes me to a small room with a desk and several chairs. Pictures of mountains and a waterfall and the familiar photograph of Admiral Nimitz with our late President Roosevelt are on the wall behind the desk.

"Take a chair," the corpsman says as he puts my records on the desk. "The doctor will be with you shortly."

In a few minutes the doctor enters. He's a tall man with graying hair and a kindly face. He sits at the desk, opens and studies my medical chart.

"How are you feeling?" he asks.

"Not too bad after my first flight."

He spends some time assessing the information in my medical records.

With a puzzled look, he says, "There's no identification on your chart. Could I see your dogtags, Lieutenant?"

"I don't have any dogtags, Sir."

"What happened to the dogtags? They're your only identification."

"I know, Sir. All I can tell you is they're lost. All I can give you is my name, rank and serial number."

"Since your dogtags are missing, we'll have to go by what you tell us, until it can be verified."

"I'm PFC Archie Morrison, 39480181. I feel like a prisoner of war giving you this information, Doctor. Sir, I'm not an officer."

"You're not a lieutenant?"

"No. I'm a private first class."

"But you have bars on the field jacket you're holding. Your chart says Lt. Morrison, no ID."

I tell him about my friend, Bob.

"We'll have to wait for verification. Tell me a little about yourself."

I tell him as little as I think is necessary: my name, rank, and serial number.

"The questions," he says, "are to verify the diagnosis I find in your chart. My job is to put you in the section of this hospital where you will receive the best possible treatment."

I barely hear him.

"I made it. I made it. Do you have any pain pills? The burns hurt a lot."

"Are you burned, Soldier?" the doctor asks.

"No, Sir!"

"What were you talking about? 'I made it, and pain pills.'"

"I didn't, Sir."

"Soldier, are you with me? Do you feel all right."

"I'm fine, Sir."

"I must place you for treatment in the hospital."

"Captain, all I want is to get my legs healed so I can get back to my outfit as soon as possible. I'm a squad leader, my men are all replacements and they need me."

"You don't want to go back to the States and home?" he asks.

It's so hard to concentrate.

"He's a great teacher, Lee is. He told me to find a young replacement and teach him like he taught me."

"Morrison, do you follow me? What are you talking about?"

"Yes, Sir. I follow."

"You don't want to go back to the States and home?" he asks again.

"No, Sir. I'm needed with my squad. I'm the most experienced man in the squad. But I'm no good with my legs like this."

I open my robe and show him my bandages.

"If I go home they won't know me. I don't know what I would do. I don't have a wife or kids. I really don't get along with my parents. I'm 19 years old now and all I know is war, the army and combat. All I've been taught is how to kill."

"Tell me what happened to you in battle. Have you lost close friends? How do you sleep? Do you have dreams?"

He's asking personal questions that I can't possibly answer. It takes everything I have to hang on.

"Morrison, do you mind if I call you *Son*?"

"Yes, Sir. I'm not your son. You can call me Arch."

"Arch, did you hear my last question."

"No, Sir."

He repeats the question.

"It's none of your Goddamned business. You wouldn't understand if I confided in you, and that's impossible since you can't possibly comprehend. It's none of your concern."

"That's all right, Son, Arch. We'll take care of you."

He examines my legs and diagnoses the problem as "jungle rot with unhealed shrapnel wounds."

"You don't want to go back to the States and you don't want to go home?" the captain asks again.

"That's right, Sir. I'm needed with my squad, as I told you before."

He tells me my legs will heal as soon as I get out of this part of the world and get adequate nutrition and rest. A corpsman escorts me to my new home—a metal Quonset hut with a large open ward and 15 beds on each side of a center aisle.

I have a bed with a table, a lamp, and a chair beside the table. The bed has blue blankets with USN in white letters in the center. There are clean white sheets and a pillow with a pillowcase. I gaze in disbelief.

I'm given a towel, washcloth, soap, shaving cream, tooth brush, toothpaste, and five packs of Chesterfields. The corpsman says I can turn my dirty clothes into the laundry twice a week, and all I have to do is ask for anything I need.

The corpsmen's station, in the center of the ward, contains file cabinets with our charts, a locked cabinet containing our pills, a scale to weigh us, and a few books and comic books on a shelf.

I'm weighed. 116 pounds!

"Do you remember what you weighed when you left the States, Arch?" the corpsman asks.

"I think I was around 160 pounds."

"You sure have lost weight. Why don't you walk around and get acquainted."

I walk around a bit, but nobody speaks to me. They just give me the thousand-yard stare that I know so well.

At the end of the ward there's a porch and a 10-foot-high chain-link fence with barbed-wire on top. The fence extends around a small yard, about as wide as the Quonset hut and maybe 15-feet deep.

Returning to the corpsman's station, I ask about the barbed-wire fence.

"That's for your protection," he says. "I'll discuss it later."

"I need the latrine in the worst way," I say. "Where is it?"

"It's the *head* now, soldier. You're in a naval hospital. It's right over there."

I stop by my bed for a towel, washcloth, and soap and notice, for the first time, that although I have shaving cream there is no razor.

The head turns out to be a very large room, with wash basins, toilets, urinals, and showers.

While I'm at the urinal I figure out why I don't have a razor. I'm in another "camp shaky," a place like Camp Ernie Pyle, where they put those who have combat fatigue or whatever euphemism they choose to use.

I escaped from Camp Ernie Pyle and returned to my outfit. But now I'm on Guam and I know there is no way I can get out of here.

"This is a nut house," I say out loud. "I'm in a place for the crazies. That's why the barbed wire. That's why there are no razors."

I wash up and return to my bed. Lying down, I look up at the ceiling and think about how and why I've landed in this place. I feel I've let my squad down. I can see, as clearly as if I were still there, that last valley where Earl was killed, where one of the twins died, where Tetsu called my name in the middle of the night. And now I've abandoned my outfit.

I have no idea where Tetsu is. Maybe he's no longer living. The feeling is devastating. I'm just existing, with no desire to do anything or to see anybody.

The next thing I know it's morning. I go to the head and a large Negro is shaving with a great big pocketknife that must be very sharp. This is the closest I have ever been to a Negro, and I'm now living with him. He puts soap on his face and continues to shave. I don't talk to him, but sit on the toilet and wonder what to do next. I decide to take a shower. I spend 20 minutes in the shower, luxuriating in the feeling of hot water running over my body.

When I come out, the Negro soldier says, "I didn't talk at all when I first came here. You don't have to talk, but if you want to you'll find me in bed 20 and maybe we could go down to the tables at the end of the ward."

He explains the reason he uses a pocketknife instead of a razor.

"I shave with my knife because I won't ask the medic for a razor. They don't know I have this knife, which I keep with me all the time."

Having spoken, he sheds his pajamas and steps into the shower.

I return to the bed. Breakfast comes on large carts. We don't go to the mess hall like normal patients. We're insane.

Most of the patients go down to the tables by the doors that open into our "pen," which is what the patients call the *yard*. It has a barbed-wire fence around it.

I watch. The Negro man rises from the table, gets a plate of food and a cup of coffee and comes down to my bed.

"I'll just leave this here," he says. "You'll feel better if you eat. Even if it's only a little hot food, it beats cold C rations."

I try some of the breakfast. The coffee is good, but I have no desire to eat. Soon after the food carts are removed, the corpsman arrives and takes me to the doctor to treat my legs. As we walk outside to another Quonset hut, I notice the hospital grounds are beautifully landscaped with palm trees and flowering hibiscus. The fragrance is wonderful after months of gunpowder and human excrement.

During our walk, the corpsman tells me he'll be taking me to see another doctor in the afternoon. He says the doctor I'll be seeing is young and doesn't know much about war, having arrived from the States only last week.

In the afternoon I'm taken to Capt. Morgan's small, sparsely furnished office in an adjacent building. It contains a small desk, two chairs in front of the desk, one nicely padded chair behind it. There is a bookshelf with several medical books on psychology, a *Reader's Digest* dated August 1943, and a *Life* magazine just three months old. The floor is covered with linoleum and the walls are white.

On one wall is the same photograph of Admiral Nimitz and the late President Roosevelt that I've seen in other offices. Presumably President Truman's photograph hasn't gotten this far west.

On the other wall is a photograph of a 1939 Packard convertible, with Dr. Morgan standing beside it. He's wearing a bathing suit and holding a surfboard.

"Sit down, Soldier." I hate being called *soldier*. I suppress the urge to say that I have a name and it's on the chart in front of you.

"How are things going? I'm Dr. Morgan. I'll be your doctor while you're here. Sit down, please."

I don't know whether this is a question or a statement, so I don't answer. I just look up at the ceiling and think to myself: I suppose this young doctor is fresh out of medical school and has completed a three-week course in psychiatry, which qualifies him to treat me. I watch him study my chart for some time.

"There isn't much here in your medical record, Soldier. I'd like you to give me a little background of your experiences on Okinawa; then I'll be able to better understand the diagnosis of combat fatigue and infected leg wounds."

"I can't," I answer.

"What do you mean you can't? Where's your home? Where did you go to school? Where did you get your training? Are you a rifleman? Have you killed any of the enemy? Have you lost friends?" He asks these questions rapid-fire.

"I'm from Okinawa, the 184th Infantry, Company C, second squad. I want you to send me back as soon as my legs are healed."

"You want to go back?"

"That is what I said, Sir."

"Are you crazy?"

"That's up to you, Sir."

"You don't want my help so you can go home?"

"No, Sir."

"I'm trained to help psychological patients, soldiers like you who have cracked up in combat. Who could not take it."

"You help? Why, you're just out of medical school. What kind of training do you have to treat a teenage killer like me? When did you arrive from the States? Yesterday? How can you help anyone when you're still wet behind the ears, full of book-learning shit? When you get back from your first beachhead, from your first actual combat, from killing your first human, from seeing your best friends murdered, then and only then can you understand and think about maybe trying to help those you say can't take it. I'll bet you've never even seen a field hospital or talked to a combat medic."

"You've said enough, Soldier."

"Don't call me *soldier* again. I hate it. I have a name. It's there on my chart."

"Don't say any more. You're speaking to a captain. I could put you in the stockade for insubordination, but I'm not going to. I'll take your condition into consideration. You know, Soldier, the stockade for psycho patients is confinement in a private room."

Ignoring his remarks, I say: "From the picture on the wall, I see you like expensive cars."

The captain takes it as a compliment. He says, "Are you into cars, Morrison? That car is my pride and joy."

"I thought so," I say. "You're one of those kids I've heard about. Your daddy gave you everything. Bought your way into USC Medical School with a deferment. You drove around the Southern California beaches in that fancy convertible with the homecoming queen. What does your daddy do—build those rotten liberty ships and bank the money or does he just give it to his little boy so he can play? I've been out here killing and losing men the likes of whom you'll never know, you son-of-a-bitch. You ought to go drown in your own shit."

"Enough, Soldier. I didn't ask to be here treating a bunch of cowards, quitters, and deserters. I would have preferred taking over a nice practice in West Los Angeles. But the army accepted me, flat-feet, post-nasal drip, hay fever and all."

He calls the corpsman, writes some orders on my chart and says, "Get this man out of here. I'll let you know what we'll do with him."

Later, the Negro soldier comes up to my bed and asks me to go outside with him to the pen. Another GI is there in navy pajamas and a red bathrobe. He's a tall, skinny guy with big eyes. He doesn't say a thing.

"How did it go with the doctor?" my friend asks.

"That so-called doctor is a kid. He doesn't know shit," I reply.

"His father's in ship-building," my friend says. "The war's making him rich."

"He asked a lot of questions, but I didn't tell him anything. If I tried to explain how things are in combat, he'd have no damn understanding of what I was talking about. He thinks we're all psychos, insane. Maybe we are."

"I wish he could spend just one day with my body-detail squad," my friend says. "He didn't even know we had body squads."

"You were in graves registration? You came up front with those trucks with high racks, where you put the bodies you collect? The bodies wrapped in ponchos at the bottom of the hills?"

"That's me. Where else do they put a Negro man in the army? Polishing the officers' shoes, maybe?

"My job was to fill out the forms. The cause of death, if I could determine it. A description of the body and, most important, the dogtags had to be fastened to the body. We filled out the forms and attached them to the ponchos. When we finished loading we trucked the bodies back to the area where graves' registration put them in wooden caskets. I don't know from there on."

"Don't say anymore. I know."

"The skinny guy here," my friend says, "doesn't remember his name or who he is. I think he knows, but he won't tell anybody anything about himself."

"I'm in the 96th Division and I want out of here," the skinny soldier says.

"I have an old friend in the 96th," I say. "We went through basic training together at Camp Roberts, then to Hawaii, and finally Okinawa. Old
Stan Curry, a great guy, about six-feet and very good-looking. When we
went to the enlisted men's club at Ford Ord, if there were girls, why old
Stan had no trouble. One night we heard Duke Ellington there. The
band introduced a new song, 'I'm Beginning to See the Light.' That was
one night I had too much beer.

"You probably wouldn't know him."

"I was in the same company."

"That's really a coincidence. When did you last see him? He's probably just as handsome and waiting to get back where the girls are. We had
some good times in Hawaii when we were stationed at Schofield."

"I can't talk about it," the skinny guy says.

"That's fair enough for me, but can you tell me if he's OK? Was he
killed or is he alive?"

The skinny man says nothing.

"Come on, you've got to give me an answer. Please, tell me what you
know."

The skinny man remains silent for some time, then he begins to talk.

"Since you know this Curry, I can tell you he's alive. The last time I
saw him was mid-July when he was sent to a hospital."

"How was he? Badly wounded?"

"He'd lost both legs."

"Both legs? Stan?"

We part company and I return to my bed where I cover my head with
my pillow.

I think of a poem in one of John's books. I feel under my bed, find
my pack, open it, and take out the book. I turn to Sassoon's "They," the
poem he had read aloud to me. I focus on the last line:

And the Bishop said, "The ways of God are strange!"

I take John's books and go out on the fenced porch. There I can find a chair and sit out of sight of those in the ward. As I read, the fence disappears and I'm once again in Tetsu's father's Zen garden. I am sitting on the stone bench by the old black pine listening to words of wisdom from Mr. Kazuki. I think about our walk in the fragrant summer air. The thought of treading lightly on the moss-covered pathway brings peace and tranquility.

The next afternoon, after a nap, I find the Negro soldier and the skinny one seated in chairs at the sides of my bed. The Negro soldier asks if I've had any dreams that scared the shit out of me.

We all know the answer, because we often awaken in the night, hearing the screams of others or the yells we make ourselves. Some patients have to be put in restraints.

I had such a dream the previous night. I saw Lee and talked to him. And I saw Tetsu the night before the big blast in Hiroshima.

We share the fact that, yes, we all have such dreams. But I don't go into details, because those things are tucked away in a corner of my mind that only I can enter.

My friends aren't able to share their dreams either, but before they leave, we make a promise to each other. If one or two or all three of us survive this war, we'll do all in our power to tell others that war doesn't need to be, that the world can't go on killing young boys like us forever.

As T.S. Eliot says, we are hollow men, we are the dead men. We are a lost generation. Another generation.

CHAPTER 30

❀

It is August 4, 1945 and I am settled into the routine of the psycho ward at the Naval Hospital on Guam.

We're now called *patients*, which is not much better than being called *soldier*. My closest friends—the Negro and the skinny GI—are seated around my bed in the middle of the ward, sharing canned fruit juice and crackers from the little kitchen the navy refers to as the *galley*.

It is early afternoon, hot and humid. All the windows are open. The three of us are in our navy pajamas and bathrobes, talking about nothing that makes sense. Most of the time we sit in silence with the familiar thousand-yard stare.

We never talk about Okinawa, combat, or home. We have never bothered to learn each other's names or what state or town we are from. We know nothing about each other's families.

Mostly we say nothing and that's OK, because we're comfortable that way. We just like being with each other.

The hospital becomes very confining when you can't go out. We are not even allowed to go for a walk.

Later in the day, I dress in my gook clothes—the same baggy pants and loose top I wore on the fishing boat—and head toward the porch, carrying a chair. I think I see someone there who looks familiar. I sit down in the chair beside him.

> The ocean is all around us and Tetsu is telling me about the killing in the hospital cave. How he was ordered to carry out that slaughter. I do not stutter while talking to Tetsu. He tells me he doesn't hate the officer who ordered him to kill all those men. The officer just didn't know any better. He was schooled to believe he must carry out the orders given.
>
> No questions asked.
>
> "Arch," Tetsu says as he holds the tiller of our boat, "we have to learn to forgive. We have to learn to love our enemies. I think Jesus said that.
>
> "We can, Arch. You and I have learned. Watch your head, the sail is going to swing around. The only way we can teach others is for them to see our example."

I see the fence again. I am sitting in my chair alone.

I walk back down the ward. I see the patients I usually ignore. Some men stay curled up on their beds like infants. Some constantly cry. Still others babble, garbage talk, not understandable. The corpsmen have to feed some of them. The violent ones are tied to their beds with restraints to protect themselves and others. Sometimes the ward is in chaos, with wails and screams and men fighting their straitjackets.

Night is the most difficult time, because night combat is so terrifying. Men awaken thinking they're still in combat and under attack. An 18-year-old, two beds down from me—a replacement who spent only four days in combat—goes through the same tortured dream every night. At about 0200, he re-enacts a banzai attack, screaming wildly at each enemy he kills.

"I shot that Goddamned Jap right between the eyes and the blood spurts out 10 feet. Here comes another Jap. He's going to get my bayonet through his gut. I killed him. What a bloody mess. This one I shot and that one I killed with a bayonet. I've got to shoot that big one and destroy his face. I stab his buddy with my bayonet. His insides come out. Pete, get down in the hole. We have to use grenades."

The young soldier describes in bloody detail how he rolls grenades out of his hole to destroy the enemy. He calls out the names of his squad members—John, Dave, Hank, Pete—telling how each became a statistic.

"Pete, get your head down."

He mimics the dying sounds we all know.

"Pete, stay down! Don't go out!
"Pete, not you too!"

The young man, we hear, is the only survivor of his squad. He is never violent with others in the ward as some are during their nightmares.

Last night the soldier across the aisle from my bed choked the man in the bed next to him, thinking the patient was a Jap. It took three of us to pull him off. Someone ran for the corpsman. It took several corpsmen to get the soldier into a straitjacket. Like others who turn violent, he was taken to a *lock ward*, a padded room where he could hurt neither other patients nor himself.

The men who are taken away to a lock ward never return. But, then, most of us are anonymous. There are no cards from family and loved ones on our bedside tables, no flowers, no visitors seated in the chair beside our beds.

I haven't seen any *Life* photographers around. Our ward isn't the one that will be featured in an article for the folks back home. We aren't likely to be interviewed by war correspondents eager to tell our thrilling stories to the world.

Most of us make it through the night without harming others. But that doesn't mean we don't have violent nightmares. I often awaken after a combat dream soaked with sweat and shaking. At such times, I go out to the pen and look up at the moon and stars the rest of the night. During these mental wanderings, I meet many of my dead comrades.

Nobody talks about such things. What's the use? Everyone is experiencing the same thing.

I figure I can endure it. But what about Mike? His twin brother is dead. I wonder what happened to him after I left him in that muddy valley. Is he somewhere in a straitjacket? Is he lying on a cot in a padded room? Did he live or kill himself?

My old squad members continue to march through my dreams. And Tetsu's always nearby. Nights are wild!

My condition has been formally diagnosed as "combat fatigue." Why can't they be honest and call it what it really is: "combat insanity?"

After breakfast one morning—we don't keep track of days of the week or the time of day—my Negro friend asks again if I've stuttered for a long time. I remember his asking about my stuttering when we met for the first time. I gave him the same answer, "What do you mean? I don't stutter."

"OK, forget it," he says, as if nothing was said. Then he proceeds to tell me about his recurring dream.

"I see my grandson," he says. "It must be in the future, because I don't have a grandson, just a son. My grandson is a good-looking young man and he asks his dad, my son, about me, his grandfather.

"'Was grandpa in the war, Dad?' the young man asks.

"'Search me,' my son answers. 'I don't even know when my dad died. I didn't know him. I don't even know when that wretched war took place or if my dad, your grandfather, was in combat. Ask your Uncle Fred, he's older and knows all about history.'

"So he goes to see Uncle Fred and says, 'Uncle Fred; can you tell me what my grandfather was like?'

"'Who?'

"'My grandfather.'

"'I don't remember. I try not to think about war. My father, your grandfather, wrote a few letters but never about the war. He never came home. You should have been taught about the war with Japan in school.'

"'Maybe they taught me about it, but I didn't know my grandpa fought in that war. Wars are boring and depressing. Nothing but guns, bombs, and battles. But, since grandpa was fighting in that war, it makes it different. How was he killed?'

"'I don't know. It's morbid to live in the past. All I know is he was killed. I don't like to focus on battles of the past.'

"The grandson answers, 'I don't think it's ancient history. It's not that long ago. There must be old men still alive who fought with grandpa, who can tell me about it.'"

After hearing the Negro soldier's dream, I'm left with a haunting question: Will anything we've done mean anything at all?

"What do you dream about, or do you even remember?" he asks.

"I don't want to talk about it."

"Come on. I talked about mine. You wake me up every night with a bunch of noisy stuff that doesn't make any sense. I promise not to tell anybody—not the corpsman, the other patients, or the doctor."

"OK, if you won't tell anybody. No telling what they'd do with me. They'd think I'm really nuts. OK, I see each of my comrades, my whole squad.

"The two who haunt me most—I can't tell you their names—but we cover each other well in combat. I hit the ground beside one of them. I can still feel the wet ground: it's rocky and uneven, and a small stump hits my belly. I give him that rap on the back that he did with me countless times when we covered each other in combat. Only this time he doesn't move. I have this horrible feeling inside, and I hit him harder on the back. My hand comes up all bloody. His blood. He's dead. I wake up shrieking. I think I didn't cover him like he taught me. I caused his death. I didn't see that Jap machinegunner. Then I'm afraid to go back to sleep, because I know it will happen all over again. If only I had been better at covering him, he'd be alive now. I caused his death.

"Then, all of a sudden, I see her."

"Who is *her*?"

"She's over in the far corner."

"Who is?"

"The Japanese wife in the picture. The picture I took out of the dead Jap's wallet. I need a light to see her, like the light we had in the cave hospital. She's calling me to join her husband, the man I killed.

"'Join him. I will give peace,' she says. 'I will take you to him.'

"I chase her out from behind the desk. She runs to the pen and right through the chain-link fence, calling to me: 'I will give you serenity.'

"I run back to bed, pull the blanket over my head, and see another squad member. I know I killed him. I fired too far to the right after Jake went berserk. I see the side of his head is gone. I see there's no eye or ear, just blood and red flesh. I can see inside his skull. I go wild. The medic comes and I even help him put me in a straitjacket, and I settle down and sleep."

"How often does this happen?"

"Almost every night. It's so frightening when I can't see everything. The enemy is in the corners of the room. I've seen them. They're real. The doctors say I'm hallucinating, but I'm not. If I don't do something about them, they'll kill me. Let's get a Coke and think about something else."

"What else is there?"

My Negro friend senses this is the time to share more of the night-mares that haunt us both.

"Do you ever get the feeling that I do at night?" he asks.

"What's that?"

"It's the covers on the bed. They get so heavy they feel like a powerful force pushing me through the bed. I haven't told anyone about it, but as the weight increases the walls of the room seem to recede from me and I become smaller and smaller. My arms and legs grow heavy. My arm is so heavy I can hardly move it. Soon, I can hardly lift a finger.

"I'm scared. Will this ever go away? I try to holler for a medic and not a sound comes out."

"That's awful," I say. "How long does it last?"

"I don't know. I don't know. When the medic comes by he takes one look at me and gives me a shot that takes me out of it for a long time. When I wake up I'm OK."

"Does it ever happen during the day?"

"No, thank God."

Mine does.

"The same thing happens to me, only I get it in the daytime too."

"I've noticed you with that thousand-yard stare."

"Yeah, that's when it happens. I just close out everything around me. I wonder if this will ever end. Is this the way I'm supposed to live the rest of my life? I refuse to accept that. When I'm in that mood, I wonder why I didn't go with the Japanese lady. But I'm afraid of her. The only way I can find the peace and serenity of her murdered husband is to let her kill me, just as I killed him. I watched and heard him die. She knows that's what I did, because he told her."

"I'm not sure anybody will ever understand us," my Negro friend says. "That's why I'm afraid to go home. Nobody, especially my family, will ever understand."

While sharing our nightmares, we didn't notice the entry of Dr. Morgan and our corpsman at the far end of the ward. When they draw close, I'm ready for the worst.

During their visits they check to see if we've performed the tasks assigned as part of our treatment. Some patients empty wastebaskets and ashtrays. Others record temperatures on patients' charts. I remember the time a patient broke a thermometer and tried to cut his wrists with it. He was covered with blood when they found him in the head.

My job is to ask patients if they've had a good bowel movement that day and record it on a chart. If a patient has dysentery—and many do—there's never enough room on the chart to put all the check marks beside their bed number.

"Where's Morrison?"

I hear my name from the other end of the ward. I walk slowly back to my bed.

"I see you haven't done your job today, Soldier."

"No, Sir."

"Refusing to carry out orders is a serious offense subject to punishment."

"Yes, Sir."

"Soldier, you have some things in your possession, in your pack to be precise, that you are not allowed to have in a hospital."

"How do you know that, Sir?"

"I know."

"Have you searched my pack, Sir?"

"I have, Soldier. It's my prerogative. I'm your commanding officer."

"Don't you dare look in my pack, you Goddamned shit. When did you do it?"

"While you were off having your legs treated. I had a corpsman with me as a witness."

"You son-of-a-bitch, you Goddamned shit. You stand there and tell me you went through my things without my permission?"

"I repeat that I'm your commanding officer, Soldier. I can do anything I want to with any of you men and your belongings. And you, Soldier, have weapons in your pack. Pistols!"

"What pistols, Sir?"

"You know very well what pistols I'm talking about. You know what's in your pack and so do I. But I'm willing to be reasonable. I could call the Shore Patrol for a violation of orders. They'd confiscate your weapons and put you on restriction."

"Put me on restriction?" I answer. "Could I be on any more restriction than I already am in this prison?"

"Try it in a straitjacket and water, Soldier. You'll cooperate. I'm willing to make you a fair offer and not report the incident."

By this time, almost every ambulatory patient in the ward has gathered to witness the confrontation.

"Make me an offer? Report the incident? You must be the one who's insane."

"No, Soldier, you're the one who's insane. That's why you're here. You, Soldier, have two choices. I'll buy those two pistols."

"What the hell do you mean I have two choices?" I holler. "You're my commanding officer. I'm your slave and you're my master. You have the power of life and death over me. Look at my chart. You'll find I have a name. I expect to be called by that name."

"My offer is, I'll give you $200 for the German Luger and $300 for the six-shot revolver. If you don't agree I'll call the Shore Patrol. They'll confiscate your weapons and you'll have nothing."

"And you, Sir, will also have nothing. You won't call the Shore Patrol. They would confiscate the weapons and their commanding officer would get them and fabricate a story just as you plan to do. You, Sir, are not deserving of the respect due an officer. You're trying to profit from a war at another person's expense. When did you get your medical degree, Captain?"

"None of your damned business."

"Wasn't it this year, from the University of Southern California? Why, you haven't even had an internship yet, just that quick course on 'battle insanity,' which provided you with all the answers. You're an instant expert in the field."

All the patients clap and laugh. One says, loudly, "Sir, it appears you got your battle experience in a Los Angeles classroom. We got ours in Okinawa killing men."

Everyone cheers.

Emboldened, the patient adds, "It appears your battle skills were learned in the Packard convertible we've all seen in that photograph on your office wall. How many pretty young women did you conquer in that car?"

That brings another outburst of laughter from the patients.

"That is enough from both of you," the captain says.

But I'm far from through.

"Sir," I say, "I know a doctor, USC class of 1941, who's a wonderful man, compassionate, honest, truthful, a true friend. He's a combat doctor who treats his patients the way human beings should be treated. He knows what happens to a mind under combat stress, because he has personally gone through the madness of battle."

Then I drop my bombshell.

"The only problem is, he's a Jap."

The ward grows quiet.

"You're displaying further symptoms of combat insanity, Soldier," says Dr. Morgan. "Hallucinations are common with shell shock, combat fatigue or insanity—whatever you choose to call your psychoses."

"You're wrong, Sir. It's no hallucination. I took a Japanese doctor prisoner and got to know him. I'll tell you the whole story, after we've settled the ownership of my personal property."

"What the hell are you talking about?" the captain asks.

At that moment, I suddenly understand what's going on in the captain's mind. I got those weapons by stealing them from the bodies of dead Japs. I want them as souvenirs of battle. The captain, who doesn't ever expect to see combat, wants to steal them from me so he can show them off as his souvenirs of battle.

"I know what you're going to do with those weapons, Captain. You're going to go home and show them off and tell your family how rough the war was. You'll tell how your field hospital was attacked by the enemy.

"You'll have to fabricate an authentic-sounding story and tell it very carefully, then you'll have to remember all the details so your damn bullshit won't be exposed. You might even be able to publish the story and make some money. I understand a lot of people back in the States are making money from war stories.

"When the attack came on your field hospital, a few 'brave men'— mostly captains, I imagine—take M-1s from soldiers lying wounded in the wards to defend the sick and wounded against a crazed enemy.

"You, the commanding officer, bravely kill two Jap officers, riddling one with bullets from a BAR. Have you ever fired a BAR, Sir? They have quite a kick and are hard to control. You can do it, Sir. The other Jap you kill by wrenching out his guts with your bayonet.

"Let's make the story better. The two Jap officers you killed were leading the attack. Many of the enemy were killed. You lead the hospital staff into battle, saving the field hospital and all the hospitalized soldiers.

"To further improve the story, you might tell how you knelt over one of the dead bodies while it was still warm and bleeding, to search for souvenirs. You find the pistol and photographs of the officer's wife and child and mother.

"Maybe you can find a bronze star to attest to your bravery and a purple heart in a pawnshop to let people know you were wounded in action.

"While you're talking about these weapons, be sure to tell your family the biggest lie of all, the one Wilfred Owen told us about—'*Dulce et decorum est pro patria mori'*—the idea that it's great, admirable and noble to die for one's country.

"One more thing. When you show your wife, children and grandchildren your war trophies, I'd appreciate it if you ended your speech by saying, 'The truth is, I took these weapons from a 19-year-old combat rifleman whose mind was all fucked up from close combat. He was the one who did the awful things I told you I did.

"That would be the honorable thing. But I don't expect you to tell the truth. You would rather take credit for being a brave man in a war you know nothing about.

"One of my dead comrades, John, used to read Shakespeare aloud in his foxhole at night. He'd say, 'To thine own self be true.' Look it up. It may come back to haunt you."

Dr. Morgan stands rigidly, his color rising. He barks to the corpsman, "Call the Shore Patrol. This soldier should be in the brig."

"Stay where you are," I say to the captain and the corpsman while I reach into my pack on the bed. I pull out the loaded revolver and point it at the commanding officer. His mouth drops open. His hands begin to shake and beads of perspiration form on his forehead.

I ask my Negro friend to go to the door and let no one in or out. He's a big man and he guards the door well.

"Now." I say, "Listen up, because I'm going to tell you what this pistol means to me. It's a better war story than you could make up.

"I stole this revolver from the body of a Jap the night of a counter-attack. That's the night that Nealy, a 16-year-old kid, got killed. That's the night the enemy came at us by the hundreds. Our outposts didn't have a chance. There were eight bodies in front of our hole. The last one dropped about three feet in front of me. Lee and I watched that lieutenant die.

"It took hours. The noises of death were unbearable. In the morning we rolled the body over. It was the first time I'd ever kicked a dead body. It was also the first time I'd touched a dead man. And it was also the first time I'd put my hand into a dead enemy's pocket. It made my stomach turn. I'll tell you what happened to me when I killed that man. I got sick. I puked up my guts. I pissed and shit my pants.

"Then I saw this pistol in his holster. I got down in my hole and used my rifle and bayonet to get the pistol out of the holster. It wasn't booby-trapped.

"The Japanese officer had his helmet on and his leggings neatly wound around his legs. He hadn't started to bloat yet. His eyes were open, staring at me. Even though he hadn't started to smell, he already had begun to attract flies, which flew in and out of his mouth and nose.

"My buddy, Lee, and I checked out the revolver. It was a six-shooter, the one I'm holding. I thought, 'My God, that's the first time we've seen one of these over here.'

"'So what do you think?' says Lee, 'Shall we take it?'

"'Sure,' I say, as I start going through the officer's pockets. There, I find two Jap flags. Usually they just carry one. We decide to take the flags, too.

"I ask Lee if he has a coin. He doesn't. So I open the Japanese officer's wallet and find some coins. I ask Lee if he's willing to flip for possession of the revolver and the flags. Heads gets the revolver, tails gets both flags. We flip it. I win the revolver. Lee takes one flag and says, 'Here, take the other one, I only need one.'

"That doesn't seem fair. So we compromise. We decide to put the revolver and flags into our packs and whichever one of us survives gets them all."

I ask the skinny, quiet soldier who has become my friend to take the wallet from my pack.

Still pointing the revolver at the commanding officer, I say, "I want you to see what's in the Japanese officer's wallet, you son-of-a-bitch."

I feel myself slipping over the edge.

The captain suddenly looks different. He is wearing Japanese shoes and his legs are wrapped. His pants are identical to those worn by the

Japanese officer I killed. He is wearing glasses and there is an enemy helmet on his head. He's a Jap and his rifle is pointed at me.

In panic, I cry out, "This revolver is loaded and cocked. Don't move."
He obeys.
"Put the rifle down."
Again he complies
I take the pictures out of the wallet, one at a time, and show him.
He says, "This middle-aged woman is my mother. You can tell your children you killed her son. The next one is my beautiful wife. You can tell your children you killed her husband."
"The last picture, please," I say to the skinny soldier. He holds up the picture of a beautiful two-year-old girl.
"You killed her father.
"What a hero you are."
The captain is suddenly back in front of me. The Japanese officer is gone. Was the Japanese officer there only for me? I go on as if nothing had happened, still pointing the revolver.
"Now for the German Luger. I'll give you the history of this piece, whether you want to hear anymore or not. I want your story to be accurate.
"I'm sure you'll want the children you have someday to be proud of their father. They can go to school and tell the other children how brave and heroic he was. Why, you could even take the pistols to school and tell about them. It's too bad I don't have Jake's collection for you. Jake cut the ears off dead Japs and knocked their teeth out with his rifle butt and put them all in a bag. That would be a wonderful thing to show the children."
All the patients roar with laughter.
"You've said enough, Soldier. Put that gun down!"
I release the safety.
"Here's your $500. I'm leaving."

"No, you're not leaving, you son-of-a-bitch. You're going to hear the story of your other stolen property.

"It happened on the hill above Yonabaru, the day before Lee was killed. It was the night of the banzai attack. The Japs blew trumpets and we could hear them coming up the hill. This was the night I killed a man so close to me that if I had waited a moment longer, he would have been the killer, and you wouldn't have a war story or be able to steal my Luger.

"He came up the hill in front of me, this Japanese lieutenant. He was leading the charge. I could see his eyes, wild with emotion, his shiny bayonet aimed at my body. I held down the trigger of the BAR and the bullets almost cut him in half. He lay there all night, looking at me, groaning and making the terrible noises of death. That morning, after the fighting was over—except for the enemy who had come through our lines and were now behind us—I was detailed to do mop up.

"'Lee,' I said, 'here's another one we know hasn't been booby-trapped.' We went through his pocket and found this Luger." I hold up a very nice weapon of the kind usually found on the European front.

"Lee and I had the same agreement as before. We put the Luger and another flag in our pack and never told anybody. That was the last day I was with Lee. As the sole survivor, these things are now mine."

I feel myself losing touch with the people in the room once more. But I press on with my story.

"So here I am now, Sir. My mind is in a turmoil. I can see the fishing boat on the blue ocean. Tetsu is at the tiller. I am midship, working with the bilge pump.

"'*Tetsu asks, 'Arch, doesn't the Bible say Jesus said to love your enemies?'*'"

"*I think so, Tetsu, why do you ask?*"

"'*Well, it doesn't work.*'"

"'*What are you taking about?' I say.*"

"'Just this,' he says, 'To love your enemies is impossible. If you love your enemy, you feel compassionate toward him. Then he's no longer your enemy, because you understand him. You can't have an enemy you understand.

"'Remember, Arch, if you were brought up in a family like your enemy's family, if you had been educated like your enemy, if you had been trained in the same way he was, you would act as he acts. The only thing that would be different is the shape of your eyes and the color of your skin.

"'If we understand each other, we can't be enemies.

"'Instead of war, there would be peace, because I would be like you and you would be just like me. That's what Jesus taught. That's what Buddha taught.'"

I see the doctor in front of me. He is now my enemy. I understand Tetsu as I never have before. Will this doctor in front of me continue the tradition and teach his children and other children the sick tradition of *Dulce et decorum est pro patria mori*? "How wonderful it is to give one's life for one's country."

I have given this doctor the props he needs to keep the traditions of war alive. Pistols. Flags. And a real war story.

Do I understand him? If I could understand his life and he could understand my life, we would not be enemies. I would not be so angry with him that I hate him.

As a doctor, he could be a force for peace. He could start by helping the men in this ward.

How can I help him? I think back to the young lieutenant who arrived as our new platoon leader at Skyline Ridge. I helped him understand what we'd been through. And when he understood, he was accepted by the combat veterans he was to lead.

Maybe there's a way to do something for this doctor. We must work together.

"Tetsu said: 'There are no sides to uphold. Every side is our side. There is no evil side. God is on all sides. We who have had combat experiences are best equipped to illuminate the roots of war and show the way to peace.'

"Today is August 5, 1945. I'm going to tell you what's going to happen August 6, tomorrow."

Everyone watches me carefully, wondering what's coming next. I wonder if I should do this? Should I tell them what I know about the devastation of Hiroshima? Should I describe it to them? They won't believe the story. They'll laugh. I'll be confined in the lock ward for sure. But I decide to go ahead.

"Let me tell you what I know. We were behind the lines, cleaning the enemy out of the pine trees. That is when I first met Tetsu, the Japanese medical doctor. Unlike our captain, he cares about his patients.

"He went to the University of Southern California, just like the captain here. His folks live in Hiroshima, and he returned there for a visit in June of 1941. He was drafted, just like you and me. He spent time in a hospital near Singapore, where he treated British and Canadian soldiers in the best way he could without his superiors knowing what he was doing.

"He was transferred to the Philippines, to a U.S. POW camp. He had one corpsman. Despite limited supplies, he did all he could to help these men. He was the only doctor on the ship that brought these men to POW camps in Japan. He told me he cried at night because he lacked the drugs and equipment to adequately treat their wounds and diseases."

The Negro soldier interrupts. "How did he tell you all this? Where did you get time to talk?"

"Sorry, I got ahead of myself. While we were mopping up, cleaning the enemy out of hiding places in the trees, we ordered anybody in hiding to come out with their clothes off and their hands behind their heads.

"Tetsu answered, 'Don't shoot, we're coming out as you ask.' I couldn't believe I was hearing English with a western accent. I took three prisoners back to the company area. Our sergeant, the acting company commander, sent the three prisoners back to the POW compound. When they were out of sight, I heard three rifle shots. Those who had been detailed to take the prisoners to the compound returned shortly after I heard the shots.

"That night, at about 0200, while I was alone in my foxhole, I heard my name called very quietly behind me. Tetsu jumped into my hole."

I relate how we deserted together, got a fishing boat, and traveled together up the Ryukyu Islands. I tell how we got to know about each other, about our families, our childhood, our religious backgrounds. Alone in a small boat on a long journey with someone who was supposedly my enemy, I found out how very much alike we were. We gained respect for each other and a form of love. No, not the kind a 19-year-old American boy normally dreams about, but a warmth, a kinship with a fellow human being that shows itself in mutual respect. I shared this feeling with Tetsu, a Jap.

I continue: "We arrived at Tetsu's home on the outskirts of Hiroshima on August 2. His folks were very kind to me, not at all belligerent. And when Tetsu told them our story, they showed me admiration and respect. They were concerned for my safety and kept me secluded during the day. I was allowed out only in the evening, when they thought it was safe. I slept in their bomb shelter, which was small, but comfortable.

"That's where I saw the unbelievable flash of light at 0815 August 6. When I finally forced my way through the bomb shelter's heavy trapdoor I could not believe what I saw. The city was completely destroyed."

The doctor laughs and says, "What hallucinations. You're insane, soldier. You're a textbook case. Now put that gun down and stop all this bullshit."

I drop the gun and fall on my bed sobbing. What choice do I have? I'm nothing but a messed-up GI, and now there is no way I'm going back to my outfit.

"That's enough, you bastard," the captain shouts as he grabs the revolver and the Luger and throws five $100 bills at me.

All the patients hoot. The captain scurries for the door. The Negro soldier lets him pass.

I take stock of my assets. I still have three flags and the ammo for the two pistols hidden in my pillowcase. I also have the wallet with the picture of the mother, wife, and baby. I also have the captain's $500.

I shove the money into the Japanese wallet and hide it. The three of us—the skinny soldier, the Negro soldier, and I—go out to the pen and look up at the blue sky and the white clouds and at the palm trees and tropical flowers beyond the fence.

We are still alive and we have each other. But we see no future. After we have stood in silence for a time, soaking up the warmth of the sun, the corpsman comes by with our medications. He has new orders for me. I'm to be evacuated immediately to the hospital at Schofield Barracks in Hawaii.

We have a little soup from the galley, then return to our beds—the walking dead—*the hollow men.*

CHAPTER 31

❀

I awake to the sound of heavy footsteps on the kitchen floor. I don't know how long I've been asleep in the bomb shelter. No one should be walking around in the destroyed Kazuki house. I pull down the stairs, climb to the trapdoor and push it open far enough to see the kitchen floor. I also see two shoes and two legs. Since they are men's shoes, I presume it's a man standing in what remains of the kitchen. I quietly close the trapdoor, sit on the floor, and plan how I will confront the person above me.

I decide that if he opens the trapdoor, there is no way I can escape and there is no way I can defend myself. The only solution is for me to take the offensive. I climb back up the stairs, quickly push open the trapdoor and let it fall with a bang as I leap onto the kitchen floor.

The person turns around as I prepare to attack. My God, it's Tetsu.

"You're alive! You're alive! How did you get here? It's wonderful to see you. I never thought I'd see you again."

"I ran back as quickly as I could after the explosion," Tetsu says. "The people are all burned. It looks like X-ray burns. There's black rain, thick smoke, and fires everywhere. The closer I got to the city the worse it was. It was hard to move against the mobs of people fleeing the city. Tell

345

me what happened, Arch. Tell me what you went through. Is there any sign of my family?"

We sit on one of the roof beams of the demolished home. I relate everything I saw and heard to the best of my ability, including the story of the boy holding his sister and asking for water and help.

"I can only hope my family found some shelter, some protection," he says. "They could be all right."

"They were in the city, Tetsu," I say. "Look at what used to be the city."

We walk beyond the shambles of the house and scan the incredible devastation.

"I don't think my father could ever come here," Tetsu says. "Everything he worked for is gone. Look where the garden used to be. Now it's just bare ground. Everything is gone.

"But I must look for them, Arch. I must look for them."

Tetsu breaks down and cries. I put my arm around his shoulder.

"Remember the night, a short time after we got home, when we raised the blackout curtains, Arch, and looked out over the city by moonlight? Now look at it, or rather what's left of it.

"I must find my father and mother, even if it's only their bodies. I'm going to look at the day-care center and the bus barn. I don't know where Tomiko's factory is located. Could you prepare some food from the emergency supplies in the bomb shelter, Arch? For when I come back."

As Tetsu runs toward the road leading into the city, I return to the bomb shelter and heat dried fish and rice on a little charcoal stove. Then I sit on the floor and wait for Tetsu.

CHAPTER 32

❁

Now hear this!
Now hear this!
The squawk box sounds at 0830 August 6, 1945.
"The war is over!
"The war is over!
"We used a secret weapon!
"It destroyed an entire city!
"The Japs are close to surrendering!
"The war is over!"

The corpsman runs into the ward shouting. We all jump up and run toward him.

Somebody calls out: "Don't give us that Goddamned U.S. b.s. We don't need to hear any more bullshit."

The skinny soldier, the Negro soldier, and I walk out to the pen, sit in some broken-down cane chairs in the sunshine, and just look at each other.

The Negro soldier is the first to break the silence. "It can't be true," he says. "The war is never going to be over. We all know that. It's probably just propaganda to keep up our morale."

The corpsman comes outside with four cups of coffee to join us. "I think it might be true," he says. "There has never been an official navy proclamation like this before. Rumors start in the head. But this is an official navy announcement."

I ask the corpsman if he has any whisky. "Yes," he replies, "in my locker. The captain gave me a bottle for my birthday."

"You're a friend of ours. Why don't you get it so we can celebrate? You see, I know the war is going to be over. I saw it on August 6, just as I told you yesterday."

"Now I know what was dropped on Hiroshima—a secret weapon. It wasn't an earthquake. There was just one airplane and one bomb. Tetsu was almost right in thinking the people had X-ray burns. They were radiation burns."

"How the hell do you know, Arch?" my friends ask.

"I don't know," I reply. "I just don't know. As I said, I was there. I saw it happen."

None of us thought we'd live to see an end to the war.

The corpsman returns with a bottle of Jack Daniels, four glasses, and a pan full of ice. He pours a large glass for each of us, adds ice, and gives us the drinks. I take a swallow. It burns all the way down my throat. I'm not used to it. There are a lot of things I haven't tried. That's why they called me "Kid" in my outfit and said they were going to get me drunk and get me bred when we got back to the States.

I take another sip of the whisky. It isn't so bad this time. I think about my old squad—Lee, Cook, John, Jake, Martinez, Nealy, and Tetsu, too, because I think he's earned his way into our squad. I drink a toast to my lost comrades, who won't get a chance to take me out when we return to the States.

I think about the cruelty of war. We didn't need Okinawa. If they had dropped the bomb earlier, say before April 1…We would have saved maybe 500,000 men and women—Japanese, Okinawan, and American. If there had been no Okinawan invasion, I wouldn't have known my squad or Tetsu…I would not have come to know the human cost of combat as I know it now. I don't know whether I would have come to oppose war. But I sure as hell would not have become one of those men who favor war as long as somebody else fights it. Even before Okinawa I knew where I stood on that question. I don't want anybody to go, no matter what the posters say.

About noon, 1200, the captain came to the ward with the official Navy announcement just as lunch was arriving. The squawk box beat him to it and he left hurriedly.

> Now hear this!
> Now hear this!
> THE UNITED STATES AIR FORCE HAS DROPPED THE
> FIRST ATOMIC BOMB IN HISTORY ON THE
> JAPANESE CITY OF HIROSHIMA.
> THE CITY HAS BEEN COMPLETELY DESTROYED.
> PRESIDENT TRUMAN HAS ANNOUNCED THAT
> THERE ARE PEACE OVERTURES.
> HE WILL ACCEPT ONLY UNCONDITIONAL SURREN-
> DER IMMEDIATELY OR A SECOND ATOMIC BOMB
> WILL BE DROPPED…
> MEN, IT LOOKS AS IF THE WAR IS OVER!

The announcement is repeated.
I go back to my bed, put my head on my pillow and cry.

Epilogue

❧

Ralph and Jim and Archie—the three men who went ashore on the island of Okinawa on April 1, 1945—survived the war and remained friends. Ralph, uninjured in the war, earned a law degree at Harvard, married, and raised a fine family. He served for many years as city attorney of Kirkland, a mid-sized town in Washington State's Puget Sound basin. A life-long smoker after picking up the habit in World War II, he died of lung cancer at age 74.

Jim lost both legs in an artillery explosion on Okinawa. He returned home, learned to walk with prostheses, and married the Red Cross volunteer who taught him to walk. After graduating from the University of Washington with a degree in advertising and communication, he was unable to find employment. He took his own life in 1952.

Some of the names of the squad members have been changed. Many died in combat.

Archie, the author of this book, left military hospitals after lengthy treatment for "combat fatigue" and fulfilled a life-long dream of going into health care by becoming a dentist. He married, raised a family, and practiced dentistry in the Seattle area. He has suffered from bouts of depression throughout his life. He is a recovering alcoholic.

Afterword

✿

Don Duncan

Although Archie Morrison's *Just Like Me: Beyond the Thousand-Yard Stare* has all the fireworks, heroism, and terror one expects in a war story, it transcends the genre by focusing as much on the psychic aspects of combat as it does on the bullets, bayonets, mortar shells, land mines, and flamethrowers that made Okinawa a living hell for combatants on both sides.

There was treatment for the physical wounds Morrison suffered on that distant island, where the landscape and the natives' tranquil, pastoral way of life were changed forever by some of World War II's most brutal battles. In fact, Morrison's shrapnel scars are hardly visible today.

The young private first class was not, however, able to rid himself of the memories of cradling dying comrades in his arms in the mud and stink of the battlefield, of wondering if an errant shot from his rifle had killed one of his best friends, of watching the life drain from young enemy soldiers that he, the product of a fundamentalist Christian home, has gunned down with vicious skill.

While in foxholes and in military hospitals, Morrison drifts in and out of reality, searching for answers to age-old dilemmas of war:

How can both sides be so positive that God, right, and justice are on their side? Why do the leaders who get us into wars always let someone else do the killing, bestow its highest honors on its most skilled killers?

In the latter part of *Just Like Me: Beyond the Thousand-Yard Stare*, Morrison's search for answers, while in the grip of "combat fatigue," takes him on a journey to Hiroshima with a most unlikely companion—a Japanese medical officer taken prisoner by Morrison's unit.

When the stunning climax is reached, many may wonder if such a thing could really happen.

Carol Lodmell

As the daughter of a career military officer who spent five years away from home during World War II, I am grateful to have been given the opportunity to read *Just Like Me*. Had I read the book years ago, it would have helped me understand the changes I observed in my father after the war and his reluctance to speak about his experience.

The reader enters the mind of a young soldier whose world is transformed so horribly that he loses his sense of reality. Thus the book gives insight into how the horrors of war produce bitterness in a young boy, thrust him into mental chaos, and shake the foundations of his religious training and beliefs. Vicariously one experiences the terror of being in battle by day and surviving in a foxhole by night.

With defense mechanism intact, the young soldier and a captured Japanese medical officer together flee the battleground. Their subsequent flight enables them to discuss their respective cultures, their philosophies of life, and the emotional pain the war has wrought.

Through the mind of the young soldier one cannot help but contemplate the inevitable questions which arise from witnessing man's inhumanity to man. The book also allows us to observe the mental deterioration of the protagonist as a result of continued guilt, fear, exhaustion, and prolonged revulsion.

Richard Prince

I have known Archie 50 years, although, in a real sense, to meet Archie is to know him. My brother and I first encountered him on the steps of the administration building at the University of Washington, all of us there to register for dental school. In the relatively brief period of conversation, Archie spoke easily and openly of life and himself. We felt we knew him. The next 50 years proved we did.

We have found Archie a man of energy and action—no half measures. For many years, in addition to his private practice, he committed himself to the Job Corps as a dentist. He donated a kidney to his son who had endured years of dialysis; he went aboard the ship *Hope* to give his services as a dentist to Nicaraguans. He climbed Mt. Rainier, Mt. Baker, and other Northwest peaks before climbing surged in popularity. As he grew into middle age, he threw himself into his ever-larger garden of flowers, vegetables and fruits, trees and extensive lawns. He annually committed himself to generous dinner celebrations of Beethoven's birthday. All the while he was the husband of a lovely wife and the proud father of three.

Yet, during these many years Archie uncharacteristically avoided one thing—his World War II experiences. Late in life, after struggling through William Manchester's *Goodbye Darkness*—for Archie, painful chapter after painful chapter—he began to deal with his own suppressed demons. He began to write this book.

Denzil Walters

Events in Archie Morrison's novel will lead readers to ask whether truth is found in what happens or what could have happened. The story distinguishes itself from other accounts of war when in the middle of combat the soldier-narrator acts on peace-time principles that war has not buried.

Morrison's account is in the words of soldiers living and fighting in holes in the earth. Seconds away from oblivion with every barrage, soldiers do not use the language of the dinner table at the homes they left. From the rough truths of death in the wasted earth, the infantryman's humane sensibilities are salvaged on the other side of what was called "shell shock" in World War I. Responses of readers will be quickened as they wrestle with the questions that come to the gentle man who is called upon to turn his back on the rules of his home, his church, and his schoolroom to obey the injunctions that go with the duties of an infantryman under fire and returning fire.

While fighting in conformity with programmed beliefs, Morrison's infantryman is drawn to act on truths that can be seen as insanity or his salvation from insanity. Ideals submerged in the practices he questioned as a boy rise in the reflections of the man.

As a novelist, Morrison has an advantage over the witness testifying in a courtroom. The writer takes the stand, raises his right hand, and asks everyone to join him in vows to look at life his way.

While ordering the world according to his design, he takes truth along with him. He builds a world close to his ideals, surmounting the objections that come with the testimony of the state's witnesses.

Notes

❀ ·

Chapter 4

For accounts of battle in this chapter I drew from my memories, rein-
forced with reading in *The Hourglass, A History of the 7th Division
in World War II, and Okinawa: The Last Battle of World War II.*

In *Doing Battle,* Paul Fussell describes the blood-thirst that rises in
close combat, a condition that changes, at least momentarily, a
man's personality. When I looked into the frightened eyes of the
enemy and he looked into my terrorized being, we were both
transformed. On reading Fussell's book, I realized that the feeling
I experienced—the rush, the high, the euphoria—was not unique
to me.

Chapter 5

"The Spirit of the Bayonet" is found in *Accidental Journey.*

Chapter 7

Statistics on death and casualties in battle are found in *The Hourglass*

Chapter 11

An account of an infantry rifleman going up the hill over and over,
appearing in *The Hourglass,* served to weave memory with history.

Chapter 18

The History of an Island People, by George H. Kerr, presents a detailed story of Okinawa, including the tombs.

"Okinawa, the Threshold to Japan," in the October 1945 *National Geographic* proved useful in describing the routine of civilians. "Okinawa, the Island Rebuilt," appearing in the *National Geographic* in 1955, provided details on clothes worn at a party.

The Girl with the White Flag, by Tomiko Higa, sets forth a record of the sickness that took many lives and a description of a farm at Shuri.

I also drew upon *The Regeneration Trilogy*, by Pat Barker, for parallels in world wars a quarter century apart.

Chapter 19

"The King's Song" is from *Okinawa: The History of an Island People*.

The description of the ship going up and down the Ryukyus is from a 1950 *National Geographic* article.

Chapter 21

The name of the pilot of the aircraft that sank the *Prince of Wales* and the *Repulse* appears in *The Rising Sun*, by John Toland.

Chapter 24

Excellent descriptions of Zen gardens appear in *The World of Zen Gardens* by Isao Oshkawa and *Zen Gardens* by Tom Wright and Mezuro Kabsuhiko.

Chapter 25

For a close look at the ceremony described here I found *The Way of Tea*, by Rand Castile, valuable.

Chapter 26

I relied on John Hersey's *Hiroshima* for the image of the wall with the imprint of a human burned in the fire following the dropping of the atomic bomb.

Chapter 32

How the outcome of the war would have been changed if the U.S. military leaders had decided not to fight the Japanese on Okinawa cannot be known for certain, I know. In my evaluation of the issues involved in that question, I weigh the statistics. The deaths of the combatants totaled 122,300, including 110,071 Japanese and 12,200 Americans. Deaths of Okinawans have been estimated at 50,000 to 150,000. The wide range of the estimated Okinawan civilian deaths creates a sad picture of a war that left the survivors in doubt about the fate of family members.

References

❀

Appleman, Roy E. *Okinawa:* the Last Battle. New York: BDD Special Editions, BDD Promotional Book Company, 1947.

Barker, A.J. *Okinawa.* London: Bison Books, 1981.

Barker, Pat. *The Regeneration Trilogy.* New York: Viking, 1986.

Billard, Jules B. "Okinawa, the Island Without a Country," *National Geographic*, September 1969.

Bradbury, Ray. *Zen in the Art of Writing.* Carpa Press, Joshua Odell Editions, 1990.

Caputo, Philip. *A Rumor of War.* New York: Ballantine Books.

Castile, Rand. *The Way of Tea.* New York & Tokyo: 1971

Diffenderfer, Hope A. "Okinawa, the Island Rebuilt." *National Geographic*, 1955.

Duncan, David D. "Okinawa, Threshold to Japan." *National Geographic.* October, 1945.

Earhart, H. Byron. *Japanese Religion: Unity and Diversity*, Third Edition. Belmont, California: Wadsworth Publishing Co.

Fussell, Paul, ed. *Siegfried Sassoon's Long Journey. Selections from the Sherston Memoirs.*
___. *Thank God for the Atom Bomb, and Other Essays.* New York: Summit Books.
___. *Doing Battle: The Making of a Skeptic.* Little Brown and Co.
___. *The Great War and Modern Memory.* Oxford: Oxford University Press, 1975.

Gard, Richard A., ed. *Buddhism.* New York: George Brazeller, 1962.

Hart-Davis, Rupert, ed. *Siegfried Sassoon Diaries 1915-1918.* London: Faber and Faber Limited, 1983.

Helprin, Mark. *A Soldier of the Great War.* New York: Avon Books, 1991.

Hemingway, Ernest. *Farewell to Arms.* New York: Charles Scribner's Sons, 1957.

Herrigel, Eugene. *Zen in the Art of Archery.* New York: Vintage Books.

Hersey, John. *Hiroshima.* New York: Bantam, 1986.

Higa, Tomiko. *The Girl with the White Flag.* Tokyo: Kidan Sha-International, 1991

Holtom, D.C. *Modern Japan and Shinto Nationalism: A study of Present-Day Trends in Japanese Religions.* New York: Paragon Book Reprint Corp., 1993.

Humphreys, Christmas. Zen Buddhism. London: George Allen and Unwick, 1996.

Kerr, George H. Okinawa,The History of an Island People (Revised). Boston: Tuttle Publishing, 2000.

Leckie, Robert. Okinawa: The Last Battle of World War II. New York: Viking, 1995.

Love, Edmund G. *The Hourglass: A History of the 7th Infantry Division in World War II*. Washington, D.C.: Infantry Journal Press, 1950.

Manchester, William. *American Caesar*. Boston and Toronto: Little, Brown and Company, 1978.
___. *Goodbye, Darkness: A Memoir of the Pacific War*. New York: Dell Publishing, 1950.
___. *The Last Lion: Winston Spencer Churchill: Visionary Glory, 1874-1932*.

Martin, Philip. *The Zen Path through Depression*, San Francisco: Harper, 1999.

Moore, Robert W. "Okinawa, Pacific Outpost." *National Geographic*, April, 1950.

Oshihkawa, Isao. *The World of Zen Gardens*. Tokyo: Gurafikkusha, 1991.

Owen, Wilfred. *The Collected Poems of Wilfred Owen*. New York: New Directions Publishing Corporation, 1965.

Remarque, Erich Maria. *All Quiet on the Western Front*. New York: Fawcett Crest, 1975.

Sassoon, Siegfried. *Memoirs of an Infantry Officer*. London: Faber and Faber, 1965.
___. *Satirical Poems*. New York: Viking Press, 1926.

Schwartz, William Leonard. "Peacetime Rambles in the Ryukyus." *National Geographic*. May, 1945.

Shay, Jonathan. *Achillies in Vietnam*. New York: Simon and Schuster.

Sherrow, Victoria. *Hiroshima*. New York: New Discovery Books, 1994.

Slawson, David. Secret Teachings in the Art of Japanese Gardens.

Stewart Sidney. *Give Us This Day*. New York: W.W. Norton & Co., 1957.

Toland, John. *Gods of War*. Toronto: Doherty Associates and Co., 1986.
___. *The Rising Sun: The Rise and Fall of the Japanese Empire 1936-1945*. New York: Random House, Bantam Books, 1971.

Watts, Alan. *The Way of Zen*. New York: Vintage Books, Random House, 1985.

Weale, Adrian, ed. *Hiroshima: First-Hand Accounts of the Atomic Terror that Changed the World*. New York: Carroll and Graf Publishers, 1995.

Wright, Tom, and Mizuno Katsuhiko. *Zen Gardens*. Kyoto, Japan: Mitsumura Suiko Shoin Co., Ltd, 1990.

0-595-22611-6

Printed in the United States
819500002B